OFFERED THE OPPORTUNITY OF THE PARDUBICE, THE GRAND NATIONAL OF CZECHOSLOVAKIA, JAGO DESPERATELY LOOKED FOR PROBLEMS AND OBJECTIONS – BUT COULD FIND NONE ...

And suddenly the prospect of four days in Czechoslovakia amidst racing people, with the smell of horses and the prospect of a crazed, hell-for-leather cross-country steeplechase, looked like an escape. Maybe he'd break his neck. It still looked like an escape. He'd be away from the squalid dealings of the town, away from the sense of failure, away from debt and love and obligation. He might, just for a day or two, be young again.

ABOUT THE AUTHOR

Mark Daniel is the son of a trainer and was brought up at steeplechasing's heart in Lambourn, Berkshire. Educated at Ampleforth College, Peterhouse, Cambridge, and HM Prison, Ashwell (handling stolen antiquarian books, since you ask), he has worked as a chef in England, France and Italy and as private tutor to the son of an Italian cabinet minister, while cutting his teeth on a host of novels for children and teenagers. Aside from his bestselling racing thrillers he is also known as an authority on skipping-songs and nursery verse. He likes oysters, fly-fishing, good company and clean air. He lives in Ireland.

Mark Daniel is the author of five other racing thrillers: *Under Orders, The Bold Thing, The Devil to Pay, Pity the Sinner* and *Sleek Bodies*, many of which are available in Signet.

MARK DANIEL

A Killing Joke

A SIGNET BOOK

SIGNET

Published by the Penguin Group
Penguin Books Ltd, 27 Wrights Lane, London W8 5TZ, England
Penguin Books USA Inc., 375 Hudson Street, New York, New York 10014, USA
Penguin Books Australia Ltd, Ringwood, Victoria, Australia
Penguin Books Canada Ltd, 10 Alcorn Avenue, Toronto, Ontario, Canada M4V 3B2
Penguin Books (NZ) Ltd, 182–190 Wairau Road, Auckland 10, New Zealand

Penguin Books Ltd, Registered Offices: Harmondsworth, Middlesex, England

First published in Great Britain by Michael Joseph 1995
Published in Signet 1996
1 3 5 7 9 10 8 6 4 2

Printed in England by Clays Ltd, St Ives plc

Author's Note:

Charlie Mann, the Lambourn trainer, joined the record books in October 1995, when he became the first Briton to win the Velka Pardubicka since Chris Collins on Stephen's Society in 1973. Charlie Mann's mount, It's a Snip, was runner-up in 1994.

This one's for Cressida

Acknowledgements:

My thanks to the 'damned few', the gallant friends of Pardubice, particularly Chris and Suzanne Collins, Marcus Armytage, Charlie Mann, Jane Walwyn, William Sworborg, David Naylor-Leland and Gavin Wragg.

Thanks too to Richard Dunwoody, to Joe Och, of Sotheby's, to Amelia Fern of the V and A, to Diana Phipps, Lord Michael Pratt and Dr Richard Overy.

'OH GOSH, I say, this *is* fun,' Paul Pickering nodded as he turned the photograph album's heavy pages. 'Any excuse to look at these old pictures again. Absolute rule around here. Pickering is strictly forbidden to open these albums without just cause. Isn't that right, girls?' He consulted the dogs who sat about him, panting. 'Quickest way to become a boring old whatsit, eh? Now – that was me in Hong Kong, my dear – would you believe it? Now, where are we . . .?'

Prince Cyril Havlik was bored and angry.

He had come to England from New York in hope of a luxurious freebie. The girl, Annie, big buck teeth, big tits, a computer-programmer, would do anything provided, he said, 'I, your prince, command it'.

She had suggested the trip, even put up the money when Havlik discovered a problem with his bank, the transfer of some family funds. She was going back home for two weeks, see the old folks' place called Weybridge, not far from London. Catch some shows. See some action. Daddy'd love to meet you.

Sure.

Daddy was a retired bank manager; carried a clipboard around the house, noting lights left on, mugs unwashed; recite the list at tea time. Tea, for Christ's sakes.

As for the mother, she was a scrawny old bat, wore bobby-sox and big pink earrings; vamped him at the table, stroking his arm. 'Oh, Prince! Ooh, you are wicked!'

It was something in the air, Havlik had decided. The parents were one thing, OK, but even Annie had turned all respectable as soon as she had inhaled Weybridge air. Not now. The walls were too thin. Daddy would hear. As for trips to town, Daddy said the least Annie could do, nine months in America, spend some time with her mother.

And she had all the money.

Havlik was grounded.

So he had flicked through his address book, sneaked down to the pub to phone, but the English girls he'd met didn't want to know. They were married or in relationships or just straight cold. Then he'd come upon this name – Paul Pickering.

Havlik had dredged his memory. Old guy, white-haired, rode races. Came up to him at the Maryland Hunt Cup, what? Eight, nine years ago? Said, 'Havlik? Gosh, you must be Pavel's nephew, right?'

Turned out this guy's father had been big buddies with Havlik's uncle Pavel. They'd partied together, flown Spitfires together. Pavel had been sliced in two by tracer somewhere over France, and when this Pickering was born, he was named after him.

'Give us a buzz if you're in England, old boy,' the old guy had said, and Havlik had pictured, the way this guy talked, a country mansion, cigars, good wine at the least.

Havlik could not believe it. He was standing in a mobile home, for Christ's sakes, whilst greyhounds sniffed at his crotch and this Pickering leafed through old photograph albums. Tea was the only drink on offer. Annie was all over the guy, thought he was sweet. Havlik was jiggling from foot to foot. He wanted to get out of here. At least he and Annie might get it on in one of these country lanes.

'Here we are,' Pickering was saying. 'Hold on, yes. There's dad with Pavel and some jolly pretty bird, I must say. What's it say? Oh, they were at Quags. Went there the other day, just for a shufti. Wouldn't recognize it. Looks like a French railway station now. 'Mazing. Ah, and here they are – gosh, don't they look dashing, bomber-jackets, scarves – that's Biggin Hill in 1943.'

'Yeah,' said Havlik. 'Right.'

'Oh, and there's another one somewhere here with mum in it. Let's see . . .'

'Is that you there?' Annie indicated a photograph of a jumping horse on the mobile home's wall.

'Hmm? Yes, yes. That was me at Bechers, oh, years ago.'

'Cyril, you rode races a bit too, didn't you?' Annie asked.

Havlik could not remember what line he had fed her. He said, 'Yeah, a bit. Not that sort of heavy stuff.'

'Well, your family, of course, comes from the place with the best steeplechase in the world for my money,' Pickering enthused. 'I'm hoping – I know you'll laugh, old fellow like me, but I've saved a bit of dosh, and – I don't know – I was rather hoping to have a crack at it this year. The Velka Pardubicka . . .' He spoke the words with dreamy pleasure. 'You should have a go at it too, Cyril, now Czechoslovakia's opened up. Family tradition. Your uncle rode there. Broke his leg at the Taxis.'

'Yeah, well, you never know,' Havlik shrugged. 'I reckon my riding days are done.'

'Nonsense, nonsense. If I can do it, gosh, you certainly can. You should think about it, old chap. Be fun. Ah, here we are. That's my mum, my dear. Well, she wasn't then, of course. I was just a twinkle in my dad's eye. There he is, the old rogue, and there's Pavel. I wonder who this Fiona was. Lovely girl, anyhow. What fun . . .'

Havlik wasn't listening. He was studying Paul and musing. 'So when is this race, then?' he asked.

'Hmm? Oh, second Sunday in October. Come on. The more the merrier, I say.'

'Yeah,' Havlik nodded slowly. 'Yeah, like I say, I'll think about it . . .'

And he thought that just perhaps this trip hadn't been wasted after all . . .

The old boy did not know what was happening. Jago thanked God for that.

He knew that he was in front of a crowd, of course. He understood that all right. That was why he was arching his neck like that, waving his tail. That was why he was bobbing, trotting at walking pace beside Cindy, his girl.

His girl. Yes. He'd have said that, had he been able to speak. His girl, just as he'd have thought of Jago as his man.

Burly owned his people.

'Look at him, bloody old show-off,' Clay Levine growled softly in Jago's ear. 'He thinks he's in the paddock, God help us.'

'Don't . . .' It forced itself from Jago, half groan, half imprecation.

Beneath the two men, the microphone crepitated and the auctioneer began his spiel. 'Burlington. Fourteen-year-old gelding, but still a lot of running in this lad. Just look at him! Familiar to all of you, on the racecourse, where he's won seven times out of twenty-two starts, including the Kim Muir Memorial and the Foxhunter's at Liverpool, and in the eventing field, where he's carried his owner, Mr Jago van Zeller, to considerable success. Fourteenth at Badminton last year. Make someone a hell of a hunter, a hell of a schoolmaster. Come on, then. Who'll give me twenty-five?'

'Oh, God almighty,' Jago moaned. It was not the only moan about that sale ring. Others, hearing the brief summary of an heroic life, tutted or sighed. You didn't sell a horse like that as he neared retirement. It wasn't done.

But Jago was doing it.

A schoolmaster? Yes, Burly would be that now. In his youth, he had been anything but. Talented, sure, but headstrong and reckless and greedy for battle. Jago had inherited him from Colin St Merryns eight years ago, in settlement of a £2,000 debt. He had hunted and point-to-pointed a fair bit back in his childhood and youth before his father went bust. Business was looking up again, and he had thought, 'Stuff it. Why not?'

Burly had been his first major extravagance. Now he was the last to go.

Once he had been castrated and Jago and he had taken a couple of ignominious purlers – once, in short, both of them had learned that it took more than enthusiasm and bold hearts to triumph in this game – they settled into a more cautious training programme.

Jago paid a large fee to a tutor in Ireland, in exchange for which he was bawled at and had dung thrown at him for a month as, with the leathers crossed over the saddle, he trotted, cantered and jumped around a tan school. He returned to London, feeling, and walking, like Catherine the Great after a good night out. He used to drive down to Lambourn three mornings a week to ride out and to school his horse. Then it was back to London and the shops by ten o'clock.

His little hobby, his folly, had turned into an exacting but enthralling occupation.

Their first victory was at Southwell, in a five-horse contest over two miles. The opposition might have been of more interest to pet-food manufacturers than to the punters. All Jago and Burly had to do was stand up. They somehow contrived to do so, and Jago felt as though he'd won an Olympic gold.

The business thrived. The financial press cooed and doted. Jago snapped up some undercapitalized rivals. Zellers opened new branches. Each was a triumph, but nothing was to equal that first gasping, steaming progress to the space marked '*Winner*' . . .

Someone on the other side of the ring seemed to be bidding now. 'Six . . .' The auctioneer fondled the head of his gavel. 'Six thousand I am bid. Come on, ladies and gentlemen. There's a lot of life left in this fellow. A seven times winner and honest as the day is long . . . Come along. Who'll give me six-five? Six-five, six-five? You can take your pick!' he almost howled. 'You want an eventer for your daughter, a hunter for yourself, even a show hack? Just look at him move. Six-five . . .' He sighed. 'Thank you, sir. Seven . . .'

Jago strained his eyes to identify the bidder. Whoever it was was still three grand short of a reserve which the auctioneers had described as 'frankly, mildly unrealistic', but, if Jago liked the look of a bidder, he would readily settle for six-and-a-half. At that price, at least, Burly wouldn't be headed for the knackers.

'Seven thousand . . . Any more for any more? No? No, sir? All done? And I'm not selling at seven thousand . . .'

The hammer thumped.

Burly was still Jago's.

Or vice versa.

'Well, that's a bugger,' Clay sighed with evident insincerity.

'I'll find the underbidder,' Jago told him. He pocketed the catalogue and set off down the steps.

'Come on,' Clay urged behind him, 'for six grand, there's no point in selling . . .'

Jago turned sideways on to squeeze through a pair of disconsolate men in Barbours. He called back over his shoulder, and theirs, 'Six-and-a-half grand, plus training-fees, Clay.'

'So give him away.' Clay ducked between the two men.

'Nope,' Jago told him. He swung to his left and into the tunnel to the open air. 'I need every penny I can get.'

'Just retire him, for God's sake. Put the old fellow out to grass!' Clay panted. He had had to trot to catch up with Jago.

Jago pushed open the door. The air outside was clean and cold, the sky milky. 'He deserves better than that,' he announced. 'Your man's right. There's a lot more competition in him. He's not ready for retirement. Not yet. God, think what a hack he'd make for a trainer, up there on the gallops where he belongs . . .'

'Sure, sure,' Clay's tweed cap nodded at Jago's elbow, 'but there don't seem to be a trainer here as wants him, does there?'

'That's why I'm going to find the underbidder.'

He jumped up the two steps to the office. He walked in fast and laid his forearms on the desk. The woman back there had a grizzled bun of hair and a broad, grey, jagged smile.

'Hello,' Jago said. 'When does the present auctioneer come off, please?'

She studied her catalogue. 'Another – ooh – five lots, dear,' she said. 'Was there anything you were wanting?'

'No no. Just wanted a quick word.'

'He doesn't really.' Clay shook his head. 'Pay no attention.'

'Yes I do. Could you tell him Jago van Zeller is in the bar next door – or, if he's in a hurry, perhaps he could just leave the name of the bidder for my horse, Burlington?'

'Don't bother,' Clay corrected. 'He's a busy man. Let him be.'

'Burlington . . .' the woman scribbled. She looked up. 'Oh, Burlington! Yes, van Zeller. Of course, I remember Burlington.'

'Yes.' Jago was as stern as he could manage. 'Well. Right. Thank you.'

He turned on his heel and strode back out into the late afternoon chill. 'For God's sake, Clay,' he grumbled as he turned towards the bar. 'I am damn near bankrupt . . .'

'No you're not. The business is,' Clay said smoothly. 'You can afford one horse.'

'I can afford nothing.' Jago pushed through the double doors. He raised his voice above the hubbub. Sheepskins and waxed cottons eddied and swirled beneath layers of smoke. Jago joined them in the Battle for the Bar. 'I've had to sell the flat and move into a cupboard,' he continued. 'The business is my only source of income. Without it, I'm done.'

'No you're not,' Clay bawled at his back. 'You've no shareholders to answer to. It's not your fault there's a bloody recession. Try working for someone else for a change – or are we too bleeding grand for that?'

Jago did not meet the challenge, but could not ignore it. In many regards, it was just. He had always been his own boss, ever since, a twenty-four-year-old rookie, he had bought back the failing family tailoring firm which his father had sold five years before.

His mother's legacy, his knowledge of the trade and his now incredible assurance had permitted him to retrieve the name and the Goldhawk Road premises.

And Zellers had prospered, riding the great, curling tube-ride of the eighties. They had prospered too fast, too far.

Jago had known about tailoring. No one, however, had ever taught him about success.

He couldn't help wondering if Clay was right. Perhaps, even at thirty-six, he did have some worth on the open market. He just didn't like the idea of testing that worth, and, perhaps, finding it lower than his estimate.

A racecourse bar is a grail, attainable only by those whose strength is as the strength of ten because their hearts are pure, or, alternatively, because they've been bonking the barmaids. The sales are not quite so bad. Jago got there within three minutes, and felt vaguely guilty to have done so. The smell of beer was strong. All about him, men barked and waved at the barmaids. Someone mumbled, 'Jago.' He could not see the speaker, so he just nodded and grinned a bit.

He obtained a tonic and bitters for himself and a glass of Guinness for Clay, quicker than, in relation to the other poor gasping punters, he deserved. He turned and shuffled back to the relatively empty space at the centre of the room. Outside suddenly seemed very dark.

Clay stood waiting for him, one corner of his mouth tucked into his cheek. His hands were pushed down deep in his raincoat pockets.

He was short and stocky. He had charcoal cheeks and chin, black eyebrows and prematurely white hair.

He was – how would Jago describe him? An attachment, a lucky charm – another luxury which, if truth be told, he could ill afford.

Clay was ten years Jago's senior, the only son of old Mr van Zeller's father's chief cutter, Dan Levine. Although Jago's father had moved to Camden when Zellers made the transition from bespoke to mass-market, off-the-peg, he had loved his old Whitechapel shop, and Jago had spent a deal of his childhood hanging about in the half-light, watching the rapid zig-zag of the needle and the sure slicing of the shears.

Clay had gone to the bad. For all his knowledge of tailoring, his quick eye and his deft hand, he had been too impatient for apprenticeship and the laborious, time-honoured process of succession. It was the seventies. Youth wanted to go in first wicket down. Clay had seen the clients – flash young men with money in their pockets and girls on their arms.

He had wanted some of that.

One day, when Jago was just thirteen, Clay's genie had appeared to grant him his every dream. A canary-yellow Daimler had drawn up outside the shop. The genie was a sleek Maltese with a big hook nose and hair like an oil slick. Jago had seen him a couple of weeks before. The stranger had ordered a navy mohair suit, double-breasted, six showing five, with four-inch step-lapels and a buggers'-muddle skirt two inches too long for his height. His name was Ricky Ricardo, a spivvy little villain who was said to run sex shops, clubs and such.

Ricardo had preened for a while before the mirrors, pursed his lips and mused as to the appropriateness of this or that feature of his suit. Jago had watched, bemused as ever by his father's and Dan's infinite patience with would-be experts. Clay had been in the shadows, stacking bolts of tweed. He had clocked the motor outside, clocked the gold on Ricardo's fingers and wrists. He knew the man's reputation . . .

His fairy godmother teetered into the room.

It is easy, with hindsight, to mock the styles of the time, but Jago thought that, even then, possessing a child's detachment from fashion, he found Leonie Lamont just a little absurd. She appeared to be made up of giant marshmallows, crammed tight together in sapphire-blue silk. Her hair was candyfloss, her eyes were black as tarantulas.

Leonie Lamont was a working-class heroine. In those days, she enjoyed a uniquely English kind of fame, the kind enjoyed by Page 3 girls and horizontal heavyweights. She was said to be a film star, but had never appeared in any but low-budget, soft-focus soft porn and rumbustious, tits-and-bums comedies. Hollywood mansions, a svelte figure and haute couture would have alienated her from her public. It was important that she was buxom, important that she hobnobbed with East End villains and boxers and was photographed eating jellied eels. She was a home-grown sex symbol, with a bit of the cockney's ideal sister and a great deal more of his ideal mother about her.

She had whined, 'Ricky . . .? Come on, doll. I mean, fuck.'

'Sorry, love.' Ricardo had slicked back the hair at his temples with the heel of his hand. 'Just hold it one, will you?'

She shrugged. She sighed. She strolled over to the counter and leaned on it. She cocked a chubby leg. She made a big, red *moue*.

And Clay popped up right there behind the counter, a slender, dark lad with a quick one-sided smile.

He gave her a thousand megawatts.

Dan Levine thought the likes of Leonie Lamont to be amongst the lowest of life forms, but Dan was concentrating on a coat, and, if anything mattered more than morals to Dan, it was cut. He protested only when Clay left in the canary motor. By then it was too late.

Clay became a gofer, a sharp little lad who hung about Lamont's yellow mansion in Esher and acted as front man in Ricardo's sex shops. He learned rapidly how to obtain drugs and girls for his employers and their friends. He was flattered. He was spoiled. He came home, lording it in suits which made dad shudder. He sneered at Dan's cautious and outraged objections. He was in the big time.

Until Leonie was found dead in her heart-shaped bed, having suffocated on her own vomit.

It was one of those deaths that don't happen to powerful people, because powerful people have them mopped up, fast. Leonie, however, was public property. The papers relished every horror: the drugs, the drink, the several varieties of semen found on or in her . . .

There was gleeful outrage. There were investigations.

It may have been Leonie who was the Jezebel, but it was Clay who was fed to the dogs. He got three years.

He had the sense to be chastened by the experience. On his release, he rejected his father's fatted calf, but only because he knew that the quiet, musty world of tailoring was not for him. He needed people about him. He took a job on Moss Bros' shop floor. By dint of acumen and charm, he rapidly became an assistant manager.

Jago returned from public school and university to find Clay always ready to mock his lah-di-dah ways. When Mrs van Zeller fulfilled a lifetime's ambition by moving to Hampshire (to her husband's horror), Clay would come to stay, help with the decorating or the mucking-out. When Jago went fishing, Clay would come along, tie the fly on the line, carry the creel and sit quietly as the fly jerked back to Jago on the water.

And when Clay was there, trout took.

Jago didn't really know if he was Clay's protégé or vice versa. Jago had the money and many of the skills that Clay admired, but then, Clay had the savvy, the ability to see through those who impressed Jago. He could also mock Jago's more grandiose aspirations.

Jago was twenty when his father's debts, so long contained, bubbled to the surface, and the stench became unmistakeable. It was Clay who saw Jago through dreary days of management training, and frequently supplemented his meagre income from his own savings. It was Clay who found Jago a buying job with Quenell's, the high street hosiers, Clay who at last pointed out to Jago that there was a gap in the market, that Zellers could fill it and that the younger man could afford to buy back the old business. Clay resigned his job and came in with Jago, though in an unspecified capacity. He would not manage a shop. He could not afford a partnership. He was happy just to lend his encouragement to Jago and to the staff, to give a hand here or there as needed. And there was still no one better at obtaining the unobtainable.

Jago would want a star to be photographed in Zellers' clothes. Clay would know the woman. Jago would want a load of rare antiques for a window display. Clay would turn up with a lorry-load and no questions asked.

Jago did not exactly pay him. It was an unspoken thing which developed over the years. Every Friday morning, Jago left two hundred pounds or so on the hall table. Sometimes none of it was there when he returned in the evening.

Sometimes only a hundred would have gone. Jago bought the meals, the drinks, the transport . . .

He could not afford Clay, but rather suspected that he was stuck with him, for richer, for poorer.

'Come on, J.' Clay now caught his eye. 'You can't do this.'

'I have no alternative,' Jago said firmly. 'Racehorses, in case you hadn't heard, are a luxury, for rich men only. I am no longer rich, and there's an end on it.'

'Just ride in the race. Just once.' Clay's grey eyes were sly. 'I'll get odds against you. It'll pay for itself, Chrissakes, and pay for the old boy's retirement. Not to mention the publicity. Gawd, you win that – think of the markets it'll open up. The Czechs, now. Big on quality sportswear. Shit, do a swap. Our expertise, their cheap labour, so on. I mean, it's got *kudos*, hasn't it, this race? And – and, yeah, I mean, OK, so you want a job with someone. Just think. First Englishman in twenty years. Only the second since the First World War, for God's sakes. Come on, mate. For the sake of six-and-a-half grand . . .?'

'And the cost of getting out there,' Jago reminded him. 'And, of course, there is always the distinct possibility, which never crosses your tiny little optimistic mind, that we might not win, or even that we might fall and the old boy might break his neck.'

'Sure!' Clay wiped spume from his upper lip. 'Sure he might break 'is neck. So? Which would he rather, eh? Stay with you, die in hot blood, doing the thing 'e likes to do, or go off to be a bleeding – what did the man say? – show hack? Chrissakes. You're doolally, you.'

'Yes, well . . .' Jago began, but the truth of Clay's remarks rudely interrupted him. The trouble was that the harebrained scheme *was* just possible. Jago sincerely wished that it were not.

'Jago . . .' The auctioneer, a youngish man with red dewlaps and rebellious black hair, approached, tweed arm extended. 'Sorry. I was told you wanted a word.'

'Yes.' Jago turned his back on Clay. 'Yes. Thank you. You had a bid for Burlington?'

'Yes.' The dewlaps concertinaed as the auctioneer nodded. His lower lip juddered. 'Yes, there was one bid.'

'You don't know who it was?'

'Yes. Yes. Absolutely . . .'

There was a long pause whilst, it seemed, he waited for Jago to say something and Jago wondered what on earth he could say. At length, the fervent fellow licked his lips and announced, 'As a matter of fact, it was a telephone bid, earlier in the day. A Mr Levi, was it? Or Levine?'

Jago's jaw wanted to drop. His teeth wanted to grind. His teeth won. It would be a moment or two before he could find some civil response.

He did not get the chance. There was a dreadful sound at his shoulder. It was like that of a donkey with a stitch, a sort of wheezing, rasping, sawing sound which Jago knew all too well.

That was Clay Levine's version of laughter.

Paul Pickering looked in the rear-view mirror. He said, 'I have no problem with exhibitionism, madam, but please make sure that the young chap does not suppurate on my upholstery.' He turned his attention back to the road over the rolling downs.

The woman in the rear seat said 'Hng', then her bespectacled head rose into view above the folded copy of *The Times*. She said, 'Suppurate? Yuk.'

The very much younger man beside her was tugging at her hand, but she pulled it away. 'No. Piss off, will you? Gross out.'

Paul's lips curled in a little smile as the young man uncomfortably adjusted his dress behind the newspaper. The pair behind him had plainly supped their lunch, but all the same, he was at a loss to explain why the back seat of an Audi and the presence of a white-haired taxi driver seemed to constitute an erotic stimulus, but this was far from the first time that such a situation had arisen. God, they must regard him as 'safe'. Little, then, did they know. They thought of themselves as daring. Paul could have shown them a thing or two.

'You're a bit posh, aren't you?' the woman was saying.

'A bit posh for what?' Paul asked mildly.

'Well, taxi driver, you know.'

'Sorry. "Wotcher, guv. String the nig-nogs up. Only language they understand." Better?'

'No, but you know what I mean. It's a surprise.'

'Why's that?' Paul drawled. 'The rich are rarely gentlemen these days, and gentlemen seldom rich. Oh, I've been there – Ascot, Henley, St Moritz, ridden in the National, hunted with the Quorn, all that. Can't afford it now, and, do you know? I couldn't give a damn.'

'Lloyds, was it?'

'No, no. Fast women, slow horses, the usual thing. Lot of fun.'

'Gosh.' The woman leaned forward now and spoke into his ear. 'Look, I'm sorry. That was silly. Too much wine at lunch.'

'Oh, I know how it feels.' The crow's feet at the corners of Paul's eyes were long and deep. 'No, you'd be amazed the things people do, they get in the back of a taxi. Had the odd proposition myself, believe it or not.'

'I bet you have.'

'No, I don't mind what people get up to – smoking, drinking, fornicating, all fine by me – but keeping the upholstery clean is damned expensive.'

The man behind suddenly said, 'You never really rode in the National, did you?'

'Matter of fact, yes. Amateur, of course. And the Swedish National, Maryland . . . Only one I've missed is a crazy contest out in Czechoslovakia, and I might just ride in that this year.'

'Come on.' The man was truculent. 'You?'

Paul was unoffended. He smiled up into the mirror. 'Yup. Me. I've got a damn good horse. Why not? I've got a little money saved up, and this morning I saw this advertisement. I rang. It sounds good.' He pulled a square of newsprint from his breast pocket and passed it back. The woman took it and studied it.

'Pardubeese,' she read aloud.

'No, that "ice" is pronounced "eetze". That's where the race is run.'

'"Sportsman with box . . ." Sounds like a cricketer,' she giggled.

'Yes. Horsebox, he means.'

'". . . will be taking his mount to the Velka Pardubicka, leaving Dover, October 6th. Seeks similar to share expenses, driving . . ." God, you really are serious about this!'

'You bet I am,' Paul said grimly. 'Deadly serious.'

'I've heard of this race,' the man said. 'Sorry, but those fences are famous. You're knocking on a bit, aren't you?'

'Steve!' the woman squealed.

'No, no,' Paul soothed. 'He's quite right, but I'll still give any of you lot a run for your money. Anyhow, it just makes it all the more urgent that I get on with it, doesn't it?'

He had been driving slowly around the outskirts of Devizes. Now, entering Long Street, he said, 'The Bear's just down there. Have a good look around the market place if you don't know it. It's pretty amazing.'

'God, I can't believe it,' the woman said. 'A bona fide dyed-in-the-wool loony romantic. I think it's great, really. I didn't think they made them like you any more.'

'They don't,' said Paul.

She moved back now, which allowed Jago to see and to breathe freely for the first time in five minutes. She made a series of little glottal stops, then a growl and a whimper as she sank down, and started to ride.

She did not look at him. She just reached over him, grasped the bed's head and pushed back, grinding her pubis against his, headed once more for just one end. With each shove, she grunted and those beautiful little breasts shook, just out of reach of Jago's lips and tongue.

He grasped her buttocks, pulled them apart, held her still. He forced her down on him so that he could get a decent mouthful at last, and his hips took over the jerking motion. Her long brown hair was moist on his cheek and forehead. She whimpered now, and strained in his grasp.

'Grrrrod!' she growled like something heavy moving on casters. 'Yes, yes, yes . . .'

Dialogue in bed is pretty uniform. In whatever language, it consists largely in invocations to the Creator and extensive affirmations, which, Jago supposed, was as it should be.

She slid off him and rolled over onto her hands and knees. 'Come on,' she ordered. Still she did not look at Jago. She stared instead at the video that she had brought over in a bid to encourage him. A woman with buck teeth and long blonde hair was getting what Julie wanted, from both ends. It did not help Jago much. 'Oh, Christ, Julie,' he sighed at the bobbing keyhole of flesh above him. 'It's no bloody good.'

'Come on . . .' she murmured, 'look at it. She's taking it. Give it to me. Oh, yes. Come on, baby, give it to me . . .'

He lay still and silent. On the screen, the woman made muffled groaning noises, the men grunted, flesh slapped. Jago liked the idea, all right, but, for the first time in his life to date, the spirit was willing but the flesh remained weak. It had been thus for the past three or four weeks now, and Julie's solicitous attempts to 'cure' him only served to make things worse.

'I'm sorry, love,' he said dully. 'It's not you. There's damn all I can do about it.'

She hit the mattress twice with a clenched fist before throwing herself hard back beside him. The mattress puffed. Damn it, her body was good. She was attractive, with that short bobbed blonde hair, those wide pale eyes and that broad, wicked mouth. He wanted to be close to her. He wanted the solace of holiday, of sweaty, mindless, Dionysian frenzy and blessed relief.

He felt impotent simply because – to be trite about it – he felt impotent. Things were being done to him. Insolvency practitioners were being called in, official receivers daily threatened. Creditors' letters piled higher and higher, their tone daily changing from unguent to pleading to monitory. Somehow, a sense of pride, a sense of self seemed necessary to the sex act – at least if, as here, it was no more than the act.

That sense had been missing of late.

Oh, Jago liked Julie well enough. She amused him, but she was hardly the person with whom he would choose to share his deepest concerns. Not the sort of person who would appreciate the hurt and the guilt which possessed him as he was compelled to let down trusting suppliers and employers.

His relationship with his suppliers and staff, no less than that with Burly, which, he felt, he had also betrayed, was founded upon many years of mutual reliance. Several of the mills and importers had supplied his father. Some had supplied his grandfather. The manageress of the World's End branch, Dorothy Garland, had been Jago's Auntie Dot back in his childhood. Her grandmother had worked as a trouser machinist in the Whitechapel Road.

After the sale of his flat, and after Customs and Excise and the Revenue had taken their various pounds of flesh, Jago now had £27,382 in his personal current account. If he wound up the business now and bankrupted himself into the bargain, he might just be able to afford to give £1,000 to each of his creditors. To some, that would be an insult. To all, it would be insufficient.

Julie was twenty-five and a model. He had met her just six months before, at one of those trade parties where you just have to pick up or get picked up if only for something to do with your hands. She was with a top agency, but had never quite made it to the top herself. She could not understand it. Jago, alas, could. To be a top model takes hard work, stamina, punctuality and vigorous self-discipline. Of these, Julie possessed only stamina.

She liked late nights. She liked sex and champagne. Jago had no objections to either, but such tastes made all the difference between that healthy incandescence possessed by the best, and the simple, two-dimensional beauty of one who seems to have stepped straight from her portrait.

Jago was not consistently cynical about these things, but a failed relationship which had endured for three years had left him cynical – which usually means frightened – when he met Julie. He knew that she valued his name and his contacts more than his sense of humour and his history, his temporal assets more than his spiritual defects. They got on. They found refuge in one another. Or rather, they had, until Jago's hitherto most wilfully and irrationally active organ went on strike.

'Don't worry,' she breathed at last, 'it doesn't matter.' Her insistently lapping finger denied her words. On the screen, the men were grunting more than ever as they carelessly discharged fluids over the woman, who feigned delight by closing her eyes and showing her teeth. Jago reached for the remote control. He pressed *Stop*. Randolph Scott was shooting at some Indians from behind a rock.

'Of course it bloody matters.' Jago pulled the sheet up over them. 'I'm sorry. So far you've come up with some stuff which smelled like hydrochloric and damn near gave me a heart attack and some film of some rather unfortunate New Yorkers with spotty bums fornicating to electric organ music. I don't need it, love. It doesn't help.'

'It's just me, isn't it?'

'No.' He risked touching her hunched shoulder with a tentative hand. 'I can promise you. If Cleopatra and Hedy Lamarr were here begging me, they'd get the same response.'

'Maybe you need psychological help,' she mumbled into the pillow. Her shoulders hunched further from him.

'What psychological help?' Jago demanded. 'Psychologists are there to tell you the reasons for things which are buried deep in the subconscious. The reasons for this are not buried deep. They're plain as the nose on your face.'

'Oh, thanks,' she sniffed. She rolled further away.

OK, so it hadn't been the most tactful of remarks, given the size of Julie's nose and her sensitivity about the subject. Jago said, 'Sorry. You know what I mean.'

'Don't touch me,' she said. 'Please. It's all right. It's not your fault.'

There was a long silence then, broken only by the distant firing of Indian guns from the television, the rushing of the traffic from the street above.

Jago had been in this rented basement at the top of

Campden Hill Square for just three weeks. There were four rooms; a sitting-room at the front, this room, in which there was barely room for the king-size bed and the chest-of-drawers on which the television stood, a shoe-box kitchen which gave onto the paved and potted garden, and an even smaller bathroom. Jago had sold all his recent acquisitions of value save for the bed and the television. He had kept only the furniture and pictures which he had inherited, and, of course, the framed photographs and paintings of him and his horses. There were still a lot of things in store.

He was looking now at a Gerry Cranham picture of him purling forward off his other chaser, Limehouse, at a Chepstow open ditch. The sky was stormy and the colour of a beaten-up face, a day or two after. Jago's red and green colours seemed bright as jewels on velvet. Limehouse was retired now, on a friend's farm in Herefordshire. He bucked and sniffed at mares and told untrue stories about his conquests, amorous and sporting, to his Shetland pony companion, who, the friend told Jago, was taking elocution lessons and had gone on a diet.

Old friends, like the furniture, like Burly, like Clay . . . Old friends who knew Jago in another life, a simpler life, when triumph had been easy and the only person hurt was him.

Julie knew nothing of such friends.

Julie knew nothing of such simplicity. To her he was a complete creature, a man, and to be judged as such. He had no irrational impulses beyond those manifest in lust or in anger, to both of which 'male' oddities she was inured – or trained – to respond appropriately.

She did not – how should she? – understand that an absurd, naughty little boy in Jago wanted to win a great, crazy race halfway across Europe. She did not – how could she? – appreciate that Jago's concern for those who had trusted him and with whom he had grown up could wither his cock.

All that was incomprehensible, because Julie believed in stasis. She believed that there were children, adolescents and adults, heterosexuals, asexuals and homosexuals, she believed in day and night, good and bad.

This did not accord with Jago's experience.

'So.' She had decided that the brisk and efficient would save the day. She rolled from the bed and, rather too quickly, pulled on her knickers, releasing the waistband with a snap. 'So, what are we doing tonight?' She stepped into a crimson body. She pulled it up with that most elegant of wriggles, fastened it with that most ungainly of poses. 'Maddy's having a do at Mortons. I said we'd drop in.'

'Oh, hell . . .' Jago covered his eyes with his hands.

'Come on. Be good for you.' She eased on a maroon mini.

'No,' he said solemnly. 'Sorry, Julie. Not tonight. You go.'

'On my own?' she squeaked. 'You must be off your head.'

'Why not!' Jago shrugged. 'You lived before you met me. Call someone.'

'That,' she said, and her voice became suddenly jagged, 'is typical. You can't get it up. OK. No problem. I suggest we go and see some of my best friends, relieve the tension a bit, but no. Call someone. Look after yourself. What am I meant to use for money? Oh, no need to worry about that. I'm no use to you any more.'

'Take fifty off the chest-of-drawers there.' Jago rolled over. 'I can't afford your sort of jollies any more. Sorry.'

He heard her completing her toilet. There was a lot of sighing and muttering and thumping in there. She had plenty of time to prepare an exit line, and he was waiting for a dilly. He knew when it was coming, because there was sudden silence. 'Well, thanks a lot, Jago. If you're not interested, all I can say is, there are plenty of others who are . . .'

That really was all she could say.

A breeze puffed the curtains inward. The door slammed. Her footfalls flapped up the stairs to join the others clicking by.

Jago sighed. He reached into the shelf at the right of the bed. He pulled out a videotape. He scrambled down the bed on hands and knees and reached out to press the *Eject* button on the recorder. It growled and spewed out Julie's tape. Jago laid it on the table and forced in the new tape. He picked up the remote-control and flung himself back into bed.

He waited then watched, Randolph Scott; flicked over, found a woman talking about ritual child-abuse; tried again, a game show, the presenter wriggling with delight at himself, the competitors looking seriously constipated . . .

He pushed the *Play* button.

There was a park of poplars and hedges. A carriage and twelve in hand trotted on the turf, bearing huge flags. The sky was pale and overcast.

Then there were horses and jockeys, riding long and sitting upright in the style of sporting prints.

'And suddenly, they're away,' said the commentator, and the horses were running – racing, damn it. They took a low hedge without problems, then another, this time with a ditch on the landing-side. Then a water – a flat water, three metres wide. One horse nosedived it, hit the far bank hard with his chest and slipped back into the water. His rider had tumbled forward, somersaulted, but somehow managed to keep a hold of the rein. He stood groggily and tugged at his horse as it scrambled up and shook itself. He remounted.

But the camera now followed the rest of the field. They had split into two as they swung to the right in front of the stands. And they were headed fast, too fast, for fence number four.

Fence number four featured in many men's nightmares.

Fence number four loomed large in Jago's.

Fence number four also played its part in his happiest dreams.

Its name was the Taxis.

It was a hedge, five-foot-six high and five-foot-six wide.

That was bad. Not impossible, but, by any standards, one of the biggest fences in the world.

And on the other side, there was a seventeen-foot drop.

The right-hand section of the field came to it first. Two horses cleared it. One pecked, sprawled and somehow recovered. Three dragged through the hedge and nosedived, their riders leaning back, one hand grasping at the air as though the gods might throw them a lifeline. As they landed, the riders were flung flailing, eight, ten feet forward.

The left-hand group were on the fence now. Two horses plunged into the great ditch. One somersaulted and rolled. Another, coming up behind, landed well but found stiff legs rolling into its path. The horse tried desperately to jump this new obstacle, but the legs of the two horses tangled. The second foundered and staggered. His rider tumbled over his head.

Five horses were still standing. Six were down. The Russian horse which had fallen at the water arrived somewhat late amidst the carnage.

He fell again.

'. . . but his rider still has hold of the reins,' the commentator was jovial '. . . perhaps we haven't heard the last of this intrepid challenger from the steppes . . .'

The camera moved on as the five remaining horses leaped onto a seven-foot Irish bank, and off again into ploughed soil . . .

Jago heard a click from the front-door. He pressed *Stop* and leaped forward to eject the tape. He forced in the nearest substitute to hand. He fell back into bed and tucked the racing tape beneath his pillow.

'Hello?' Clay called softly out there. 'Hello? J?'

Jago cleared his throat. 'Oh, hi, Clay. Just having a rest. Come on in.'

'Yeah, yeah. I saw your rest leaving. Nice, that Julie; you like 'em with erectile noses.' He stepped in and sniffed as he looked around. He was in a double-breasted blazer now, a pale blue polo neck and baggy cream trousers. 'Nah, sorry to bother you, mate. Gawd, this place is tight as a tight-rope walker's bum. I mean, get the bed in – no space for anything else, is there? Priorities, I suppose.'

'Did you want something, Clay?'

'Yeah.' He paused and casually pressed the *Play* button. A pair of heaving white buttocks appeared on the screen, framed by raised legs in stockings and high heels. ''Allo . . .' Clay bent to peer at the action. 'Gor. She's all right. Sooner be in that than in the Scrubs. You like this stuff, do you, J?'

'Not much,' Jago sighed. 'Switch the bloody thing off, will you?'

Clay obliged. 'Yeah, well,' he shrugged. He reached into his inside pocket. Clay's inside pockets resembled Harpo Marx's. At any moment, he could be relied upon for railway timetables, tobacco, pens, envelopes and newspapers full of human interest stories. 'Cop a load of that,' he said. He tossed over a folded *Horse and Hound*.

Jago feigned indifference. 'Derby Day showed much of his sire, Superstar's, presence when shown in hand by young Deirdre Spencer . . .' he read.

'Come on, J.' Clay leaned over the bed, exasperated. 'Not that. Look.' He stabbed with a thick, stiff finger at the magazine.

Jago saw the fluorescent pink square, and within it the bold heading: **PARDUBICE**. He closed his eyes.

'Come on. Read it at least.'

Jago read. 'Pardubice: Sportsman with box will be taking his mount to the Velka Pardubicka, leaving Dover October 6th. Seek similar to share expenses/driving. Please contact . . .'

A moan forced its way up from somewhere near his groin. He leaned back on the pillows. 'So?'

'So it's obvious, innit?' Clay's voice was high-pitched. 'So there's you, whingeing about every bleeding penny, and there's this guy offering to pay half the fees! Jesus, man! Snap out of it. You've got the horse. Do it!'

'Clay,' Jago told him patiently, 'look at my diary for the next four weeks. I have appointments with the receiver, suppliers, the receiver, builders, the receiver . . .'

'Yeah, but not on the last Friday, Saturday or Sunday, have you?' Clay was smug. 'There just 'appens to be a big gap there, doesn't there?'

'He is proposing to leave on October 6th, Clay. That's a whole week he's allowing. I haven't got a whole week. Three days isn't enough.'

'Oh, yes it is, Mr I'm so effing poor and noble. Oh, yes it bloody is.' Clay stood upright. He started to pace to and fro the three narrow yards at the foot of the bed. 'You arrive on the Friday, settle in, look round Prague. Saturday, you exercise 'im, walk the course. Sunday, you ride the race.'

'But *someone's* got to drive the bloody animal!' Jago howled.

'Sure.' Clay nodded. 'Well done. And my diary – you'll not believe this – but my diary is totally empty between the sixth and the fourteenth. So. See any problems?'

Jago glowered, but considered. He looked for problems and objections. He could find none.

And suddenly the prospect of four days in Czechoslovakia amidst racing people, with the smell of horses and the prospect of a crazed, hell-for-leather cross-country steeple-chase, looked like an escape. Maybe he'd break his neck. It still looked like an escape. He'd be away from the squalid dealings of the town, away from the sense of failure, away from debt and love and obligation. He might, just for a day or two, be young again.

He took a deep breath. He said through tight lips, 'Sod you, Clay Levine,' then he grinned. 'Go on,' he laughed. He picked up the telephone by the bed and flung it onto the bed. 'Ring the silly sod.'

Clay raised a heavy eyebrow. 'You'll do it?'

'Yes, yes. All right.' Childish glee possessed Jago. 'Go on. Ring him.'

'Yeah, well . . .? Clay slowly smiled.

'Yes?'

'Well . . . I don't need to, do I?'

'What? You mean – you've already rung?'

'Er, no. Not exactly.'

'Well, what . . .?'

'Well, I don't 'ave to ring the silly sod, do I?' Clay was only mildly rueful. 'I mean, I'm talking to 'im, in' I?'

'You mean . . .' Jago stared. He licked his lips, found voice and breath. He roared, 'You mean you put that ad in?' The walls rang. The window panes buzzed.

'Well, you could say . . .' Clay hummed. '*And*, before you say anything . . .' He was assertive again. 'Don't bother, 'cos the ad got an answer, and Mr Paul Pickering is just delighted to share the expenses and the driving, thank you. So.'

Jago looked around for something to throw at Clay's leering, happy, ugly face. By the time he came up with a copy of *Middlemarch*, however, that leering, happy, ugly face was gone.

Middlemarch bounced off the door.

Jago was going to Pardubice.

Goldhawk Road was the centre of Zellers' operations now.

Jas. van Zeller's was a traditional East End tailor's until the late fifties, when Jago's father, a rebel in his time, started to make frock coats for the Teds and, later, to buy and restore military tunics for the flaneurs. His own father disapproved of the styles and the clients, but very much approved of the cash coming in.

When Jas. himself retired, Jago's father kept the traditional business going, but opened outlets at World's End, in Goldhawk Road and in South Molton Street. He became a rich man. He drove a Ferrari. In 1961, he married Elizabeth Gibb, the daughter, as the papers said, and oft repeated, 'of wealthy county Brigadier Fred Gibb.' Jago's mother was a would-be actress at the time, a popular girl on the party circuit.

Jago was born in 1963, the intended heir to a thriving and fashionable business and a burly red brick, white-coped mansion on Primrose Hill. He was sent to a smart Hampstead school and then to St Paul's. The van Zellers, whose progress had been pretty consistently downward since their Huguenot ancestor first arrived in London, were on the up again.

Tailors were suddenly trendy. They found themselves invited to the very parties for which, in the past, they had made their clients' clothes. Jago's parents were at the centre of all this. His mother, of course, took to it as of right. She loved the risqué parties, the rock-star friends, the attentions of the press. His father was never so happy as a trendy, but he played the part in his diffident way, and Zellers (the 'van' had long since been dropped) when it ceased to be strictly fashionable, had a big enough name to attract the high street aspirants, the country cousins who pursued as ever, and, as ever, failed to catch up.

It wasn't until 1975 that even that source of punters turned to a trickle and dried. The West End leases lapsed and were not renewed. Zeller's name was now its curse, inevitably linked with an age long gone.

But Jago's mother was bright. She had noted the rise of androgynous fashions for working women. She had noticed the absence of decent building and tailoring in even the most expensive of women's jackets, coats and trousers. She had noticed, too, the traditional tailor's reluctance to work for women. The reasons were simple and silly. Traditional tailors *liked* the old-fashioned, all-male ambience of their shops. They did not like taking women's inside-leg measurements. Above all, they could fit and cut men's clothes with their eyes closed. Adapting to women's contours and women's conventions entailed work. Not a lot, but work, all the same.

Dan Levine was prepared to do it.

Zellers went upmarket again. They made chic, traditional men's suits to measure. They made them for women. The market was small, select and rich. You could not walk a hundred yards in Gray's Inn without coming upon a Zeller suit. The market may have been small, but the margins were high. All could – all should – have been well, had it not been for Jago's father's Peter Pan complex, his reluctance to grow old and to return to anonymity, had it not been for his inevitable mistress.

When it all came out, it proved that that mistress, a former dental hygienist by name Sorrel Ransome, had cost him, and the van Zellers, fifty-four thousand a year over the past ten years. He had set her up with a flat in Stratton Street, just off Piccadilly. He had paid a Spanish maid. He had equipped Sorrel with wines, crystal, furniture and paintings. He had taken her on holidays all over the world . . .

Jago could not entirely blame him, once the initial anger had died. His father's pretensions had developed in reaction to his wife's. She had insisted on the rectory in Hawkley, the horses for herself and her darling son. She had created for herself a world in which he felt uncomfortable and inadequate. They were both hooked on their brief experience of fame and irresponsible wealth.

Zellers rationalized, which means, basically, that they flogged off everything. The business and the three shops were snapped up by booming couturiers Macaire. The shops became Macaire outlets. The Zeller trade name and workshop were simply allowed to die. The North London house was sold at a bargain price.

Then Clay had made his bright suggestion that Jago should buy back the company, and again Zellers supplied the barristers and high-flying City women of the eighties with their working clothes.

It was raining on the Goldhawk Road, but then, as far as Jago was concerned, it always rained on the Goldhawk Road, just as the Whitechapel Road was always, in his mind, washed by watery autumn sunlight or flushed with winter warmth.

Zellers occupied three floors out of four just the other side of the footbridge on Shepherds Bush Green. The ground floor was still the shop. It had deliberately been kept small and dingy, with half-made-up garments, aged fashion plates and occasional pages from *Vogue* in the windows against a draped black catafalque. Inside, too, lighting was barely adequate. The right-hand-side of the shop was lined with bolts of fabric. On the left, Cindy Clarke stood slouching behind the counter, the tape measure slung about her neck like a badge of office. More framed, yellowing fashion plates hung on the wall behind her.

Cindy was the daughter and grand-daughter of tailors. If her eye was not yet perfect, her hand was as quick and adept as any in London. Jago was giving her retail and fitting experience, because he reckoned that she did not belong at a bench. She was Cockney, cocky, bright and pretty, with a pale blonde fringe and wide grey eyes on which she wore huge pink porthole glasses.

'Morning, Cindy,' he greeted her. 'How's business?'

'Booming,' she answered, as ever. 'Cop the raging mob, would you? Thought I'd be engulfed. Nah. One bag lady, one copper and Miss Sniffy upstairs – oh, and two reps with flannel I'd not use in the bath.'

'Gawd.' Jago dropped into the vernacular. 'It's the weather, I suppose.'

'Yeah,' she said sarcastically. 'That'll do it every time.'

Zeller's shopfront was not dingy because its proprietors had never been able to afford to brighten it. On the contrary, they could at any stage – save, perhaps, this one – have turned it into a dazzling ice cube filled with fluorescent light and peacock fire. Exclusivity, however, and the ambience of a place in which craftsmen were at work, had served both the image and the margins very nicely.

At the back, beyond the changing rooms, the light in the white-painted stairwell and the kitchen were bright enough to make Jago blink.

He clattered up the uncarpeted stairs to the work room, where John Duhigg and Neil Green cut and stitched and argued and bitched and added considerably to the company's telephone bills by calling Ladbrokes to lay generally losing bets. Jago deemed this a legitimate business expense. He doubted that the current inhabitant of the third floor would agree.

Roberta Kelly, aka 'Miss Sniffy', aka the consultant in insolvency, was solid as a pillar. Not an ounce of her appeared loose or yielding. Her cheeks were apples; her chin twin walnuts; her bust, which defied the imagination to divide it into its constituent parts, a tight, hard parcel, like the extremities of a bean-bag when the labradors are asleep at its centre. So it went on. Her bum too was a single hemisphere which shifted, rustling, with her every step. Her calves were balustrades beneath their slick of grey nylon. Even her iron-grey, bobbed hair seemed immobile as a helmet.

'Good morning, good morning, good morning!' Jago hailed her, in hope that repetition of the arcana might undo her brown magic. No chance.

He shed his raincoat and flung it over his desk. 'So, my dear Miss Kelly, are we bankrupt yet? Should I adjourn to the library to do the Decent Thing, or can we throw a tax-deductible wake for the House of Zeller?'

'You are in serious trouble.' Roberta Kelly did not look up from her ledgers. 'I cannot believe these books.'

'I feel the same about most romantic fiction,' Jago agreed. 'Haydn was, perhaps, just a trifle fanciful, but honest. It's a case, I'm afraid, of Haydn's somewhat messy truth being rather stranger than most companies' antiseptic fiction.'

She sniffed. Roberta Kelly had only met Haydn Jones twice, but Jago guessed that she had come very cordially to hate him. This was unjust. Haydn had been a fine cutter until, at sixty-three, his eyes had failed him. He was a widower, and retirement would have been lonely. To give him a job doing the books twice a week had seemed natural to Jago. It gave Haydn a role in the company for which he had worked for over twenty years. It gave him beer money. And the accounts were never that complicated.

Until Haydn got his hands on them.

Jago had not realized how far his eyes had failed.

'I am not a cryptographer, Mr van Zeller,' Roberta Kelly told Jago, not for the first time. 'And what, pray, is this entry? Sundries, thirty-four pounds?'

'When's that?' He peered over her shoulder. 'March 9th? Oh, whisky, I think.'

'Whisky?' She was a Lady Bracknell with no trace of shrillness.

In the corner, beneath the window, Diana Osborne, Jago's personal assistant, appeared to be having trouble with her breathing. She was rocking slightly, and her shoulders were jerking up and down.

'Yes, whisky and smoked salmon sandwiches. I had a winner at Worcester. Rang up and told them to have a drink on the house.'

Roberta Kelly shuddered. 'That will be your horses, I suppose?'

'That's right. Don't forget, Miss Kelly,' Jago allowed himself just a trace of a menacing growl. 'This company is mine. That money was mine. You may accuse me of folly, but not of malfeasance, I think. Please don't sniff and tut at me. Save me if you can. Call in the receiver if you must, but please don't treat me like the Robert Maxwell of the tailoring world.'

'Oh, it's nothing to me,' she sighed. 'If you want to throw money about . . . Well, you can see where that sort of thing gets you.'

Diana glanced quickly over her shoulder. She caught Jago's eye. She gritted her teeth and her eyes rolled heavenward.

Roberta Kelly's analysis of the causes of Zellers's downfall was entirely unfair, but Roberta Kelly would never understand a business like this. She liked everyone to be answerable for everything. When at last she had begun to crack the Jones cipher, she made some shocking discoveries. She had been working for two days before at last she had plucked up the courage to ask Jago why he or his staff consumed so much cabbage – 'not just hundreds, but thousands of pounds' worth!' On this occasion, she had allowed emotion to enter her voice. Waste she disapproved of, but could understand. Profligacy she deplored but expected of irresponsible, rich young men like Jago.

Profligacy on green vegetables, however, was somehow deeply shocking.

He had had to explain. 'Cabbage', he told her, 'is the tailoring term for those bits of fabric left over after cutting. By ancient convention and guild law, the cutter is entitled to his cabbage, so we must build the cost of cabbage into any assessment of our profits.'

'But – but that means', she had spluttered, 'that a cutter could deliberately leave as much – cabbage – as possible, to his own benefit!'

It had been Jago's turn to sniff. 'Cutters,' he had explained, 'are craftsmen. Please do not suggest such a thing again.'

To date, Jago had derived no perceptible benefit from Miss Kelly's laborious studies. To judge from her constant tutting and sighing, however, she had not, in Haydn's labyrinthine records, found the Rembrandt which would save the mansion.

'So,' he now said, with due solemnity and sobriety, 'what do you reckon? Have we got a chance?'

'I repeat,' Miss Sniffy rustled viciously at him, 'you are in serious trouble. I will be unable to arrive at a comprehensive assessment for another few days. Obviously, in the present climate . . .' She shook her head sadly as though delivering a tacit prognosis on a dying child. 'You seem to have precious few realizable assets, Mr van Zeller. Aside from the Whitechapel Road premises, you have two leases close to expiry, excessive stocks of fabric, and your personal property, the car, the van, your horses . . .'

'You can forget the horses,' he told her briskly.

She looked up. 'Hardly the indulgence for someone in your position, surely, Mr van Zeller?' she hummed.

'I have one hundred and twenty pounds,' he told her, 'for the mare's carcase. I shot her last weekend.'

Roberta Kelly shuddered. 'And the other – the racehorse . . .?'

'He didn't reach his reserve.' He wandered over to the window, gazed out on scurrying shoppers, on grinding, shuddering buses, smudged by the rain. His hand lay on Diana's shoulder. 'In fact, Miss Kelly,' he swung round and told her with a smile, 'he may just be the Rembrandt in the attic.'

'Bloody nags,' Ian Johnson puffed. 'You're sure you want to break your bloody neck out in some hell hole behind the Iron Curtain?'

'The Iron Curtain has been drawn, Ian,' Jago reminded him. He wrapped his tweed Ulster closer against the wind which hummed tritones, playing at ghosts. 'It's our ancient friend and ally Czechoslovakia now, or rather, the Czech Republic. And yes. I've wanted to ride in this race since I was sixteen. We all have one dream that survives all the friction of a life. I hope we do, anyhow. This one's not only survived intact, it's become smoother and brighter with the years. It's perfect. I've got a friend, you know, decided when he was eleven, read Stevenson, right, he was going to live in Polynesia some day. He collected books about Polynesia, even bought things for his trip, stored them in the cupboard under the stairs. He worked hard, got a seat on the board, reared three children, got 'em through school . . . He's been gone three years now. Got a postcard from him the other day. He's got as far as the Marquesas. Well, this is like that for me. God, have you seen the films of that race?'

Jago had been raising his voice against the growing thunder. Ian's eyes had slowly narrowed. Now the amorphous thunder split up into separate mama-dada drumrolls. There was panting, too, from the horses as they burst over the crest of the hill, the jingle of harness and the odd ragged word from the lads.

They flashed by like a magic lantern show, then the screen was blank again save for the white sheen on the dun grass, the clasping junipers and the Rokeby Venus swoop of the downs.

'Humph,' Ian said. 'Yes, yes, I've seen the films. Looks like a bloody hard way to commit suicide, you ask me. Bloody long way to go, too. What's wrong with drowning yourself in the village pond?'

Jago grinned as he followed Ian down the hill to where the string now circled, puffing steam. 'But what do you think of his chances?' he asked.

'I dunno, do I?' Ian waved a gloved hand. 'I mean, sure, he can jump well enough, but – what sort of animal d'ye reckon you want?'

'Well,' Jago considered as he had considered the question many times before, 'you need a racehorse because it can get rough out there. You're racing all the way, and certainly up to the Taxis . . .'

'You can't fault Burly, not when it comes to getting in amongst 'em and fighting.'

'No, well, but then, you need an animal with wide experience of different sorts of obstacles – a cross-country horse, a horse that's hunted . . .'

'Full marks so far.' Ian's voice jolted as he walked.

'A lot of the animals that run there are lean and weedy and inexperienced.'

'That, then, will be your greatest danger – mind, it usually is. The other bugger. And fate, of course, She's a bitch.'

'"I' faith, she is a strumpet."'

'Exactly.'

Suddenly, the two men were surrounded by horses which circled them, steaming, just feet away. Steam arose from the riders' lips, too.

Burly looked – well, burly. He had consistently put on condition as he grew older, furnishing an already substantial frame. If Jago had not known better, he'd have thought to find a vast pair of swinging balls between those balloon-shaped hams.

'Right, bit of schooling now,' Ian called up. 'Judith, you take Golden Lad; Steve, the youngster. Mr van Zeller'll lead you on the old feller.'

Jago tied the throat strap on his skull cap and walked over to where Raff, Burly's lad was dismounting. He handed him the reins. Jago smiled, nodded. Raff's head was at the level of his breastbone. The lad said, 'Gassy as all get out, for a geriatric, sir,' and Jago wondered, as he bent to flick him up into the saddle, whether he referred to him or to the horse.

The saddle was warm. Jago folded the reins at his crotch and dropped the leathers by seven holes. Sometimes he was asked why, of all diversions that he could have picked, he, at six foot two, chose race-riding. He could never think of a very good answer, save that there is no gentlemans' basket-ball, that steeplechasing always appealed to him and that he seemed to be good at it.

Not as good, however, as those whom he was supposed to lead over the three schooling fences. That, he would never be. Judith Stead was Ian's secretary and one of the most successful girl professionals in the country. As for Steve Daffen, he was one of the Holy Trinity. At any time in the past twenty years, there have been just two or three riders who make the remainder of their fellow professionals look silly; who, on a moderate horse, will always beat their confrères on a halfway good one; who are worth your money, on the average day, just because they know the right way round.

And of the current Trinity, Steve was the big boy. He had been champion three times now. He had won the Gold Cup twice, the Hennessy three times, the King George three times, the National once. He was a serious player.

And Jago was to lead him.

The wind wriggled past them and over them like a stream. Burly was high-stepping like a hackney, barely deigning to touch the turf with his each footfall. Jago glanced over his left shoulder. 'All set?'

Judith nodded. Her dark hair splayed behind her, then whipped about her mouth and chin. Steve, on a skittering, side-slithering flame chestnut, called, 'Show us the way, Jago!'

He leaned forward and clicked his tongue. Burly had seen the fences. He needed no encouragement. He rocked easily into a hack canter, but had to pretend that he was above such sluggish progress. He shook his head against the bit's restraint. He snorted his protest. He was all *machismo*. He knew his business.

Jago did not need to count down to take off. Burly did it, in general, a damn sight better than he. Nonetheless, just from habit, he was alert for errors. 'Three, two, one, and . . .'

There was silence as Burly's back stretched and the grass grew suddenly distant, a crackle as he clipped the top of the plain fence, then a loud 'houf!' as his forefeet clove the dew-soaked turf. Jago sat square in the middle of the saddle, just leaning forward a little to add impulsion, rocking back as a counterbalance as Burly descended, gathering him up in readiness for the giant stride that he always put in as his hind legs caught up, his rear end dropped, and he kicked for the next obstacle.

Behind them, like echoes, there were crackles and thuds as the others took the fence. Jago was not nervous, not even self-conscious any more. He was alone with his horse on the downs, far, far in space and time from Consultants in Insolvency and piles of bills and dingy shops on dirty streets.

And that, he supposed, was why a six-foot-two business-man chose this for a diversion. Nowhere else was he so little – or so much – himself. Nowhere else did he feel so dissoci-ated from the world and its problems. If power without responsibility be the prerogative of the harlot, this was Jago's Belle de Jour adventure. He had no power save Burly's, which let him fly. He could hurt no one save himself, so was free of responsibility. That was a rare freedom.

The second was an open ditch. The birch loomed between Burly's bobbing ears, and suddenly Jago gulped and gasped. Burly should have stood off. Instead, his forefeet were teetering on the very brink of the ditch as, at the last moment, his muscles bunched and he somehow projected himself almost vertically up at the obstacle.

His forefeet hit it hard. Jago lurched forward. The rough maned neck punched him in the teeth, making his head snap back. His right hand rose for balance. The horse descended steeply, with Jago lolling forward on his neck like a straw doll. He saw the turf through a fast and powerful zoom lens. Suddenly it was rushing backwards in detailed close-up. His hands fumbled and flapped, found the loose rein and closed on it. At his near side, Judith was already landing. Jago pulled himself back up in the saddle, not for the first time thanking God for long legs and wondering how those less generously provided for in this department ever stayed on a jumping horse at all.

Burly raised his head. He shook it, for all the world like a drunk trying to clear his vision. Then he saw the plain fence ahead. Of course, *that* was what he had been doing. Winning the Grand National. Silly of him. He bounded like a playful greyhound.

'Listen,' Jago said to Steve as they walked their mounts slowly back to the string. 'How would you approach a fence five foot six high and five foot six wide . . .?'

'Carefully.' Steve raised one black eyebrow.

'. . . with a seventeen-foot drop on the landing side,' Jago finished.

'Seventeen . . .?' This time Steve's eyebrows damn near jerked up to his widow's peak. 'I wouldn't approach it at all. Not without a parachute.'

'Say you had to,' Jago persisted.

'If I had to approach it,' he considered, 'I would do it . . . in tears, I reckon.'

Jago was to meet Mr Paul Pickering on his way back to town. He assumed that this must be *the* Paul Pickering's son, because *the* Paul Pickering had been something of a hero in Jago's childhood. He had been a rich playboy and a first-rate amateur rider back in the sixties. Jago had read of his exploits in the papers when he was at prep school. Pickering had vanished without trace, and Jago had assumed that he must be dead.

Diana had arranged the meeting amidst fits of giggles. She was helpless for a minute or so after putting the telephone down. 'Oh, he's a charmer,' she explained 'A right character. He lives in a mobile home, only he says it's not very mobile because it's on bricks, behind a sawmill just outside Hungerford, and he says he lives with twelve greyhounds and two horses and he'd rather not meet at a pubic house – he really did say that – because he has problems with the sauce, and if it wasn't too far out of your way . . .'

Jago said, 'God save us.'

It was exactly as she had described it. Incredulous, he steered the XJS to the left onto a light industrial estate, and wound his way through various huge white sheds until he found the one marked Lloyds of Hungerford, Sawmill. 'Take the little track to your right,' the directions read, 'and you can't miss it.'

He took the little track at his right. It bumped along to a wire fence, then hooked to the right again to run alongside the wire. And there, beneath the sawmill, perched on stilts of bricks and overlooking the ischial folds of the valley, was a long, tatty, blue and white mobile home. There were large gas cylinders about the wooden steps to the only door. There was a wooden hut, too, at the left of Mr Pickering's home. Everything seemed a little worn, but orderly and clean.

As Jago stepped from the car, still frowning, a gap opened up in the Venetian blinds at the right of the door. A second later, the door swung inwards. Mr Paul Pickering sauntered out into the sunlight.

He had to be fifty. His hair was white, his skin tanned the colour of last year's penny. There was not an inch of spare on his frame. His legs, though encased in cavalry twill, were those of a gangling adolescent. His jodhpur boots gleamed – the deep gleam of a military spit-and-polish job.

'Hello,' he said. 'Hello, hello.' And he strode towards Jago, one long hand extended. 'You'll be Jago. God, good. Super. Glad you could make it.'

As they shook hands, Paul gazed at Jago's face with narrowed eyes as though it were on a distant horizon. His smile dragged his lips roguishly to the right. His teeth were perfect.

'Nice motor,' he drawled, and Jago could not believe that that twanging, Leslie Phillips, sixties Lothario accent had survived. Paul Pickering was a human Madagascar. He had somehow developed untouched by all adjacent evolution. He strolled round the car. He ran a loving hand down the sills. 'Used to have an E type myself,' he mused. 'Lovely old girl. And my dad had the old SS100, you know? Leather strap round the bonnet, all that? Gosh.'

He snapped out of his reverie. 'So. Yes. No. Jolly pleased to meet you. Read about you, of course. Saw you did well in that Swedish thing. Rode in that myself back in – what? Sixty-eight. Came an almighty cropper at the second big ditch.'

'God,' Jago grinned, 'I can't believe it. You rode the first horse I ever backed. Ballinteer. I won five pounds. You must be one of the principal reasons that I ride at all.'

'Ah, Ballinteer. Great old pal. Yes. Now. Sorry. You'll be wanting to get into the warm. Come along. Meet the family.'

He led Jago across the pitted yard and up the three steps. He stood back to allow him in. 'Not a lot of room, I'm afraid,' he said, 'but enough for my needs. Used to have space, you know, big house, big farm, the lot, but I can tell you, I've never been happier than I am here. Just me and the dogs. No need to worry about insurance, all that. Sit down, sit down, please.'

He indicated a utility armchair. Jago sat. It was surprisingly warm in here. In front of him, there was a double bed on which three big greyhounds lay, two brindles and a grey. They did not growl. They did not move. They just lay there, looking at him, and their eyes wrinkled in those most beguiling of canine smiles. Their tails thudded on the Paisley counterpane.

Paul said, 'Won't be a sec.' He walked through into the room behind Jago. Water chuckled. A kettle clanged. A match puffed.

Jago looked about, still bemused. There was a smoked glass and chrome coffee table and another armchair. A Swiss cheese plant stood in a rather surprising heavy green jardinière complete with stand by the little telephone. There were a lot of books which seemed to range from the calf-bound and gilt to the tattiest and sleaziest spy thrillers of the fifties and sixties. Two mounted trout rods and what looked like a massive split-cane salmon rod, still in its Farlows canvas case, stood in an old brass mortar shell, together with a selection of blackthorns and a fine umbrella with an engraved gold band. The walls not lined with books were almost as comprehensively covered with framed photographs, of horses and their riders, of young men in white ties and of pretty girls with softened edges and naked shoulders.

'I thought you had twelve dogs!' Jago called above the soughing and rattling of the kettle.

'Yes, yes, absolutely!' he called back. 'No, these are my privileged ladies. The other nine are out in the kennel.'

'They didn't bark!'

'No, no. I told them not to. If you'd just been a stranger, they'd have barked the house down, but, you know, I told them you were all right. No, it's funny,' he came through with two chipped mugs of coffee, 'I'm usually at work at this time. I'm a one-man taxi firm, you know? School runs, things like that. Keeps the old bod and soul together. And they're quiet as mice, unless a stranger turns up. Soon as I get back, of course, they're crazy with excitement. Know the sound of the barouche.'

He sat on the very edge of the armchair. His left knee jiggled constantly. 'So,' he said gleefully, 'Pardubice. Just four weeks off. Can't believe it.'

'Yes,' Jago was inclined to share his incredulity. He was cautious. 'Well, like I said in the advert, my horse and Clay – that's my sort of friend and assistant – will be setting off on the Monday before the race. I'll be flying out on the Thursday or Friday. Forgive my asking, but . . . it is you we're talking about, isn't it? Riding, I mean?'

'Oh, absolutely, absolutely. Bloody silly, I know. Just one of those things I've always wanted to do but never got the chance. You see, old chap,' he tapped Jago's knee, 'I was jolly lucky as a young man. My mama had a pile in Rutland, you know the sort of thing, so, as you know, I got to do a fair bit of the old upsy downsy back then. Melton Ride – you ever do the Melton Ride?'

'Yes,' Jago smiled. He had won the Melton Ride three years ago.

'Team chases, all those chaps. And lots and lots of lovely girls. Anyhow, seventy-one, I go and marry one of them. Silly boy, eh? Two children, farm, all that. And my wife doesn't like me racing, so, that's that. Eight years on, the – lady dog, I would say, but it might offend my girls here – absconds with the next-door neighbour. Well, between her and the lawyers and a chum who screwed me for sixty grand, then topped himself – poor chap, not really his fault, gambling, drink, you know, there but for a brace of Cod, eh? – I'm cleaned out. So I think, well, bugger all that. Don't want anything to do with it. Let them have their damned intrigues and their griping for money Me, I've got everything I want here. The dogs – much nicer than people – the coursing, warmth, food, a job. Perfect.'

He picked up his coffee. He raised the mug. 'Here's to us,' he said; 'those like us. Damn few.' He drank.

'Damn few indeed,' Jago smiled.

'But there's always been this niggle, this one thing still left to do, you know? I was meant to ride at Pardubice back then, in my last year of freedom, but I fell out hunting. Horse got out there. I never did. Of course, it was all communist in those days. But now . . . Well, I've got the horse. Little fellow. Avocet, he's called. Goes like the proverbial off the shovel in team chases, point-to-points, and Czechoslovakia's opened up, and I'd never qualify for the National – and who'd want to, now that they've buggered about with the fences? And – well, I've got a few thousand saved up, and I thought, well, come on, Pickering. It's now or never. Then I saw your ad, and that put the lid on it. Mad, I know. But even if I put down at the first, I'd like to be able to say, "Damn it, I did it. I rode in the Velka Pardubicka." So. Crazy, I know,' he shrugged, 'but there you are.'

'Not so crazy,' Jago said slowly. 'I suppose my story's none so different, only, thank God, I never got trapped by a bloodsucking woman . . .'

'Wise chap.'

'But it's always nagged at me, too. The big one. And now – hell, it's got to be worth a crack.'

He still could not work out if Mr Paul Pickering was for real or not. If, however, his horse and his nine silent greyhounds proved imaginary, Jago thought that he would still feel sympathy and affection for his Mitty dreams. Maybe Paul had not fallen from the heaven of his memory, but it was plain that he had fallen from grace, yet had taken grace with him, within him. He had fallen with the light-footed blitheness of the philosopher, and still had some dreams intact. In some ways, Jago actually envied him his untroubled existence.

'Have you been out there before?' Jago asked. 'Eastern Europe, I mean?'

'No, Berlin, though. Been to Berlin.'

He stood and pulled down one of the framed photographs on the wall. He handed it to Jago. Three smiling young men in white tie and three smiling girls in ball gowns. Two of the men wore military tailcoats. The last, in the livery of the Cottesmore, was Mr Paul Pickering, blond, lean, but still with those stalker's eyes, narrowed as if against the sun.

'That was Berlin,' he smiled happily. 'Big ball. Great gas.

She was a lovely girl.' He pointed to the brunette on his arm. He was lost again. 'Lovely girl,' he drawled softly, 'lovely girl . . . Now,' again he almost visibly shook himself, 'come and see the beasties . . .'

Receivership was easy – one might almost say painless were it not for the years of hope and hard work which had gone into constructing the company and its reputation.

No, it was painful, all right, but there was nothing shocking or sudden about the pain. That was all internal. Externally, it was a mere formality. Jago registered a death. The clerks nodded.

It was, in fact, a process so workaday, so matter-of-fact, so tawdry that he felt cheated. The appropriate documents were signed, Miss Sniffy, like a one-track feminist glaring at a widower, indicated to him that the company's demise, evidence or no evidence, must be the fault of the spendthrift managing director. He rode horses, didn't he? Well. There. And drove a fast car? She rested her case.

And that was that.

Clay said, 'Shit, Cindy, Diana, I'm really sorry. That's really bad luck.'

Cindy just shrugged. 'Ah, well. Back to the streets. What was good enough for mum is good enough for me.'

'Whoa, now. Hold it,' Jago told her. 'Not yet awhile, any road. The receivers will keep the business going until they can sell it, wind it up with all creditors paid, turn it back into a going concern, or, if all else fails, simply fold. That's their business.' He eyed Miss Sniffy. She had never lost a business in her life because she had never started one. Or, Jago thought viciously, a baby. She sat chewing something and studying papers.

'It is also their business,' he spoke loudly, 'to save jobs where possible. Isn't that right, Ms Kelly?'

She shrugged. She was now in control.

'Anyway, if that day comes, we'll get together and form a co-operative in a country cottage. No. Listen. What it comes down to is that Zellers is under new management. I'm out on my ear.'

'Well, *bollocks* to that,' announced Diana. 'I mean, what do these guys know about our business, eh? We've failed because the market's all arse about face. Fine. They can do better? The only chance we've got – the only chance is *us* guys, who know what we're doing, waiting for things to pick up again or waiting till we see an opening. That right or not? Jeez, I mean, look. Successful business. Old Mr van Zeller comes up with the goods, right? Then everything goes bad. In comes Jago, turns it all around. Why? 'Cos he's one of us, right? He knows the trade. Everything works great until . . .' She flapped her open hands twice. She pouted. 'Well, fuck the lot of 'em, I say.' She inhaled deeply. Her lower lip trembled. Then she spun round and fled for the Ladies.

There was a murmur of sympathy, which made Jago feel good.

'For your information,' Miss Sniffy looked up from her ledger, 'Mr van Zeller will be retained in an advisory capacity. His expertise will, of course, be invaluable. Oh, and Mr van Zeller . . .?'

'Yes?'

'If I could have your passport, please . . .'

He joined the workforce then, in staring down at her over-stuffed face. He rested his forearms on the desk. He milled and spat out the words in chunks. 'What the hell are you talking about?' he growled. 'I am a British subject. I retain my rights.'

'Read the regulations.' She reached for a leaflet and tossed it to him without raising her eyes.

'Stuff the regulations, madam.' Jago picked up the leaflet and ripped it in two. 'I have damn near bankrupted myself in fulfilling my guarantees, as well you know. I have shown myself willing in every regard to assist in this process. There is no question of any impropriety. I am perfectly willing to keep you posted as to my whereabouts, but no way do you stop me from travelling where I will, and I guarantee that your superiors will back me in this. For your information, in just under a month from today, I will be going to the Czech Republic with my last few pence in order to ride a horse in a race there. Just see whether your bosses are prepared to try to stop me. Bluff called, Miss Kelly.'

And her bluff had indeed been called. Jago did not know the regulations, but he was confident enough that he was in the right of it, and her face told him that she knew it too. Her mouth worked like an eager caterpillar. Her eyes were sullen and stubborn. 'We shall see,' she said, as the ragged chorus of cheers and catcalls from the staff swept over her. 'We shall see.' And she mustered what dignity she could. Rustling like a parcel and, followed by whoops and applause, she waddled from the room.

'Right,' Jago announced when she was gone. 'We are going to have a wake. It's been a good life and the old thing deserves a rousing send-off. I have all of two thousand pounds left in my account. That won't pay a quarter of your outstanding wages. What I propose is – I'm riding Burly for the last-but-one time at Sandown on Saturday, and he's in with a chance. With your permission, we're all going down there and we'll have a decent lunch and drink a few bottles of champagne to the memory of Zellers. And if there's a bob or two left over, we'll shove it all on Burly, who's been with us almost as long as I have, and if he wins, we might get seriously, disgustingly drunk. Alternatively, of course, I can give each of you a few quid and wish you a fond farewell. So, with not a single reference to St Crispian, who's game for a day at the races?'

The cheer that went up gave Jago fleeting pleasure. He was offering extemporized *panem et circenses* as the empire crumbled. Nonetheless, on that cold afternoon, with great, swagging black clouds grinding across the London skyline, they all felt hopeful again. They were united. They were friends.

'And God help my friends,' thought Jago ruefully.

Prince Cyril Havlik knelt up on the bed in his New York apartment. His naked body was very white and thin. 'Go on,' he said, 'go on. You'll love it.' He grasped the nape of the blonde woman's neck and pushed it downward.

She turned her head so that her cheek rested against the other woman's pubis. 'No! I'll gag. Honest. I'll vomit!'

'Bullshit. Come on. Shit, millions of girls eat pussy, Christ's sakes. What's wrong with you? You like it, don't you, Fliss?'

'I love it, baby,' the black girl yawned. Her right hand was idly pumping at the kneeling prince's engorged organ. Her left plucked at the blonde girl's hair. 'Shit, kind'll take it OK but not give it.'

'No, I . . . OK. OK, I'll try . . .' The blonde girl stuck out a tentative tongue. She grimaced, but persisted.

'That's a good girl,' Havlik soothed. 'Open it up, Fliss. Let her get at it.' He moved behind the blonde girl, licked his finger and felt his way. He groped amongst the litter on the bedside table, found a condom wrapper and raised it to his mouth. He ripped it with his teeth whilst his left hand yet probed. 'That's a good little whore . . .' He eased on the condom and, holding his cock straight, slid it into the blonde girl. 'You like it, don't you?' he breathed. 'Course you do. You love it, don't you?' He brought his open hand down hard on her right buttock.

She nodded frantically. Havlik's left hand grasped the nape of her neck again and pushed down hard. He sneered. Again he spanked her, and the black girl beneath them smiled. 'That's it. Give it to the little bitch . . .'

She was the only one of the three who did not start when the door slammed inwards and two men moved smoothly and silently to take up positions on either side of the bed. One of the men was tall and black, the other stocky and white, with crewcut grizzled hair. Both held handguns in both hands.

Havlik yelped and doubled up. He grabbed up a crumpled corner of sheet and pulled it to his groin. 'No?' he keened. 'No? Please? Come on, guys . . .'

The blonde girl lifted her gleaming face, saw the guns, whimpered just once, eyes bulging, and rolled from the bed onto the floor. She curled up into as tight a ball as she could contrive, and lay shivering and rhythmically squeaking.

The black girl kept smiling. She remained spreadeagled, knees raised. She licked her middle finger and took up the duty so lately done by the blonde girl's tongue. 'Hi, guys,' she said languorously. 'You come to join the party?'

Hers was the most efficacious strategy. The white man gulped. His eyes remained fastened on that dipping, clicking finger. A child could have taken him at that moment.

'Ah, our noble prince.' The dark voice buzzed in the bare boards. 'I always like to see aristocrats at play.'

The man who strolled in was taller than the black man, broader than the white. He wore a charcoal-grey herring-bone overcoat over a black and white dogstooth sports coat, an open-necked button-down Oxford and grey slacks. His brown brogues looked expensive and well-tended.

His body was that of a heavyweight boxer barely beginning to go to seed. His stomach was concave, but only just. He stood straight. His skin was tanned and glowing, his hair a smooth, shiny skullcap. If ever his nose had been broken, it had been expensively mended. His head was the only incongruity. It looked absurdly small and soft atop such a body. The cheeks were plush, the lips full and dry. It was a baby's face on a killer's body.

'What's this all about, man?' Havlik's voice cracked and shook. 'I mean, busting into my apartment . . .'

'My apartment, I think.' The man strolled to the foot of the bed. 'And my girls. That's right, Felicity, huh?'

'That's right, Mr Ward.' The dark girl made a moue and her eyes grinned wickedly up at him.

The big man reached down and grasped the blonde girl under the arms. He lifted her effortlessly up and appraised her hanging, wriggling body. 'Don't know you. You mine?'

'Please . . .' the girl implored.

'Are you mine?'

'B-Billy Jink's,' she drooled.

'Billy's?' The big man smiled a slow smile. 'I don't think so. You're nice. Far too nice for the Jink. Six o'clock this evening at the Troubadour, right? Leave Billy to me. You know who I am? Paul Ward. Mr Ward to you. Now, girls, I got to have a little word with our noble prince, so please be so good as to get.'

'Ah . . .' Felicity moaned, 'we was having fun.'

'Out.'

The blonde girl scampered gratefully to the scattered

clothes at the centre of the room. Some she examined and dropped. The others she pulled quickly over trembling limbs. Felicity was less hurried, but both girls were ready at the same time. They walked out like strangers.

'Now, Prince Havlik.' Ward dusted a chair and sank down on it. 'They say you got a plan you want to discuss with me.'

Havlik had pulled a sheet up around him. Shock had chilled him. He hugged himself and shook. His short mouse hair was splashed in spikes. He looked sullen. 'I got a plan, yeah. Didn't know it was you. Shit, why'd you need all this stuff? Guns, busting things up . . .? Just a business discussion, a meeting . . .'

'When I have meetings, Prince, people sometimes try to put one over on me. Often they owe me money. Sometimes they heard of guns too. This way, I talk to Felicity, she unlocks the door, I know what you're going to be doing when I arrive, right? You got no clothes on. There are no surprises. I don't like surprises.'

'These guys have to keep pointing guns at me?'

'Hmm.' Ward made much of considering. 'No. He's right, boys. You can ease up. There's a TV in there. The prince's video collection should be interesting. Just listen out, OK? I call for you, you just come in and blow my friend here away, OK?'

'Sure.' Both men spoke as one. They shoved their guns under their armpits.

'That high yellow's somethin',' the crewcut man mumbled as he walked past Ward.

'Felicity?' Ward mused. 'Fifty dollars off the week's wages, you can take her night off.'

'You got it.' The man clenched his fist and slapped it into his palm.

'So, now, prince.' Ward leaned forward and rested his forearms on his thighs. He was all charm. He purred like an idling Rolls. 'Tell me about this "plan".'

'I get to put on clothes?'

'No.'

'Shit. OK. Listen. So I owe you money . . .'

'A lot of money, prince. Felicity doesn't come cheap, nor does that nice white powder over there on the dresser. It's been a while, huh? Expensive habits. Lot of credit there.'

'No, no, sure. So, listen. I used to do a bit of race-riding, you know? And there's this race over there. The Pardubice, right? That gives me a reason to be there, OK?'

'Certainly, but why should we want you out there? We send our own men in, there's no problem.'

'For me there is,' Havlik mumbled sulkily. 'OK, a lot of it's yours, but I tell you where it is, how'd I know I'd ever get any of it?' His own audacity made him gulp. 'I mean, what we got here is a standoff, right?'

'I don't see it that way.' Ward showed his teeth.

'Sure. You can kill me, whatever, but what good's that to you? I'm the guy knows where the stuff is stashed, right? I'll go in and get it, but I'm not telling.'

'There are ways of squeezing that out of you, prince.'

'Yeah, but I lie, you're fucked. Even if you get the stuff, I withdraw my provenance, you're back with scrap value, aren't you? I'm part of the prize.'

'I'll grant,' Ward nodded, 'that you have your uses. So, you ride in this race . . .'

'Yeah. Only I won't have to do more than the first couple of fences, 'cos I've heard there's gonna be this big demonstration, stop the race before they get to the big fences, which is fine by me. But I take out a mare, right? The stuff goes into the mare, yeah? They can't X-ray a mare's uterus. Makes her sterile, OK? So how many customs guys are ready to get behind a race mare, shove their hands up her cunt, huh? Shit, I'm a US citizen. There's going to be press and things about. Diplomatic suicide, forget getting kicked to hell and back.'

'It's a thought,' Ward conceded. 'It's been used for narcotics. It's worked. Mare has a hell of a space in there. Only problem is, you're marked over there, right? Soon as you arrive, you got a thousand Stasi or whatever they're called on your tail.'

'Sure.' Havlik nodded eagerly. 'No, sure, but the whole point, this race, there's guys, English, French, German . . . I know this sort of guy. They think, "Great. Adventure. Save the legacy of a great aristocrat dynasty". They – they're all kind of Indiana Jones. Way they're reared.'

'Yeah? Tell me about these people,' Ward said sombrely.

'OK. OK. Sure. There's this English guy I know. Old guy, crazy. Met him at Maryland, I was just eighteen, but he knows my family, right? His dad flew with my uncle, Battle of Britain, all that, OK? He's like all those David Niven characters in the "Bandits, dive, dive, dive" movies. He's like out of another age, yeah? I get him to go for me, dig the stuff up, right? He brings it back to me, I shove it in the mare, we're away.'

'And what if he won't do the job?' Ward was mild.

'There's another one. Another English guy. I got friends know him. English are best. They still believe the world belongs to them. Tailor, would you believe? Rides horses in his spare time. Going bad. You think he's not going to jump at a thing like this?'

'Give me the details.' Ward slapped his thighs. 'In theory, I'll buy it, though I still don't get why you won't let us find the stuff.'

''Cos I don't trust you guys,' Havlik snapped. 'There's still some change owed me. I need it.'

'I am insulted.' Ward slowly shook his head. 'Still, your interests and mine are the same in this business. You want out. I want the stuff. If you can persuade me these guys are right, you go ride your race. You cross me, I presume you know, you're quite seriously dead. You've had your fun. It's time you paid your dues.'

'Yeah.' Havlik nodded fast. He licked his lips. 'Yeah, sure. I know that. Come on, man, I'll not cross you. Am I fucking crazy or what? I owe you. Shit, being a prince may not mean much these days, but I pay my debts.'

'You better, Prince.' Ward stood. This was a lengthy process. Such a frame needed time to extend. 'Olcese! Moreton!'

'No? Shit!' Havlik had pulled the duvet up and now cringed down, biting the mattress.

'Easy,' oozed Ward with a grin. 'The prince has sensitive

aristocratic genes. Now, prince. The details about these messengers of yours?'

When Jago rode his first winner, he decided to record the fact with something more serious than the little silver cup with which he was presented. He went to Sotheby's where, for five thousand pounds, he acquired a Sartorius oil in a black frame. It showed two jockeys riding a close finish. They rode like Jago, sitting almost upright, with long rein and long leathers and vaguely alarmed but resolute expressions on their faces. The rider nearest to the painter had his whip raised high. He was a neck behind his opponent, but that crack might just engender a last-stride surge which would bring him upsides.

Jago had speculated about that finish through many happy hours. It was the perfect race because it would never know a conclusion, though the post was clearly visible at the right-hand-side of the canvas.

He loved that picture.

Now, however, the finish had become abstract, conceptual, minimalist, worthy of a Turner prize at least, because all that Jago had to gaze upon was a blank space on his bedroom wall.

Yesterday, he had taken the painting down to a Bond Street gallery with a reputation for honesty.

Honesty, needless to say, was relative. It was very relative on the racecourse. It was exceedingly relative in the City. In Bond Street art galleries, it barely meant the same thing as elsewhere. It was a word much used, as though its use might furnish the establishment with probity, replacing the thing itself, but it was something like gentleness in a knackers' yard or selflessness on stage. The trade precluded the virtue. This dealer was merely thought to be a gentler death-dealer, a less ambitious actor than most.

He was young, with a Billy Bunter belly and a splash of black hair, and roses in his cheeks. He said, 'Honest, Jago, I wish I could help. I mean, it's a lovely thing, and two years ago – God, easy. I mean, I could have got you twelve, fourteen, no problem. But the market's dead. I mean, look. I've got this Seymour. Now that's a serious picture, am I right?'

Jago eyed the vast canvas. He understood Chris Owen's term. It was indeed serious, with a cast of some twenty horses and humans milling, rearing, galloping and jumping in a great landscape.

'Can I shift it? Not for love nor money. Honest. Two years, I've had that. When I bought it, I reckoned eighty easy. Now it's marked down to forty-five and there's not even a Jap or a Swiss on the horizon. No. I mean – well, you know. You must have been suffering. All I can say is, whatever you've been suffering, we've had far, far worse. Half the boys round here have had their cheque books taken away. There must be a hundred million hanging on the walls of this street, and it's all dead money.'

'I'm a dealer,' Jago told Owen, 'I know the song. How much?'

'God . . .' He looked down at the canvas on his desk. 'I mean, it's embarrassing . . .'

'So blush.'

'I mean, it is a lovely thing. God, it should be worth far more . . .'

'Please.' Jago sighed. 'I know how things are. What's the score?'

'Well,' Owen turned, desolate, to Jago, 'I could do you seven, and that's top dollar. Honest. Even when I've had it cleaned and restored. I'll be lucky to make a grand on it, and it may sit here for the next five years. No. No, I'd keep it for stock, see when the market takes an upturn.'

He shook his head, disconsolate. He really did not want to buy the picture. He really did not like pictures. He would love to go off and become a hermit, perhaps keep a few bees, live in a sackcloth habit. He was bound to this art-dealing business by a vengeful Fury, like Sisyphus to his boulder or Tantalus to his apples. It was his cross.

Jago tried to barter but, to his astonishment, Owen stuck at seven thousand.

Jago did not look at his painting again as Chris wrote the

cheque, ripped it with a flourish from the book and, with further apologies, saw him to the door.

Jago had no income. To all intents and purposes, he was unemployed. He had no assets save an aged horse, a horse-box, a few articles of furniture and eight thousand, seven hundred pounds. Of this, two thousand must go to Clay, who needed expenses for the trip and was owed a month's wages anyhow; two thousand to the staff party; nine hundred to Ian for training fees and vet's bills. He allowed a further two thousand for rent, electricity, telephone and petrol up to the end of October. The return fare to Czechoslovakia was £450, then there were hotel bills, the cost of a hire car and so on.

The Pardubice, then, was the end of the road. He could not see beyond that, nor had he the least idea how he would survive thereafter. His ticket guaranteed that he would return to England, but he would do so bust up, bust to the wide, or both.

In his colours and cover-coat, Jago bade them farewell.

They cheered.

They would have cheered, he suspected, if he had dropped dead.

One case of champagne, an acre's worth of asparagus and several large salmon had given their all to create this bonhomie amongst the staff and associates of Zellers. Jago had invited Charlie, who ran the local wine merchants, Frank and Pat, who ran the local pub, Dario and Theresa, who ran the local restaurant, and various reps and suppliers who had given long and conscientious service to the firm. He had also invited Miss Sniffy who, to his surprise, had accepted the olive branch and now sat, arms folded and legs crossed beneath the open-topped bus, gazing out over the racecourse with a glazed, expectant look in her eyes.

The Zellers staff were conspicuously well-dressed. It was for occasions like this that Zellers had existed. Coats and jackets were cut, built and stitched better, Jago thought, than any modern designer could contrive. They were cut soberly, conventionally, yet with a romantic flair which, to his eye, was distinctive. Dan had had the gift. He had passed it on to Neil, and he in turn to Cindy. It lay in the snugness of the shoulders, the darts which made a coat's skirt flare in a soft swoop from the small of the back, the generous allowance of fabric which gave the garments fluent movement.

Jago was proud of his defunct firm, its products and its staff, for all that Diana was alternately sniffing and giggling where she sat on the rug and Neil was swaying as though the suite was adrift on a swell.

In order to make the occasion more memorable, Jago had sent down to the weighing-room to invite a few pros to the bus, so it was in elevated company that he now left and ducked beneath the rails to cross the course. Steve Daffen was at his right hand. He had been cornered by Diana and cried upon, informed by Miss Sniffy that she was much struck by his proficiency, fawned upon by Neil and John and taught how to ride by Clay. At Jago's left hand, Nick Storr, another of the top pros, was giggling happily. Cindy had told him that she'd give him a ride anytime, and Haydn Jones had mistaken him for his father and berated him about an animal which failed to win the Hennessy in 1969 or something.

They strode out onto the racecourse and, with childish pride, Jago relished the moment. They were three jockeys, shoulder to shoulder, three fittish, youngish men united by knowledge and by acceptance of personal risk. People greeted them as they passed and they nodded and waved. Jago knew, of course, that most of them were greeting Steve and Nick, heroes of the course on a daily basis. He did not care. He enjoyed his temporary co-opted membership of the Musketeers.

This, after all, was to be his last race, aside from the mad apotheosis of his riding career in Czechoslovakia. Whatever the future, it was unlikely to involve the sort of income needed to sustain an amateur rider.

It was a sad thought.

To many, never again to have to jolt through flying mud, mist, rain and snow at considerable personal risk may seem eminently desirable. Those who have done it don't see it that way. Jago would sooner give up a forty a day habit.

It was that every horse and every race was different, and that each contest entailed a flood of adrenalin such as he had never known elsewhere. It was making mistakes and thinking, 'next time I'll do that right,' and reliving each stride in your head. It was the companionship, with the horse and with the other riders. It was the awareness that each fence just might be your last. It was walking into a restaurant or an office feeling somehow detached and superior because you had been on the edge whilst others had been safe and sure. And it was horses; old friends whom you longed to ride because they were old friends, and, worse, progressive types whom you longed to ride because the two of you were going to get it right this time. Worst of all, there were the stars, superhorses, the animals blessed with courage that you could only briefly borrow, and a surge like a Guy Fawkes rocket when the touchpaper has sizzled down.

To hang up your boots feels like the most definitive step towards the grave.

They strode into the weighing-room past journalists and trainers. Trenchard, the plump little correspondent for the *Echo*, bearded Steve at the door. Nick and Jago strolled past the scales and into the changing room.

Here was subject matter for an artist – subject matter for a whole exhibition. There were young, ingenuous faces with clear bright eyes and toothless faces wrinkled as walnuts in which sharp, shifting eyes seemed the only things alive.

There were scrawny bodies, dimpled buttocks and stringy calves and thighs. There were shoulders like striding ridges, backs like thick rope. There were men in jock straps, men in long johns, men in breeches, men fully dressed. And all about there were the distinctive changing-room sounds – the flap of fabric, the rustle of breeches, the snap of elastic, the puff and the deep clang as locker doors shut, the burble of conversation, the occasional bark of laughter or bellowed joke.

Jago removed his coat and hung it up. He pulled down his whip, his cap and goggles. He was set.

'Best chateaubriand I've 'ad in years,' the little blond man behind him was saying.

'What's the difference between Sarah Carswell and spaghetti?' the big man with black hair on his arms and shoulder-blades shouted.

'No, I mean, fuck it. You plant hazels, I mean, they grow here naturally, right? You just shoot the squirrels, get students to harvest, and – shit, I mean, they've got a shelf-life of three years . . .'

'Richard's got a nice bitch. You should ask him . . .'

'Spaghetti moves when you eat it!'

'No, pig tries to run out at the open ditch. I tell you, that type's always bad news . . .'

Jago sat silent, and enjoyed the rough warmth. There are times when a night well-wrapped in the open can be infinitely more restorative than the deep peace of a Claridges double bed.

The riders were summoned out to the scales and so onto the course. It was a pale grey day, shiny as polished pewter. The trees and the rails of the winners' enclosure dazzled. Four or five autograph hunters assailed the group as they made their way to the paddock, a sudden oasis of relative peace amidst the hubbub. There was still some whiteness in the grass where boots had not trodden.

'Nothing to say, really, is there?' Ian greeted Jago with characteristic grumpiness. 'Oh. Cheque? Thanks. No, I mean, horse knows his business, well in at the weights. That thing, Swan Upping, has the beating of you if he gets it right, but, otherwise, Burly should be there or thereabouts. He's ready for it.'

Jago folded his arms and they stood side by side, watching Burly as he danced, head down, about the tan oval.

Burly's mane and tail were plaited, his quarters wisped in neat checks. Age had given him no gravitas, but it had given him weight and added presence. He looked bigger than his opponents, but then so did Jago. 'Yes,' he said, and his spine was crawling, his tits taut with anticipation. 'He looks great. You've done a great job.'

'Well, all you have to do is sit tight and let him do the business.'

Jago was not affronted. He knew the extent of the truth of this statement and the extent of its inaccuracy. Burly *could* run the race blindfold. He did know how to keep out of trouble and how to deal with it when it occurred, but then Jago also knew how to keep out of trouble. Just somehow he never managed to do so.

No, Burly's problem was sheer, boisterous coltishness. He wanted to be first at all the cakes, the jellies and the bouncy castle. He wanted to beat up all the boys and kiss all the girls. When first the thrill of the racecourse took hold of him, he could not really see the point of jumping and galloping, jumping and galloping. He preferred the idea of standing off and flying the whole course. Far less laborious, and far more in keeping with such a, well, such an altogether powerful, virile, super sort of horse.

It was no use Jago's fighting him. That simply made him bloody-minded. He fought back, and, with his mind on showing Jago who was boss, he would not notice such minor problems as open ditches. Jago had to console him, soothe him, remind him of all that he had learned over the years. He had to channel all that energy and aggression to one end.

So, yes, that meant sitting still, but sitting still in a certain way. There is more to horsemanship than the mechanical. Thought comes into it too.

Once, and if, he contrived to get Burly's back down, he could relax – almost.

Burly was being led towards Jago now. He put in a couple of quick bucks as he drew near, just to show that he meant business. The crowd behind him, though five yards away, backed away from the rails. Raff, Burly's lad, merely smiled and croaked, 'Whoah. Silly old fart.'

'Right, Jago.' Ian bent to give Jago a leg-up. Jago gathered the reins. Burly snorted and resumed his firewalking. 'Off with you, and good luck.'

As Raff led them out onto the course, Jago heard 'Good luck!' from Clay and from Cindy, who materialized at his near heel, then horse and rider were through the rails, the clip was released, and Burly sprang.

The process started now, as they cantered up to the start, with the washy bay quarters of the favourite ahead of them and the black heels flicking up gobs of turf, and Burly striking out with his forehand, nodding his heavy head, already wanting to be up there in what he saw as his place: Leader of the Pack.

Jago kept the reins crossed beneath his crotch, exerting even, steady pressure on the long reins, just bending the horse's neck a little, containing him.

And he talked above the rapid chopping of the hoofbeats. 'There we are, boy . . . out on our own. That's a find, bold boy . . . We're OK, aren't we? Sure we are. Sure we are. We're fine. Lovely day. No problem. That's a feller. Long way to go yet. Easy now. Easy. *Doucement*. Take it nice and easy . . .'

Burly heeded him – or maybe not. One way or another, he went steadily enough up to the three-mile, five-furlong start, slowed to a trot when Jago bade him, walked when he bade him. He was far from settled yet. Another horse cantered up behind them. Burly's arse dropped and he spurted as though goosed. A pigeon broke from a hedge twenty yards ahead of them. Even Burly could not pretend that this was alarming enough to justify shying, but he stiffened, raised his head and pricked his ears.

Jago went on with the soothing nonsense as they circled, and he appraised the opposition.

They were at Sandown, so none of the opposition was exactly negligible. On his or her day and in the right conditions, each of these could win a fair race. Several of them had done so.

Nick Storr was on a lovely iron-grey mare named Zingara who had scored in many a Northern Handicap chase and had twice completed the National. Kevin Doyle, the vet and Irish ex-champion amateur, rode Outfromunder, his compatriot, a solid, stocky sort of juvenile who had won a bumper at Leopardstown and had failed to quicken in two two-mile chases at Gowran and Fairyhouse. He had crossed the water now to be trained by George Godley. This was his first outing in a stayers' chase. He looked the type. Then there was the favourite, Swan Upping, a consistently genuine, honest, clean-jumping handicap chaser who, for five years, had run precisely true to form, winning when the handicapper allowed him. The handicapper was close to allowing him today. Burly, however, eight pounds better off, had the beating of him on a line through Swallowtail, who had beaten him by a length at Warwick at the back end of last term.

But Burly was lumbered by Jago; Swan Upping bore Steve Daffen. That made something of a nonsense of the handicap, because if, by any strange chance, they should jump the last upsides, Jago reckoned that you could add two stone to Burly's payload. Steve had the balance, the ferocity, the fitness and the expertise in a finish to make Jago's gangling attempts look, as Clay had it, 'like a Great Dane fucking a Yorkie'.

Jockeys were counted. They roughly lined up. The starter bellowed, 'Come along now. All ready?' Burly's neck rose, his quarters bunched, his forefeet kicked in a fast trot that made Jago feel as though he were a far from easy rider on a Harley.

The flag dropped.

Burly was on his way.

And the worst of it was, he broke clear of the field. Jago wanted the consoling presence of the others about him, the sound of their breathing, the grunts, the snorts and the tinkling and the rattle all around, like he'd been put in a wooden barrel and rolled over shingle. He wanted the sweet smell of horse grease in his nostrils and a nice solid rump bobbing before his horse's nose.

Instead, they were out on their own. That tattoo of horses was distant. The smell was of rotting autumn leaves and broken wet earth. The breeze was loo-paper and comb, *piano*.

They were four lengths clear.

Jago wanted to know that he had the pace right. He had never set it, still less won off it. That was for the guys with stopwatches in their heads.

Then he thought, hell, Burly's galloping well within himself. He seems to be happy enough to get his nose cold. He's not straining because he's where he reckons he belongs. And what do you mean, you want to know if you've got the pace right? You've hunted him, haven't you? And next month, you're proposing to take him over four-and-a-quarter miles. You can't judge the pace? Hell, Jago. So they're sluggardly. Enjoy it.

So he eased him to the inside, steadied him and told him that he was a fine fellow again.

Burly wasn't about to disagree.

He took the first in his stride like a hurdle. He disdained it. Jago noticed regretfully that there were no photographers by the wings. Never had he taken a steeplechase fence with so little change of posture. He remained crouched forward, sitting into him, and barely noticed the break in the regular churning of his stride. He thought that he looked beautiful then.

Burly bouldered on. The verb is not in the OED, but it should be because that's what Burly did. He trundled, only trundle is ponderous. He rolled, only roll is spherical. He rumbled, he careered, he . . . he *bouldered*. It is a sound word. It has much which is solid about it, much which is rounded. It reflects the sound of what he was doing, as well as the substance. It has connotations of 'bold' and of 'shouldered', echoes of 'burbled' and 'bubbled'. It speaks of those great, bouncing rocks which unarmed savages in movies let roll down hills towards brutish invaders. Anyhow, that was what Burly did.

At the second, he told his rider that he had it right, but put in a short one at the last moment which almost had Jago toppling out of the front door. Jago had been preparing for another Gerry Cranham photograph. He had seen himself riding a leaping chaser like one of the flat boys riding a finish, all poised and forward thrusting.

But Burly put in that little, hiccoughing hop, said 'Ha!' – inaudibly to any save him – then cleared the fence by two feet.

Had Gerry Cranham been by that fence, he'd have

snapped the amateur par excellence, a twisted swastika of long limbs on a horse which was – or appeared to be – executing a perfect jump.

The wind was in their faces now as they swung into the straight. It softened Jago up with little soft-gloved jabs.

He thought that no one who had not ridden a long steeplechase could really understand the process – how you were racing all the time, racing even when you were lengths clear or lengths behind, racing, and plotting racing tactics, even as, in a slow-moving cluster, you moved up or dropped back an inch.

Many an athlete, equine and human, had failed simply because he wasn't a racer, just as many a doughty racer had failed for want of speed. You saw those elegant young men loping about the athletics track and you thought – or Jago had, at least – that it was merely a matter of speed. Then it was pointed out to him that, in that case, races could be run by different athletes in different countries. All that you would need was a stopwatch.

No. A sports physiotherapist had once told Jago, 'You can run like the wind, but if you don't know what to do with your elbows, you might as well stay at home.'

The same was true here. Choosing a pace and a position, balancing your mount before entering the fray, then impressing your superiority and their unworthiness upon each of your opponents in turn, conserving energy whilst at all times keeping him balanced, holding yourself ready at every turn to cope with the sudden, stride-breaking side-nudge (horses do it by nature, jockeys too), you were always racing.

Battle was always half show, and the horses were engaged in show no less than the would-be chivalric knights on The Field of the Cloth of Gold. They were showing off as they ran side by side. Each in his way was staking his claim to be boss, and it was for Jago and his fellows to encourage them in their aspirations whilst checking their excesses.

So when, after the water, Jago found two animals hot on Burly's heels and Burly set his ears back and struck out resentfully, he had to tuck him up, tell him, 'Easy, now. Let's just think about these fences, shall we, for now?'

Burly did not like it. He liked it still less when Jago collected him as they approached the big open ditch and Nick Storr drew alongside so that they took off in the same stride.

Burly took it low. It was like barging through a giant hairbrush. His chest hit it hard. Jago was knocked rear-wards. His feet were shoved backwards by the birch which made a sort of 'ouff!' sound even as Burly did. He rocked forwards again, sprawling. The first leg to hit the turf buckled. For a moment, Jago was perched precipitously on a see-saw tilted to the front at forty-five degrees, watching muddy hoofprints, too close, skidding towards him, then, before he could roll, Burly found his footing and levered him upwards. There was thudding and grunting all about him now as he gathered up the reins and shook his head.

Burly needed no urging. He was shaken, but not winded. He had just received an object lesson in the merits of concentration and the dangers of its opposite.

There were three ahead of him now, two of them occupy-ing what had been their position on the rails, Steve, in blue and red crossbelts, crouched at their outside.

As Jago shook Burly up, another animal came up on either side. They were part of the pack now, jockeying and jostling.

It was a case now of being wary, wary of the animal that might swing across to unsight you, wary of the faller who can bring you down, wary of the half-length trap, where an animal half-a-length up on you takes off for the jump and your fellow follows suit, too soon, too far off.

Burly jumped like an electro-cardiograph. His experience told over his ebullience. He was no longer picking petty fights. He was racing against the field. He had remembered the purpose of all this.

Jago was aching and short of breath, but Burly seemed full of running. At the last plain fence, before they entered the straight, the Irish beast, Outfromunder, held the lead. Nick's animal was on his heels but running down to the right at every fence. His ears were back. Nick had to give him a crack down his near side to get him over. Then came Steve on the favourite, unflappable, nigh unmoving, staring straight ahead of him with the single-mindedness of an air ace in battle, yet, like those of an air ace in battle, Jago knew that those narrowed eyes would be flickering this way and that, taking in every potential source of danger.

A lean dun animal was at Burly's offside now. The rider was puffing worse than Jago.

Burly stood off and put in a monster jump which had Jago, amateur that he was, instinctively reaching back with his right hand – 'hailing a cab', it is called. It is not injurious, just undignified.

There was no need. Burly gained over a length in that leap, and his weaker opponent, trying the same thing, hit the fence with his forefeet. Jago and Burly were still in the air as, beneath Jago's heel, the dun hit the ground with head skewed, and slid on the greasy turf. His rider was flung forward and unwillingly ran, pushed in the small of his back by his own volition. He sprawled with a grunt as the earth hit his ribs, another as the earth hit his chin.

It was time now that they made their move.

Burly was not blessed with a great turn of foot, but he had a fourth gear, if not a blistering overdrive.

Jago engaged it.

They were side by side with Steve as they approached the second last. Steve took up the challenge. He decided to make his race here. He knew Burly of old, and his decision was a sound one from the point of view of the horses. It was, however, unduly flattering to Jago. Burly's handicap would be his rider in a finish. Jago knew that. Steve, more self-effacing, might not have been so confident.

They were going at full lick as they rose to the obstacle, and the wind was strong now in their faces. They took it perfectly. Their mounts' forefeet cleaved the turf at the same moment. Both riders had double handsful as they set off for the next. Nick's animal had veered to the right and skewed over the fence, trickled over it almost. He was a spent force. Jago and Burly left him behind them.

Only the Irish horse remained, two lengths ahead at Jago's near side.

Burly's many races stood him in good stead. He was not going to obstruct Steve, but neither was he going to give him an inch of room. Jago's left knee was just inches from Steve's right as they crouched down, pushed out, and the two animals puffed with every stride and their footfalls became a roll, not a beat. Their heads bobbed. Between Burly's bobbing ears and through the mud and sweat which bleared his vision, Jago saw the stands and the crowds as an amorphous, pointilliste blob. The scratchy noise of shouting was all of a piece with the rasping of his breath and the creaking of leather.

Burly had it all worked out. If he had the speed, if he caught the Irish brute, Steve would have to pull out to get past.

A deep growl was pushing its way up from somewhere deep inside Steve as suddenly they were on the Irish animal. They were four strides off the final fence. Burly's nose was at the Irish horse's quarters. Jago had to make room, pull out further, or any error by his opponent would be paid for as dearly by him.

He told Burly something like 'Gaah!' and the horse gathered his strength, went back on his hocks like a good 'un, projected himself upwards and forwards, sedate and studious as a solitary animal in an indoor school, and Jago knew then that, notwithstanding his burden, Burly was not to be denied his swan-song.

The Irish horse at Jago's nearside dragged through the fence. His hind legs had to swing sideways to clear the birch. Burly landed cleanly, crisply, leaving Steve to swerve past a tired, confused horse in inexpert hands.

Jago said, 'Come on, you old bugger. We're not there yet.' He crouched forward, studying his style.

Burly said something like '*You're* telling *me?*' and he went for the post like the baby grand the Pickfords men let go.

Jago was deliciously aching as he returned to the Zeller's shindig. His shoulders kept shifting as though he were urging on his horse. Climbing the stairs to the top level of the bus was a laborious business.

They had all been down in the winners' enclosure, clapping and slapping, squealing and sobbing, bringing some raucous London enthusiasm to sober Surrey. Steve had followed Jago into the weighing-room. He had laid one gloved hand on his shoulder. 'One hell of a horse, that,' he said. 'Ian's well chuffed. Doesn't show it, but an old servant like that . . .'

'Couldn't have a better, could you?'

'Wouldn't swap one of him for twenty flash-and-flop merchants. His rider's no slouch either.'

'It's the legs,' Jago said. 'Link the feet beneath him, you see, so you can't fall, hold onto the saddle. He'll do the rest.'

'Nope. If you'd taken it up earlier . . .' He wiped his eyes on his sleeve. He sat on the scales. 'No, you're a lucky guy, Jago.'

And, Jago reflected now, as he pulled himself wearily up the last steps, he was right.

Oh, he'd missed out on the wife and family bit, thus far at least. Money and business had somehow prevented him from meeting his kindred spirit. If she existed, it was not in the world in which he moved. Still, there was time, and maybe poverty would have its consolations in that regard. But he had friends, he had enjoyed the company and the bodies of some beautiful women, he had ridden in some memorable races, he had had a lot of fun.

He would not use today's prize money to finance his renaissance. The £8,500 would not buy him more than breathing space. He had no need of that. No, it could go into the kitty, pay a few wages, make good a little of the damage if, as seemed certain, Zellers went to the wall. He had enough for now, and was happier with the idea of starting again with nothing than with that of husbanding an ever decreasing pittance.

'Freedom's just another word for nothing left to lose,' wrote Kristofferson. Well, Jago had never tried that. It sounded good.

Champagne was pressed on him as soon as he appeared

on top of the bus, pressed so vigorously that it soaked his sleeve. Neil Green and John Duhigg were sitting slumped on seats littered with empty bottles and glasses, sodden betting tickets, racecards and newspapers, arguing about horses in great, florid outbursts which rapidly dwindled into drivel.

'No, what I say is, you've got Arkle, right?'

'You've g't 'rkle. 'Sright.'

'And you've got your Miller. Am I right?'

'Cer'nly. Miller.'

'And your Miller won the National and your Arkle dn't. So. Stands to reason, dunnt?'

Clay was talking animatedly to Miss Sniffy. Cindy was pouring tea for Auntie Vi. Diana was having a fit of the giggles at some joke of Ian's. There were two races more to come.

Yes, Jago thought, he was a very lucky man indeed. He was blessed with a tribe, and that made him more blessed than most in an alienated Western world.

He could not stand the idea of losing that luxury.

'Hal-lo?' said the female voice at the end of the line. Jago knew that it was a foreign voice. In English, 'Hello' is a salutation. In every other language, it seemed, it is a query – are you ready to be greeted?

He raised his voice, as you try not to but inevitably do with the deaf or with foreigners on the telephone. 'Hello! Jago van Zeller here?'

'Hallo, is Mr van Zeller who is speaking.' No query here.

'Yes! Hello. *C'est moi*. I am Mr van Zeller!'

'My name is Stojna Pavla. I am welcoming to Velka Pardubicka and very much waiting to meet you.'

'I am very much waiting to meet you!' he called, less from the exquisite courtesy which makes you excuse yourself when the duchess farts than from imitative reflex. 'Thank you!'

'You are arriving on Thursday afternoon, yes? British Airways, yes?'

'Yes.'

'You want we arrange you hotel?'

'Thank you. No. It's all organized. I have a friend who is travel agent who has arranged it. I am staying at the Hotel President on Thursday evening.'

'Is good hotel. Very modern. Very clean.'

That sounded like hell to Jago, but he said, 'Good.'

'I will send to Hotel President the papers.'

He frowned. 'Papers?'

'Yes. Accreditations for enter the racecourse and also there are soirees before the race and after for to you are invitarted.'

He admired the inversion. So much tidier than 'you are invitarted for to', as sloppier speakers might have put it. 'Thank you!' he bellowed, as though the telephone were a stage-prop.

'You are more than you?' she shouted back. It was catching.

'Um – yes. Yes. My friend, Clement Levine, will be driving the horse out.'

'He will be invitarted also.'

'Great. Thank you, Pavla.'

'For nothing, sir!'

He wondered about this. English schoolchildren were always taught to say '*de rien*' or '*de nada*' in response to thanks. It seemed that foreigners when learning English were likewise taught a response unheard of from the lips of natives.

'These soirees – do I need a black tie?'

There was rustling then, and breathing. Maybe 'black tie' merely meant funerals in the Czech Republic, in which case she must be considering Jago still loopier than she might with reason suppose a man about to ride in her country's most famous race. 'Dinner jacket!' he called. 'Le smoking!'

'No, no. Just normal. Vest, you know. Trousers.'

'Oh.' Jago nodded. 'Good.'

'I am very much waiting to meet you. Good bye,' she announced briskly.

He was about to repeat the formula when the telephone clicked and buzzed. He imagined Stojna Pavla dialling the next number on her list of riders and trainers. If she could communicate with them as well as she had managed with him, she was some linguist.

Prince Cyril Havlik was clipping his toenails on the bed, the phone wedged between his jaw and his collarbone. He said, 'Well, Lou, it's on. You done your bit. It's my turn now.'

'God, sooner you than me.' Lou Robinson's parents had anglicized their name from Rubinstein. Lou had been brought up in and around New York, a good all-American boy with all traces of Jewry expunged from his life, yet still Havlik thought that he discerned the stage-Jew wheedle in that voice. 'So when do you reckon you'll be back?'

'Yeah, I got a flight gets in Mexico City – what? 1940 local time, Tuesday.'

'Great. OK. Yeah, I'll be there. I've taken the whole week off, but the guy's ready to transfer the money soon as he sees the stuff. Wednesday afternoon we should be millionaires. Good kind of thought, hey?'

'The best.' Havlik clipped the little toe on his right foot, shifted the receiver to the other side and started on the left. 'Shit, you're a millionaire already, Lou.'

'I wish,' the other man laughed. 'Listen, now, this has cost me. You're not going to try anything, are you? 'Cos I warn you . . .'

'Hey, Lou, it's me you're talking to, right?' Havlik protested. 'A Czech like you, yeah? A prince. Do princes break their words? And listen, man. How'm I going to pull one on you, huh? How'm I gonna sell the stuff without you? I'm gonna walk into Sotheby's, say, "sell this for me"? Sure. I get a bullet in the back two seconds. And you got insurance every which way. You're the only guy knows the plan, right? So you go to certain people, tell them what went down, I'm dead. You know that, I know that. We got to have trust in a thing like this; but, man, you stand to lose bread. Me, I stand to lose one hell of a lot more. Am I right?'

'Yeah.' The voice was sullen. 'Yeah. You're right. And I'd do it. Don't think I wouldn't.'

'Sure you'd do it. Christ, I blame you, guy tries to rip you off? Listen, what I'd like . . . We can't meet, but I'm, like . . .

I go in at night, I want to be quadruple sure where I'm going . . .'

'I told you . . .'

'Sure, you told me. I know you told me. You think I don't know you told me? It's like, I know in theory, but it's not going to be fucking theory, I get there, is it? What I – I mean, this fountain thing is one complicated mother. What I'd like, you draw me a little map. No names, nothing, just, you know, fountain, trees, house. I'm out walking, your street, say seven o'clock? You, right, bang on seven, you're somewhere up from that wop place on the same sidewalk, right-hand-side. You screw up the map, throw it in the gutter. I'm behind you. You do that for me?'

'Shit, I give you a map already. You think all I got to do is run around town dropping paper? I got an opening tonight. Gallery sells post-modernist installations, Christ. That's seven. I got to be there.'

'So fine.' Havlik leaned forward as though to urge the decision. 'You arrive on time, you're gonna be a post-modernist installation. They're gonna walk round you, think you're an exhibit. How long'll it take? Twenty minutes, get from your place to a downtown gallery? Outside. Perfect. So that's where you're going. You want a little exercise, you walk to find a cab, get down the waistline. Yeah, you gave me a map, but, shit, a spastic spider done better maps. Anyhow, girl was round here the other day, had this big mutt, wolfhound. You ever been there? You're fucking, suddenly there's this long hot tongue licking your balls? You know what? She's only trained the fucker. She goes, "Come on, it's fun!" I mean, fuck, you've got your balls I mean that far away from these big yellow teeth and a fucking wolf, I mean, mouth like a dead man's fridge, just there? Fun? I kick the booger out. What's he do? He only eats my billfold, your map. Come on. I need you. I'll be there seven.'

The man sighed. 'No games?'

'I want games now? Shit, I told you. There's two of us in this. I need you, you need what I bring out. What do I want with games now? Tomorrow I'm flying to Germany, pick up the horse. Next day, Czechoslovakia. Our home, right? I want games now?'

'OK, OK.' The man was too pissed off to be scared, which was just how Havlik wanted it. 'I'll be there, but seven means seven. I'll not hang about. You're not there seven, forget it. I walk on.'

'Sure, Lou, sure. I told you. I'll be there. See you in Mexico, huh? And the drinks are on me.'

'You bet they are,' said Lou Robinson drily, and was gone.

Havlik laid down the receiver and leaned back on the pillow. It was all set up. He was surprised that he did not feel more excited or apprehensive. It was merely a thing that had to be done.

He had never done it. Not knowingly at least. Thus far, such victims as he could claim had been delivered oven-ready, plucked, trussed and stuffed.

Nor did the prospect fill him with glee. It was a tedious essential. There was no other way, that was all. If it came to the ultimate calculation, it seemed self-evident. Others must die sooner than he. It was necessary. He had spent his life trying to avoid this thing, sure, but it was not such a big deal, not when it came to it.

Would his nerve fail him? Why should it? His fathers had not baulked at the messy bits. He cared nothing for his proposed victim, though *Where have all the Flowers Gone?* was among his most requested turns when he slung his guitar. If it came to a choice between a Havlik and another, there was no question as to where his duty lay. Thousands of years, many generations, had been distilled into this last of the line. It was hard, sure, but lots of first times were hard – losing virginity, learning to swim.

Murder would be no different.

Nor was it. At seven o'clock, he saw the little man in his flapping overcoat, strutting quickly down the leafy street towards him. He selected precisely the point where he could mount the pavement without fear of hitting a tree. He eased the car from its parking-place without lights and cruised slowly down towards him. He turned the lights on full when he was just twenty yards away. The man raised his arm to cover his eyes. Havlik changed into third, and put his foot down.

The man had a chance to stagger back against the palings. Havlik saw his eyes white as spit-gobs, his teeth linked by gleaming strands of saliva gossamer. He wanted to make sure, so he swerved away only at the very last moment. His nearside headlight caught the man in the groin. The man flew, head flung backwards, mouth still open in a silent scream. The palings buckled and collapsed beneath his weight. The man lay in a flowerbed. Laths fell onto him, obscuring his head and chest. His knees rose just once, then started shaking and convulsively kicking. Someone up there was screaming, but when was someone not?

Havlik had no need to climb from the car to know that Robinson was dead, nor to collect the map. He had Robinson's original in his breast pocket.

He had got a result, Havlik told himself proudly as he climbed aboard the aeroplane an hour later.

He was free and clear. He was on his way to a new life.

The day came closer. Jago's apprehension and excitement grew. For some reason, the Pardubice appeared to be receiving more than the usual publicity this year, or maybe Jago simply had not noticed in years gone by. 'More than usual' was not a lot, but two reporters rang, and two two-inch columns duly appeared on the racing pages the following day, stating that no less than three British riders, Jago van Zeller, veteran Paul Pickering and one Richard Miller, would be contesting 'the Czech Republic's daunting two hundred-year-old steeplechase'.

Jago and Paul must leave early. They must pass through or by London. As a final bit of inducement or man-management, Jago had promised them breakfast at the Connaught to set them on their way.

He walked through Hyde Park to find the horsebox already in the hotel car-park, Clay and Paul snugly and smugly installed in a bow-window of the restaurant.

In their tweeds and jeans, they looked happily, even

rebelliously provincial. Clay was cackling as Jago entered the room. 'J!' he shouted. He flung down his napkin and strode across the room to take Jago's hand. 'God. Come on, come on. This guy's – where'd you find the bugger? Jeez. He's amazing. A-ma-zing. You ought to listen to this guy. He's been richer than all of us, and he's happy being poor. He's ridden almost every race. He's – how'll I say? he's – Jesus, he knew, I mean, he'd never say he'd bedded, but I reckon, I mean, Ava Gardner, Christ's sakes. He knew her at least. What would I give to say "Hello" to Ava Gardner? I *mean*. Jeez, we're talking, I mean, Frank Sinatra sang "I'm a Fool to Love You" when she left, slammed down the piano-top and stalked out. We are talking *history*!'

'She lived down the road,' Jago refused to be impressed, 'in Ennismore Gardens.'

'Well, no fucker told me. Last time Paul was here, Aly Khan was here, I mean, Jesus, Aly Khan!'

'The two concepts are not naturally related,' Jago said softly. 'Jesus, I mean, and Aly Khan.'

'Oh, lah-di-dah.' Clay's voice was rough and derisive. ''E tells me, Aly Khan, I mean, seriously famous, kept three women 'appy, or un'appy, I suppose, different floors of the Ritz, said to 'im, 'e was a boy, "Paul, always think of elm trees". Whass 'e mean by that, then? You bedding Rita Hayworth, you think of elm-trees? Jesus, I don't know. Been missing a trick, I guess. 'Mazing.'

'Glad you're getting on.' Jago grinned at Clay's obvious excitement. He shared it. 'So,' he said as he reached the table, 'Paul, all well?'

'Fine, fine. No problems. Nice horse that one. Both went in sweet as a nut. No. Well, we're off, eh? Bloody good. Can't wait.'

Jago sat. A waiter pushed in his chair and unfurled a napkin on his lap. 'You two are fizzing so much you might burst,' Jago laughed. 'It feels like the last day of term.'

'Exactly what it does feel like,' Paul nodded. 'No more Latin, no more French, hunting tomorrow, cocking the next day, Christmas is coming . . . Funny, actually. This is where I used to meet my mum at the end of term. School train from Marlborough, taxi here, slap-up lunch, go to the theatre, Christmas time, *Where the Rainbow Ends, Peter Pan,* tea at Fortnums. *Eheu fugaces,* eh? Gosh.'

'See?' Clay beamed proudly. ''E goes on like that non-stop. Don't understand 'alf of it, but it sounds good. What's cocking, any road? Doesn't sound like the sort of thing my dad arranged for me after school.'

'Oh. No.' Paul faintly blushed. 'No, woodcock. Had a couple of bogs. No, sorry. Talk too much.'

'So, have you ordered?' Jago asked.

'No, we waited for our gracious host,' said Clay.

'You must be starving. Let's get down to it.'

Clay contented himself with bacon, eggs and puddings, Jago with kippers. Paul had to be apologetically difficult. 'Terribly sorry,' he said to the waiter, 'not on the menu. Probably can't do it. What I'd really like – perfectly understand if you can't, but it would be a treat, used to have it here in the old days – herring roes, soft roes, you know? Fried, with bacon. Oh toast. Sprinkle of cayenne, lemon juice, salt, pepper. Yum.'

'Certainly, sir.' The waiter was unfazed.

'And three glasses of Buck's Fizz,' Jago added.

'Gosh.' Paul considered. 'Oh, why not? Once in a while. Big day. Can't do any harm. Super.'

At first, Jago felt inappropriately avuncular towards the two ebullient older men. As breakfast proceeded, however, he was infected by their enthusiasm. By the time he slipped Clay an envelope of cash and prepared to start farewells, his face ached with grinning. He envied them their careless adventure. It would hurt to return to Miss Sniffy and gloom.

The three men strolled contentedly from the restaurant. Suddenly Paul beamed and bounded. 'Clare!' he enthused. 'Bloody good of you, really so good, come and see us off. I was wondering . . .'

He embraced the girl who rose from the gilt chair. She kissed him once, then turned her fine, sharp, startlingly white face towards the lights as he hugged her and swung her round.

He set her down, but still held her hand. 'Jago, Clay whoops, wrong way round – Clare, my dear. So sorry. Clare, this is Jago van Zeller, Clay Levine. Clare is my dearly beloved daughter – and this . . .' he knelt smoothly to grin into the pushchair, 'this is my one and only grandson, aren't you, George? Yes – you – are . . .'

The child chuckled. He was perhaps eighteen months old. His skin was soft brown, his hair thick, black and curly. For all that his Afro-Caribbean paternity was evident, he, as his mother, had the pale Pickering eyes.

Clare cast a glance at her father and her son before turning back to Jago and Clay. She had very black hair and she was dressed all in black. The only colour about her came from those eyes and from a big oval tiger's eye which gleamed on her little finger. She raised it to her forehead, pushed back a heavy hank of blackness. She said, 'He's not called George and dad knows it. He's just being his usual impossible self.'

'Well, he answers to George, don't you, George? Course you do.' Paul continued to play with the child. 'I just can't get my tongue round that other pig's breakfast of a name. Sorry.'

'What is his real name, then?' Jago asked.

'Darren,' she said. 'It's beneath dad.'

'Mind if I take him out of this thing?' Paul looked up.

'No, no. Your responsibility if he breaks something priceless, that's all.'

'Oh, he won't break anything, will you, George?' Paul stood and heaved the boy up in his arms. 'Course not.'

'You should have come earlier,' Jago told Clare. 'We've just had breakfast. Can I get you anything – coffee or something?'

'No, honestly. No, listen, I just dropped in, literally. I haven't got long.'

'Have you come far?'

'No, no. Primrose Hill. No, I just thought I'd see dad off, wish him luck, sort of thing. I mean, I think he's mad at his age, but . . .'

'I want a drink!' shrilled Darren.

'Please,' prompted Paul. Clare's lips twitched.

'I want a drink please.'

'Of course you do,' said Jago. 'What would you like? Orange juice, milk, apple juice, absinthe . . .?'

'Orange juice!'

'And orange juice you shall have. Come on, Clare. Stop for a second, have some coffee.'

She looked from Jago to Clay. Her shoulders rose once, then sank. She smiled, and was then more than ever her father's daughter. 'OK,' she said. She pinched her son's cheek and gritted her teeth in mock savagery. 'Ten minutes, no more, right?'

They sat in armchairs. Jago ordered the drinks. Over the next ten minutes, it seemed to him that Clare was cautious – not sullen or sulky – but nervous with her father, rather like a mother whose child might at any moment disgrace her. Her smile was an occasional twitch, her laughter sudden and as suddenly checked as a drunkard's song. Her fine white hands must always be plucking at something. She rolled and unrolled her napkin. She picked up a biscuit only to roll it between her fingers. Her dramatic eyes skedaddled about the table from one face to another, never settling upon one for a second. When she spoke, it was to make polite remarks about the coffee or to chide her father. 'Oh, dad, you do go on!' 'Dad, you never will grow up, will you?' 'Trust dad, mad as a March hare . . .'

'You will take care of him, won't you?' she said softly as the horse-box at last lumbered off towards Park Lane.

'Oh, I reckon he can look after himself pretty well,' Jago grinned.

'Yes, but no. He's crazy. Things always happen to him. Always have, and if he sees a tidal wave, his first reaction is to look for a surf-board. You know he captured a U-boat with a tin-opener when he was four years old?'

'Don't be silly.'

'I'm not! No one believes it, but I've seen it in the books. It's true. He went up to his grandfather's place in Scotland for the duration. A U-boat gets beached, the Germans sit there waiting for the tide to refloat them. Dad's not having that. Clambers up with his tin-opener and hacks away at the conning-tower. Some stage, the local priest comes along and lends a hand. By the time the tide's come in, the boat's unseaworthy – least, they can't submerge, and the crew has to surrender! It's true! There are pictures!' She grinned, but then was suddenly sober. 'No, I mean, he shouldn't be riding in this thing. Not at his age, but you try telling him that.'

Jago glanced down at her. Her eyes were still fixed on the corner long after the horsebox was gone. 'You're fond of him, though, aren't you?'

'Oh, God. How can you not be?' she sighed. 'I'm a bit like him, which is why I've spent my whole life doing things which won't meet with his approval. Difference between us is, I try to restrain that madness, and I'm not half as nice as he is. You know?' She cocked her head. 'I think he's the nicest bloody man I've ever met. Never held a grudge, never neglected a courtesy or failed to pay a debt. It nearly drove mum to a breakdown. She couldn't live with him, but she couldn't justify her exasperation. He was just so tooth-achingly nice. She became really brutal in the end. She'd lose her temper, do the vilest things, he'd say, "Steady, old girl. What can I do to help?" That would make her scream. Oh, I don't know.' She shook her head. 'What do you do with a man who tells supermarket checkout girls that they are fairer than the day and expresses the hope that the fruit of their loins may be tall and strong as the young oak tree, then insists on spending an hour listening to their problems with their love lives? Just – just try to keep an eye on him, OK?'

Jago was still smiling. He said, 'Of course I will, as best I can,' and wondered why everyone cast him in an avuncular role. 'Well, better be getting back . . .'

'Yeah.' She took the handles of the baby-buggy. 'Nice meeting you. You know, I wish I could be in your position . . .'

'Why's that?'

'I wish I could ride a tough race against dad, and beat him. I'd feel close to him then . . .'

But of course, she could never have done such a thing,

Jago reflected as he set off down Mount Street, because girls, for Paul, were to be cherished and served. His gallantry had alienated his child.

That afternoon, 'the whore correspondent' called.

In Jago's business, it paid to be polite to the media. He would very much have liked to make an exception in the case of Gary Greenaway. A pretty, nippy little man with a bouffant barnet so perfect that Jago strongly suspected him of wearing a hairnet, Greenaway, the 'Society Columnist' for the *Echo*, claimed to have been a war correspondent. It was widely rumoured that his only experience of atrocity was when his arm got jogged and he spilled his Cinzano down his dress-shirt's lacy front, five hundred miles from the nearest war zone, a tragedy which had traumatized him to this day.

He was a crashing snob with precisely no justification, if justification there can be, having come from a family which barely so much as claimed Brian Boru amongst its antecedents and a public school still more minor than Jago's. When Jago was going out with the Hon Julia Freedman, whose father was then a Cabinet Minister, he was 'Dashing St Paul's educated tailoring tycoon'; when he was staying in with actress Fiona Farmiloe (it's catching), who also happened to be the ex-Mrs Greenaway, he was 'Cockney serge-snipper'; then Greenaway lost out at Lloyds and Jago took up race-riding, and he suddenly became 'sartorial doyen and gentleman-rider, Huguenot horseman and nephew of royal portrait-painter Sir David Devaney.' He was more loquacious, more practised in ingratiation than in invective. Jago would sooner have had the invective.

'Jago. How *are* you?' Greenaway purred with a drawl like a cartoon cat.

'Gary. Hello.'

'Hello. Hello, indeed. How are things, then, Jago?'

'Fine, thanks, Gary.'

'Good, good. How's Julie?'

'Julie who?'

'Don't be naughty, Jago. Julie who. No, just ringing for a little chat about this Pardu – how do you pronounce it?'

'Par-du-bitsy,' Jago said slowly, 'as in teeny weeny polka-dot bikini. Most people pronounce it as though it were Italian, as in "She's a bitch, eh?"'

'Very good!' he said, and his smile flattened his vowels. 'Very good! Never lend to a writer, Jago. I'll use that.'

'Fine.'

'So, tell me about it.'

'Try the library, Gary. I don't know much. It's a race, that's all. Horse and rider who arrive soonest at the finish are the winners. Big jumps.'

'*Very* big jumps, from what I hear.'

'Some are very big. Yes.'

'Bit dashing, though. Old horse, no chicken yourself . . .'

There was silence. Jago let it ride.

'So sorry about the firm, Jago,' Greenaway resumed. 'Bugger, this recession, isn't it?'

'Yes,' said Jago.

'So, this is sort of the last big extravagance, the last splurge, is it?'

'No. This is something I've wanted to do for a long time. I have next to no money left, but I've sold a picture, and I'm heading out on my own money and under my own steam. Look, I've got to go now, Gary . . .'

'Sure, Jago. Just a second. So, sorry. Can I get this right? This race is a bit like a suicide attempt, from what I gather.'

'I don't think so.'

'But it's pretty crazy, right?'

'I don't think so.'

'Would you describe it as frivolous, then?'

'A moment ago, you wanted it to be a suicide attempt. Suicide attempts may be humorous, but never, I think, frivolous.' Jago cursed himself for speaking too much, cursed Greenaway for his undoubted skill. It reminded him of the 'yes/no' game of childhood. You lost if you said, 'yes', or 'no', shook your head or nodded.

Every child should play that game. A yes, a no, a nod or a shake constituted a lifeline for the likes of Gary Greenaway.

'SUICIDE CAN BE HUMOROUS, SAYS CZECH-BOUND JAGO,' read the headline. 'There are some very big fences out there,' said dashing gentleman-rider Jago van Zeller, 36, of his attempt on Czechoslovakia's Pardubice (pronounced Par-du-bitsy, not, as certain ignorant aspirants have it, Par-du-bitchy), a crazy, cavalryman's version of the Grand National to be run on Sunday. But suicide can be humorous, can't it?

'Jago, who inherited a multi-million-pound tailoring empire from his father, has not proved a success in the world of cutting and stitching, and has been feeling the pinch of late. "I have no money to speak of, Gary," he told me last night, "but this is something I've dreamed of for a long, long time. My business may be going down the tubes – recession is a bitch – but I've sold a painting and I'm on my way."

'NOT SAFE IN TAXIS'.

'Ex-St Paul's man Jago, who has escorted Cabinet minister Julius Freedman's daughter, Julia, and stunning Bond girl Miriam Dainty, has been experiencing ill fortune with his business and his love-life of late, which may explain his tendency towards felo de se. Of late, he has been seen around with leggy model Julie Fanshawe, but, when I called Julie, she told me, "Jago thinks suicide is funny? Yes, well, in his case, I could see the joke."'

'Whoops.

'The Pardubice, featuring the monster fence, the Taxis, has only once been won by an Englishman since the First World War, when lanky Aqua Manda toiletries tycoon, now Hanson director, Chris Collins bore home the laurels in 1963.

'"I wish Jago every good fortune," said Collins last night. 'It's a marvellous race."

'Two other Englishmen, dashing veteran Paul Pickering, 56, and Lincolnshire farmer's son Richard Miller will also be lining up at the start of the four-and-a-quarter mile marathon, but, of this unprepossessing squad, Jago, on his doughty mount Burlington, is reckoned to stand the best chance of getting round in one piece.'

It is an art, tabloid writing, not unakin to converting Krug into urine.

A thousand honest, even lofty passions, hopes and dreams were distilled in those few words into their basest constituents. Barely a word was untrue, yet the whole thing was a monstrous calumny. Jago was a failure in business who still claimed the freedom to indulge in grossly irresponsible extravagance. His love affairs became brisk sexual encounters. He was a libertine, and a bad one at that. As for the race, it was transformed into a ghastly sick joke, contested by a geriatric, a tailor and a 'farmer's son'. How was it possible to instil those two innocent words with such contempt?

For all that he knew the truth, the article nonetheless depressed Jago and made him feel cheap and absurd.

It got noticed too.

Clay rang, as pre-arranged, at six o'clock that last night, to report progress. Paul and he were making better time than they'd anticipated. They had cancelled their reservation at a Kulmbach hotel and had passed over the Czech border to a place called Cheb. Jago's finger followed their route in the atlas open on his lap.

Burly, Clay reported, was calm and well. Paul had given both animals a mile-long gallop at half-speed this morning. Friendly farmers had allowed them to graze for an hour this evening. The word Pardubice, it seemed, worked wonders out there. Paul would meet Jago at his Prague hotel on the evening of his arrival. Clay had no interest in sightseeing. He would stay with the horses.

Jago had barely put the telephone down when it shrieked again. He sipped the whisky which, with its twin, would constitute his sleeping-draught. He was planning an early night. He picked up the receiver. 'Hello?'

'Hello, Jago. Father Ignatius.'

Jago was surprised, if not displeased. He had no reason to suppose that they had his number down there, but the

Lord's servants worked in ways nigh as mysterious as their master's.

Jago was that improbable creature, a Huguenot Catholic. His grandfather had not been a man of high principles or deep grudges and, when he married an Italian girl, was happy enough that his children should be brought up in her faith. Jago was a frequent, if not regular churchgoer. He went to St Jude's for the motets and the Gregorian chant and the Vittoria mass. He went for the incense and the resonant Latin spells of the Tridentine liturgy, the memories and the magic. He went because, for a while there, his thoughts attained some sort of simplicity and serenity. Whether that state was any nearer to God than the quotidian, he had no idea, but, if not, he had no idea what God might be.

In Dom. Ignatius Beresford and his brethren, too, he had found worldly wisdom and a sense of proportion far beyond that which could be bought from analysts. The saints were the best support group he had come across.

His response to this call, then, was warm enough. He said, 'Father! Good to hear you!'

'When are you off?'

'Tomorrow morning early.'

'Ah. Sorry. Are you busy tonight?'

'Not busy. Thinking of sleeping mostly. Why? Can I help?'

'No. Just hoped for a word, that's all. Before you went.'

Jago was puzzled. For all his apologies, Father Ignatius was not backing off. Jago shrugged. 'Well, drop by, if you can make it before, say, eight thirty.'

'You couldn't make it down here, could you? Sorry. It's silly. There's someone I'd like you to meet, that's all. He's a little old. He's a Czech, actually.'

So, Jago thought, because the atlas was still open at that page, are 15,280,147 other people. He did not say so. He put the monk's request down to an unworldly disingenuousness which he had not hitherto suspected. With only a trace of a sigh, he conceded defeat. 'OK, father. It'll have to be quick, though. I'll be over in a quarter of an hour.'

'Splendid!' It burst from the priest. 'I'll open a nice bottle, give you a send-off. I won't keep you long, Jago, I promise. Thank you.'

St Jude's was a large church manned by a small Benedictine community. It was, in essence, a Hall of Residence for seminarists and Catholic scholars, attached to London University. So far as was possible in a tall, maroon-bricked house on Fulham Broadway, the eight or nine monks who ran the place and their resident seminarists attempted to maintain the ordered regime of their mother abbey in border country. Every morning at half-past five, they were awoken by a rap on the door and a bellowed '*Benedicamus Dominum*', to which they croaked back a more or less sincere, '*Deo Gratias*'. The canonical hours proceeded as prescribed, from matins to compline, but such were the demands of London life and academe that terce, sext and nones might often be sung by just one solitary worshipper.

Jago arrived five minutes early. Through the right-hand first-floor window, he saw black-robed figures moving back and forth in the brightly lit dining-room. He would let them finish their supper. He pushed open the western door of the church, and strolled into the vaulted gloom.

There was low lighting from the recesses along the nave. Low spotlight beams clashed like sabres up in the tower. The sacristy lamp was a ruby twinkle.

Jago's footfalls scampered like children in and out of the arcades. The door behind him whooshed shut, and the traffic was suddenly hundreds of miles away.

Ghosts haunt places, not people, which rather gives the lie to the idea that ghosts are the conscious undead, wandering the earth with a mission. Musicians hear ghosts, painters see them. Most of us just feel their presence. They were everywhere here, pressed close about him, consoling, reassuring, family.

He sank down on his knees there, suddenly grateful to Fr Ignatius for reminding him.

These ghosts were as near as he would ever get to home.

He prayed.

He prayed that everything would go right, that he would

win the Pardubice, that he would make a mysterious million, that he would meet a millionairess who would prove his soul-sister, that, above all, he might be carefree, and so free to make others so.

He thanked God for all that he had. A good trick for happiness.

He visualized a bit more of it, because that seemed to work too.

He commended his soul and his fortunes in the race – if not to God, then to something more important and enduring than Jago van Zeller.

The ghosts helped the message on its way.

He felt better and lighter as he stood and crossed himself, more from reflex than devotion.

He turned. He strolled back to the little transept door which led into the hall of the monastic house.

He climbed the steps and pulled the door towards him. Suddenly his lungs clenched. He raised a hand to ward off the horror which lay on the other side. He staggered back down the steps. He flung the door shut again.

He had relaxed too much. His thoughts, such as they were, were full of superstition. When, therefore, he opened that door to find a bent, black form with its head grimacing at groin level and a long, heavily veined hand clawing at his crotch, reason was on hold. His unconscious mind, at least, was now programmed to believe in cockatrices, basilisks and men with heads beneath their arms.

He righted himself. He said, 'Um, sorry.' He flicked through the expressions file and drew out an idiotic grin.

Fr Ignatius, in full habit and cowl, had been pushing a wheelchair through the mushroom-gill gloom on the other side and bending forward to speak to his passenger. The passenger, meanwhile, an old, old man with a triangular face so welted that it read as coppiced, had leaned forward to grasp the door-handle. At that moment, Jago had opened the door from within.

Now Ignatius looked up, and smiled. He threw back the cowl. The only real light came from behind Jago. The only reflective surfaces were the two men's faces and the old man's hand. Ignatius said, 'Ah, Jago,' and his voice was a fat thud.

'Sorry,' Jago said again. 'You were at dinner. I thought I'd spend a while in there.'

'Splendid. Splendid. No, we saw the car, assumed as much. Delighted you could make it.' Ignatius pulled the chair back from the doorway. 'Come on in, come on in. We're waiting for you in the sitting-room. Bottle, as promised.'

The hall was painted white, but they husbanded energy here. The narrow columns seemed dull pink, the floor-tiles pink and black, the paintings and the ceilings muddy purple, like a bruised plum. From outside, a swinging headlight beam painted chequers on the walls. A huge purple Judith at Jago's right hand held forth Holofernes's hairy head. She looked like a child-star who had executed a good tap-dance. He looked gloomy, as well he might. Last time he gave head. They receded into darkness.

The room into which they showed Jago was, by comparison, inordinately bright. There was a pink sofa. There were armchairs in cornflower blue brocade. There were apricot-ceiling-to-floor silk curtains. The carpet was oatmeal. It felt like walking on oatmeal.

Ignatius pushed the wheelchair towards the high window and spun it round. The old man's white hair was cropped square to within a quarter of an inch of his scalp. His ears were large and angry crimson. His eyes were large and bright and blue. The rest of his head looked as though it had been hung out to shrink long since.

'This is Father Bernard, Jago, Father Bernard Hacha.' Ignatius walked over to a mahogany card table. He picked up the dusty bottle like a grail. He eyed the label and sighed. 'Now, then,' he said. He picked up a claret glass and held it up to the light. He squinted.

Jago walked across to the wheelchair. He held out his hand. He smiled. 'Father Bernard.'

His hand was taken by something which felt dry and fragile as a Dead Sea scroll. Suddenly, the little old man convulsed. His whole frame shuddered. A husky little giggle like a hacksaw on steel seeped from his sunken lips. His hand tightened about Jago's.

Jago flicked a quick, concerned glance at Ignatius. The portly monk merely continued to pour claret with no sign of concern. He did not turn from his duties as he announced, 'Fr Bernard comes from where you're going tomorrow, Jago.'

'Pardubice?' That hand was still clamped fiercely about Jago's fingers. It was like being dog-tied.

'Well, Bohemia, anyway.' Ignatius puffed. His habit swished with every footfall as he lumbered towards Jago. His high pate gleamed between two cloudy puffs of sandy hair.

'Bohemia,' the little man echoed. His voice was a twang like a broken string. His eyes flashed upwards. He looked down at their clasped hands. Very slowly, one by one, his fingers released their grip. Jago stepped back gratefully, resisting the temptation to wipe off the old man's touch on his trousers.

'See what you make of this, Jago.' Ignatius was smiling, proffering a glass. 'Sit down, please.'

Jago took the glass over to the sofa. The wine was very tawny at the edges. He sniffed, tasted.

It was a bit like meeting Joe Louis in the last days of his life, or listening to Wagner in echo. This was a wine which, ten years ago, could have blown you out of your socks. It had been strong and rumbustious at every level, a *liaison dangereuse* in which every element had melded and married and lived in potent harmony. The harmony was still there. The potency was gone.

'That was once quite something,' Jago said. 'I'm glad to have had the chance to taste it, sad not to have been around when it was in its prime.'

'Hmm.' Ignatius leaned contentedly back in his armchair. 'So often the problem with community property. One has to tend the community's assets, husband them, only open the best bottles when there is a genuinely good excuse. Unfortunately, "because it's at its best" is not seen as sufficient excuse.'

'And my going to Pardubice is?'

'Well, why not?' Ignatius chortled. 'Why not indeed . . .'

There was a long silence then, whilst they sipped their drinks and adjusted their legs and waited for someone to speak.

'Pardubice,' Fr Bernard said at last. 'Very funny horse-race. You ride, yes?'

'That's right, father.'

'I see many years ago,' the old man's hand beat time on the wheelchair's arm, 'all riders and horses fall down.'

Jago said, 'her her'. So did Ignatius. They both looked towards the little old man, awaiting more, but he had shot his bolt. His right hand shook as it raised his glass to his lips. Wine trickled down his chin. Some found its way between those thin lips.

'Fr Bernard had a living with a great family in the old Czechoslovakia,' Ignatius at last volunteered. 'Dispossessed, of course, when the Communists arrived.'

Fr Bernard very deliberately laid his glass down on the sofa table at his side, then convulsed a bit more.

'He was lucky to get out himself,' Ignatius continued. 'As you probably know, the Communist Secret Police gave the priests a hard time. Even in the poorest parishes, they suspected the presence of great treasures–works of art, church plate, manuscripts. They tortured the priests, then packed them off to die in the Uralian mines. There were three such mines, named, I hate to tell you, "Liberty", "Equality" and "Fraternity". Isn't that right, Fr Bernard?'

Fr Bernard nodded like a grebe swallowing an outsized fish. 'Equality, Liberty, Fraternity . . .'

'And Bernard's family, Bernard's church, really did have treasures, didn't they, Bernard? Yes. He was lucky to get out.'

'Lord,' Jago said to the old man, 'the things you must have seen. I can't imagine it was easy under Heydrich either.'

'What?' Ignatius frowned.

'During the war. I've been reading about it. How Chamberlain and Co threw the Czechs to the wolves, the Nazi occupation, all that. The first Protector of Bohemia and Moravia was von Neurath, who made much of being an old high German Protestant. Then Heydrich took over, the nastiest and most brilliant of a very nasty mob. He invented the Final Solution. He didn't like the Church much. Anyhow, he got blown up in his car by two Czechs dropped in from London. Good riddance, but appalling reprisals . . .'

'Ah, that Heydrich,' Ignatius rumbled. 'Of course. Here. Let me fill your glass, Jago. Yes, well, I think everyone under the Nazis had a pretty horrid time, but at least they were cultured men. Oh, I'm not saying that that is any sort of defence, just that the Nazis tortured and killed, but that the Communists tortured, killed and destroyed beautiful things.'

'Well, one way or another, your country's had a pretty hard time of it, Fr Bernard. I'm told it's very beautiful. I look forward to seeing it.' Jago looked down at his watch. 'Look, I'll have to be going soon, so . . .'

'Yes. No, of course.' Ignatius had barely resumed his seat. He sprang to his feet again. 'It's been very kind of you to come down at such short notice. Hasn't it, Bernard? Send us a post-card, and drop in; let us know how you got on, when you return, hmm?'

Jago was standing. His hand was being pumped. He was being herded from the room. He was bemused. Surely there had been some purpose to this visit beyond giving the two priests an excuse for a piss-up?

It appeared not. He waved goodbye to Fr Bernard and was escorted back out into the gloomy hall. Ignatius opened the front door. 'Keep your eyes open out there, Jago,' he rumbled softly. 'If you get the chance to render some assistance, further a good cause, I'm sure you'll do your best.'

'I hope so,' Jago said uncertainly. 'Why . . ?'

'Course you will! Course you will! No, as I say, just remember, if you get asked to render some small service, we approve. It will be to the benefit of the Church. So, good luck, Jago. God bless you.'

The door shut. Jago van Zeller was left standing at the top

of the steps, gazing back at the doorway and wondering just what had happened in there, just what he had missed.

Jago had set the alarm for half-past six, but was already wide awake at six o'clock, filled with pleasurable anticipation, the almost forgotten thrill at the prospect of adventure.

He had read in a newspaper recently of a study they'd made of seals. It seemed that seals enjoyed the preparation of their food, the games that their trainers made them play and so on, far more than the food which was their reward. They claimed to know this because they had measured the endorphins squirting around in the seals' systems at both times.

He did not know whether to believe this, because he would not believe the sort of people who go round measuring endorphins in seals if they told him the time, but if it were true, he reckoned that he had a lot in common with your average seal. The prospect of a holiday, a big deal, a meal, an adventure had kept him happy through months of drudgery. Over the past few years, rather as in a wearisome losing game of Monopoly, there had been no bright prospects to enliven the decline of Zellers – and his – fortunes.

Today, then, was a treat.

He lay enjoying an overdose of endorphins and a mug of tea in a biting hot bath.

He shaved in the bath, climbed out and dried himself to a tuneless rendition of 'It's All Right With Me'. He made another mug of tea, then dressed quickly and, as he thought, suitably for a steeplechase in Eastern Europe: an open-necked, pale blue Sea Island cotton shirt, a brown Prince of Wales check pullover, a single-breasted Irish twist worsted suit and McAfee's lace-up ankle boots.

He switched on the World Service which soon made way for *Today*. He packed six more shirts, four changes of socks, his sponge bag, the breeks from the same tweed suit, sweaters, jeans, ties and a dark grey double-breasted silk and wool suit against the soirees to which he was 'invitarted'.

Then he sat on the bed and fidgeted.

Occasionally, he picked up a magazine only to lay it

down again. Occasionally, he got up, stretched and paced the length of the room a few times. He switched the wireless to Capital. Michael Jackson came on, so he naturally switched it back again. He washed up the mugs in the kitchen. He hoovered the flat. He paced a bit more as the darkness thinned and the traffic-sounds thickened.

It was a great morning. Endorphins by the gallon.

At eight, he gave up the bid to be patient. He picked up the suitcase and his overcoat and switched off the lights. He double-locked the front door. He trotted up the steps into the square.

The sky was polished bone. The trees in the gardens beneath him snuffled and softly moaned. The puddles sneezed beneath passing tyres.

A taxi shuddered by within five minutes. He hailed it and clambered in. 'Heathrow,' he told the driver. The driver nodded once and shifted into gear.

Jago was away.

He might return to these sad grey streets in an ambulance or even in a box. He did not, at the moment, care. He had no dependants. He did not even, to all intents and purposes, have a business. His debts were paid. He owned nothing save some furniture, some nice clothes, a horse and an airline ticket.

It felt just fine.

If your average seal were forced to wait for his herring for as long as Jago was forced to wait for that flight, he might just find his endorphin-induced euphoria waning a trifle.

He had done the usual things – checked in, bought books and newspapers, eaten breakfast – and, bang on five past eleven, had been summoned by the departures board and the tannoy to boarding gate 12. *Now Boarding*, the board flashed with unseemly urgency. Jago believed it. He ran.

As usual, the heating was turned up to maximum. Jago was agitated and dripping sweat by the time he reached the metal-detecting barrier. As always, the damned thing beeped as he passed through, so he had to empty his pockets. A long-lost key in the breast pocket proved culpable. And still that *Now Boarding* legend flashed.

Years of experience should have taught him not to get flustered, but he always persuaded himself that today, for the first time, they might leave on time and without him. He was flushed, therefore, and wild-eyed, and his suit trousers and shirt were clinging like seaweed when at last he arrived at the gate.

He slumped down into the nearest chair. He groaned. The woman at the tannoy must have seen him coming. At that moment, she chimed on air to announce that she – only she adopted the royal plural – regretted that, due to minor mechanical problems, the flight would not be boarding for another twenty minutes, or, she portentously added, so.

Jago told her under his breath that she was a silly, stuck up bitch, and why the hell could she not have told him half an hour ago, before he started the five hundred metre hurdle which had resulted in his present condition.

'They always do this, don't they?' A girl sat down beside him. Her voice was rich and soft, like wind across a bottle-neck. Her hair was pale brown with an overlay of gold. It curled from her brow to her shoulder in an attenuated S. She wore faded jeans, a dark blue Guernsey, a white shirt with a leg-of-mutton collar, and very white trainers. 'Have you been running?'

'Like a hare.' Jago nodded. 'Oh, I know that they're not going to take off without me, but it still always has that effect.'

'I know.' She leaned forward, forearms on thighs, hands clasped, and looked back at him like a cyclist. 'You on business?'

'No. Couple of days' fun and games. I'm in a race out there.'

'Race? Well you're not going to win it if a run through the airport does that to you.'

'Not that sort of race,' Jago laughed. 'I don't do the running. A horse does that. I just sit on top and cling on for dear life.'

'You're a jockey, then?'

'Well, not a professional, no. It's a sort of hobby, that's all. There's this gallant little race over in Pardubice, four-and-a-quarter miles over some seriously hairy fences.'

'Yuk,' she shuddered. She looked up as another woman, similarly dressed, approached, a black jacket slung over her shoulder. 'Cora. Here. Did you hear we'll not be going for another twenty minutes?'

'Yup. I heard.' The other girl sat heavily on the other side of the first.

'This is a jockey. Sorry, I'm Holly. Holly Byrne.'

'Jago van Zeller.' He held out a hand. Holly took it, and a large amount of the tension which had been accumulating at the back of his neck seemed to slither away.

'And this is Cora. Cora Sanderson.'

'Hi.'

The other girl was well built, heavy-set, even. She was bigger and older than Holly. Seeing Holly full-face now, Jago put her at twenty-eight, maybe early thirties. It was a funny sort of face which narrowly avoided beauty and as narrowly avoided ugliness. The eyes were pale, wide and wide-set. The brow was almost oblong, the nose small and snub and the cheeks that Valentine's heart-shape more usually associated with the sort of face commonly described as 'impish'. A smile turned the heart into a big diamond.

Her friend was a deal closer to conventional handsomeness, but she had statements to make with her appearance. Her eyebrows were thick and unculled. She wore no make-up, and dark hair grew above the corners of her lips. Her hair was brown. It poured straight from a centre-parting.

'But I thought jockeys were knee-high to a grasshopper,' Holly was saying; 'didn't you, Cora?'

Cora nodded.

'Not over fences,' Jago smiled. 'The length of leg is an advantage for us guys. More to hold on with. So, what are you guys doing in Prague?'

'Oh, a working holiday.' Holly nodded down at her coat. She shifted it with a foot.

Jago saw the familiar shape of a fiddle case, the still more familiar shape of a camera case.

'Which is which, then?' he asked. 'Which is the fiddler and which the photographer?'

'Oh, I'm both,' Holly said. 'Well, amateur photographer only. Cora's the brains. She's educating me, and not before time. My education was a little one-tracked. She's taking me in hand, making me into a serious person, aren't you, Cora?'

Cora's lips twitched just once.

'Oh, don't get too serious,' Jago grinned. 'Frivolous people are usually the ones who do the most good on this earth.'

'Ooh. Don't tell that to Cora.' Holly flashed a grin at her friend. 'No. She's right. I've made enough of a fool of myself in the past. Anyhow. No. I'll play the streets to earn my keep, see if I can get some good shots. I mean, Prague; I've read so much about it; heard so much about it. I had friends at college who came from there. And I'm into Mozart in a big way. Thought I'd better get there before the Germans buy the place and reassemble it as an amusement park in Frankfurt.'

'And you, Cora?'

'Oh, I have friends there.' Cora did not look at Jago. 'I've been longing to go there for years.'

'Tell me something.' Holly's voice was concerned. 'Sorry. I want to ask you. You don't mind, do you?'

'Dunno. Fire away. I'll tell you.'

'OK, so you can hurt yourself, but what about the poor horses? Don't they get killed and things?'

'Sure,' Jago nodded. 'Sometimes.'

'But what do you feel about that? Isn't it rather unfair?'

'Nope.'

'Well, I think it is.'

'Am I allowed to explain?' Jago begged.

'Of course. Explain away.'

'OK. Look.' He slapped his damp thighs. 'A horse – any horse – is stronger than I am. I can't make a Shetland pony do what it doesn't want to do, any more than, without violence, I can make you do what you don't want to do. A pony can buck, it can rear, it can fall backwards and roll on me. Listen. It can refuse, right? What horses do, the way they survive, is to run. In the wild, the slowest is dead. They compete from the moment they're born, and they jump ferocious obstacles. A horse isn't a hunter. He's a specialist runner and jumper. As for racehorses, they're superspecialists, preservers of a highly select and important part of the gene-pool. They're like fighting bulls. OK. So some of them get killed, but so they would in the wild, and because we actually enjoy seeking perfection in a horse, we pamper them and keep that priceless gene-pool going. They're volunteers, those horses, and they get royally paid for what they do. End of lecture. Sorry.'

'I suppose so,' Holly nodded. She cast a quick glance at Cora, who appeared deep-sunk in brooding reverie.

'So. You're a professional fiddler, then. Classical?'

'Anything,' she shrugged. 'Yes, I play in an orchestra, but I've got a folk band too.'

'Nice way of travelling,' Jago mused. 'Have fiddle, will travel, and welcome wherever you go.'

The tannoy jangled. The complacent female voice requested that passengers in rows ten to twenty-one should now board. Jago stood. 'Well, that's me. I'll see you in Prague, then.'

The girls were gathering their things. 'That's us too,' said Cora.

Holly said, 'Oh, my God, I hate this,' as they shuffled down the metal tube to the aircraft.

'What? Flying?'

'I'm afraid so. It's ridiculous, isn't it? I'm always convinced – I don't know – it's not crashing, it's storms, being struck by lightning, I don't know.'

'You'll be fine.' For the first time, Cora smiled as she laid a hand on Holly's shoulder. 'Don't worry.'

'I know. It's crazy. Don't worry about it. What row are you in, Jago?'

He studied his boarding-card. 'Fifteen.'

'What are we? Eighteen. Oh, well.'

But when Jago and the girls had taken their places, he could not resist a quick reassuring smile over his shoulder at Holly. She returned it, and he noticed that Cora was leaning back by the window, Holly was at the centre of her row, and the aisle seat was still empty. He vaguely hoped that it might remain so, then told himself that it was bound to be filled, and what the hell. The girl would survive without his gallant ministrations. He faced front.

But they taxied and took off, and still a glance told him that the seat was empty. He waited a while, then turned solicitously and caught Holly's eye. She cocked her head at the seat. She signalled. She raised her eyebrows. He nodded. He unfastened his belt and slowly strolled back to her row. Cora just kept staring through the window as though her friend's choice of companion was of no interest to her. 'How're you bearing up?' Jago asked as he sat beside Holly.

'Oh, OK,' she nodded, 'but I'm glad to have you to gabble at. I always gabble when I'm nervous, and it drives Cora mad, poor thing.'

'You're not worried by flying, then, Cora?' Jago tried to involve the other girl.

'No,' she said without turning from her study of the clouds. 'I'm fine.'

'Cora's done a lot of flying.' Holly nodded a bit more. 'You like to think when you're up above the clouds, don't you?'

'Yes,' said Cora.

Jago decided to quiz Holly to keep her occupied. After the first couple of questions, little more prompting was necessary. She was indeed a gabbler when nervous. Jago sat back, content to let it all wash over him. It beat the in-flight magazine.

She talked of music and her childhood.

It had never struck Jago before just how cruel musical talent could be. Music was innate – a language to which common mortals could listen, entranced, but could never speak better than haltingly. Holly had been born nigh fluent. At four, she had enrolled in a Suzuki course. At eleven, she had won a scholarship to the Menuhin school, and the whole family had moved south from Parkgate in order to assist her progress. Her father, a doctor, her mother, a dental assistant, her two brothers, all had been enslaved by this monster gift.

And she, of course, had grown up aware of the sacrifices made for her, aware of the special nature of her talent.

And then, 'I was good, but I'd never be great,' she told Jago with blithe resignation.

The gift which had separated her from the ordinary run by miles now separated her by inches from big money and the sort of adulation which she had enjoyed in childhood. A century earlier, she would at the least have been feted within her own community. Now, in the days of the CD, she was merely an also-ran.

'But doesn't it make you feel a bit sick?' he asked her. 'I mean, some twelve-year-old pops up, playing as a soloist, and there you are, all those years of hard work, playing for him or her in an orchestra?'

'Nah.' She grinned. 'It's all music, isn't it? Someone's really good, really really semi-divine good, it gives me a buzz just to get close to them.'

They were already over the Czech Republic when he asked the two girls to dine with him that night. Holly turned to Cora. 'What do you reckon, Cora? Night on the town?'

Cora's shoulders rose and sank as she sighed. 'That's very kind. Can I think about it?'

'Sure, sure!' He was munificent. In reality, although he liked this girl, found her amusing and attractive, and liked the prospect of dinner with her in a strange town, the brooding Cora might just mean more trouble than pleasure. Dinner with Paul, or even on his own, might prove just as agreeable in the long run.

Paul Pickering sprang up the steps of the Hotel President. He was grinning as he loped into the foyer and made his way to the reception desk. He laid his overnight case on the thick carpet. 'Hello,' he twanged. The blonde girl looked up. 'Hel*lo*,' he drawled. 'You don't speak English, by any chance, do you?'

'Yes.' The girl gave him a smile warmer than mere professional courtesy required. 'I speak English.'

'Good. Gosh, it was difficult to find my way here. The

signposts are incomprehensible, and no one understands a dicky-bird. Still, I made it. Paul Pickering. I have a room booked.'

'Oh, yes, Mr Pickering. Of course.' She swivelled the register. 'If you'll just sign here.'

What with the business of completing his address, nationality, passport number and so on, and the twinkling banter which he at once initiated with the receptionist, Paul was far too busy to notice the young man behind him as he rose from his armchair and strode swiftly but smoothly to the lift. The young man pressed the button. The lift doors opened instantly. The man stepped in. He pushed another button and stepped back so that his back was against the wall. The lights above the doors would have told the curious that the lift rose only to the first floor.

When, therefore, having completed the formalities, Paul summoned the lift, it was half a minute or so before it moaned to a standstill and opened its maws. He stepped in, whistling. He twirled the key around his index finger. He saw the young man, vaguely registered jeans with a frayed hole at the knee, a big sloppy rust sweater, flopping honey-coloured hair, then turned away. Paul pressed the button marked '3'. The young man stepped quickly forward and pressed '2'. The doors sighed shut. The lift jerked and sped upwards. Almost as soon as it started up, the young man stepped forward. He reached very deliberately into his jeans back pocket and pulled out a bent and grubby envelope. He thrust it out under Paul's nose.

Paul blinked. He frowned with one eyebrow. The same corner of his lips jerked up towards his ear. 'Sorry? Some mistake, I think.'

'You,' the man nodded. He pointed. 'You.'

'No, no, old chap. Whatever it is, I don't want . . .'

The lift stopped. The doors slid open. The young man dropped the envelope, turned and scampered out onto the landing. 'Hold on!' Paul called after him, then murmured to himself, 'What on earth is going on?'

He shrugged and knelt as the doors once more closed. He

picked up the envelope and smoothed it out. 'Good heavens,' he whistled as he saw the name on it. 'What on earth can this be?' For the envelope was addressed in a bubbly spume of a hand, '*Paul Pickering, Hotel President*'. He tore it impatiently open, and stood reading it even as the lift stood open at his floor.

Hi, Paul.

Sorry about the mysterious stuff. Well, I took your advice, and here I am! Remember me? Listen. I urgently need your help right now. Can you come to the astronomical clock just before six? Sort of sidle up as though you're looking at the clock, then just say sort of, "Wow, this is amazing" or something. I'll be wearing a red baseball cap. Please help if you can. It won't take more than a few minutes. Please be really discreet, OK?

Yours, Cyril Havlik.

Paul raised the heel of his hand to his brow. He shook his head fast. He suddenly realized that the lift was standing open. He snatched up his bag and stepped quickly out. He laid down the bag again almost immediately and resumed his blinking down at the missive.

'Good Lord,' he breathed, 'there's a turn-up. Havlik. Funny chap. Heavens. What fun!'

The thought that someone might be pulling his leg and that he would find himself observed at the astronomical clock by a bevy of scoffing jockeys flickered across his mind, almost at once to be snuffed. The Havliks were a great family and, after all, his father had been a chum of Cyril's uncle. This was for real. The fellow must seriously need his help. Paul continued shaking his head as he strode to his room and let himself in. He sat at the desk, pulled out a sheet of hotel writing paper and wrote, '*Dear Jago . . .*'

He wrote for a minute or two. When he looked up from his work, his grin was still broader than ever.

The sky was the clearest, brightest blue. In the shadow of the aeroplane, the cold wrapped around them like water, seeping into collars and cuffs. In the brilliant sunshine, heat spread like whisky in the blood.

Cora was the first to step onto Czech soil. She marked the occasion by saying, 'So.'

'Right, so what about this evening, then?' Jago asked.

They walked side by side towards the waiting coach. 'So, Holly,' Cora said to her feet.

This was a strange 'so', neither apparently interrogatory nor consequent. It stood on its own like an ancient monolith, evidently pregnant with meaning, though that meaning was now unclear.

'I don't know.' Holly laid a hand on the taller girl's shoulder. Cora strode. Holly had to put in two steps for her companion's every one. 'It would be fun. What do you think, Cora?'

Cora's eyes swivelled towards Jago beneath those thick eyebrows. 'You know Prague?'

'Nope. I'll just ask at my hotel – which is the best typically Czech restaurant.'

'Come on, Cora. Why not? We've got nothing else planned. Chance to see the town.'

'I have plenty planned.' Cora clambered onto the bus. She swung round with her fingertips in her jeans pockets, her hips thrust forward. 'Still. If you want. I may not stay long, but all right. If it amuses you.'

Holly had climbed up after her. 'So where do we meet?'

'Well, where are you two staying?'

'Why?' Cora's eyes flickered towards Jago, veered swiftly away.

'Well, so that I can pick you up, of course.'

'I thought you had already done that,' Cora said flatly and under her breath, but nonetheless audibly. 'We are not sure where we will stay. We have some telephone calls to make when we reach the centre. It would be better if we came to your hotel to pick you up.' She seemed to enjoy this idea. Her mouth curled in what could, in a deceptive light, be taken for a smile. It vanished as though erased with one smear of the board-rubber. 'Where are you staying?'

'Um – a place called the Hotel President. I don't know anything about it. A friend runs a travel agency. He booked me in.'

The doors folded with a groan and a double thud. The bus jolted forward. Holly rocked back against Jago. Her hair was soft for a second against his lips. 'OK,' she said as she pulled herself back towards her friend. 'We'll come to the Hotel President at – what, Cora? Seven-thirty?'

Cora shrugged. 'Seven-thirty,' she confirmed.

'Great. I may have a friend with me. How far are we from the town, anyhow?'

Cora shrugged again. Holly had no idea. A man in a seat in front of them turned his head. 'Half an hour, forty minutes,' he volunteered. His accent was American.

'Do you want to share a taxi?' Jago asked the girls.

'No, that will not be necessary, thank you.' Cora spoke in a precise monotone. 'Some people are waiting for us here.'

Holly, Jago could see, had known nothing of these 'people'. She looked up at him with apology in her eyes. It was her turn to shrug. Then she smiled. 'Thank you, anyhow, Jago.'

Suspicion fizzled in Jago's brain only to be extinguished. He did not believe in these mystery 'people'. Cora merely wanted to get her little plaything away from him and, probably, to lecture her on the evils of men in general, Englishmen, jockeys and Jago in particular. He would continue to hope, but he would not lay long odds against the girls' being there tonight.

The outskirts of Prague were unprepossessing. Aside from the odd brilliantly painted house, Jago could have been in Swindon, say, right down to the Apple computers logo atop what looked like a corner-shop.

Suddenly, however, as the taxi descended a hill with forest to the left, Prague proper emerged beneath him. It would be nice to think that he might have said something original, something worthy of the Dictionary of Quotations. Instead, he said 'Wow.'

The driver, who had thus far been silent, nodded approval.

'Is Praha very good,' he said.

'Is Praha very good indeed,' Jago agreed.

Oxford might have its dreaming spires. Prague appeared to have a thousand more, and not just spires, but domes, minarets and battlements, towers and turrets. Black stone, white stone, grey, green and ochre glowed in the sheer light, and everywhere little specks of gold glittered. It was like looking down on a great mediaeval army in the plain, armed to the teeth with swords, lances and helmets above gorgeous livery. And through the middle of it all, a crinkled strip of tinfoil, flashed the winding Vltava river, spanned by five striding bridges and one great white feathery weir.

'This Mala Strana, Prague Lesser,' the driver volunteered as they wound downwards. 'There Prague Castle.' He indicated a massive complex about a towering black Gothic cathedral topped with verdigris copper and winking balls of gold. 'And on other coast, Starometska. Old Town.' Jago looked over to the opposite bank, where the greatest concentration of towers was, and reflected that a fourteenth-century cathedral which called its neighbour 'old' was quite seriously showing off.

And then they were in the thick of it, on gleaming cobbled streets, amidst grand Empire and Deco and glittering baroque. Even modest houses and shops were painted with geometrical designs, religious or chivalric scenes or adorned with statuary.

Jago had expected just Skodas and Trabants, but his expectations were long out of date. BMWs jostled with Volkswagens and Audis in the streets, though the traffic seemed sparser than in other great cities that he had known. With a loud clanging, a tram sped by at their off-side. And everywhere about them there was decoration, some grand – those straining caryatids on the corner, that glittering mosaic façade – some modest, like the statue of a kneeling girl above that doorway, the black and white chevron pattern with which that little mediaeval house had been painted.

Jago had wandered around Rome for weeks, and later had discovered that the only way to see Venice was to approach by sea and then to walk, but never had he seen so much statuary. Prince Charles, he thought, would love this place. Every period seemed represented, and the scale was human, not forbidding. Every building was distinct from its confrères by reason of ornamentation.

The Hotel President, after all this, proved a disappointment. It was a block, barely distinguishable from the Inter-Continental block next door. Both hotels were of the sort which flies faster than you can. You leave one at Heathrow, catch Concorde to any destination in the world, and the hotel has got there first. There is no escaping Death or Inter-Continentals.

Nonetheless, the President had its advantages. It stood on the riverside with its back to the Old Town. Staggeringly, on the other side of the river, there was nothing but a tall bank of forest. The President's foyer was warm and the receptionist spoke English.

She handed him two envelopes. He opened the first in the lift. It contained two invitations – one to a soiree the night before the race, the other to a dinner afterwards, optimistically supposing that he would still be capable of attending. It also contained passes and accreditation documents for the racecourse, a colourful racecard and a detailed timetable. On Saturday, for example, at 2.15 p.m., there would be 'jockeys' meeting and dedication of Velka Pardubicka. Please read here our prayer enclosed.' The prayer enclosed was scarcely a prayer. It read, 'We dedicate this race to the memory of the gallant Captain Poplar and we pledge that we will compete in a fair and sportsmanlike manner.'

Jago was in his room by the time that he opened the second envelope. It contained a single sheet of Hotel President writing-paper. The copper-plate hand was small and neat.

My dear Jago,

Sorry about this, but I'll have to miss the six o'clock appointment. Just arrived and the most extraordinary thing has happened. Intrigue and mystery and whatnot.

Great gas. Got to go and meet a chap I know vaguely, nephew of an old family friend, also here for the race. His name is Prince Havlik, just so as you know in case it's some sort of joke. Thought I'd have a stroll before my assignation. Chap says it shouldn't take too long, so I'll hope to be back so we can meet for a jar. Wonderful place, this. I'll call if I'm delayed.

Yours, Paul.

Jago sat on the windowsill. He gazed up river, past two gilded angels atop pillars, towards Prague Castle. He smiled as he thought of Paul. He *would* find himself a mysterious prince within minutes of arriving in Prague. Just as stories seem to happen to certain journalists, so the world would adapt to Paul's outdated perception of it. If there was romance yet to be had in the world, Paul would sniff it out. Things like that did not happen to Jago. In general, he thought, he was glad of it.

He looked at the racecard. Burlington, he noted, was rendered as 'Barlington' and Paul as 'Paul Pickeling', and there, at the foot of the field, was a German horse: Kalliope – owner and rider, Prince Cyril Havlik.

Jago laid down the card. He was not tired. So far, the day had fulfilled its early promise. He had met a nice sort of girl and come to a magical city. Paul's mystery assignation with a fellow rider seemed altogether in keeping. He glanced at his watch. It was twenty to four. He would wash, change into something more casual, find out about restaurants and book a table, then wander the streets.

Paul Pickering was enjoying himself. He had acquired a map from Reception and was headed for the only place that he had ever heard of: Wenceslas Square.

He never got there.

He got to the Old Jewish Cemetery all right – a poignant, peaceful, higgledy-piggledy mass of gravestones crammed close, leaning at impossible angles to accommodate late-comers. He got to the synagogue, with its stepped roof. He got to the Old Town Square, and grinned and breathed

'I say' when assailed by the bubbling baroque magnificence of St Nicholas's gleaming white cathedral on the one hand, the gaunt Jan Hus memorial, the rose Kinsky Palace and the grim fourteenth-century spires of Our Lady of Tyn. Ahead of him, the Old Town Hall, a single square tower, again Gothic, stood tall above the square next to its contemporary, shorter, pink companion, like a bridegroom with his bride, forever frozen at the church door.

And for the rest, just beautiful town houses in pinks, yellows and greys, some of them arcaded, each of them with different lines to their roofs and different architraves or embellishments about their windows.

They were pretty, they were opulent, they were elegant, they were frivolous, even – a happy family beneath the dour gaze of its older, battle-scarred patriarchs.

He wandered on, now thoroughly mesmerized, a sightseer through and through. Free enterprise was everywhere – not visible here in brass plates indicating that private houses had been taken over by corporations, but by masses of temporary stalls set up on the cobbles – stalls selling postcards and posters, stalls selling cigarettes, stalls selling hand-painted dolls, wooden toys, Russian military caps and badges, sausages, beer . . .

He passed the astronomical clock on the Old Town Hall. He strolled aimlessly through the narrow streets, admiring Bohemian crystal and marvelling at the prices, gawping into shop-windows filled with sausages and hams of every variety, stopping at antique shops to reflect that if only he had a juggernaut and a factual rather than fictional book of cheques, he could carry home a fortune in furniture and garden statuary. He happened on the Festival Theatre, a glorious late eighteenth-century green and white confection which had seen the premières of *Figaro* and *Don Giovanni*.

Cobbled street led to cobbled street. He wandered in perfect contentment, grateful to the builders, grateful to steeplechasing, without which he might never have come here, grateful, even, to the Nazis and the Russians. Even they had stayed their hands rather than despoil this loveliness.

He was approaching Wenceslas Square – was looking out at its vast expanse – when he happened to catch a glimpse of a clock through the windows of a Bureau de Change.

It said that it was seven minutes short of six.

He said, 'Damn', and he meant, 'Damn mister bloody Havlik for so rudely awaking me from my reverie.' He turned on his heel and paced quickly now, dodging stalls and idiotic, aimlessly wandering tourists, back to Old Town Square.

A crowd had already gathered in front of the astronomical clock. They gazed expectantly upwards. Paul nodded. If you wanted a meeting to pass unobserved, there were worse times and places than this.

He strolled past the front of the crowd, looking for a red baseball cap. He found two. One, at the forefront, was worn by a little boy. The other, worn by someone taller, was at the very back, almost beneath the arcades.

He made his way casually round behind him.

Havlik was tall and spare. Paul could not see his face, but the hair beneath the cap was dark blond, the colour of wet sand. His right leg jiggled beneath the yellow check trousers as if he needed a pee. His right hand opened and shut again and again by his side, then clenched and beat thrice at his thigh.

'Whoa, there,' Paul said softly at his shoulder. 'Got your note. Good to see you here. Amazing place, this, isn't it?'

'I think I've shaken him,' Havlik whispered without turning. 'God, I hope so. Thanks for coming.'

'Sorry, shaken whom?' Paul frowned. He had just spent the past two hours wandering freely through the streets of a sunny city without let or hindrance. This fellow seemed to think that they were still in the murky, paranoiac world of the Quiller Memorandum.

'Shit, I don't know,' Havlik murmured, and his shoulders just shifted beneath the green blouson. 'He was on my tail from the minute we crossed the border. Jeez. Thought, great, the old country's free, just sneak in, sneak out. Hell I can. Old system's still here. Still goddamned efficient too. That's why I'm riding in this so-called horse race. Jesus. Fucking bloodbath, you ask me.'

'I'm not with you, old chap.' Paul shook his head, exasperated. 'Could you start at the beginning and sort of work your way towards the middle?'

'Not here. There won't be time. Look. Best bet. You speak French?'

'Well, a bit. Schoolboy stuff.'

'OK. Can you go to the Club André tonight as a Frenchman? There's no one there speaks more'n a coupla words, so you'll be OK. No credit cards or anything. Call yourself – I dunno – Jean Dupont, anything. Get there round – what? Eleven? I'll come in round twelve. I got myself a little friend, Russian chick, name of Orla. She'll help. Can't miss her. Shoulder-length brown hair, big swoopy sort of eyebrows, brown leather mini-skirt. She knows what's wanted. Christ knows if I can trust her, but I got to take a risk here.'

'Sorry,' Paul winced, 'but I'm still way off the pace. First, how did you know I was coming here?'

'What, to Prague? Simple. I checked with the organizers which hotel you were staying at and asked them. Otherwise I'd've had to head down there this evening. Saved me a lot of hassle. Easier in a big city.'

'And second, sorry, but why on earth should I race around town picking up girls for a chap I barely know when I don't even know the reasons?'

'Oh shit,' Havlik sighed. 'Because it's thanks to you that I'm here and in this fix, because we're both jocks and I claim the great freemasonry of hunters and riders, because your father knew my uncle, because it's an adventure, and if you're the sort of guy rides horses over seventeen-foot ditches, you'll not say no to an adventure. Is that enough?'

'Well . . .' Paul struggled for a second, but the result, he knew, was a foregone conclusion.

Havlik, however, did not know his man so well. 'Oh, and – you need another because? Try 'cos there's a ten per cent minimum share of six million dollars for you, everything works out.'

There was a lot of creaking then, from the great fifteenth-century clock and from Paul's stomach.

A skeleton raised his arm and brought it down, ringing the bell, *memento mori*. One by one, each of the carved apostles, carrying his symbols, emerged at the doors above and swung on round. The crowd shielded eyes, pointed, gasped. The final stroke tolled. The gold cock crowed.

Time had most definitely passed. Death and judgement were so much nearer.

'I say,' Paul said softly. 'No. Of course. Club André. Gosh. Right. Absolutely.'

Cyril Havlik's hand fumbled behind him for Paul's. He nodded once. 'See you midnight.'

And, hands twitching, he strode away with the dispersing crowd.

Paul was still gleefully rubbing his hands together as he bustled back towards the hotel. Head down, he had already overtaken Jago without noticing when the voice hailed him from behind. 'Paul! Hey! What's the rush?'

Paul turned. 'Oh, oh, hello, old man.'

'So what's all this high adventure stuff?' Jago smiled and dropped into step beside him. 'Isn't this place amazing?'

'Fantastic,' Paul agreed. 'Absolutely bloody fabulous.'

'So, Prince Havlik. Riding in the race, I see. Ruritanian, I suppose. Trust you to find a mystery.'

'Hmm?' Paul was abstracted. 'Oh, yes. Well, it really seems to be a mystery, I can tell you. Well, I can't, of course. Tell you. At least, I don't think I can. Top secret, all that, but no. Amazing. Got to go and meet him late tonight, find out more. His uncle was my dad's best friend. Think I told you. RAF. The Few, you know? I was called after him, matter of fact. He was a Pavel, hence Paul. Nice young chap. Absolutely bona fide prince, all that, even if he is a bit – well, American, if you know what I mean.'

'I know what you mean,' Jago laughed. 'Now, you're not getting dragged into anything silly, are you, Paul? Anything a bit dodgy? Remember, we are strangers in a strange land.'

'Oh, no, no. I don't think so. Not a Havlik. No, all above board. Come on. I'm not a child.'

'OK, OK. So,' Jago pushed open the hotel's glass door, 'bring me up to date. Sorry. I haven't got long. I've somehow found myself a dinner engagement tonight. You could come along if you fancied it?'

'Um, no. No, thanks, Jago. Not tonight. Good of you. No, but, you know, this assignation. I need my beauty sleep. Just take it easy, I reckon.' He led the way into the red-walled bar. 'Now, what'll you have?'

'No. Let me do this.' Jago spoke from habit. 'I dragged you out here.'

'Damned good of you, must say. Orange juice, please, Jago.'

Jago ordered an orange juice and a glass of beer. 'So,' he leaned on the bar and turned back to Paul, whose hair glowed in the pink light, 'news from Pardubice. All well?'

'Oh, all brilliant.' Paul nodded enthusiastically. 'Wonderful trip, wonderful. God, that course is beautiful. Damn pretty birds here too. Brilliant stuff. That chap of yours, he's a treat, isn't he? What housemaids used to call "a proper caution".'

'Clay?' Jago laughed. 'Yes. Yes, you could call him that.'

'Absolutely. Real old-fashioned NCO sort. Salt of the earth. Fancies himself as a bit of a trainer, though, to be frank – and I'm not, of course, as you know, I'm Paul – I don't really think he knows which end bites and which feeds the roses. No, I've been exercising your fellow – I hope that's OK?' He took his drink and went over to a low table.

'God, yes.' Jago sat. 'I'm honoured. I should think he is too.'

'I thought we'd do a bit of upsides work. Got this Czech boy in. Good lad. Comes from the school of jockeys. Clay says things like, "Right, just take him four furlongs off the cuff." I say, "Don't you mean 'on the collar'?" He goes, "Gor, I don't fuckin' know, do I? On the collar, off the cuff . . . Bugger don't understand a dicky-bird anyhow."'

Laughter burst from Jago. Paul was a first-rate mimic. He reproduced Clay's voice and facial expressions to perfection.

'Oh, Lord,' Jago gulped. 'You're sure he'll not take it into his head to exercise the old boy over the full four miles?'

'Oh, he would have done.' Paul smiled a little sheepishly at Jago's laughter. 'No, don't worry. I've given him a strict timetable, even got it translated by the hotel receptionist and gave a copy to the boy. Strict instructions: don't listen to Mr Levine. Follow these orders or die.'

'So how's your animal, Avocet?'

'Oh, fine. Very bonny. Busting out of his skin. 'Mazing. Knows this isn't just another day's hunting, that's for sure. No, they're both fine. So, you'll be down tomorrow morning?'

'Well, tomorrow, anyhow,' Jago equivocated. 'I've barely scratched the surface of this city. I'd like a good look, if the animals really are OK.'

'Absolutely fine. No problems. Security at the racecourse and the stables is tight as a newt's whatnot. They seem pretty jumpy. Hangover from commie days, I suppose. No. Relax on that score. Well,' Paul drank deep and suddenly slapped his thighs, 'sorry to be anti-social, but I'm not used to these late hours any more. If you don't mind, I'll take myself off to beddy-byes for a couple of hours. Extraordinary trip, this. Greatest gas.'

He stood and reached down a hand to Jago. His lips were curled downwards in an amused smile. His eyes, as ever, glittered. 'See you at breakfast tomorrow, right?'

Jago took the hand and pulled himself to his feet. His left hand lightly clasped Paul's upper arm. 'Take it easy,' he said.

'And you.' Paul wheeled and loped with that increasingly familiar, springy gait, out into the foyer.

Jago sat again. He shook his head in mild amazement, and waited for the girls.

'This', said Holly with a wicked grin, 'is fun.'

'I agree. Let's stay here. Let's tell the world to go hang. Let's buy a modest little palace and we'll grow our own wine and you can play me lullabies on your fiddle . . .'

'And you can ride your poor old horse down the hill to the village for provisions . . .'

'And shoot wild boars and rabbits for dinner . . .'

Jago knew as he spoke that he had blundered. Holly's eyebrows rose in the centre. Her lips twitched. Her shoulders slumped. She said, 'Yuk.' Cora, who had hardly spoken so far, tutted and sneered.

'Sorry, sorry.' He held up his hands for peace. 'Someone has to do it, though. Anyhow, let's steer clear of contention tonight. I'm free of Miss Sniffy and you're free of . . . well, and you're free too. Nobody knows us. We don't know anybody. We can do everything and anything without fear of gossip and slander. Do you wish to dance upon the table? You shall do it. Is there a word – "district nurse", say – that you have always longed to say but never dared to say in public? You must have. Everyone has. I, for example, have never had the opportunity to use the words "terrapin" or "theodolite" in cogent conversation.'

'Or "gusset",' Holly volunteered.

'Oh, I have had cause to say "gusset" in the highest circles. "Bollard", however, try as I might, has eluded me. Unless you hit one, there is no socially acceptable reason for mentioning bollards. "I say, look at that fascinating bollard," just doesn't ring true. "There was I, standing by the bollard, when who should I see but my old friend Mauricc . . ." It doesn't sound right.'

'Yes,' she giggled, and Jago liked the crow's feet at the corners of her eyes. 'Bollard is nice. No. You're right. I haven't been silly in public for years. Can I have some more wine?'

Jago reached for the bottle. He said, 'Sorry.'

'You should be careful, Holly,' Cora warned.

'Oh, it's all right.' Holly held forth her glass. 'It's only a short walk back. Come on. Just once.'

Jago poured the Czech white, of which he had never heard but which had proved fruity, nicely acid and bigger than most of its kind. Apple with apple skin and apple jelly – the sort which, as the French say, 'drinks itself'.

The restaurant was all white arches, like a cellar. The windows were covered by black wrought-iron lattices.

There were only two other couples eating there.

The menu had held surprises and problems for them. To start off with, it was in Czech and German, and Jago was getting used to the startling – if, for an Englishman, salutary – fact that these were the only languages which Czechs, in general, speak. Czech appeared impenetrable, and his 'O' level German availed him little.

Cora, they discovered, was going to have a hard time of it in the Czech Republic. She grew more and more annoyed as the nature of the dishes on offer became clear. The only vegetables advertised, aside from sauerkraut and potato dumplings, of course, were 'sterilized peas' and 'sterilized carrots'. Cora was a committed vegetarian.

With the faltering aid of the only waiter who knew a smattering of English, however, and a deal of farmyard impersonations, they had discovered that '*fleisch*' was invariably to be translated as 'pork', and that the menu consisted largely in variations on a theme of pork with potato dumpling and sauerkraut. It was a reflection of past privations that the precise quantity of *fleisch* used was printed by the name of each dish – so you got 150g of pig in your Chinese *fleisch* and 200 in your *gulas*, which even the English could understand.

'No pork for me,' Jago announced equably. 'I never eat a pig that I have not met socially.'

'Right.' Cora thumped the table. She spoke evenly. 'I don't think there's much point in my staying. I approve of that principle at least, Mr van Zeller. I will abide by it. At least I can say that I have met you socially. Enjoy yourself, Holly.' She pushed back her chair, stood, gave Jago one last, scornful long-distance header, and strode out.

'Cora . . .?' Holly called after her. She too leaped up and scampered after her friend.

Jago sat twiddling his glass between thumb and forefinger. He was not minded to get up and apologize. He had, to his mind, done no wrong, and if these two girls meant this sort of irritation, he had better people to befriend and better things to do. Any relationship, he knew, in which there was subservience and dominion, was in part a sexual relationship. Holly, for some reason, then, was involved in a sexual relationship with this sulky, resentful PC houri. Maybe Cora had even physically seduced Holly, but that did not make Holly a lesbian. There was some reason why Holly needed what Cora could give. He genuinely liked Holly. He reckoned that she liked him. He was not, however, going to fight dragons to wrest her from the thrall which she had embraced. Jago had not been brought up to knight errantry, and his adolescent attempts at the genre had been signal failures.

The waiter arrived, with a bowl of vegetable soup for Holly, of chicken soup for Jago and a plate of crudités for Cora. Jago pointed at the door, where the girls stood making a noise like distant Bob Marley. The waiter understood that. He nodded, winked and left the crudités.

'She's hurt,' Holly announced when she strutted back to the table. 'Not by you, just by men.'

'Men don't exist.' Jago shook his head sadly. 'They're not a class or a club. They're as diverse as dogs or . . . They include Jesus Christ and William Wordsworth and Jimi Hendrix and Stalin. Jesus! If I started generalizing about "women" . . .'

To his gratification, she unfolded her napkin and sat. 'I know,' she said fiercely, 'but she's got her problems. You're everything which annoys her. She's kind.'

'She's doctrinaire,' Jago sighed. 'Doctrinaire can never be kind. She wants to be loved. Join the club. We all want to be loved. Actors get up on stage and get applause. That's a substitute. No demands. She, with a half-trained mind, says things which sound right without having thought them out. I'm sorry. A totalitarian with high moral principles is a damn sight worse than a totalitarian with none. She's sad.'

'She's helped me so much,' Holly mused. 'All right. Can we leave it and enjoy ourselves? Please? This is meant to be a holiday. You're a needless complication. God, why are all my friends so aggressive?'

'Because you want to be led.' Jago grinned at her. 'Right. Food. Come on. Let's have fun.'

They settled, in the end, on carp for Holly and quail for Jago, with an agreement to share and swap. Having discovered that they could eat a large meal in what was, supposedly, the best Czech restaurant in Prague, for less than two English pounds a head, and having discovered the wine to be good, they gave up worrying about Cora and the quality or variety of the food.

In fact, when it came, it was good. Holly's carp had a blackened skin and a strange black sauce and was fresh and firm, whilst Jago's birds, as he told her, had plainly lived well and died fulfilled.

'I wish you wouldn't say things like that – all jokey like that,' Holly complained.

'Sorry. I shall adopt funereal tones in future. I thought we were celebrating liberation.'

'Yes, OK. But when you talk about things dying . . .'

'I reveal myself an unfeeling brute?' Jago sighed. 'No. Listen, love. I meant a little of what I said this afternoon. We do have a place in the food chain and a responsibility to uphold. We do have to cull deer and control foxes and selectively breed and tend migratory fish and domestic animals. I hate cruelty, but most of the serious cruelty done on this earth is done by greedy, supposedly respectable farmers and Kennel Club breeders, but you don't object to them because they aren't seen to enjoy what they do. They sure enjoy the profits, though. We plainly enjoy the activity and don't see any profits. So what's wrong with enjoying a necessary activity? Is there something immoral about an undertaker whistling while he works? I don't understand that, I'm afraid. It's deeply envious and puritanical. Sorry.'

'Shit,' she said, and she stared solemnly at her half-eaten fish. She reached for the clutch bag on the bench beside her.

Jago thought, 'Well, done, van Zeller. You've blown it good and proper. She's going to storm out now . . .'

Instead, she pulled out a paper tissue and angrily dabbed at her right eye.

She picked up her knife and fork again. 'Oh, I don't know, I don't know, I don't know,' she sighed. 'I don't know what I believe. I wish I could just say "I don't care", but I *do* care. I feel that I have to care one way or another. You do. Cora does. And your views sound right but feel wrong, and her views feel right, but . . .'

'The woman lies sleeping,' Jago said softly. It was his turn to lay down his knife and fork. 'Above her, a masked man raises the glittering blade . . .'

'What are you . . .?' she frowned.

'He brings it down and precisely slices from her chestbone to her pubis. Blood spurts but is quickly staunched as he delves further . . .'

'Jago . . .' She had backed against the wall. She was genuinely alarmed. 'What in God's name . . .? Are you mad?'

'Feels wrong, doesn't it?' He smiled as soothingly as he could. 'But we add a quick spoonful of knowledge, and all that I've described is a surgical operation. Aesthetic morality won't do. If I show you an appendicectomy or a circumcision or an abortion on film, it looks ugly. Doesn't mean that it's wrong, does it? Same thing here. Cora shows you the slaughtering, the blood, the viscera. I give you the perpetuation of a species, the placid, natural life on the hillside or in the forest. I . . .' Then he was reaching for her arm as her lower lip shook and curled and her face collapsed and she raised her hands to her face and stumbled to her feet. 'Holly?' He too half stood. 'No, please. I didn't mean . . .'

'Please,' she keened, and tears splashed on his hand. 'Please, let me *go*.'

He let her go. With one big sob which shook her shoulders and a desperate moan, she lurched for the door and pushed her way out into the night.

'The Great Bloody Seducer,' Jago muttered. 'Jesus.'

He downed his wine and flung five hundred crowns onto the table. The waiter would have cause to be grateful to Holly.

He was cursing himself bitterly as he walked out into the winding street. Where in God's name had he found the depths of stupidity necessary to educe tears and bitterness on a rare, precious night of carefree fun? Yes, it was true that he cared, but that was a bloody poor demagogue's excuse for ruining a night out.

He actually punched the wall as he strode out.

She had not run away. She was right there in the next doorway, a hunched little figure with her hands over her face as though she feared that it might trickle away with her tears.

'Holly?' He found it difficult to speak. He swallowed. 'Listen. I'm sorry. I didn't mean to get on my hobby horse. I was wrong. I'm sorry. Really.'

He had stood a couple of feet back, wary of flying hands and flailing feet. Suddenly, however, without straightening, she swivelled and flung herself blindly at his chest. His arms folded around her.

She was rubbing her cheek on his chest. Her sobs ran up a short staircase then jumped from the top with a sudden jerk. The top of her head was against his lips, so he kissed it gently, said, 'Holly. OK, OK, I'm sorry.' The smell about her was good and clean, and her cheek was cool as grape-skin where he stroked it. 'Sh,' he soothed. 'Easy. I'm sorry. Don't worry . . .'

'Oh, fuck.' She took a deep breath and stood back with blinking red eyes and a little smile. She sniffed deeply and blinked up at the black sky. 'Oh, God. I'm sorry.'

'No, it's my fault.' Jago still held her hands.

'No, it's not!' She sniffed again. 'It's just – God. I'm glad you're not representing British interests abroad.'

'Tactless, eh?'

She squeezed his hands tight. Her giggle was husky. 'You could say . . .' She let go his hands then, and turned her back to him. 'Oh, God. It's not your fault. I'm just so bloody hypersensitive, I . . .' She shrugged. 'It's not like me at all. It just keeps coming back and sort of – turns everything upside down.'

'We walk?' Jago suggested.

She turned her head. She bit her lower lip. She nodded. 'Yes please.'

She took his arm. They walked.

'It's just so – like, you know, you always think of tragedy as grand, but when it comes, it's like, you know, an orgy or something. Seems great and dramatic and it'll be a purging and so on. In fact, it's always so tawdry, so squalid. You know, like the charlady at Elsinore. Not exactly high tragedy for her, was it? Just mucky and a bore. And that's how it feels. I wish I could dramatize it, make it all heroic and poor little me, but what it comes down to is, it's just a squalid, commonplace little story and nothing special at all. You guessed, of course?'

'Abortion.'

'Yeah. I mean, so what? I did it, wanted to do it, woman's right, all that, but just sometimes, it comes back and punches you square between the eyes, you know?'

'Jesus,' Jago moaned, 'I just cannot believe . . . I see what you mean about me and diplomacy.'

'No. Come on. You weren't to know. Anyhow, even if you did – it was a good bit of debating. I admired it. I'd use it myself if I could. It just – it's just, I suppose here, on holiday, being frivolous, I'd let my guard down, you know? Dangerous thing to do. I always have the worst blues on holidays and things.'

'Tell me,' Jago ordered as they entered the Old Town Square.

'God,' she said, echoing his thoughts. 'It is as amazing as it was an hour ago.'

'Yup. I spent the afternoon saying "Wow" and wishing I could think of anything better.'

'You could always try "bollards".'

'Why not?' Jago grinned. He squeezed her arm. 'Makes as much sense as "wow". OK. Bollards. Now. Tell me.'

'Oh, God. There's nothing to tell, is there? Same old boring, irrational story. You know, we never see ourselves as others do. God knows what reason, but someone's said the wrong thing or something, and it sticks in your mind, so everyone's telling you, like with this weight thing, you know? Bulimia, all that. Everyone's telling you, God, you're thin, you're stunning, wow . . .'

'Bollards.'

'Right, and something – some vile little boy who teased you once or something – is sitting there at the back of your head calling you "fatty!", so you don't even believe the mirror. Well, I don't know. Self-esteem is a problem. Why, Christ knows. I mean, for me, I mean, there are all these people without special talents, without a loving, supportive family. It's crazy. In fact, it's outrageous. I have no *right* to have that problem. All my life, people have been telling me how wonderful I am . . .'

'Uh uh.' Jago shook his head. 'All your life, people have been telling you how wonderful your talent is, and you know, better than they, that, while talent is a wonderful part of you, it isn't you. It comes from nowhere and you can see no reason why it shouldn't vanish just as readily. Easy come, easy go. And your parents making all those sacrifices for you – great, only somehow you were made aware that they were sacrifices and that your brothers were suffering for you. I'd feel bloody guilty if I were you, I'd feel like a fraud. You know, you're only worth anything, you're only loved with a fiddle in your hand. And you've got to suspect that what they love is the fiddle, not you . . .'

She was frowning up at him. She said, as though asking a surprised question, 'Yes. That's it. It was always, "my wonderful daughter, just listen to her play," not, "my wonderful daughter, full stop." Pathetic, really, isn't it? How do you know?'

'Because I adolesced with a similar curse,' Jago told her. 'I had lots of money. People love you for that too. That's why the rich usually make friends with the rich. It's not snobbery. It's fear of disillusionment.'

'Yes.' She was all dreamy now. 'Maybe I should make friends with the rich too. Anyhow, don't ask me. All my adult life, it's been – first it was, like you said, sort of adolescent rebellion, testing people, you know? *Now* do you love me? I gave up music, took up dope, got booted out of school, then men – I mean, shitty, really obvious creeps, you know? And this guy – Christ, I mean, if you couldn't see his problems six miles off – I mean, an arrogant, strutting bully, what? Nineteen years older than me. Twice married. Everyone tells me to keep away – so what does old clever clogs do? Move in with him, of course. Sort of guy, one minute he's crying, the next he's stamping and shouting. Convinced I spend all my waking hours in bed with every man I see. Stops me wearing make-up, tight jeans, short skirts – anything. Follows me around at parties, sort of snapping at anyone who even smiles at me, then gets me home and beats me up because I'm meant to have been encouraging them.

'Jesus, I don't know. You look back and you say, "Why in hell did I stick it for four years? *How* did I stick it?" And the nearest I've got is just good old lack of self-esteem.'

'On both sides, by the sound of it,' Jago said sadly.

'Yeah. Mmm. I don't know. I haven't got there yet. I'm only just at the healthy "God, what a bastard" stage. I don't know why. I'd always thought someone like you – jockey, all that – would be insensitive. Jock straps. Showers. Haway the lads.'

'Ah, well,' Jago smiled. 'Deep down, of course, I'm a closet marine commando. No. I know what you need, that's for sure.'

'Oh, of course, and of course you can give it to me,' she snapped suddenly.

'Oh, no,' he sighed. 'I very much doubt that.'

'Sorry,' she gulped, then, 'What, then?'

'Not now.' He checked himself. 'Go on.'

'Nothing more to tell, really.' She was airy. 'I wanted commitment, or thought I did. He says, sure, let's make it permanent, only he never gets round to doing anything about it. So the biological clock is doing its thing. I get pregnant. He comes back pissed, says I'm trying to trap him, beats – is it seven bells? – well, beats the hell out of me. That's why I thank God for Cora. She patched me up, got me to the hospital, all that, organized about the . . .'

'Terrapin,' Jago suggested.

'Yeah. She was good to me. And her crowd of friends. I mean, it feels good to have people who understand, who've been through it too . . .'

'Sure,' he agreed, 'as long as their conclusions are hopeful, not vengeful.'

She looked sharply towards him, then sharply away.

They were entering Wenceslas Square at last. They looked around. They saw a vast oblong full of stalls and taxis, crowned with thorns of neon.

'Non-bollards,' Jago announced.

'Yuk,' she admitted regretfully. 'Come on. I've given you enough gloom and doom to last a lifetime. Let's go back and do something stupid.'

'Like what?'

'Well, I know what would be really stupid . . .'

'Good.'

'Let's go back to Mozart's theatre, then I'll tell you.'

'OK,' he shrugged. 'Now, you said you fly back on Tuesday morning, same as me, right?'

'That's right.'

'Good. Come with me.'

He swerved into the Bureau de Change where Paul had earlier seen the clock. He pointed at the poster on the wall.

'You've got a choice, then. *Don Giovanni* at the Estates or *Otello* at the State Opera. Speak.'

'You . . .' She grinned delightedly. She pushed her hair back behind her ear with the outside of her hand. 'You mean . . .'

'Come along. Haven't got all night.'

'But I can't afford . . .'

'I can,' he said, 'just,' though he doubted that Miss Sniffy would agree. 'Come on. *Otello* or *Don Giovanni*?'

'No contest,' she said. 'Mozart in Mozart's theatre, please.'

Jago nodded. He walked to the counter. He engaged in some lengthy sign-language negotiations. He emerged with two stalls tickets in his hand.

Holly was exhibiting considerable powers of co-ordination, clapping, skipping, beaming and thanking him all at the same time. He held out the tickets. 'You hold onto them,' he said. 'Just in case.'

'In case of what?' she frowned.

'Oh, just in case you've forgotten the little matter of a race I've got to ride on Sunday. Don't worry. Usually, I bounce. I'll be there. And if, for any reason, I'm not, you can take dear Cora. Whoops. No. *Don Giovanni* is seriously non-PC.'

She took the tickets and pushed them into her clutch bag. 'The only problem is,' she looked coyly up at him out of the corner of her eye, 'the stupid thing I wanted to do may not be so stupid after all.'

'What's that, then?'

'Come here.' She led him to the Lion, Witch and Wardrobe-style lamppost beneath the Estates theatre.

'No,' she said solemnly. 'Of course it's stupid. It's probably the stupidest thing I've done in years. Still.'

And, with a matter-of-fact shrug of resignation, she reached up, clasped her hands behind his neck, and did it.

'*Viva la folia*,' he murmured a minute later.

She said, 'Shut up.'

The taxi-driver seemed to have no doubts as to the nature of the Club André or as to the nature of Paul's business there. He winked a cobwebbed eye and leered. He studied Paul in the rear-view mirror. '*Bist* English?' he asked.

'*Non*,' some cautious reflex made him answer, even here. '*Français*.'

'Ah. *Franzia. Bonsoir*.'

Paul feared for a moment that he had engaged the only polyglot in Prague, but it seemed that, with this sally, the driver had shot his sole French bolt. He sank into silence as he drove out into what seemed to be the suburbs of the city. Paul grew ever more alarmed as they sped out into the realm of tower blocks, trees and terraced villas.

It was in front of one of these last that the driver braked and announced, as though he had produced it from a hat, 'Club André.'

Paul peered out through the window. There was a fence of high white railings and a gate higher still. Beyond, he saw crazy paving and a fishpond with a fountain, then a white villa with a white light in its porch. A burly man in a dark suit stood with his legs planted wide in the doorway. Another, only slightly lighter of frame, stepped forward from the gate to open the taxi door.

Paul stepped out. He nodded to him and tried to look like a high-roller. He paid the taxi-driver what seemed to him the enormous sum of eight hundred crowns – damn near twenty pounds – and the big man pushed open the gate. It creaked.

The second man, who towered above Paul, flexed his muscles as Paul sidestepped the fishpond and approached the door. This man too gave and received a nod, then Paul was inside the hall.

A mustachioed man whom he would have taken elsewhere for an Arab sat at a small desk. There were pink roses on the table beside him. The man said, '*Guten abends.*' Paul nodded to him, too. The man smiled and showed him a large gap in his teeth. One of them was all gold. His left cheek was strafed with pocks. Paul stepped into full light. Again he was at once asked, 'From England?'

Paul shook his head. '*Suis Français,*' he corrected. '*Vous parlez Français?*'

The pockmarked man shook his head. 'English, yes. German, yes. French very leetle.'

'We speak in English, zen.' Paul gave it the full Clouseau bit.

'You pay to me two hundred crown, please.'

Paul sighed. He paid him his two hundred, reflecting that Mr Havlik was chewing substantial holes in his budget for this trip. That Paul could only blame himself in no sense made it better.

He walked on into a modest sized, brightly lit bar which reminded him of the anteroom of a restaurant or the health bar attached to a swimming pool. It was cheerful rather than comfortable with its dark yellow walls and its white ceiling. Secrets here would have to be spoken very softly. Had it been a restaurant, you might have crammed six tables in.

All that he saw was girls. There was a neat, air-brushed air hostess figure behind the bar, her blonde hair wound up into a bun. At the bar, two more girls lounged on the high stools. One would have passed for a blonde English horsewoman in her tight white breeches and her black boots. The other, a pale brunette, wore a sparkling purple dress. You could see the plush white pouch of her knickers as she moved.

In the main part of the room, down a step at his left, two more girls sat quietly talking on a banquette. Five or six more girls sat at a table swapping jokes.

He ran a finger around his collar. He felt conspicuous as he walked across to the bar. 'Er, *bonsoir,*' he said again to the three girls there. 'Good evening.'

'Good evening,' they answered in chorus.

'You want drink?' the air hostess asked.

'Yes. Thank you. Um. A beer.'

She poured a bottled Pilsner whilst the other girls made desultory stabs at conversation. 'You English?'

'No. French. But I speak English. You?'

One shook her head and giggled. The other, the one in breeches, said coolly, 'No. She English *spreche,*' and she headed an invisible ball at one of the two girls on the sofa.

This was his contact. He was sure of it. She looked up at him. He gulped. Her glance was slow, serious, deep and dark, the sort of look that somehow seemed to burrow deep into the darkest regions of your thoughts whilst at the same time drawing you into the depths of her like a maelstrom.

It was not that she was as pretty as half the girls in the room. She was older than most. Her mouth was wide, her chin weak, but those eyes spoke of knowledge of ancient, dark arcana beyond the reach of magi. They would be still and would thus scrutinize, it seemed to Paul, any wildness, any madness with infinite pity, infinite humour. It was the still, haunting gaze of a little girl but a little girl who was now forgiving mother to all aspirant, eager, fumbling, brutish, angry, pitiful men.

Paul shook himself. He was going mad. This was a Prague hooker, for Christ's sakes, not the Mona Lisa. Yes, as Havlik had said, she had dark glossy hair with slight auburn highlights. She wore a loose-fitting white cotton shirt with a foaming jabot front and a short leather skirt. Her legs were, by any standards, lovely, her ankles fine.

He looked back to her face, to her ironic smile, and it started all over again.

He buried his nose in his beer for a second, then strolled towards her. 'Hello,' he said. 'I am told you speak English.'

'A little,' she said softly. She tapped the banquette beside her. 'Siddown. What your name?'

'Paul um . . . Dupont,' he whispered. He cleared his throat. 'Sorry. Paul. I am French.'

'Paul who is French,' she said, 'I Orla. This my friend Katushka.'

He glanced at Katushka. She was a dumpy, dowdy little thing with short mouse hair. She looked nice. She looked as though she had fed largely on potatoes. He smiled quickly. He turned back to Orla. Once again, he travelled down a zoom lens into darkness.

'You are Czech?' he asked.

'No. Russian.'

'From Moscow?'

She shrugged. 'Moscow, yes. Ust Kamensgorsk. What you like.' She stretched. The ruffled cotton outlined full breasts. The arms and hands seemed impossibly long and fine. 'What would you like?' she asked innocuously, and her smile was warm and bright.

Paul glanced quickly over his shoulder, then back at her. Their eyes met. She made no movement, yet those eyes seemed to tell him that she understood, not merely what he was doing here, but damn near everything about him. 'Can we go somewhere quieter to discuss that?' he croaked.

'It is three thousand crowns,' she said.

'Oh. OK.' He nodded.

She said 'Good,' and she laid a long hand on his. 'We have very nice time. Yes?'

'Yes,' he nodded obediently. 'Absolutely. Thank you.'

She giggled. 'You thank me already. Maybe I should thank you.' She was suddenly a playful little girl. 'Come.'

Paul stood and smiled at Katushka. Orla's hand held his as she led him past the bar and through a beaded curtain.

They were in a dark corridor with doors at either side. There was music in here of the strained syrup variety, gleaming strands of it separating, wavering and melding. 'We go in here,' she said and ushered him ahead of her into a dimly lit room.

The room was mostly bed. Its ceiling was a mosaic of mirrors.

Orla pushed the door shut, and suddenly she was in his arms and kissing him as, he had always understood, tarts never kissed. Her body pressed hard against his. Her hands stroked his cheek, his sides, his buttocks. Her hair held the scent of something exotic and musty, the scent of an Egyptian tomb in his imagination, the scent which an orchid would have if orchids had scent. It was like being in a jacuzzi filled with warm raw liver. It was very near to bliss.

He pulled away from her. 'Er. Gosh, I'm mean, *excusez moi*. Jolly nice, but . . .'

'Sh,' she whispered against his lips. She pointed at the table beside the bed. 'You have the money?'

'Yes.' He reached for his wallet and counted out three one-thousand-crown notes. She said 'Thank you,' and kissed him again, lightly this time. 'You take off the cloths and take the shower in next door. I recome back, all right?'

'All right.' He frowned. He remembered to readopt his pidgin. 'I do.'

She left him then, to wonder just how far this charade must go.

He had visited whorehouses just twice in his life before today – once when he was seventeen and in Amsterdam where he had stared, transfixed with terror, at a bush that seemed to him the size of a Newfoundland dog and, with muttered apologies, had run for his life; and once, in Liverpool, twenty years back now, when a gang of professional jockeys had conducted him after the Turkish baths closed to a remarkably similar establishment. Here a black girl with a Brummy accent had recited a menu of activities with much the same enthusiasm as a waitress running through the puddings for the fourth time.

He had chosen the least expensive option. She had shown manual dexterity which would have stood her in good stead in a milking-parlour, but an unseemly impatience. ''Ere, come on, will you? I got a living to make. Most men just want to, you know, it's down with their trousers and bingo.' Paul had told her to forget it.

He had not avoided tarts out of any profound moral conviction. On the contrary, it had always seemed to him that a man who pays for his pleasures avoids all the worst consequences of aberration. The married man who rented it earned greater respect from him than the little shit who screwed his secretary or his neighbour in the name of love.

No. He knew little of brothels only because his sexually hyperactive years had coincided with a freak period in history, when contraception, antibiotics, the theories of women's lib and the economic emancipation at once of the young in general and of females in particular had combined to create the happiest hunting-ground that ever a randy young man could have wished for. If he had liked a girl and she had liked him, they had gone to bed with one another, and if it had occasionally seemed, as Robert Frost had said of free verse, 'like playing tennis with the net down', he had not cavilled back then. The male impulse was to spread seed, and the world had seemed made of John Innes.

He clutched the tiny napkin of a towel to him as now he walked, otherwise naked, to the shower cubicle next door.

He enjoyed the shower. He always relished the chance to take his clothes off in a city.

Suddenly, however, he froze and adopted a fighter's crouch. A shadow with bulk lumbered past the frosted glass door. The footfalls were heavy. The breathing was shallow and husky. It sounded like an old buffalo with emphysema. The wool or tweed of the coat crunched like snow as the man touched the door and the walls.

Paul was alone here, under an assumed name, in half darkness and a thousand miles from home. He was enclosed in a tiny cubicle. He was damned near powerless.

He had no desire to have it recorded that he had finished his existence naked in a Prague cathouse.

The footfalls lumbered on. The puffing subsided. A woman called something in Czech and her slimmer form clicked past the door. Another door out there swung shut. The music and the steam swirled around Paul.

He hastily switched off the shower, dabbed himself with the towel, and scampered back to the mirrored room.

Orla came in a minute later. 'You 'ave shower?' she grinned.

He nodded. '*Oui*. Sorry. Yes. I have shower.'

'Come here,' she said, all maternal, and she drew him to her. Paul found himself toppling sideways onto the bed. Her tongue was probing softly into the back of his skull. She rolled so that she was on top of him. He pushed ineffectually at her and tried to speak, but she kept her mouth attached to his. He could feel the warmth and plushness down there against his thigh. She was reaching across with her right hand to do something on the table by the bed. Suddenly she moaned, 'Oh, yes,' only she couldn't have done, because her tongue was still intertwining with his. A man said, 'So beautiful . . .' at Paul's left ear. Orla sat up astride him, her finger against his mouth. She smiled. She raised her eyebrows, querying.

Paul glanced at the little tape recorder on the table, and understood. She had taped one of her professional encounters, and a vigorous one, by the sound of it, so that anyone bugging the room would hear nothing untoward as Paul went to meet Havlik. He nodded. She clambered off him. Paul banished the momentary pang of disappointment and swung his legs from the bed. Any rustling as he pulled on boxer-shorts and trousers was of a piece with the slapping and groaning on the tape. He reached for his shirt, but Orla shook her head, pointed at her watch and took his forearm. She pulled him towards the door, opened it a mere crack and peered out.

Quickly now, she opened it and squeezed out into the corridor. Paul followed her. She closed the door softly behind him. She led him down to the end of the corridor. Again she opened a door and, very gently, pushed him out into the open air.

The door shut behind him.

He was naked to the waist, and the night air was cold.

He was in a small back garden with a high fence all about it. There was another still fountain at its centre. Plants bristled in beds about the garden's perimeter and in pots elsewhere. The sky was blue satin, shot through with sulphurous urban glare.

He looked to right and left, then went down the steps. They were mossy and cool beneath his bare feet.

Cyril Havlik emerged from the shadows at his right, softly striding in white sneakers over the paving stones. Somewhat to Paul's chagrin, he was fully dressed.

'Hey, thanks for coming, man.' He was more relaxed now. The jitters had gone.

'Yes, well,' Paul said, 'I have to say that you owe me quite a lot of spondulicks. What with admission to this place, a taxi, paying Orla . . .'

'Nice girl?' Havlik grinned.

'Very, so far as I can see, but I'm not here for fun, and I'm not flush with cash. Pay up.'

'OK, OK. I'm pretty darned broke myself. Still . . .' He delved into his back pocket. 'Five thou. That should fix it.'

'And if you're so broke,' Paul rolled up the notes and shoved them into his back pocket, 'how come you can go round offering large fortunes?'

'Yeah, well, that's the point, isn't it?' Havlik leaned on the fountain's wall. As Paul's eyes accustomed themselves to the darkness, the boyish, grinning face beneath the baseball cap became visible. The eyes were the shape of Dover soles and very protuberant. The nose was hooked and strong. 'Listen, we got to be quickish. Orla's tape. Kati's got one too. They last twenty minutes or so, then we got to be back in the rooms saying, "Gee, that was great," and that. That way, these guys don't know we've ever met – unless someone's following you, that is.'

Paul was becoming exasperated. 'For heaven's sake, of course nobody's following me. Why on earth should they?'

'Yeah, well. They would if they knew we'd met. I'll tell you that for nothing. Listen. Your dad knew my uncle Pavel, right?'

'Yes. You know that. I showed you the pictures, remember? They were brother officers, best friends. Flew Spitfires together. I was called after him.'

'Right, so you know that my granddad was a bona fide prince, had palaces here, in the country, all over. My grandfather and my gran and my dad, they were trudging out when the commies came in '48, stopped for the night in a ditch, right? And he was this tall, beautiful guy, my granddad, lovely hands, high cheekbones, you know? And for a minute, grandma kind of breaks down, says, "But Alfie, we lost everything!" "Hmm," he says slowly, "Yes . . ." And then he goes – and he has to be the last man ever to say this – he goes, "but I *think* there's a palace in Venice." Was too. Palazzo Havlik. It's a consulate now.'

It was a nice yarn, but standing half naked in a strange garden in a strange capital city in mid-October did not make Paul feel like bedtime stories. 'Splendid,' he said, 'but look, old chap, on my first night in Prague, I have come at your behest to a knocking shop. I want to go back to my hotel. I want a drink and a warm bed. I'll give you just five minutes to explain.'

'OK, OK!' That grin flashed again. His hands rose to check Paul's protests. 'Hey! All right! So my family's dispossessed, right? And now, technically, we get it all back, after a lot of negotiations and that. So what do we get? A palace that's fallen down in the country, a palace that's been demolished in the Old Town, a lot of land, only they won't kick out the collective farmers there. One day, perhaps, it'll all be worth something. For now, it's worth doodle-squat. *But*, there's the family jewels and silver, right? My grandfather buried them before he set off, and, when he and grandma died, only my father knew where. Uncle Pavel didn't know, of course, 'cos he was over in England throughout the war, and he had money over there.'

'He died in '45 . . .' Paul nodded.

'Right, so no one knew, 'cept my grandparents and my father and, now, me. Not in one of our houses. A cousin's place, on the way out. Just the known jewels, the famous ones – you want a list?' He ticked them off on his fingers. 'A river of cabochon emeralds from Richelieu, a Fabergé egg of rhodochrosite and diamonds, a brooch of the Hapsburg arms in yellow diamonds and enamel presented by Maximilian himself, a necklace of brilliant-cut diamonds and star sapphires which was famous in its own time – just those things are reckoned to be worth six million dollars. There's a hell of a lot more. Church plate, shit, a hell of a lot.'

'And – you're saying it's still there?' Paul gasped, then, 'Oh, come on. Someone will have dug it all up.'

'Why should they? Just buried in farmland out in the country? None of them has turned up on the market, and the spot is undisturbed.'

'Well, I have to say . . .' Paul stopped. 'Oh, dear. It's a sad fact, and I wish it weren't so, but I have to say that, in my experience, the poorest people – and I'm amongst 'em – are the ones who believe in hundred to one winners and buried treasure. Anyhow. OK. So go dig this stuff up.'

'Yeah, yeah. What do you think I did? Soon as I can get a visa, hell, two years ago, I'm in. I think, same as you, fine, no hassle. Slip in, head quietly down to the place, dig 'em up, whisk 'em out. Sure. You seen customs here? They hardly look at you, right? Sure, but they see me, my name, and – shit, I mean, I see the guy five minutes later. Maybe it's real secret police, you know, want these things like for national heritage, treasures of the nation sort of thing. Maybe the guy's an ex-commie doing a bit of free-market speculation, thinks, OK, use the old networks, follow this guy, steal the goods. I don't know. All I know is, there's this guy with eyebrows and he looks mean, and he and his friends follow me everywhere I go. No chance.'

'I suppose that might give credence to the idea that the jewels are still there . . .' Paul mused.

'Right. So then I meet you and you mention this race. I done some riding back there in the States. You know that. I mean, not like you, man, Grand Nationals, that sort of heavy shit, but you mention this race, and I get to thinking, right? I buy a horse in Germany, drive it over the border, ride in this race, it's good cover. Sneak out one night, dig up the jewels, and away. So then, I reckon, I drive back over the border, gallant jockey in the great Pardubice, the first

Czech exile, the first prince sure as hell-fire, ride in the race. And we're stopped? Fuck. They'd never dare. You get it?'

'Oh, I get it,' Paul drawled. He perched on the fountain wall. He folded his arms. He crossed his legs. 'But you're still being followed?'

'Moment I arrived. Not a chance to get near the things.'

'So what's wrong with employing someone to go in and dig the stuff up? Why involve a relative stranger?'

'Ah, now. You think about it. Sure, I've got friends. They could come into the country. No one follows them, I give them the directions, the map, everything. I sit in Manhattan. I wait. You've got friends, too. How many of them, you say, here's – what? – even at breakdown value, two, three million – you can be sure they'll come back? Shit. Two million dollars'll buy you the life of a king here. Why not take it, stay on? Particularly if you've made a friend with my pursuer, my little bristling friend with the eyebrows. He'll sort out any law suits, any "Hey, that's mine" stuff. They split the proceeds. I raise objections, Jeez, buy you the life of a king, it'll sure as hell buy you the death of a prince.'

'You've no family?'

'Nope. Only son. Mother and father dead. Pavel, as you know, died in the war. Otherwise, just great-aunts and such.'

Paul damped down the hope which flared in him. This man was unstable, his story vague and wild. 'Let's get this straight,' he said, with as much firmness as he could muster. 'Your family baubles are buried. You want them back. Fair enough. You can trust me because I'm a friend of the family and because I'm riding in this race. That makes a crazy sort of sense . . .'

'Yeah, what I figure, like, we're brothers. We ride over fences. We gamble. I look into it. You're a straight guy, and you have a bona fide reason for being at Pardubice. No suspicion there. English-speaking jocks stick together. And you understand. I'm this stuff's provenance, right? I bring it into Sotheby's, sure, the Czech government kicks up, but it'll be the sale of the decade, right? Everyone wanting a little bit of buried history. Without me, it's just so many rocks, and it has to be sold under the counter. It makes commercial sense, give you a decent percentage.'

'OK. I'll buy that. What I don't understand is why you can't go through the normal procedures. Property's being restored to exiles left, right and centre. You tell the Czech government where the jewels are, you stake your claim . . .'

'Come on, man!' Havlik rolled his protuberant eyes upwards. 'You imagine the bureaucracy involved? Jeez, it'd take decades. And who'd I tell in the Czech government? Who'd I know? Who'd I trust? This sort of money, you tell the wrong guy, you vanish, the jewels vanish. No, I reckon, you dig the stuff up. You bring it back to me. We ride this damn-fool contest. I get what's rightfully mine out of the country. Let them sue me, not the other way round. Shit, it's my only goddamn chance,' he sighed. He looked down into the water, an Aubrey Beardsley Narcissus in a baseball-cap and trainers. 'So what I'm saying. You go out there – tomorrow, say. You do some digging. You bring the stuff back to this goddamned racetrack, meet me at the riders' reception, I take it on from there. We meet in London, New York, wherever. Make sense?'

'Hold on . . .' Paul looked for objections, but a story like this greeted the likes of Paul Pickering like a long-lost twin. 'You say it's farmland?'

'That's right. Out in the mountains. Only guy nearby's a farmer, Sadovy, lives in one wing. We're talking a good hundred yards from the house.'

'Hmmm.' Paul's mouth became a long straight slit as he considered. 'Yes, but what happens if one does get caught? I mean, behind the Iron Curtain. I mean, I know it's not like it used to be, but still . . .'

'Nah. It's a normal democratic country now, man. Check it out. Trespass is all. Slip the farmer ten thousand crowns, he'll offer you his wife into the bargain. If it's anyone else, hell, call the consulate. You think hick police out in the mountains gonna detain a guy like you for *trespass*? It's not even a felony. It's a misdemeanour. I mean, try, sure, to cover your tracks, lead them away from the real site, but, worst comes to the worst, you're just an eccentric guy thought you'd dig up a bit of Czechoslovakia. They find the hole, that's my bad luck. We have to go through the courts, but it's got to be worth a try.'

Paul was intoxicated. He was wringing his hands and shifting from foot to foot. 'You know, I think I'll try. Gosh, what a giggle. Bloody marvellous. Course, I'll probably dig all night and find nothing except Australia, but I'll give it a spin. So, where do I find this boodle?'

'Zichy Palace, near Susice, southern Bohemia, edge of Sumava. Couple of hours from here. Here.' He held out a hand. Paul, now broadly grinning, felt paper crackling in his palm. 'I like to keep it this way. Anyone's listening, they know where but they don't know the details. They get the details, they don't know where it is. Read this, memorize it, burn it, eat it, whatever.'

Paul nodded. 'God,' he said, 'I hope I know what I'm doing. God, what fun.' He pocketed the note. 'Madness, but give it a whirl. Sorry to ask this, but – we really are talking about *your* property, aren't we?'

'Come on, man. Your dad's stories! Was Pavel ever short of a buck? We were something in this country. And how'd I know where the things were? Look, you saw me at Maryland. I'm a member of the hunt club! Look. Check with your friend van Zeller. He knows some of my friends, Maryland, Virginia, all that. They'll tell you.'

'No, no. Of course,' Paul mumbled, 'Sorry. No need.'

Three minutes later, Orla, now once more dressed, sent the two men plunging into the shrubbery. She beckoned.

Paul walked back into the Club André confused, enchanted and vaguely convinced that he was being taken for a monster ride. The only thing that he could not work out was what Havlik stood to gain from such an exercise. His suspicions were founded upon one simple premiss. According to Havlik, he was now privy to the whereabouts of a king's ransom in jewels, and things like that didn't happen.

Orla led him back to the room. He cringed at the now urgently passionate noises emerging from the tape recorder. Orla grinned. She helped him to the shower.

Ten minutes later, fully dressed, he nodded to the girls at

the bar. He kissed Orla's cheek. He smiled at Katushka and kissed her hand. He pushed open the door. A burly man in black tie escorted him to a waiting taxi.

He had wanted games to play.

There were games aplenty for the playing, if still he wanted them.

He rather fancied that he wanted them. It had been a long time.

'Jago?' Clay's voice was clogged as minestrone. He was very cockney tonight. He was always very cockney when he'd sunk a few. 'Bloody 'ell, but we been 'aving a good time. Shit, I mean, I thought as this place was cold and stiff as a bishop's dicky and you'd 'ave to sign in triplicate before you could scratch your balls, but shit, I tell you, there's some bints over 'ere, and the casinos – Christ, costs you nothing and you play all bleeding night. Lovely grub. Just got back. Won two thousand, seven hundred and sumfin' crowns. Shit, I mean, that's – what?'

'Sixty quid or so. Not bad.'

'Not bad for four hours' gas, that's for sure. And the course – you ain't seen nuffin like it. It's – it's like – I dunno, sort of Versailles or somefin'. I mean, you know, streams, 'edges, and those trees you see in French pictures . . .'

'Yes, I know.' Jago leaned contentedly back on cold pillows. He knew that at the end of his life, when his prostate was swollen and his eyes were weeping, he would look back on today, on Holly and Prague, all given Acapulco Gold edges by the prospect of a great steeplechase, and he would smile. 'So, can we get back to the reasons for which you're here? My horse, for example. Burly. Paul tells me he's OK.'

'Ah, 'e's 'appy as a pig in shit, mate. Really. Eaten up well every day. Cushy stable. Had a canter this morning. Busting out of 'is skin. So, the Colonel found you, did 'e? Gawd, 'e's a barrel of laughs. Bit of a goer in 'is day, I reckon.'

'Bit of a goer still, I'd say.' Jago smiled. 'So, what's the hotel like?'

'Bit stuffy, but OK.' Clay sniffed. 'Know something odd?

They 'aven't 'eard of double beds 'ere. Ask for a double room, you get two sort of box affairs at right angles to each other. How Czechs get little Czechs, I don't know. No Czech mating in these beds, eh?'

'God, but that was laboured, Clay.' Jago sighed without rancour.

'Yeah, well. One-thirty in the morning, what do you want? So. You be 'ere tomorrow?'

'Yup. But give me time. This is some city. You've got this boy to ride him tomorrow morning?'

'Yep.'

'Right, well, Paul and I'll be there mid-afternoon, early evening, I reckon. I think I'm owed a day's holiday. I want to see Prague.'

'No problem. They're looking after us well.'

'Great. If you're not at the hotel, I'll make my own way to the course.'

Jago laid down the telephone. He reached for the bedside lamp. Almost at once, as though the knocker had been listening, there came three light knocks at the door. Jago softly moaned. He threw back duvet and counterpane. He reached for his dressing-gown, shrugged it on and walked to the door.

'Sorry, Jago, old chap.' Paul grinned meekly. He looked very thin, deferentially bent against the dark green wall of the corridor. He ran his fingers back through his white hair. 'Phew. I've got a story. Can you spare me a second?'

'Yes, fine,' Jago lied. 'Come on in. Mind if I go back to my pit?'

'No, no, old boy. Just sorry to disturb you. I just have to tell someone. It's – oh, hell. Actually, I can't tell you much. Just, OK, let's hypothesize. Put it in general terms. You mind? Right. Where'll I start?'

He sat on the bottom left-hand corner of Jago's bed. He started.

Jago slept long and deep. He was awoken by the telephone. It was half-past nine. The central heating had been on and the windows were sealed. His head seemed full of sponge.

'Jago?' Holly sounded bright. 'Hi. Thanks for last night. What's on your agenda today, then?'

'Tourism,' he said. 'Idiotic, gawping, goggling tourism, plus food, drink and shopping. That's my plan, anyhow. You?'

'Suits me fine. Where should we meet?'

'Wherever. You come here or I come and pick you up?'

'Better I come there.'

'Cora,' he said.

'Well – yes.'

'OK. Look, I'm still in bed. I'll get up, do the necessary, stroll elegantly downstairs and see what Czechs have for breakfast. Give me an hour, will you?

'Order extra coffee. I'll be there.'

Czechs, for breakfast, eat pig. There were sausages and hams various strewn on the buffet table, together with various cheeses, bread and boiled eggs. Loyal as ever to pigs, Jago took a bowl of cereal and two boiled eggs back to his table. He ordered coffee twice. Holly arrived before it did.

She looked whimsical and pretty and funny. She carried her fiddle-case. She had donned a skirt today, about eighteen inches of wrap-around tartan rug which Jago believed to be Ralph Lauren, and a brown polo-neck which he knew to be cashmere. She had her hair up in a couple of twists of purple velvet.

'How long can you give me?' he asked.

She shrugged. 'As long as you can stand me.'

'I haven't got that long,' he told her. 'Cora didn't object, then?'

'Oh, she objected, but we've got to be allowed our own lives. She's busy plotting the reform of the world with her friends. It's just not me. Maybe I'm blundering again, but that's my business. I told her so.'

'Good girl. Well, unfortunately, I've got to be away this evening at the latest.'

'What?' She laid down her cup. 'To this race place?'

'Yup. It's just a hundred kilometres east of here. Tomorrow I have to exercise my animal, take a look at the course, have a fit, ring mummy and ask her to take me away, things like that, then, Sunday, it's the race.'

'God, it sounds terrifying.'

'It is terrifying. I suppose that's why we do it. The ultimate test sort of thing.'

'Like wars.' She was solemn.

'Yes, I suppose so, only this hurts no one except us willing participants. And, God, the glory to be won! And it's a very special sort of glory, the only sort worth having, I reckon. No one in England will know or give a damn save the very few who care about such things, the other guys who've had a crack at it or dreamed of doing so. Except here in the Czech Republic, where you're a hero forever after, it's the sort of glory that only initiates understand. If we win, a few people all over the world will be nodding with approval at the names Burlington and van Zeller. It's a very smart sort of glory.'

'You want it. I hope you get it.' She touched his hand. She smiled. 'Really.'

'What's with the fiddle?' He nodded towards the case at her feet. 'Do I get a personal command performance?'

'You and all Prague.' She pushed back a wisp of hair. 'At some point, I've got to make some money. And don't tell me that you've got enough. I don't work that way.'

'I wouldn't dream of it.' He drank the black, granular stuff which here passed for coffee. 'I'm managing director of a company in the hands of the receivers, King of nothing. When I get home, I'm going to have to look for a job. I've never had one of those.'

'Really?'

'Well, jackeroo in Australia for six months, if that counts, but that's about it. No. I've been lucky.'

'Yeah, but . . .' She cocked her head.

'But what?'

'But, you know, us poor beggars, we lose everything, we don't mind much. We've been there before. It's like Italy, Ireland. They live so well because they've made getting by into an art form. They've learned to make haute cuisine out of flour and potatoes. Somewhere like England, rich as all get out, run out of beef and everyone's jumping off high buildings and wandering around being gloomy. What do you think you'll do?'

'I don't know. What can a thirty-six-year-old new on the market do? Something to do with tailoring, I suppose, though that's not so easy these days. I mean, most clothes are machine-made and mass-produced now. I wouldn't mind being a buyer for a department store – otherwise, I suppose, I'll just have to be a shop assistant, a manager or something; measure inside legs and suggest that sir might find the fawn more to his liking. I don't know. I've got some friends who might help. We'll see.'

'You seem quite blithe about it.'

'It's virgin territory, isn't it?' Jago laughed. 'No point in moping. I've had a hell of a lot of fun.'

They took a taxi to Prague Castle, where they were treated churlishly, presumably because the stout women at the ticket-booths had been in those same booths throughout the communist era and therefore could see no profit in smiling or in offering a service.

They walked back over Charles Bridge, the world's loveliest sculpture gallery, adorned on both sides by black bronze saints and subjects religious and mythological. They found a building with many grimacing gargoyles. Holly gleefully screwed on her telefoto lens.

'Look,' she said, 'great for postcards. See this fellow with his tongue out, looking sick? That's "*Dinner was delightful*", then this guy, all crushed like that – what? "*Under stress*" or "*I'm overwhelmed*". He's got to be "*I'm sorry . . .*" or maybe "*So thrilled*", depending on whether we're being ironic or not – oh, lovely.' Her Nikon clicked and whirred, clicked and whirred. 'What do you think? Commercial winner?'

'Distribution would be the problem . . .' Jago started, then kicked himself. 'Actually, I think it's brilliant, but don't tell it or sell it to anyone. Gargoyle Greetings Cards plc, distributed through petrol stations and post offices. Nice long shelf-life. Yes, there's gold in them thar hills . . . Come to think of it, Prague's a gift. Everything you want to say, you've got free models just waiting to be snapped. Grab it, girl, while you have the chance, and before some other smartarse gets the idea. I'd back you if I had any money.'

That, then, was how they spent their hours in Prague. It was as good a theme as any for a tour. They hunted sculptures and gargoyles whose images could express some message. They found perhaps sixty of them, and the motor-drive on Holly's camera must have been red-hot.

They lunched on goulash and white wine, then Holly begged Jago's pardon, consigned her camera to his safekeeping and, moving a few yards away from their table, spread out a patch of maroon felt. She opened her violin case and pulled out a fiddle which gleamed like beer. She nestled into it as if into a lover's shoulder. She closed her eyes.

She started to play.

It was all to do with the circumstances, Jago told himself. It had to be. It was a consequence of stress and of apprehension, of sunshine and of an all too brief absence of worry. It was to do with Prague, too, and the magic which enthralled the city.

Somehow, it seemed to him that he had never heard a fiddle before.

She played Bach. Within minutes, Jago had heard that clear, strong voice mourning like a widow and giggling like a gaggle of schoolgirls, singing a dulcet love song and arguing with vehemence.

Maybe he had never really listened to a violin, never considered, that is, that it spoke in virile, even strident tones rather than merely making a pleasant soothing sound, but then, he had never known a violinist well enough to be interested in what she had to say, nor known the tranquillity in which he could listen.

The last note seemed to sing long after Holly's bow had left the strings. Several of the onlookers clapped. Coins and notes fell onto the square of felt. She cast a brief, amused glance of complicity at Jago, then, with her eyes still sparkling, struck up some sort of fast and jaunty jig. A young Czech couple at a table beside Jago's stood and started to dance with more enthusiasm than formality. Passers-by stopped and clapped in time with the music. Where Holly had been still during the Bach, now she bobbed from the waist and her right foot tapped on the cobbles.

As the notes swooped and scampered around him, Jago reviewed his conversation with Paul last night. For all his liking of the man, he had increasing suspicions as to his sanity, and had been able to make little of the various hypotheses which Paul had raised – 'I mean, if a friend – or, well, not a friend, but the son of a friend, say – obviously a good sort, references, all that – asked you to do a favour, you'd do it, wouldn't you?'

'It would have to depend on the nature of the favour, but in general, yes, if I could.'

'What if that something was – not illegal, exactly, but, say, contrary to bye-laws, that sort of thing?'

'Depends on the bye-laws. If you mean illegal parking or picking municipal flowers or something, of course.'

'Yes, but . . . Suppose what you were doing would bring about justice by sidestepping red-tape sort of thing?'

'Again, in general, no problem, provided that's all you're sidestepping and you're certain it's justice.'

'Oh, dear . . . I'm a bit at a loss, I have to say, Jago . . .' Paul had made a brow-mopping gesture, though his brow was dry. 'I'll have to sleep on it.' He had stood and given a little flapping wave. He had turned towards the door.

'Paul.' Jago had yawned, as much to smother a smile as from fatigue. 'Listen. You're older than I and probably a darned sight wiser. I can't tell you what to do. In these terms, I can't even advise you. I'd look at the people involved. If you think this guy is straight and what he wants is basically desirable, go for it. If you aren't certain about him, forget it. You'll have more fun just enjoying your holiday.'

'Oh, I'm sure enough of *him*.' Paul looked down at hands which writhed about one another. 'No. Damn it, he's a prince. He knows everyone. He's got – he said check with you. You have friends in Virginia and Maryland who know him. And his family, as I say. No, I think he's all right. It would be wrong not to do it just because you were a bit frightened of inconvenience, wouldn't it?'

'Not necessarily,' Jago shrugged. He passed a hand over his mouth in order to wipe away a splutter of laughter which threatened at Paul's assumption that any Central European prince must automatically be a decent chap. 'I don't know what *it* is. That's the problem.'

'No, of course you don't. Oh, damn it. I'll think about it. Sorry to bother you, Jago. Bloody silly.'

And with a quick, 'good night', he had let himself out.

Jago had slept largely unperturbed by this exchange. On balance, he was inclined to believe in this prince and his relationship, by birth at least, with Paul. He was less certain that the two men had met, or that, whatever problem the prince had raised, it was as inconsiderate as Paul insisted on believing.

Paul was an anachronism and a romantic. Jago loved him for that. But that very insistence upon seeing the world as the world, for better or worse, declined to be, distorted Paul's view. A modern woman might deny that she was a damsel, still less in distress, but Paul's hand would never leave his figurative sword-pommel until he was satisfied that she was safe. Time and again, women and friends had done their best to disillusion him, but he had no desire to lose his illusions or to become bitter. He preferred to preserve the illusions, and be happy, regarding those who had let him down as unfortunate aberrations.

Paul's mention of bye-laws had given Jago momentary cause for concern as he snuggled down into bed again, but a bye-law, after all, was but a bye-law. If, as he suspected, Paul was being embroiled in a little local smuggling, no great harm could be done, and Jago was confident that he would know all before Paul set off for the border again. Paul was not the taciturn sort, nor – and of this, knowing Paul, he was confident – would he use Jago's box for the purpose without first consulting him.

The man was dramatizing. There was an end on it.

Jago had not seen him at breakfast, but had simply assumed that he had chosen to take a lie-in after his unwonted late night. He had left a message at Reception, therefore, asking Paul to be ready to set off for Pardubice at four o'clock this afternoon. He had set off with Holly without a qualm.

Qualms would have been in order. As Holly started to play that afternoon, Paul was emerging from an ironmongers, armed with a spade and a slashing hook. He shoved them in the boot of the car.

It was all very well Havlik talking about slipping the farmer ten thousand crowns, he thought as he walked round to the driver's seat and strapped himself in, but, what with the cost of the hired car, these implements and, presumably, a hotel bed somewhere tonight, he would be lucky if he possessed ten thousand crowns at the end of the day. Paul's predecessors had needed but a lance to ensure mobility. Today's adventurer, alas, needed a gold card and an overdraft facility.

Paul was not one to fret. After soul-searching and tossing around the alternatives for the better part of the night, he had made up his mind, and, when once his mind was made up, all qualms were shelved. He was going to enjoy this.

He had organized that the hire-car would be delivered at two o'clock. He had bought a road map from the hotel shop. He had then retired to the quieter, upstairs bar. Literary composition never came easy to him, so he had started with the simpler task. He had written a brief note to Jago, explaining that he had once more been delayed, and would make his own way back to Pardubice.

The second letter, also to Jago, was altogether more difficult. He had to rack his brains as to exactly what he should put in, and what leave out.

It was not so much that Paul feared for his own safety as that he mistrusted Havlik's appraisal of provincial bureaucracy. Paul's chiefest fear was that, due to the officiousness of some rural functionary, he might be kept from the race on Sunday. If he were arrested for what was, admittedly, a trivial offence, he might yet find himself slammed up on suspicion of something graver, and denied a telephone with which to reach his friends or his consulate. This consideration would, indeed, have kept him from performing Havlik's mission had it not been for one persuasive factor.

Any old friend of Paul Pickering would have scoffed at the thought that he might need financial inducement to undertake an adventure. Paul, it was well known, cared nothing for money. He had had it, had lost it and had renounced its pursuit. Paul's doctor, however, might more readily have divined the reason for which this least ascetic of hermits might now hope to acquire a nest-egg for his daughter and his grandson. He was dying no more than another of his age. The moment might yet be some years off, but he knew, at least, the name of his most likely assassin. The doctor had divined it last year, the same brute that carried away 'that charming chap, met him a couple of times, matter of fact, David Niven'. Motor neurone disease was a bugger. Could bide its time or come at you out of nowhere like a tidal wave. If there were a chance, however slight, that he might provide for the extenuated incapacity of his last years or for Clare's future, he must take it whilst he was fit.

He must take it, but he was damned if he would miss the Velka Pardubicka, even in so worthy a cause.

It had been half an hour before he at last picked up the screwed-up balls of paper from the floor and flushed them down the loo. He had re-read the letter, folded it and slipped it into an envelope. He had written, '*To Jago van Zeller, Esq.,* **Only to be opened if I am not in touch by 2 p.m. Friday.**' He had taken both letters down to Reception, paid his bill, and tapped his foot as he awaited the hire-car.

He drove out into the country now with his window wide open so that the wind could tug at his hair. His eyes were narrowed, his lips drawn back in a broad rictus. Excitement shuddered through him. He sat forward and hit the wheel with his extended right hand. 'God,' he gloated, 'I am so bloody lucky!' And he laughed.

*

Holly finished her playing with a breathless flurry of notes which evoked a ragged cheer from her audience. She bowed low. More notes floated down onto the felt. She played two more melodies. The first, Jago recognized. When his father sang it, it was known as '*Passengers Will Please Refrain/ From Passing Water When the Train/Is Standing in the Station, Parlez-Vous*'. When Art Tatum spun it into a floss of dreams, it was called Dvorak's 'Humoresque'. The second, Holly would later tell him, was called something with fewer vowels than the Welsh for diarrhoea and was by Janacek. This appeal to patriotism, like most appeals to patriotism, proved profitable.

Holly smiled happily then, gave one more deep bow and laid her fiddle in its case. The concert was done.

'I am impressed,' Jago clapped as she approached the table, 'very, very impressed. God, but I envy you.'

'Envy me?'

'Yes. Really. I wish I could say anything that clearly. Just to be able to pull out that instrument and make people feel things – let alone earn your keep . . . How much did you make anyhow?'

'I don't know,' she shrugged. 'At a glance – what? Twelve hundred crowns? What's that in English?'

'Thirty quid or so.' He whistled. 'Lord, if you can make thirty pounds in – what? Three quarters of an hour?'

'Yeah, but it doesn't work like that. Not really. Unless you're happy to be an itinerant, which I'm not. No, but it's a great gift all right. I'd be desolate without it.'

'It's funny, that. Most of us, we'd only be desolate if we lost someone we loved. You, it's like having a loved one always with you. It must be difficult to hurt you, really hurt you.'

'Don't you bloody believe it,' she said sharply. 'Don't glorify an ability, please. I've had enough of that. It's not a friend, it's not a lover. It's an ability, that's all. I can be hurt just like anyone else. You'd better believe it.'

'Sorry.' Jago sat back, shaken by her vehemence. 'It's difficult to imagine, really, what it must be like.'

'You said yourself,' she relented, 'it's like having money.

Yes, it's pleasant. Yes, in some ways it gives you confidence, but it's frightening too. It gets in the way of normal relationships. Sometimes, you must have felt like a sort of animated piggy-bank. Sometimes I feel like a performing monkey. That's all.'

'You're right. I was stupid.' Jago looked at his watch. 'Bugger. I'm going to have to go. I've got to pay the bill, round up Paul . . . I could stay here forever. Are you going to play again? Because I'll have to love you and leave you here . . .'

'Can I come with you? Tonight, I mean?'

The question came from nowhere. It followed so fast on her plaint that he had to blink and shake his head. He said stupidly, 'What?'

'Come with you. To this race. I'd – I'd like to see it and . . . Well, I think perhaps – you grow out of people, don't you? It's cruel, but you must. Cora and all her crowd, their ideas are fixed, and they don't want me around. Not really. God, me discussing politics and so on. I just get in the way. They sort of sneer at me because I don't know my Kropotsis-name from my Heidegger or whoever. And we get on . . . Well, I like you, what I can see, at least, and . . . well, we've been having fun. It'll mean I'll have to get a taxi and pick up my things, but that won't take more than twenty minutes, max. I mean, I'm here for a holiday, and as long as it's not all phoney and you don't automatically assume that, you know, this gives you rights or something . . . I wouldn't get in the way.'

Her wide grey eyes were very solemn. Jago found that a broad, involuntary grin had split his face. Her lips twitched. She too smiled. Her hand was soft and warm on his. 'Yes?' she said softly.

'Yes,' he nodded. He grasped her hand tight, then remembered his manners. 'Please.'

Jago paid his bill and collected his bags from a receptionist whom he had never seen before. Holly returned, breathless and glowing. They sat in armchairs in the foyer and waited for Paul.

It was ten minutes before a brisk blonde woman, bustling across from the dining-room area, stopped short before them and said in a voice of professional sweetness, 'Ah, Mr van Zeller. I am so sorry. I was called away. Emergency in the kitchens, I'm afraid. I have two notes for you, from Mr Pickering. He has left.'

'Left?' Jago winced.

'Yes.'

'Sorry.' Jago pushed himself to his feet. He took the envelopes. 'But we've been waiting here . . . We could have missed these altogether! Why weren't they at the desk, for heaven's sake?'

The woman's mouth wriggled. She gave a little, reflex, deferential bow. 'I didn't want . . . The other men did not seem nice . . .'

'The other men? Sorry. You'd better explain. What about other men?'

'No, sir. Soon after Mr Pickering left, two other men came in wanting to know where he had gone. I did not think them nice. I told them that I didn't know. They asked if there were any messages. I said "no".'

Jago shot a quick glance at Holly. He frowned. 'Quite right,' he reassured the woman. 'These men, were they Czechs?'

'Yes, sir.' The woman looked thoroughly disapproving. 'The one that spoke was a Czech. A provincial Czech. Or, at least,' she added with pedantic precision, 'he spoke like a provincial Czech.'

Alarm bells were shrilling faintly at the back of Jago's skull. 'Sorry about all these questions. You did exactly the right thing. These men - could one of them have been a rider in the Velka Pardubicka?'

She almost allowed a smile to crease her perfect, foundation-primed face. 'No, Mr van Zeller. Mr Pickering, I know, is old, but he could ride. You, you are tall. You could ride. These men, no. One is old, older than Mr Pickering, and he has the belly – so. The other is tall and thin and weak. He wears glasses. No. I am sure. Neither could ride so far.'

'Jago, what's the matter?' Holly stood. Her eyebrows

rose at the centre. Her lips were slightly parted to show two sparkling teeth.

'Thank you.' Jago smiled at the woman. 'Thank you very, very much.' She smiled and bowed and minced towards the desk, soundless despite her heels.

'What is it?' Holly insisted. 'Jago?'

'What's the bloody fool gone and done now?' Jago asked through gritted teeth. He tore at the first envelope. He read. He sighed and passed the single sheet on to Holly. He looked at the proviso on the second envelope. 'Stuff that,' he said simply, and ripped it open.

He read, and, as he read, sank back into the armchair with a groan. 'I can't believe it!' he said at last. He passed this letter too to Holly. 'It's like having a bloody juvenile delinquent on one's hands! And there are already people after him! Bye-laws! Christ! He's only starting World War Three . . .'

'Sh!' Holly sat. She flapped a hand at him. 'Let me get this . . .'

She read, and she frowned, and she giggled.

Jago. Thanks for your help last night. You know how silly things always look bigger at night? Case in point, I fear. Just in case – highly improbable, but if anything should go wrong, I'm damned if I want to miss the contest, so I'd be grateful, if you haven't heard anything from me by now, if you'd give the consul a tinkle and put him in the picture. It'll sound a bit silly to you, of course, because you're a hard-nosed businessman and a stuffy old fogey at heart, but here goes. Young Havlik tells me there's a family fortune in jewels and whatnot hidden on some estate (used to be the property of a family called Zichy, anyhow,) near Susice, southern Bohemia. He's being followed, of course (his name gives him away at once, you see). So I'll pop down (the stuff's almost certainly gone, of course, but it must be worth a try) and have a root around. Stopcock housing of some fountain, he says. Miles out in the sticks, so I can't see any big problem, but a farmer lives at the place now, and might get wind of me, so it's as well you should know.

Good luck, Yours, Paul.

'The man is simply mad!' Jago squealed. 'He lives life like a Henty or Weyman hero. Why do things like this happen to him? Because they see him coming, I suppose. God. You want someone killed, tell Paul you're a dispossessed princess and your victim's the Napoleon of crime, and he'll do it! In a sabre duel, of course. God. The man's a romance waiting to happen!'

'Sounds like fun,' Holly grinned.

'Fun?' Jago stared. He nodded. 'Sure. I suppose. I hardly know him, but he's a nice guy. Straight as a die, courteous, courageous, honourable to a fault, but where does that leave *us*? You really think there's a fortune in jewels out there? This is the late twentieth century. More likely he's an unwitting drugs courier or something, but he just charges in . . .'

'Come on, Jago,' Holly said. 'You're being cynical. There are lots of fortunes out there. I've read about them. Works of art coming to light, things buried when the communists came in. The late twentieth century doesn't mean the same thing here. It is possible.'

'Oh, it's possible, and it's possible that I'll win the pools. The likelihood, however, and I like to play the odds, is that . . . All right . . .' He checked himself. 'OK, you're right. It may be OK. As he says, he'll go out there, find nothing, everything'll be all right, but suppose – just suppose there is something there. Fine. These noble families are getting their property back all over the shop. Why does Havlik or whatever he calls himself need Paul's services?'

'Like he says,' Holly pointed at the letter, 'because people recognise whatsisname's name and follow him.'

'Why?' Jago demanded. 'I mean, why is there any need for all this skedaddling about? The stuff is his. He goes to the government, says, "this stuff is mine". He proves his claim, he scoops the pool. Oh, hell. You're right. We should leave the old bugger to his own devices, but . . .' He breathed out long and hard through his nose. He nodded grimly. He came to a decision. 'Right. I'll tell you what. What's the time in New York now? Must be elevenish. One of your man's excellent references, apparently, came from my friends in Maryland and Virginia and so on. I'll try a few. If they tell me he's straight, I'll leave it at that. If not – God, I don't know. Talk about an innocent abroad . . .'

He leafed through the addresses in his Badminton diary as he returned to Reception. He asked if he might telephone on credit, then retired to the telephone box. He checked the American codes, and dialled.

Connie Macleod, in successive incarnations Connie Rea, of Lincolnshire and Fulham, then Lady Constance Rushbury of Newmarket and Cadogan Square, now the owner of a Maryland estate, a lot of first-class racehorses and a Degas-papered shack on Long Island, was in the bath. 'Havlik? Christ, Jago, he a friend of yours or something? I should hope not. His dad was a quiet, academic sort, nice manners. Sexually nobody home, if you believe in such a creature, which I do not. Friend Cyril – I'd stay clear. Flash little shit. Gambler, I believe. Drugs? I don't know. Could be. Reputation for being pretty mean with women, any road. Nasty mean, not nice mean. No, I reckon, probably not much cash, certainly no property to speak of, just runs up credit on being a prince and on the famous Havlik treasure. Load of crap, I'd say. Pardubice? Havlik? You've got to be joking. Windy, you ask me . . .'

And Mark Lambert, the City type, a contemporary from school and who was now in New York with a merchant bank: 'Havlik? *Cy* Havlik? What d'ye want to know? Cy's all right. Bit useless, perhaps, but you don't need to be useful if you're a bona fide prince, do you? Tell you about the family treasure? God, I'd like to get out there with a bloody metal detector, I can tell you. Cy got pissed one day, tells me he knows where it's all stashed, he'll cut me in for a percentage if I'll loan him five K. Well, if anyone knows where it is, it must be him, I mean, his dad's dead, and there's all this dosh. I'd have taken a flier on it, only you wouldn't trust the little bugger as far as you could spit . . .'

And Isobel Rostock, fashion writer and friend, if a hundred

times trendier, grander and more sophisticated than Jago. 'Havlik? Yuk. Leave well alone, Jago.'

'How well do you know him, Isobel?'

'Too well. How well do you?'

'Not at all. Tell me about him.'

'You haven't met him?'

'Nope. Just checking him out. A friend's got involved with him.'

'Christ. OK. Bug-eyed, antsy, can't stand still two seconds. The guy's pure poison.'

'Enlarge,' Jago called.

'Please, no. Don't say that, OK? Elucidate, I'd rather. Just – general spoiled brat little shit. Beats up on women, lives off his title, likes to wind other people up, stand back, watch the damage. His idea of fun, you know, put a hundred-dollar bill on a thread and snigger at people's greed, pull out on the highway, then nip back in when a truck's approaching, introduce a married closet gay to a beautiful transvestite. Friend of mine, no names, first time she came up from the boondocks, crazy on culture and history and ballet and all things European, right? I mean, a prince? A Bohemian? Flat on her back before she'd let go of his hand. God, I had to help with that little mess. Please.'

Jago was clutching his brow by now. 'What does he do, Isobel?'

'Do? Shit, nothing. Hangs around looking for little boys and girls with money or bodies available for a gallant prince. According to Barbara, damn it, I said no names, forget I said it, no, he's got a nice little apartment on Bunk Street, and he's never short of cash, but God knows where that comes from. His father was bust when he died. There's always the talk of the treasure. Maybe someone's found it and is dishing it out to him piecemeal. I don't know. But I've talked to a couple of guys know the score, and the Havliks were big cheeses back in old Bohemia. Perhaps there is a treasure. It's in the books, anyhow. Shit, emerald necklaces, church stuff . . . Anyhow, the company he keeps – we are talking seriously nasty gangland types, dope-dealers, extortionists, you know?'

Jago frowned. Cold things were trickling down his spine. It got worse and worse.

'Listen, Jago,' Isobel went on, 'slander suits I can do without. Let's just say . . . You say a friend of yours got tied up with him?'

'Yes.' The word was a quiet thud. 'So, you're saying Havlik proposes a deal with you . . .'

'He's planning to fleece you, or set you up. Something fucking devious. That man – even if there's a profit in doing it straight, he's one of those'd feel he was missing something if he wasn't doing it crooked, you know?'

'I know,' Jago groaned. 'Oh, God help us. Thank you, Isobel.'

He walked back into the foyer with shoulders slumped. His footfalls were slow and heavy. His hands hung loose at his side. Holly looked up, and knew. 'Bad news,' she said quietly.

Jago nodded. He slumped into his chair. He clasped his hands. He looked down at them for a while, then up at the ceiling. 'The good news, which will please you, at least,' he said at last, 'is that there well may be a Havlik treasure out here. The bad news is that Paul's noble prince is a crook who hangs out with gangsters and dope-dealers and may well be wanted by the police and, apparently, couldn't lie straight in bed.'

'Oh,' said Holly simply. 'So, what's next?'

'I don't know . . .' Jago mused. 'Oh, damn it. I can't let that old fool Paul career off to disaster. Sorry, love. I'm going to have to go down to wherever this place is, see if I can head him off.'

'Do you know where it is?'

'Not exactly. Southern Bohemia. I'll have to get a map. I'll have to call Clay too. Bugger.'

'Need a navigator?'

'You don't want to waste your time chasing round after a senile delinquent. This is my problem, though I can't for the life of me think why. Actually, if you could find your way to Pardubice, there's an empty hotel room waiting, if you wanted it.'

'No. Come on. I'd like to help, and I'll get to see a bit of the country. *Please*, Jago.'

Jago stared at her. At last he shrugged. 'On your own head be it. I'd like the company, I must say.'

'So, buy a map, make your call and let's go.'

Jago grinned at her. He saluted, said, 'Aye aye, ma'am,' and got going.

The worry remained, but, no less than for Paul, who had passed this way a mere two hours before, it did not take Jago long to reduce his fears to the level at which they became tolerable. Just as Paul enhanced reality to match his fantasies, so Jago scaled his fantasies down to his perception of reality.

What, after all, was the worst that could happen? Paul would seek his treasure, fail to find it, and return beneficially (to Jago's mind) chastened. Or again, Paul might find his treasure and have it taken from him by his pursuers, or, be there treasure or no, be arrested, questioned and, with Jago's assistance, released. However Paul might strive to avert the commonplace, it was inevitable and inescapable as death.

Jago too, though not without occasional mutterings of 'stopcock housing of a fountain', and 'bloody half-baked treasure hunts', started to enjoy himself.

Here he was, after all, in a rented car with a lovely, gifted girl at his side. The sun, though sinking, was bright. There was the prospect, however dubious, of a bit of excitement and of a glorious race two days from now. He had seen Prague. He was now seeing Bohemia.

The gods were holding Christmas early.

Of course, whenever benisons were showered on him, Jago felt fear and disbelief. The gods also had a habit of Indian giving, as he knew too well, which is why, at such times, he was inclined to salute a lot of magpies and never walked under ladders. He could see when the gods were kind. He remembered to be grateful. What he found difficult was enjoying their gifts without clasping them too close to him for fear of their loss. Good fortune was so inexplicable and so transient that, at moments like this, he was already anticipating – and, perhaps, thereby hastening – its apotheosis and its passing.

'As long as we're there before it's pitch dark, I reckon we're OK,' Jago murmured. 'Susice doesn't look like a big town on the map, does it?'

'No. Medium.'

'We might even catch Paul wandering about the streets. If the farmer's the only bogeyman, Paul won't be going in till after nightfall.'

'Do farmers have guns over here?'

'I imagine so. All farmers have guns, don't they?'

'And dogs, generally. This could be very nasty,' she said slowly.

'Nah,' Jago reassured her, and himself, 'farmers don't shoot first and ask questions afterwards. Not usually.'

'No, but if he asks this Paul a question in Czech, he's not going to know how to answer, is he? Can't we sort of decoy the farmer away?'

'Bright ideas gratefully received,' Jago said, 'but how exactly? We don't speak Czech either and we haven't got long. What we don't want, too, is anyone calling the police because we've done something suspicious. I think it's best to keep it simple. Look. Let's face it. The overwhelming likelihood is that there'll be no problem and there's no treasure there. If it ever was there, it's probably been found long since. If we get to the town in time to find Paul, well and good. If not, we go out to this hunting lodge place and just watch out, play it by ear. Bloody man.'

'You like him.' She smiled up at him.

'Of course I bloody like him,' Jago conceded. 'He's a one-off. He has faith and enthusiasm. Those sort of things are infectious. Everyone else – me, for example – started off like Paul and then learned that goodies weren't necessarily goodies and didn't necessarily triumph even if they were. We all learned to compromise. Paul learned to compromise with financial misfortune, but not with his dreams. God bless him for that, but God damn him for involving us.'

'He didn't, Jago,' Holly pointed out with another sly smile.

'Of course he did.' Jago drove on in silence for a moment. 'Well, all right, he didn't. Not directly. But . . . I mean, why would strange Czech men be looking for him? Why would Havlik pick him? Because he's the obvious candidate, is why. He's being set up. I'm sure of it. I don't know why or how. Maybe it's just a malicious joke. Either way, I'd like . . . Damn it, someone's got to look after him.'

They had been speeding through ever more undulant farmland and forest. The sky was bruised and puffy now. Every so often, in a high place, some great castle or palace gleamed as though possessed of its own light against the backdrop of dark trees. Every few miles, too, they passed through a small town. There were plain Lego towerblocks in the outskirts, then rows of dowdy peeling houses, then they came to the old central square which was invariably tree-lined, invariably contained houses with ornate decoration and complex curves to their roofs, and a church which was generally baroque, and far larger and grander than appeared apt.

Night began to fall, blue not black, and the urban glare of a great city suffused the sky ahead of them like a blush.

'That'll be Plsen,' Holly said.

'Of which I know precious little, save that it has four consonants to one vowel in its name and it's where Pilsner beer and Martina Navratilova come from.'

'Not a bad record for a provincial town I've never heard of.' Holly laughed lightly, then, 'Jago?'

'Yup?'

'Is life always like this when you're around? Lethal races, treasure hunts, macho stuff?'

'Christ, no!' he snorted. 'Listen, there's you with your fiddle. You can travel anywhere. You probably have, busking at festivals or in strange cities, touring with your band. More than that, you can close your eyes and play, and God knows where you go then. Out of yourself, that's for sure. I saw you. Me, I have a business to run – a lot of customers who are waiting for my product, a lot of employees who depend upon me for their livings. They, and I, have precious few escapes on a day-to-day basis. We go to work, we work very hard, we might have a jar in the pub, we go to bed and off we go again. This – racing – is just my one loony, lone, fuck-you activity, it's also a buzz for all those guys who work for me or with me. There *is* life out there. We *can* have a bet on something uncertain, rather than just depending on the wage-packet. It's a little fairy story in the midst of a very dull soap opera. No. Sorry. This sort of thing, for me, is a treat, a once-in-a-lifetime jaunt. Meeting you, all this . . . I'm having fun.'

Her hand was suddenly cold on his. He cast a quick glance at her. She was watching him with that serious, wide-eyed stare, though her eyes were mere hollows in the lamplight. Jago smiled. She sat back. She pulled his hand onto her thigh. The lycra was slick, the flesh beneath it warm. Very slowly, she unravelled his fist, plucking out the fingers one by one.

'I don't know,' she said sadly.

'You don't know what?'

'Just I don't know.'

The road dipped down into the city. Tall houses puffed as the car passed. Jago had to change down. He squeezed her hand and gently pulled his away. Having done the business, he put his hand back where it had been. It lay still on her thigh. Her hand covered it.

'No,' she said. 'It's all illusion, isn't it? It's like it snows in December and March is spring. We still believe it, though it never snows in December and it often does in March . . . You know, it's like . . . The rich, you know? We assume so many things. It's all so simple. Robin Hood, that sort of thing. But there's no such thing, really, a class called the rich, the poor, thinking alike, doing things alike.'

'Ah, well,' Jago told her. 'People like classifications. They like to see things as static, prefer to pretend that a river is ice. Someone once said to me, "God, you public school types are all so bigoted." It makes life seem simpler, but it's all so much crap.'

'I like you,' she said pensively. She stared out of the

window. Jago watched her reflection in the glass. She was frowning. Her fingers suddenly tightened about his hand. 'Oh, sod it.'

'I like you.' Again he withdrew his hand to change gear. He followed the signs to Klatovy. 'Is that such bad news?'

'Yes,' she said. 'Hand, please,' and she shivered.

Paul pulled in beneath a street lamp in Susice. He consulted the little map which he had propped on the dashboard. He nodded, replaced the folded scrap of paper and drove slowly up the main street. The church loomed at his right. He ducked down to read the signpost, nodded again, and turned left. Almost at once, he was in the country and climbing.

At first, there were just expanses of flattish farmland bordered only with ditches, then maize crowded in on either side, a peasants' revolt of sickle-blades. Forest was just a distant blur. It closed in suddenly. Pine trunks flashed by and puffed as they passed. Pine fronds tapped and scraped at the car's offside.

He bore right at a fork, and acknowledged the justice of the sinuous line on the map. The forest road climbed steeply, doubling back on itself in a series of hairpins. A cross stood at the third of them, no doubt marking the spot at which some poor soul had lost control and careered into a pine trunk or plunged into the darkness. Withered flowers on the cross looked like screws of brown paper.

Halfway up the mountain, there was a sudden clear patch where a hunter's hide stood on its stilts. Deer, Paul thought. Then, no. Wild boar. Maybe bear.

He did not want to break down here.

Suddenly, he was out in the open. The moon was a quarter, but it was bright white and the night was clear. The car's shadow was an outrider. The road began to dip.

Pasture now bounced down at the car's left into another deep valley with a crown of wispy mist. Down there at the right, he knew, must be the hunting lodge, for there the slope was gentle and the pasture would be well drained, and down there, he could hear a river run.

Halfway down the hillside, he saw the house for the first

time, an oblong block of darkness. Beside it stood a smaller building – a chapel, he supposed, with an Ottoman onion dome, topped by a golden ball which gleamed in the moonlight.

It was perhaps half a mile away.

He passed a ride at his left. He braked and reversed. The car groaned and moaned, but he drove it up the hard rutted ride until, twenty yards from the road, another ride crossed it at right angles. He circled it round in the clearing, then drew in at the right, out of sight of the road.

He climbed from the car. He shut the door quietly. He stretched.

He suddenly felt just a little bit silly.

Maybe, after all, this was a trifle unwise, scurrying around the countryside in search of buried treasure on the say-so of a relative stranger. He felt certain that tomorrow he would be cringing with embarrassment at the memory of this fanciful jaunt.

It would have been better had he had a coil of rope, an axe or a gun. Such props might have afforded him something of the seriousness expected of an action man. A blacked-up face or a pair of black sneakers might have served to convince him that he had something about him of the hero. Dressed, however, in a dark blue polo neck and jeans and a tweed coat, and armed only with a spade and a hook, he felt keenly aware that he was what he was, a fifty-six-year-old taxi driver, an amateur, a bungling Brit.

He waited for perhaps ten minutes, then had a sorely needed pee and set off. To have crouched, as doubtless he should, and scampered from cover to cover, would have made him feel still sillier. He feigned casualness so that he need not laugh at himself. He leaned on a tree by the side of the road. He gauged the lie of the land.

To his left, the road wound north and west to pass the northern side of the house. Beneath him, meadow fringed by forest ran down to the river. On the far bank, the ground rose sharply. There were two terraced plateaux then, both of them apparently planted with crops which grew right up to the walls of the building.

Havlik had drawn the house as a broken oblong, an 'E' without the central stroke. There was a courtyard, now a farmyard, in there, with views over the terraces to the south. Mr Sadovy occupied the further, westerly wing. The fountain was also to the west, beyond the house itself, presumably beneath the rocks which brooded there, a black backdrop to the building. In theory, then, Paul could stroll along the road, over the river and past the gate of the house, then look for some way over or through the north-westerly wall into what had been the garden. That way, he would be separated from Sadovy by the bulk of the house until he scrambled into the garden.

The problem with that plan was that he did not fancy running into a restive farmer patrolling his land, nor being seen by locals returning home from the pub.

The alternative, then, was to skirt the building on this, the southerly side. He would have the cover of the forest's fringe down to the river. He would then have to ford or wade the river, depending on its depth and speed, clamber up the bank and skirt the terraced fields to approach the orchard from the far side.

He shouldered the spade. He carried the hook in his left hand. He very nearly whistled in his bid to be casual as he set off down the springy meadow. As he neared the river, the ground began to squelch beneath his feet. Every footfall set up a crackling like ants on cellophane.

He looked down at the stream beneath him. He sighed. It was some twelve or fifteen feet wide. It looked shallowish. In the dark patches where the moonlight did not strike, he could see pale pebbles and shifting fronds of weed. There was white spume about the few black rocks. The surface chuckled above the water's prolonged gasp.

He sat down on the damp turf. He removed his boots and socks and pulled the cuffs of his jeans as high up his calf as they would go. The socks he shoved in his pockets. The boots he tied together with their laces and slung about his neck. He picked up the spade, took his first step down the bank.

The grass was greasy. His back hit the bank. His teeth

jolted together. His left hand clasped uselessly at wet strands of grass as he slithered downwards. He ended up sprawled and damp, his extended left foot just inches from the water.

He stood cautiously and flapped at the dampness at his seat. Just upstream, there was a flat rock perhaps five foot into the current. He poked at it with the spade. It grated and sang on the stone. He flung the spade and the hook across the river.

He stood back, sighted, and jumped.

His front foot clutched at cold wet rock, slipped, held. His back foot caught up, but his weight was too far forward. For a second, he lurched and flailed. His options were limited. He could take a small step into water or he could jump for the far bank. What he could not do was stand still.

He jumped for it. The bank was beyond his range, but he aimed for a pale patch just one large stride from home.

He then said, rather plaintively, 'Oh, fuck.'

It was not a thing that he often said, but the circumstances seemed to justify it. He had taken the pale patch for shallow shale, but his foot just kept on plunging downwards. Water rode up to the middle of his thigh. It splashed his lips. It was icy. He said, 'Oh, really . . .'

The riverbed, he was glad to find, was firm, but it still took him three grunting, spluttering, splashing strides to drag himself clear of the water's clutch.

He sat on the far bank. He spent a couple of minutes in vainly wringing at his trouser cuffs. He then started cursing Havlik, his ancestors, his nation and any of his issue as yet unborn and unbegot. When that was sorted out, and he was sure that he had covered all aspects of the family Havlik, he pulled out his dry socks and pulled them on. He untied the boot laces with trembling fingers. When he stood, it was clear that his attempts at stealth were to be seriously compromised.

He picked up the spade and scrambled up the bank. He glanced quickly from side to side, then pulled himself to his feet.

The first field was planted with some winter crop only inches high. The ruts left by the plough were still deep, so his progress was uneven. As he stumbled up and down, up and down, his already damp boots collected a great deal of the field. He would no longer have had a spring in his step had he been walking on the moon.

The moonlight contributed to his impression that he was walking across a First World War battlefield rather than a cornfield. Every rut seemed a trench. He was panting when at last he reached the ditch which separated the two fields. Sweat made his shirt cling almost as tightly as his jeans. He flung himself down into the broad grassy ditch and, for a minute or two, just lay there, spreadeagled, until his lungs stopped heaving and the stars stopped spinning.

He sat up then and scraped slabs of the thick clay from the sides and soles of his shoes. He could not in honesty claim to feel optimistic at that moment, but he did allow himself to believe that the worst of this absurd journey was over. The field above him was planted with apparently orderly rows of head-high maize. It would provide him with cover most of the way. He estimated that he must follow a north-westerly course for about three hundred yards. The rows were too closely planted to permit of diagonal movement, so he would have to follow a low westerly tunnel, looking all the while for gaps into the next tunnel on his left.

At first, this plan worked well. The dry plants swooshed and rustled as he brushed past them and the chaff crackled beneath his feet, but he tried to ensure that his steps were regular and he concentrated on shifting his weight slowly and carefully from heel to toe.

Then the moon went in. It was almost pitch black.

What with the flapping of his wet trousers and the crashing of the plants as he reeled against them, he sounded, to himself, at least, like elephants copulating on a bed of cornflakes. Twice more he stumbled and almost fell. The second time, he reached out with his left hand to save himself.

His hand touched stone.

And the moon, as though she had been watching him, slid from behind a caul of cloud.

The moonlight cast his shadow on the masonry. The

moonlight caught the curved or jagged edges of broken glass in the great, tombstone-shaped window above him. There must have been forty leaded panes in that one black casement. Every one of them was gone now save one at the top left, which had somehow survived war, revolution and counter-revolution. Once clear and bright, it had looked down on the intrigues, seductions, labours, sports, antics and rituals of a great aristocracy. Now that aristocracy was gone, dispersed and diffused about the globe. Its heirs comprised gum-chewing New Yorkers in baseball caps. The house was neglected, overgrown and shattered. The tapestries and the paintings, the furniture and the chandeliers had been broken up or sold to the progeny of those who had pressed their noses to such panes. A culture – privileged, gallant; at its worst, no doubt, inequitable; at its best, fine – had died, but that pane still winked in the moonlight.

Paul turned his attention to the open land at his right, beyond the maize. There was a narrow strip of heavily overgrown lawn, then a balustrade of which only two pedestals stood intact. Beyond and beneath, not thirty yards on, Paul saw the bulging wall of rock and, beneath it, three pouting black grottos surrounded by a huge broken basin of stone. Within the basin, there were pedestals which had once borne sculptures but were now truncated to mere nipples.

Paul slipped back into the shelter of the maize and made his way down past the house. A single strand of barbed wire had taken the place of the balustrade here. He slid under the wire and slithered down the ten-foot drop. He thanked God for the moisture. Had it been dry, the grass would have crashed like cymbals.

He turned back, then, and could see how it all was and how it all had been.

He was back in rough, tussocky pasture. The terraced lawns had once run around three sides of the house – one broken oblong, this one reversed, enclosing another. Paul was looking at the outside of the western wing, and the relative sparseness and simplicity of the windows indicated that most of the living and entertaining done here had been within the courtyard. This might have been a stable-wing, perhaps with a granary or servants' quarters above the horses. Light trickled onto the grass from wounds in two ground-floor windows. That was where Sadovy was, not a hundred yards away.

And directly below that light, on this lower terrace, the fountain had been constructed, presumably because that wall of tumbling rock was there. The stopcock housing was down there, to the right of the basin. There was no cover save scrub.

Paul sat on the ground. He would have to wait, at the very least, until the moon went in. The task looked very daunting, but he knew that he could never walk away having come this far, any more than he could back out of a race at the last minute, because the thought of what might have been would banish peace and sleep for the rest of his life. He had to give it a go. But not yet. He would wait. Until the moon went in. Until the light in the house was extinguished, perhaps. At least until the chill had left his veins and enthusiasm once more possessed him. Until he was himself again.

Susice was in a deep, thickly afforested basin. Jago drew up beneath a yellow lime tree in the central square. A hotel, apparently called simply 'Hotel', stood ahead. It was a classic Western saloon, lit by bobbing festoons of fairy-lights. Light spilled onto the cobbles from the latticed windows of a bar at the right. The terrace tables were empty.

'So. Hotel or bar?' he asked Holly.

'Hm,' she considered, 'think about it. Hotel safe and stuffy, bar rowdier but more anonymous. Bar for my money. Better for our purposes. More fun, too, I'd guess.' A car spluttered by. Its lights slid across her face, like veils. Her jaw was set firm. Her upper lip almost eclipsed the lower. Jago wondered what thoughts caused this resolute, pensive look.

'Bar it is.' He unfastened the seatbelt and opened the door. 'We'll have to be quick.'

'But not so quick as to arouse suspicion,' she told him across the car's roof.

The slamming of the two doors shocked the placid square. Jago and Holly strolled side by side across the square and under the bar's striped awning. He pushed open the door and stepped in ahead of her.

The bar was basic – so basic that it did not so much as boast a bar. There were five small tables and one long refectory table, flanked on either side by benches, up against the far wall. There were a lot of bums in creased and crumpled fabrics on the benches. They spread like punctured tyres. Three of the tables were occupied.

The Czechs, it seemed, regarded beer-drinking as a unisex activity. Half of the drinkers were women. All of them were large. Egalitarianism, however, did not extend to age. Everyone here was over forty. The walls were pale green and entirely bare save for a calendar featuring a provocatively posed Massey Ferguson.

The drinkers were not a rowdy crowd, nor convivial. Their conversation was desultory and confidential. It started and stopped. It rumbled and sometimes squeaked. It was like something very heavy being moved across boards on ill-oiled casters. An old man with a giant belly caught Jago's eye as he entered. He nodded. A woman with hair the colour of dried blood glanced at the two strangers over her shoulder. She wore a white and orange print three sizes too small for her. The fabric strained and gaped to expose cream flannel. Jago and Holly sat at the nearest table.

'Sheesh!' Holly murmured. 'We walk in on a house of grief or what?'

'Not a lot of tap-dancing, I'll grant you.' Jago looked about him, head raised. Esperanto body language: '*Not that I want to trouble anyone, but is there some chance of service?*'

The woman in the orange print finished what she was saying. In profile to them now, she pursed her lips and raised her eyebrows. She nodded sagely, censoriously. More Esperanto for the deaf: '*There's an object lesson for us. If people will behave like that, what can they expect?*'

She planted her hands on the pitch-pine surface. She

shifted from ham to ham before pushing herself to her feet. She sidestepped down the bench and waddled over. Her bare arms and legs were mottled pink and white, like attenuated alabaster eggs.

'*Bitte?*' She swept the table with her forearm.

'Ah. *Zwei bieren, bitte.*' Jago hoped that two raised fingers were not also Esperanto.

She pulled a card from her pocket. She slapped it disdainfully on the table. It was a faded typescript list. From the repeated 'Plsner' Jago divined that he had a choice of at least twenty beers. He had committed a solecism not unlike asking for fish and chips at the Cipriani.

He pointed at a glass on the next-door table. '*Schwarz,*' he said. 'Um, *das bier schwarz.*'

The woman's neck expanded widthways. She scribbled something with a pencil stub, tore off a square sheet of paper and thumped it down inches from Holly's elbow. It bore a legend like one of the more esoteric passages from the Rosetta stone. She waddled away. Her buttocks looked like a fat man chewing.

'Trouble is,' Jago murmured, 'I ask for directions to this Mr Sadovy's place, chances are, he or his daughter or his cousin'll be in here, wanting to know what our interest is.'

'So just ask for the Zichy place. You could be – I don't know – an historian or something.'

'At ten o'clock at night?'

'You've got a tight schedule. You're American.'

'I don't know how to say all that in German. Oh, well. It's a half-baked, bungling business. Here goes.'

The orange woman was approaching again with two tall mugs of foaming beer. She banged them down one by one. '*Danke.*' Jago smiled what he hoped was an honest, engaging smile. 'Er, *wo haus Zichy, bitte?*'

He thought that the burble of chat subsided just a little. The woman slapped her hands as though flapping off dust. She shrugged. She turned to the big table and released a clogged jet of babble. Thick eyebrows rose and frowned. There were scowls. Opinions were volunteered. Fingers pointed. The woman nodded. She leaned over Holly's shoulder. She retrieved the original scrap of paper, turned it over and started to draw a map. '*Hier Hotel,*' she pointed. Her stubby finger nigh obscured the whole map. '*Ja?*'

'*Ja,*' both Holly and Jago obediently nodded.

'*Links . . .*' she drew. '*Kase, recht, im bergen . . .*' Her German was little more fluent than Jago's.

Her hand sketched a wriggling road. She called a question without turning. Answers were shouted. She nodded again. She drew with quick little darting movements of her bulbous wrist. '*Und so,*' she announced at last. She drew an X. She stood back.

Holly, who had been crouched beneath the woman's bosom, breathed a soft sigh and sat up straight.

The map was primitive but clear. Jago smiled up at the woman. He said, '*Danke schon.*'

'*Warum?*' She affected casual curiosity.

'*Warum?*' Jago echoed.

'*Ja. Warum gehst . . .? Warum wollst du . . .?*' Her hands slapped on her thighs. Her inability to communicate angered her.

'Ah. *Historische.*' Jago pointed at his chest. '*Ich bin historische.*' He was uncertain as to whether this made him historic or an historian. '*Architekturale,*' he added lamely, '*Englander.*'

'Ah.' She sniffed. She turned away. She squeezed into her former place at the big table. She leaned forward to confide her discoveries. Eyes flickered towards the two interlopers.

'Right,' Jago said softly, 'we'll just quaff this little lot down . . .'

'It's delicious.' Holly wiped foam from her upper lip.

'High praise from a woman with a name like Byrne.'

'Ah, it's nothing like Uncle Arthur's. It's lighter, brighter, sharper . . .'

'Mmm.' Jago supped. 'Right, so, we drink this down, head off . . .'

'The whole bar knows where we're going.'

'I know,' he protested, 'but what else was I to do, for God's sake? I'm not bloody James Bond. Paul was hardly precise in his directions, was he? Anyhow, they don't look too interested. We'll keep an eye open, make sure we're not followed.'

'They've heard of the telephone here.'

'Damn it, I know!' He suppressed a wail. 'What do you want to do, wait for the libraries to open and look up "Bohemian country houses"? We can only find the place and hope for the best. You ready?'

Holly nodded. 'Right. Set.'

'And let's pray to God we find the old sod before anyone else.' Jago threw a banknote down onto the table. They both stood, smiled at the assembled company and tried to look casual as they walked to the street.

The door swung shut behind them, and they ran.

The wind was getting up, and the trees were stirring uneasily like extras saying 'rhubarb'. Up there in the sky, the clouds were scudding still faster. There would be no long-term cloud cover. Paul pushed his fingers back through his hair. He flexed his lips with a crackle. 'Ah, well. The hell with it,' he muttered.

He stepped out into the open.

The spade in his hand grated on a flint.

He inhaled with a hiss. He crouched low, watching that light up at the house. A shadow moved towards the window. A hand curled about the curtain. A dark head appeared in the yellow frame. There was a moment's stillness, then the curtains were drawn together again, this time so that they overlapped, leaving only a puritan's décolletage at the top.

He counted to twenty, then he counted to twenty again, then he gave it twenty more, just for luck.

If Sadovy were that alert, he had problems.

He pulled himself up, but not far up. He remained bent as he scurried across to the fountain's side. He crouched in the shelter of the stone basin. He again found himself panting.

He raised his head. It was as though he were on the brink of a fat punk's loo. The rock bellied out above him. Above that, grass spurted out like unkempt hair.

The moon was not in, but neither was it out. It was cruising along the very edge of a long, ragged cloud. In its diffuse light, the shapes of the rocks and broken pedestals within the fountain's basin seemed twisted and fluent, like wrought and wrenched clay. The grottos seemed infinitely deep and dark.

According to the map, which was anything but precise, the stopcock cavity was some twenty feet to Paul's right. He turned his head to survey the area. The map plainly showed the apple trees there, and indicated that the stopcock housing was this side of them. It roughly indicated, too, that it was on the side of the terrace nearer to the house, but the X was drawn so casually that that might be no more than an approximation. Nonetheless, he would start over there in a patch some six feet square, then move on to a similar area. He suddenly wished that he had brought a trowel rather than a spade. He could have continued his work lying down.

He made his way over to his chosen area on hands and knees, pulling the spade behind him. He started to quarter the ground like a setter, ready at any moment to drop flat. Twice he pricked his hands on thistles and winced. Once, up above him to his left, a car's headlight beams scanned the sky then dipped like deferential swords as someone drove down the mountain road on which he had come. He waited, ready to run back into cover, but the lights swept down the hill, vanished behind the house and emerged seconds later to climb another afforested hill. The beams had come nowhere near him.

He checked his bearings against the house. He double checked against the North Star. No doubt old man Havlik had chosen this spot, or somewhere near it, because he had been out of sight of all the windows in the main house. He had not foreseen that the main house would be empty and that his hiding-place would be in full view of the only inhabited wing. The fountain, plainly a magnificent seventeenth-century confection, must have long been dry when the jewels were hidden. Probably the Great War had sounded its death knell, as so many others.

Paul scrabbled at the soil as he crawled. How much dirt would have accumulated since 1948? He had no idea. Had the stopcock housing been set in a dip or dimple, leaves and soil would have accumulated, rotting down to loam. He could only hope that his fingertips would penetrate deep enough to find the stone or metal cover. Twice his fingers touched what seemed flat stone, and he knelt up to cut turves with the spade, only to find that the stone sloped away beneath his hands.

He moved on to the second area which he had chosen. Again he scratched at the cold turf. Again, though once or twice his heart jumped, he found only random flints.

He sighed. This could take forever. He would have to stand, and probe with the blade of the spade.

He pulled himself upright. A door slammed somewhere up there. He doubled up as though punched in the gut by the sound. He tried to swallow himself. He scurried across to the fountain and squatted in its shade.

Little feet pattered, then stopped.

Paul moaned, 'Oh, Christ.'

A dog's form appeared on the balustrade above him, then stretched and dived down into the darkness.

Paul knelt on one knee. He clasped the spade tight across his chest. He tried very hard not to breathe.

He did not see the animal at first. He merely heard a deep, low, gravelly rumble like a rolling boulder. He pictured the flash of pink as the upper lip curled back above jagged yellow teeth. His stomach made appeasing whimpers.

Then he saw the patch of white in the grass just six feet away. He saw the moonstone flush of the eyes, the telltale crouch of the collie. It was better, at least, than the Dobermann or German shepherd that he had imagined. Better, perhaps, but not good.

He resolved to bluff it out. He lowered the spade. He stretched out a hand. 'Hello, old chap,' he soothed, 'how're you doing? There's a fine fellow. There's a boy . . .'

The dog did not understand English. It kept on growling.

'Whoa, now. What's up with you, then, feller?' Paul chivvied and cheered. 'Out for walkies, are we? Or d'ye spend the night out, hey? Don't you worry, lad. Got company now, haven't you? You can help me digging, hmmm? Find a nice juicy bone, eh?'

The dog crept forward. It sniffed Paul's hand. Its tail swished in the grass. Paul told his hand to remain steady as he scratched behind the dog's ear. The collie lowered the other ear to the ground and raised his rump in a sort of twisted salaam. He sniffed at Paul's trouser cuffs, and Paul thanked God that his jeans had not been washed since he had wished the greyhounds farewell. He had made a new friend.

Paul resumed his work. The dog watched his every movement, but made no further complaint. Paul's technique was simple. Every six inches or so, he inserted the blade of the spade and slowly, carefully leaned on the handle until his whole weight was on it. Whatever depth the spade had reached, he then worked it backwards and forwards until he was satisfied.

He was almost beneath the branches of an apple tree when he found what he was looking for.

The spade sank without resistance and grated on stone. Paul started his wagging motion with the handle. The spade merely slid onward. The surface was flat, and nothing but rotten and rotting leaves lay above it. Paul dropped to his knees and swept them away. His signet clinked against metal. Paul breathed, 'I say . . .' and, with ever more urgent movements, pushed aside the soggy leaves.

He needed no more light than he had. Beneath him was a three-foot-square slab with a metal ring at its centre. He paused then. He sank back on his hunkers, panting. His heart was thudding far faster than his exertions warranted. Hope crackled through him, to be smothered by realism, only to surge up again.

Just feet away, there might be – there wasn't, of course – but there might be, a hoard of historic jewels, untouched in fifty years. Of course, there wouldn't be. They would have been found and broken up years since. But there might be. Or Havlik was having him on. Torches would appear from somewhere, and laughter rattle at him like machine-gun fire.

He pulled himself back, scrambled to his feet, reached down to grasp the ring. And pulled.

'That'll be it down there.' Jago pointed as the car crested the hill.

'Where?' Holly straightened and strained.

'Down there. See the onion dome? I wonder how much of this fountain is left. God, poor Paul, scouting round in the gloom for diamonds and things. I'll lay odds that the "treasure" is very well wrapped, so that Paul need not know what it is. Drugs are a damn sight more likely than jewels.'

'Shame.' Holly's shoulders sank. 'Oh, well.'

Jago shifted into third as the car nuzzled down into the forest. 'If he's in there and I'm going to find him fast, we're going to need to distract this bloody farmer and his family while I look for him.' Jago changed up as the car crested the hill. The valley beneath was deep. 'Ready for your little concert?'

'Sure.'

On the drive from Susice, Jago had outlined a possible plan of action.

'Suppose I drive past this place,' he had said. 'I'm a Czech giving a tourist a lift, right? Maybe we've had a row or I've tried to molest you or something. Anyhow, I stop for a second, drop you off, you're stranded in the depths of the countryside.'

'Bastard.'

'Yup. So, I drive on, park at the first place I can along the road. Gateway, even on the verge if I must. Then, while you play up a storm, I can sneak in and have a look around.'

'What if Paul won't come with you?'

'Then I'll drag him out,' Jago had said grimly. 'I'm not having this trip ruined by nursemaiding duties. If all is well, I'll just knock on the door and retrieve you. If for any reason we're separated, the car'll be just up the road. I'll leave the keys in the car. You do drive, don't you?'

'Just. This is fun. So where do we meet up?'

'You must make it back to Plsen. Not Susice. If we hang around Susice, I mean, there only seems to be one hotel.

There's no guarantee we'll find rooms. At least in Plsen . . . Try that big place we passed on the way in. International, Continental, whatever it was called.'

Now Holly pointed at the lighted windows. 'God, is that it?'

'Must be.' Jago nodded. 'Right. Ready? Got the fiddle? See you soon. Good luck.' He leaned across and quickly kissed her. He aimed for her cheek, but Holly turned, alarmed, towards him. Their lips met. He pulled back fast. She nodded, and fumbled as she reached for the door-handle. 'Bye,' she said from reflex and to no one much. The door opened. Her feet crunched on tarmac. The wind droned. It whisked her hair into floss. The door thumped shut. Jago shoved the car into gear. He made the most of second gear's acceleration.

Behind him on the verge, Holly flicked open the catches on her fiddle case. She reached down and in one smooth, practised movement, plucked out the fiddle and its bow.

'And if Paul is in there digging,' she muttered, 'here comes the fright of his life.' Her eyes twinkled, then closed.

Paul lay flat so that he could reach still further in. Even as he did so, another set of headlights appeared up on the mountain. They descended very slowly. The drone of the engine became a pudder like distant wingbeats. He raised his head. The car or truck sort of gulped as it passed behind the house, and for a moment he thought that it had stopped. He prepared to run, but, a moment later, the engine roared and the headlights emerged and climbed. He sighed in relief.

Right. This was it. He blew on his hands and rubbed them together. He reached into the hole to the full extent of his arms. His fingers clawed at nothing. He sighed. He withdrew his arm and rolled over on his back. He would have to go back to the fountain. The hook might serve its turn. For a moment, however, he lay there, staring up at the torn and frayed clouds. The sky seemed to wheel. He did not give himself the luxury of believing that beneath him lay hidden millions, but, if faith was denied him, hope nourished him, refreshing as water after a night on the tiles.

He wanted to dive down that hole headfirst, drag out whatever was in there and empty it out on the turf. It was very like lust.

Later, Paul would worry about that passion. He would nurse a suspicion that, had Sadovy happened upon him and challenged him at that moment, he would have laid him out with the spade, and Paul was no expert in relative skull thickness.

He gathered up his knees and jumped to his feet. He returned to the fountain and reached for the hook. He scuttled back to the stopcock cover and knelt as though in prayer. 'Come on,' he whispered to the jewels or to himself, 'come on, come on . . .'

It was then that the music started.

The dog jumped up, barking, and scuttled back towards the house. Paul sprang up, transfixed for a second, gazing up at the lighted window as the violin coughed, then sang like crystal. He muttered, 'What in blazes . . .'

He heard the click of the doorlatch. He risked a glance up at the house. The door was open. A woman's plump figure stood in the frame of yellow light. A man's bent form pottered around the house to investigate. The dog was a shadow at his heel. A gate clicked and whined. The music very suddenly stopped. There was a flutter of voices, then footfalls chimed on the tarmac.

The door shut again. What in God's name was going on? Was music delivered in these parts, like ice-cream at home?

Paul stood gaping for a while. The fiddle was groaning up there, this time more muffled and richer than before. The groan turned to a squeak, and the fiddler was away, playing some sort of frenzied, footstamping Irish jig.

Paul was bemused, but that was quite normal. He felt happier. The music seemed to bless his venture. He whistled quietly as he returned to his work. He reached down the hole with the hook. It touched nothing. It seemed the stopcock itself had been removed. He leaned further in, lowering his head into darkness which smelled strongly of damp dog. The blade of the hook touched something which sounded metallic and yielding, like tin. Paul reached still further in, until he was in danger of tipping in entirely. The hook caused something to flap and rap against that metal surface. He was reminded of his father's deed box. If, then, he could get his fingers, or the blade, beneath that handle . . .

He thought he heard something close by and immediately raised his head but saw nothing. He dismissed it as the moaning of the wind. He continued to fish for that handle.

It was a frustrating game, and it was made no easier by the necessity that he should again and again pull himself from the hole to listen to the melody. He was making a lot of noise down here, with the steel blade scraping against the stone or thudding against the tin, if tin it was. He wanted to know when a melody was drawing to a close. There were, of course, always those tunes which caused paroxysms in disc-jockeys by ending suddenly and *in medias res* . . .

All in all, Paul counted three gypsy-style pieces, all frantic business and wind-in-the-woods chords, before at last he contrived to slide the hook's blade, at the diagonal, beneath the handle, turn the hook to the vertical and start to pull. The box was tightly wedged in there. He had to squat and strain and rock the box, and still it only rasped and groaned against the stone, but it was coming. With every jerk it moved more readily . . .

It started to rise.

He saw the two cars before he heard them, saw the headlight beams of the first scanning the hillside, saw the dull glow of metal in the headlight beams of the second, as, like giant horned beetles, they crested the hill and slid down its side. Then the growling of gears came to him on the breeze.

It was their speed, the slickness with which they were driven in tandem, the power of which those engines spoke. He knew that these were not farm vehicles.

He knew that these were not tourists.

He knew that they were there because of him.

He had no doubt about it, not for a second, and it took him only a second to decide what must be done. He had hooked the treasure, if treasure it were. He wanted it with all his heart. Like a mother partridge protecting her young, he must draw the predators away.

It hurt him to do it, but he let the box, with the hook, back into the hole. The violin still keened. The car lights had vanished in the dip. Any minute they would emerge on the level.

He gazed wistfully at the darkness of the grottos as he hauled the stone cover roughly over the square shaft. He shook his head. He must decoy them from this area. He snatched up the spade and he ran.

He ran, regardless now of noise, back to the shelter of the maize and round onto the scrubby flat land which had once been the courtyard. He was headed towards the main body of the house. He took the steps up to the great front door in one leap. He tried the iron ring before he realized that there was a little postern in the vast sheet of adzed oak. He pushed, and it gave, but there was a weight behind it. He pushed harder. The something against it – a tea chest, he guessed – scraped over the boards, hit the wall. He was through.

He was in a high hall. The flagstones were chequered by the blue moonlight. There were faded murals there. Running deer, horses, dogs, and, high above the shattered fireplace, a ghostly starburst where a panoply had hung.

He ran to his right. His footfalls around the gallery sounded like a blundering, panicked bird. He pushed open another door beneath a white broken architrave.

He was in another giant room – or, at least, the light made it seem giant. It might have been a banqueting hall or a drawing room. Moonlight through the windows projected fancy surfboards on the walls. Fabric clung to the walls in peeling patches which cast axe-head shadows. Chains hung loose from mouldings on the ceiling. The branches of some plant tapped at the window as though seeking admission.

Paul found what he was looking for. Or, at least, this would have to do. All that he must do was persuade his pursuers that he had been searching here. He had not time to dig a hole. Here, he found one waiting for him.

In the far left-hand corner, beneath another creeping

plant which had stolen in and was now pretending to sustain the ceiling, someone had pulled up floorboards. The cavity was perhaps five foot deep. Paul saw broken laths. He saw rocks beneath. He saw a lot of darkness too.

He dropped the spade in, then let himself gingerly down.

He found a firm foothold. He grasped the nearest floorboard. He pushed upwards until he felt that his neck must burst, but the board rose. It groaned and squeaked in protest, like someone rudely awoken after a hard night. A nail gave, then another. The board spat as it split.

The next one yielded more readily.

And that, Paul thought, was the best that he could do. Outside, cars sighed as they settled. Doors clunked shut. Someone shouted.

Leaving the spade, he pulled himself up and started to run again, back towards the front door and out into the cool moonlight. He swung left, swerving to crash into the maize as he went. He very much wanted them to know that he was here. He turned the corner to face the road, and a barrage of three, maybe four torch blasts smashed the darkness, not twenty yards away. He raised an arm against the dazzling light. He stopped, arms windmilling, and spun round. Someone shouted and something rattled. He hoped very much that it was not a gun.

His own weight and speed carried him wide around the corner. There was a lot more shouting behind him, a lot more rattling, and now there was the clatter of running feet.

Another dark figure suddenly loomed up out of the darkness ahead of him. Paul could make out that it was big and human. That was all. He did not stop. He ran as if to pass the man on his left-hand side. The shadow bought the dummy. Paul lunged hard to his left. He felt a plucking as the shadow's hand made a despairing grab at him, but Paul plunged into the high maize and smashed his way through, heading back towards the ploughed field. A rapid riffling sound, like a cardsharp many times amplified, mystified him for a split second, then he realized, incredulously, that someone was shooting, if not at him, then towards him, and that somewhere down to his right, maize stalks were pattering and crackling as bullets whiffled them down.

There was another quick burst. That was all he needed. He flung himself flat, sniffed in damp earth smells, and waited. Treasure was good, but life without it, he discovered, was better. He had never been shot at before. He did not like it.

Whatever else they might be, these were no hunters. They crashed and bellowed and cursed and their torchbeams scythed through the stalks. Had Paul been armed, he could have picked off three of them before they even saw him.

They knew him to be unarmed, then, or they were rank amateurs.

He disliked the implications of both possibilities.

The man who found Paul quite literally tripped over him. He was shoving at a maize stalk and moving at a trot when his torch dabbed Paul with light. The man stopped, too fast, made a vomiting sound and fell across Paul's back. He gabbled something fast and furious as he steadied his torch-beam on Paul's face, then he pulled himself to his feet and shouted something full of gutturals and 'z's to his comrades.

They gathered about Paul. They clutched his shirt and tugged at him until he stood. Then they jostled him and prodded him as though to prove to themselves that they were immune to any magic contained in this venerable stranger. None of them seemed to be less than two inches shorter than Paul.

There were four of them, all dark-haired, two of them wearing moustaches, he saw in the criss-cross torchlight. Two of them carried guns – little square frames which ran over their wrists and along their forearms. Machine-pistols, he assumed, in that he had heard of such things, and these were far smaller and more toy-like than any machine-guns of his experience. Three of the men wore leather jackets. One wore jeans and a thick blue sweater.

They shouted at Paul. None of them seemed clearly to be the leader, though on two occasions the others looked to one of the mustachioed men, who had a creased and punctured face like that of a plump Charles Bronson. Paul discovered why when this man hushed them with upraised hands, gulped twice, wiped his moustaches on his sleeve, spat, gulped again and said 'Wheres?'

The wind made the corn whisper. It raised the hair from Paul's brow. He frowned. 'Sorry? Not with you. Wheres?'

'Wheres gems? You, speak me wheres.' He had plainly looked 'gems' up in the dictionary. He pronounced it with a hard 'g'.

Paul did likewise. 'Gems? What gems? Sorry. I'm not with you.'

'Gems you dig wheres?' The words emerged slowly and with great effort, like droppings from a constipated dog. The man gritted his teeth and pointed a stiff finger at Paul. He stabbed hard at his chest three times. 'You speak me wheres or we gunning.'

The gesture drew a murmur of approval from his comrades. They got the gist. One of them stepped forward and jabbed his pistol in the area of Paul's liver. There was a moment of shocking clarity as Paul's mind registered this. His mind sent signals: to his bowels to evacuate, to his knees to buckle, to his sweat glands to start pumping. The sweat glands did as they were told. The bowels whimpered, and his arse gulped like his interlocutor, but held. The knees wavered, but again refused to yield.

It was a thing you learned from riding horses. You're scared, but you must never let them know. Paul's conscious mind, in so far as it was conscious, told him that this moment of weakness must not recur, or these men would be on him like jackals on a straggler. He badly needed another shot of adrenaline. He silently cleared his throat. He said, 'I say, please don't do that, funny little Czech person,' and he swept the gun away with his forearm. To his astonishment, the gun did not yap at him nor return. He said slowly, and with triple underlining, like a granny's letter, 'Now, I do not know at all what you are talking about. I ride in Velka Pardubicka. I come down here to see Beautiful Czech Architecture. I am a Very Important Englishman. Jolly good chum of Princess Di. Go away.'

He did not know how much of this animated Dalek-speak

was understood. Certainly it evoked a lot of rattling question and answer from the boys. There were sneers and snarls. Hands clasped like claws. The men with guns growled. One of them jeered and released a fake laugh which sounded alarmingly like a machine-gun. 'Princess Di' obviously hit home. The words peppered their speech.

There was a moment there when nothing much happened. The men kept glancing back at the house, where more torches flickered. They were uncertain as to what to do next. If they were bemused, Paul was still more so. He vaguely assumed these men to be police or government agents. This was only in part consoling. The Czech police might now be, officially at least, democratically accountable, but old habits die hard, and the old habits of the totalitarian days were bad ones. Paul had no doubt that Her Majesty's Ambassador in Prague would have some very stern words to say if he should be found shot dead on a Bohemian mountainside, but stern words would do him precious little good, and a police force, he was sure, could readily cook up proof of a hunting accident or even disappear him altogether. Communist police forces were meant to be good at disappearing people.

Paul did not want to disappear. Not before Sunday's race.

How had these people known of his intentions? Had someone, after all, been listening to Havlik in the garden of the Club André? It was not impossible, and would explain why they knew that he was here but did not know precisely where he had been searching. Alternatively, he supposed, the authorities had been waiting for someone to go treasure-hunting in the area. The only other possibility, which made no sense at all, was that Havlik had set him up and informed upon him . . .

His speculations were cut short by a shout from the direction of the house. Paul breathed a fervent prayer that someone had found the hole and the spade. A torch wagged its light as a man over there ran from the front door towards them. He was panting when he arrived. He had a red beard and wild hair. He held Paul's spade high. He indicated Paul and pointed back at the house. He coughed a bit, but managed to get his message out. The Bronson lookalike grabbed Paul's arm. 'You come,' he said.

The keenest of the gunmen again jabbed Paul in the back with his weapon's muzzle, so Paul did as he was told.

Jago had been tiptoeing along the uppermost terrace towards the house's main door when he had heard the cars. He had presumed that the fountain would be a common or garden Versailles-style ornament, and that the courtyard was the obvious place for such a thing. The house, therefore, had been too close for him to have seen the cars as they swept down the valley, but he too had known at once that they meant trouble. He had called, as loudly as he dared, 'Paul? Paul!' He had headed downwards, into darkness. He had vaulted the balustrade and crouched down below the terrace.

As the cars' brakes wheezed and the car doors slammed, the music from the house had very suddenly stopped. Footfalls had rattled further along the terrace, and a man's figure had burst from the darkness, running upstairs, towards trouble, in long, leaping strides. 'Paul!' Jago had called again, but the man was already gone. Jago had swivelled round to watch over the terrace's edge as the door became darker and the man's footfalls rang inside.

He had seen Paul run out again, this time without the spade, had seen him crucified for a second against the spray of torchlight as he rounded the corner, skidded to a halt and ran back, his white hair flashing in the torchlight as he ducked down and sprinted round the house. He had heard the crash as Paul threw himself into the cornfield, he had cringed and muttered a prayer as the gun had clattered. He had breathed out only when he had seen Paul led out captive, but there had been nothing that he could do. Not with four men, apparently armed, out there.

He watched now as Paul was half pulled, half dragged through the house's front door. He longed to get up, walk in there, tell them, 'that's quite enough of this sort of nonsense', but he suspected that his dormitory-monitor style would not serve here. Paul, of course, would not have hesitated. He would probably have been looking even now for a suitable chandelier on which to make his entrance, but that was why Paul was where he now was. Jago estimated odds, and if that made him craven, so be it. The odds here made the National Lottery look like a Good Thing.

Cramp made Jago straighten his left leg. He swivelled round to rub it. As the pain eased, he looked up. The moon picked out the wall of tumbling rocks, the broken basin, the deep dark caves. There was Paul's fountain. He had a faint urge to scrabble down there and himself hunt for this mythical treasure, but he must keep an eye on that door in hope that some opportunity might arise to lend assistance.

He waited for another ten minutes before men and torches again appeared at the door. Two men walked out briskly. Another staggered out and fell. Others followed. Their torch-beams showed the white hair of the man on the ground.

One of the men walked towards Paul and kicked him. Jago flinched, but did not move.

Another man reached down and grasped Paul's collar. He pulled him up. Paul stooped and sagged between them. One man took his either arm and half carried him along the façade and around the corner. They passed the light from the farmer's window. The garden gate clinked. Car doors clunked. The other men, still at the front door, briefly conferred then returned into the house.

The car's engine started up. Headlight beams thrust up the hill, receded, returned, dazzling, pointing directly above Jago, receded again and pointed back in the direction from which the cars had come. The car roared. Jago watched the headlights as they broke free of the left-hand side of the house. They bored onwards for some half a mile, then swivelled to the right and lurched as the car bounced up some ride or rough track. They vanished behind trees, emerged again as a dragonfly glimmer, vanished again, emerged again. Somewhere up there, perhaps a mile up the hill, they stopped moving. Jago waited.

He was straightening when the lights swung round, high up there on the hill. Now they bobbed downwards, coming ever nearer. They swung left onto the road and drew closer and closer. The car braked hard behind the house. Again doors clunked. This time, just two men marched round the corner to the great door to join their colleagues. Somewhere up there, they had lost Paul.

Jago groaned.

He considered his options. None particularly appealed. He could not just leave Paul, even if, as he supposed, he were dead. He could, in theory, knock on the door of the farmer's house and retrieve Holly, but he had no guarantee that his appearance would not cause the farmer to start hollering. A farmer's family might accept and even shelter a nice-looking girl with a fiddle who had been deserted by some brute, but if that brute turned up asking for her back, they were likely to baulk. He could take the car, then, and drive up to where he had last seen the car's lights, but that would leave Holly stranded. With the place crawling with unidentified armed men, she needed to get away fast.

He had two choices, then. He could wait until the men departed and Holly emerged, and only then go in search of Paul, or he could set off on foot. He recalled Paul's weakened, sagging body. The man had taken a beating. He could not leave him long in the cold night air.

He sighed deeply. He hit the grass with a clenched fist. He said again, '*Bloody* man!' and, clinging now to such cover as there was, he slunk towards the road.

The car door opened with a gasp. Paul drooled a protest, but was answered by a shove and another prod with the gun. He slumped into the passenger seat. The gunman climbed in behind him. He smelled strongly of stale sweat. He rested the gun's barrel on the back of Paul's seat. Paul was vaguely aware of it, vaguely hoped that the safety catch was on and that the roads were smooth. The overripe Bronson strode briskly around the car and slid in at his left.

The car tilted. The man tapped out a cigarette and pulled it with his lips from the packet. He lit it and exhaled before turning the ignition key. Smoke exploded on the windscreen.

Paul lolled in his seat as the car executed a rapid three-point turn and spurted up the hill-road towards Susice. He rocked helplessly as the car swung hard to the right. His temple struck the window. He licked blood from his otherwise parched lips.

He had not known this feeling, halfway between pain and blissful oblivion, since some chums had bought him a one-way ticket to Inverness and deposited him on the train after a big dance in London when he had been too tight to protest.

It was difficult to force his eyes to focus. There was only a dull, smoky blur. It was a minute or two before he realized that, even when he was frowning with all his strength, there was still only a dull smoky blur. He had assumed that they were headed for the local cop-shop. He was startled, therefore, to realize that they were climbing a narrow avenue, straight as a perspective exercise, through thick forest. They were rocking and bouncing. They were on turf . . .

The temptation to close his eyes was overwhelming. His eyelashes buzzed like hummingbirds' wings. He had been hit in the stomach and the kidneys. He prayed that no internal damage had been done. An elbow had slammed into his temple. For a minute after that he had been in veering darkness. Boots had rattled and thumped about him. The rattle of the guns had been amplified a thousand times. 'Where's?' the roar had come at him down a long dark resonant tube. 'Where's where's where's?'

It had not been heroism, after all. There had been no point in telling them, and anyhow, by now, it had become a linguistic tic, a habit to reply 'Under the floor. Where the spade . . . There . . .' To have described the fountain or to have found the word 'stopcock' would have been altogether too much effort.

He became aware that the driver was driving one-handed whilst tapping at a telephone in his lap. He hadn't a hand spare for his cigarette. Ash purled down the leather of his jacket. A lot of breathing was being done in here. The windows were heavily misted.

'Where are you taking me?' Paul demanded, but it came out as a sort of garbled miaow.

The driver said 'hmph'. The gun-muzzle jerked against the nape of Paul's neck.

''re you police? Polizei?'

Another 'hmph', another jerk. All attempts at communication had ceased.

The car slowed. It passed a pile of pine logs at the right. Its engine gulped and gasped, gulped and gasped, like an old boozer taking the first shot of the day, over and over. Then suddenly the headlights picked out nothing. Their beams became endless bars, and all that they showed was a smoke of motes and the odd moth which flickered like a screwed-up scrap of tinfoil. The car bucked as it stopped. Ahead, there were just a few feet of crusty ruts and pebbles, then nothing.

The driver was out of the car before it stopped rocking. He held the telephone in his left hand. His right paddled along the bonnet as he marched around the front of the car, pressed close. There was something out there, beyond and beneath, to which he had no desire to get too near. Paul suspected that that something was a whole lot more nothing.

Paul's door was wrenched open. The man outside said something which must have been 'Get him out,' because the gun-muzzle jerked at the nape of Paul's neck and the door behind him opened too. If he were to make a break for it, it must be now, but he could see no way, not if this man were willing to shoot. There was only one way to establish that.

He staggered out, and immediately knew that he had been right. The lights picked out no reassuring hillocks down there. There was only darkness deeper than that in the sky. The breeze which combed his hair and feathered his cheeks came from below. He was on a cliff's edge, miles from anywhere, in what was, to him at least, a strange landscape in a strange land.

He remembered Havlik's consoling words, his assurances that the worst to which he was likely to be subjected was a charge of trespass, but local JPs did not tote guns, or conduct their business on the edges of precipices, however conveniently situated.

Paul searched his turbid mind for possible explanations for the choice of just these circumstances. The first was that these two men intended to scare him.

The second was that he had every reason to be scared.

The mustachioed man laid a hand almost protectively between Paul's shoulder-blades. Paul felt like a child in his powerlessness as he obeyed the pressure of that hand, the prodding of the gun.

Neither man said much. There wasn't really much need. The message was clear enough. Beneath Paul, not two horizontal feet from his toes, was the brim of the void. Should he step out there, it might be months before his mortal remains were ever found, by which time such mortal remains would be seriously diminished.

Paul did not like heights at the best of times. He very much hated this one. He said things like 'No . . .' and 'But . . .' and 'Look, what the bloody hell is happening here?' He pulled backwards, resolved that, at the very least, they must go to the trouble and expense of a bullet.

Incredibly, the bloated Bronson was talking into his mobile phone and holding up a hand, at once hushing and consoling. He winced as he tried to hear his interlocutor above Paul's protests. He nodded at Paul, as though to say, 'Yes, yes. We understand. Don't worry. We're not going to murder you yet.'

This was how the old-fashioned business of murder was done in the nineties – chatting on a mobile phone in the chiaroscuro of headlight beams.

Paul's doom would be decided by committee.

If someone else called, no doubt these two thugs would be said to be 'in a meeting'.

The telephone was babbling now, and the shoulders of the man holding it drooped. He put in a few protesting monosyllables which were swept away on the tide of words from the other end of the line. Paul slumped back on the car's bonnet. He knew from the covert glances which one man cast at the other that they were being torn off a strip. It afforded him some small satisfaction.

The man at his left suddenly thrust a hand towards Paul's face. Paul swung his head away by weary reflex before he realized that the man was holding the phone out to him. 'You speak,' he was saying.

Bemused, Paul took the telephone. The cold gun-muzzle resumed its sniffing at his neck. A voice at his ear said, 'Ah, Mr Pickering. You have had a busy time. Whoring one night, archaeology the next. Well, well.'

The voice was heavily accented, husky and strangely high-pitched. Peter Lorre playing a Ruritanian. Paul did not believe it to be natural. No human larynx, with the possible exception of Janis Joplin's, could stand such constant strain.

'I – I just came down to see the house,' Paul enunciated as clearly as he could with his swollen lips. 'This is a free country now, isn't it?'

'Why that house, Mr Pickering?'

'I – I don't know. Why not?'

'And why with a spade?'

'Spade?'

'Yes, Mr Pickering. Please don't be needlessly obtuse. You were sent to the house by Cyril Havlik, weren't you? What did he tell you? That there was treasure there?'

'You seem to know it all,' Paul said, mentally washing his hands of the whole business. 'Yes. All right. I met Cyril Havlik. He said, go down to the Zichy house and look under the big hall. I thought, well, why not? An adventure. He promised me a percentage. Far as I knew, the stuff belonged to his family, so why not? I didn't realize people would be chasing me with guns and things.'

'Hmmm.' Saliva crackled. 'That is very much what we thought . . .'

'Who is "we"?' Paul asked as cordially as he could contrive. 'Are you police or what?'

The other speaker ignored him. 'You see, Mr Pickering? It is not wise to get mixed up in things which do not concern you. I am sorry to have interrupted your little – adventure.

Now, of course, we must wait to find out if Havlik told you the truth or not. If the things you were looking for are found, we'll have a problem, thanks to those weirdos with you. God, don't you hate menials who try to think for themselves? Yes, we could not have you returning to England and telling everyone of what has happened . . .'

'I can't see why anyone would be interested,' Paul put in helpfully. 'Anyhow, I only know what I've been told. You let me go back to my car, I go off, ride in the Velka Pardubicka, go home again. OK, so I blundered into something, got into trouble with the police. I'm sorry if I've caused trouble. So far, I'm all right. Bit bruised, but nothing serious. On the other hand, you keep me here, kidnap me, keep pointing guns at me, all that, I really have got a story to tell.'

Again, the man seemed not to hear Paul. 'If the things are not found, of course, our argument will be with Mr Havlik, not with you. So, we wait. It should not be long now. How specific were Havlik's instructions, Mr Pickering?'

'Oh, absolutely,' Paul shrugged. He looked out into the darkness and a sudden cold gust of wind wriggled past him like an icy current. He shuddered, and knew beyond doubt that his ancestors had walked on all fours by the way his hackles stirred. He swallowed. 'The north-west corner of the big hall, he told me, no more than six foot from the walls, no more than five foot deep.'

'Hardly probable, hmmm?'

'Why not?'

'You don't suppose that everyone was not looking for treasure at the houses of the old aristocracy? Of course they were. The secret police, the historians, every curious passer-by . . . There must have been a thousand metal-detectors passed over that room.'

'So someone has found it, sold it secretly. I told Havlik that that was likely.'

'So you did.' The voice suddenly dropped in pitch. 'So you did.'

'So you were listening to us at the Club André,' Paul

nodded. 'Then you know that I knew nothing about the whole business. I was approached that evening and thought, well, why not? What harm can it do?'

'Certainly that was the impression you gave, Mr Pickering. An ignorant amateur. Don't worry, please. I'm sure all will be well.'

Paul resented the description for the barest millisecond, then he acknowledged its justice. 'Sorry,' he said, 'but what's all this drama about? Guns, beating people up. Bloody outrageous.'

'I agree with you.' The man gave a soft, husky little laugh. 'They are ignorant jerks out there, greedy and ignorant, and I strongly suspect that they watch too many of the worst sort of American film. Movies lost all soul and style when they moved into colour and out of the studio. Don't you agree?'

'Of course,' Paul snapped. 'What's that got to do with anything?'

'I'm sorry. Why on earth did you let yourself get involved, Mr Pickering?'

'Oh, you know. The money, bit of fun, bit of old-fashioned romance.'

'Romance!' The man laughed, and his laugh was undisguised. It was deep and rough. It sounded like a saw on a shuddering plank of timber, held only by the carpenter's knee.

'Yes.' Paul was affronted. 'OK, so you think it's silly, but it's like why I ride races. Tradition. Risk. A challenge. I don't see what's so strange or funny.'

'No, no. I'm sure you're right. I'm just an old cynic, I'm sure. So, you have no moral qualms?'

'What qualms? The communists were thieves. Havlik's family hid their property. If a family isn't entitled to pass on what it has earned . . . It doesn't matter to me if it's our royal family with billions or the Havliks and their jewels or you having the right to pass on your silver to your child. It's the same principle and the main motivation for doing anything. I don't see anything wrong in trying to restore property to its owners.'

The man was laughing again. Paul found it annoying. 'Oh, nor do I,' the man gasped between chuckles, 'nor do I.'

'I don't know anything about the Havliks,' Paul persisted defensively, 'well, not much, but at some point or other they must have taken big risks, served their people, tended their lands, all that. You don't get and keep estates and land like that without jolly hard work and responsibility.'

'Oh, yes, indeed. You're right of course, Mr Pickering.' The man gulped back his laughter. 'So, you don't respect the State's claim on the Havlik property?'

'Nope. We don't respect the State very much, not where I come from.'

'No. You respect romance. And tradition.'

'And people, yes . . .'

There was shrilling in there, like that noise which partying Brazilians make. The voice at the other end of the line said, 'Excuse me.' There was a clatter as he laid down one receiver and picked up another. He spoke one word, which sounded like '*Vlozh*'. Thereafter, he spoke just twice more, again in monosyllables. Paul looked at the men on either side of him. They looked sullenly away from his gaze. They blamed him for their discomfiture. They were waiting. There was another, higher 'beep' as, presumably, Paul's interlocutor signed off. 'I am sorry, Mr Pickering,' the voice resumed, still in that straining, rasping voice. Paul did not like the sound of this. 'It appears that nothing has been found. This is annoying. May I speak to . . .? May I speak to those idiots there?'

'Hang on!' Paul protested. 'These apes don't speak English! What are your plans? What's going to happen now?'

'Don't worry, Mr Pickering. Please let me speak to my colleagues . . .'

If he thought it out at all, it was no more than you think out a slip-catch or a snap-shot before the event. If reasoning there was, it was only to the effect that it was easier for followers not to kill than to kill without their leader's authority, and that any surprise which Paul could engender must be to his advantage.

Had he had more time, he might have taken the fifty-fifty

odds that they might simply have left him here to find his way back to Susice. He might, on the other hand, have reflected that thugs like these might lose restraint with their tempers, and accepted the voice's 'don't worry' as sincere reassurance rather than mere soothing to render the victim acquiescent.

As it was, he flung the telephone like a grenade out into the darkness.

It seemed a long time before it clicked and clattered on rock. His guards gazed stupidly after it.

Paul lurched somewhat clumsily to his left and shoulder-barged the bloated Bronson. The shorter man grunted. His arms rose and flailed. For a moment, Paul saw deep shadows in his stretched, pockmarked cheek, a deeper shadow where his mouth had been, and thought that he had, albeit inadvertently, consigned him to the chasm beneath. Instead, the man sat down hard. He had too little space to allow himself to roll, but his left hand was already on the ground, pushing his bulk up again.

Paul made to kick him, but there was a bark and a rattle behind him. Arms clamped tight about him, pulling him back.

Whenever Paul read accounts of fights, the antagonists always seemed to know what they were doing – 'I dragon-kicked to his knee-cap . . .' 'I jabbed at his Adam's Apple . . .' His experience of fighting was limited – a few brawls at school, a tussle with a would-be mugger in Barcelona, this encounter – but all had about them a deal of indignity and uncertainty. Jaws hit elbows and groins hit knees as much as the other way round. There was always a lot of shoving and wrenching and flapping.

That was how it was here.

Paul used his strength and height to rid himself of the man on his back, but by now, the other man had again attained his feet. He aimed punches at Paul's stomach, but they slid off his forearms.

Paul's head jerked up and his crown smashed into the man's jaw, which probably shook one man as much as the other. Meanwhile, the man behind him was kicking at the backs of Paul's knees. All this was accompanied by puffing and grunting and wheezing. Paul had no idea as to exactly what he hoped to attain by all this activity. He had vague thoughts, he supposed, of winning his freedom and out-sprinting his assailants for the cover of the trees. That was as far as strategy went.

Had there been just one of them, he might even have made it, but a deep blow to his already bruised kidneys made him wince and gasp. A forearm which jolted first against his jaw, then against the side of his nose, caused all sorts of exotic phosphorescent fish to swim around inside his eyelids. Then one of those kicks found its mark, and he found himself toppling forwards, clinging to the fat man's leather jacket for support, finding no handhold and slipping downwards to his knees.

He swayed for a moment, like a drunken worshipper in a storm at sea. He half raised an arm against the expected boot or bullet in the face. His ears sang.

It was very still now, but for the sighing of the breeze, the puffing and clattering of the men above. One of them resentfully snarled something down at him. Paul felt very sick. He swallowed hard, then blinked to clear the smears from his vision.

He need not have bothered.

There was a grunt from above him, a whoosh of air in fabric. Paul's hand reached and grasped the boot only after it had clunked into his skull, only after the *Dr Who* theme had started playing at full volume in there. He vomited before skewing sideways. The *Dr Who* theme echoed on and on. Dirt was on his cheek and grass up his nostrils. Air burst from him and seeped as his knees rose almost to his chest, then suddenly straightened. He lay still.

He did not know that the man above him spat down on him and snarled.

He knew no fear when the car started up and rolled forward until the right tyre almost touched his hair before reverse gear bit, and the car drew back as though it too suffered vertigo.

He did not hear the dwindling sound of the engine.

He lay very still whilst, about him, the forest seethed.

It was working, Havlik thought gleefully as he drove out of Prague towards Pardubice. Ever since he had arrived in the country, he had been followed at every turn. He had expected it, if not the sheer quantity of men crowding him wherever he went.

Since this morning, he reckoned that the team of followers had been reduced to four. This afternoon, the man with the white eyebrows had gone. That left just three, the youngest three.

It had not been difficult to shake them. He had taken trams all round the city tonight, forced the followers to abandon their cars by walking across Charles Bridge, then doubled back to hail a taxi.

He had booked the hire-car on the telephone from the airport.

Oh, they would catch up with him. They were welcome to, but he had an hour or so. He would make full use of it.

He pulled off the main road when he saw the sign for Hradec Kralove. The pursuers would be expecting him at the Hotel Slatovice in Pardubice. They would have to wait. Havlik had a little sightseeing to do.

Lou Robinson's directions proved precise. Havlik drove across the plain towards the high hills. He passed through a couple of small villages and found himself descending a gentle slope to a narrow stream. He crossed the bridge and turned sharp right. The car bumped along the stream's bank. Down at his right, the water twinkled in the moonlight. He saw the mill wheel before he saw the black shape of the house beyond. The wheel was turning, dripping pearls. The sound of the mill-race would drown out any other.

Havlik parked the car. He stepped out casually, pulled up his jeans, pulled down his jerkin. He polished his shoes on his calves.

He smiled, just for practice, then pushed open the little garden gate. It squeaked. He walked up the narrow path between two small vegetable beds. The furrows on the right were lit by a ground-floor window whose top right pane had been replaced with cardboard or plywood. Havlik looked for a bell-push or a knocker. He found neither.

He rapped on the door with his knuckles. For what seemed two or three minutes, there was no sound save the thunder of the mill-wheel.

There was a scraping then from inside, the latch clicked and the door opened inwards.

An old man stood in the door-frame. The white hair on his egg-shaped cranium was afterthought wisps. The white stubble on his chin was profuse. His eyes were mere slits, his mouth a jagged wedge. Havlik thrust out his hand. He said, 'Mr Filip! How are you?'

'What?' The man jumped backwards. 'Sorry, who are you?'

'Sorry, Cyril Havlik. I wrote to you, remember?'

'Yes, I remember.' The old man turned dolefully away. 'Havlik. Yes. A friend of yours came to visit me.'

'That's right. Lou, Lou Robinson. He said you had some things of the Havlik family and you'd not sell them to him.' Havlik followed the old man through the narrow porch into the room at the right.

The floor was of green concrete. The walls were shiny yellow. There was a plain pine table, two upright chairs and a little oak bureau in the corner. A solid-fuel stove burned in the chimney-breast.

On the right, a television blinked in monochrome at a wounded armchair. There was a long work-surface topped with red formica, a flat oblong sink and a wooden draining-board beneath the cardboard-patched window. 'So, you know, I was just passing, thought I'd drop in, have a word, see if I could take a look.'

'You are interested in family history, Mr Havlik?' The old man felt for the oak swivel chair before the bureau. He sank into it with a sigh. A grey cat jumped down from the armchair and up into his lap.

'Sure. Sure, I am. You, now. You grew up with my dad, didn't you, Mr Filip?'

'I would hardly say "with".' Filip attempted a smile.

'Hardly "with". I was brought up in the village, yes. My father was a schoolteacher, as I have been. Your uncle Pavel was my friend, I think. My father taught us English together. I was sad when Pavel was killed. He was a good man.'

'Yeah, so I heard.' Havlik walked over to the sink. He leaned on its rim and gazed through the window. There was a neatly folded J-cloth on the draining-board, two cabbage-heads and the pane from the window above, broken in four. A plate streaked with some sort of gravy lay in the sink. It was very cold in here. 'So, you keep teaching all these years?'

'No, Mr Havlik, I did not,' the old man droned. 'I was not allowed to teach. My ideology was suspect. People with suspect ideology were not suitable to teach. I worked on a farm.'

'Hey, that's bad luck.' Havlik swivelled round and rested his bum against the sink. 'I mean, really.' Rumlova's eyes were open now. The irises were very pale and very blue, the whites dirty at the corners and scrawled with red. The lower lids sagged like pouches. His gaze was unmoving. It made Havlik fidget. He put his fingertips in his jeans pockets and walked the length of the room. 'No,' he said, 'so, no family?'

'No, Mr Havlik. I had a wife. She is dead.'

'So, these things . . . Hey, I'm sorry. That's really . . .'

'These things,' the old man reminded him.

'Yeah, well, I'd heard, you know, you had these things – papers, household accounts, that sort of thing, right? My dad told me. He said, "Old man Filip" – that'll have been your dad, I guess – has the contents of the munitions room . . .'

'Yes,' Filip nodded. 'Your father gave them to my father.'

'To look after, right?'

'No. Your father knew that he would not be coming back. My father asked if he might have the papers. He was an historian, you see. Your father said yes. He would have burned them otherwise.'

'Yeah, but . . .' Havlik's hands worked together. 'Yeah, OK. No, it's just, that's why I wrote. You know, looking into the family history, I thought, you know, great to get these things back, right?'

The old man swivelled the chair so that he was facing the desk. He pulled open the second drawer.

He extracted a sheaf of papers in an embroidered folder, then two long vellum-bound ledgers, then a little leather-bound octavo volume. He placed them on the desk. He said, 'As you can see, I have looked after these very carefully. So now perhaps you can tell me why you want them, Mr Havlik, and what they are worth to you . . .'

Havlik nodded, gulped, and inwardly cursed.

Once on the verge, Jago jogged.

When the moon was out and the turf was aluminium, the road touched with silver, he saw each little drain as a gaping crevice and each indentation as a chasm. When the moon was in, he slowed, foundered and staggered, groping his way like a blind man.

He passed two dark avenues or rides and had to stop, panting, waiting for moonlight to show him his position in relation to that gleaming orb on top of the dome. At the third, he was satisfied that this was the route which the car had taken.

He was grateful to be off the road and out of sight of any passing cars. The running here was easier too. There were deep tyre-ruts which were in large measure level. The problem here was the darkness. It was nigh absolute. Even when the moon came out, it barely penetrated the tops of the trees. He could see no more than six feet ahead. Again and again, he tripped on the rut's edge and staggered. Three times, where the ruts levelled out, he found himself in amongst the trees, with branches scraping at his face and hands, and had to grope his way back to the track.

The trees seemed to crowd closer in about him as though he were in some anatomical canal which resented the alien intruder.

He was not running now, but stumbling, faltering, feeling his way. All this, perhaps, he had known before in English woods, but he had never known sounds such as those which here assailed him. There were strange, high-pitched shrieks so close that he started. There were mysterious cackles from high in the trees. There were lumbering, crashing sounds as heavy-footed creatures lumbered through the undergrowth. There were rattles as birds took wing.

The forest sounded like Bartok.

He could not believe that yesterday morning he had been in Campden Hill Square nor that, this afternoon, he had been calmly sitting in the sunshine listening to music in Prague. Now, suddenly, he was amongst strange men with guns and, almost worse, amongst wild animals in a wild forest. All this he owed to the man whose name he called as he proceeded through the blackness.

He would find him. Then, if he were not already dead, he would kill him.

'Paul?' he called, and more birds clattered. 'Paul!'

Paul Pickering grunted. He said, 'Ooh, I say. God. Help.'

He gathered his legs beneath him and knelt up. His hand rose to his head. He swayed. He blinked at the darkness, which spun.

'Ow?' he winced.

He shuddered. He was very, very cold.

He was not sure quite where he was, though he knew the smell of pines and of soil. He gathered up such memories as he possessed. Avocet. Pardubice. Prague. Havlik. Jago.

He recalled the lorry which he had narrowly missed on the drive down. There was something about a fountain, but he transposed that to Prague. Beyond the lorry, there was such confusion that it properly and obviously belonged to dreams.

He raised his other hand to his throbbing kidneys, then to his mouth. He said 'Yeeuck!' like a child. He sniffed the hand and irritably wiped it on the grass. There was cold sick there. He retched air.

The convulsion made him rock forward. He extended his hands to take his weight.

His skull had become an echoing bell, but the alarms were louder than the echoes.

He started back, and his intake of breath punched him in the throat. His heart had been playing rhythm for lullabies. Suddenly it invented rock'n'roll.

His mouth opened in a silent scream.

His hands would not have touched the ground.

There was no ground there to touch.

He reared like a horse at a snake. He flung himself backwards so hard that he sprawled. The luminous fish before his eyes were dead now, and bobbing upwards through the darkness.

When next he opened his eyes, he was clinging to the turf as though it were the mane and the earth a powerful horse, and the bit had snapped. He drooled and whimpered.

Paul Pickering stepped onto the scene. 'Come on, come on,' he told the child who lay on his side, stuffing his mouth with his fist, knees pumping. 'For heaven's sake, pull yourself together, old boy. Out in the woods? What's the problem? Done that, before, for goodness' sake. Had a bit of an accident. Happens. Come along. Gentleman and all that.'

He very suddenly clambered to his feet. He swayed backwards, then forwards, then about-turned. 'Right,' he said. 'Absolutely. Off we go.' He lurched a little. 'Come along, Pickering,' he burped, and careered into the grove. 'Road . . .' he said, looking around. 'There we are. No problem . . .'

The road was a bouncy track of parted grass. It made good walking. He leaned forward and careered in spurts down it, laughing when he found himself embracing a tree trunk or staggering through beaded curtains of pine-needles.

'Come along, Pickering,' he murmured. His broken lips shifted against the bark of a pine. His teeth even touched its scales. 'Quite enough fun for one night. Serious business . . .'

And somewhere down there at his left, someone was calling 'Paul? Paul!'

They did that a lot these days.

Jago's voice was becoming hoarse. He knew that he was close, thought that he might even be past the spot where the headlights had been extinguished when he stepped out into the clearing and suddenly felt the wind whiffling up from below. He knew at once by the silence and the wind that this was the end of the track. He padded gingerly forward.

The moon came to his aid, suddenly emerging to encrust the edge of the cliff. Jago walked to within feet of it. He gazed sadly down. He was sure that they had come here simply to dispose of the strange Englishman who had stumbled upon some intrigue which he had not even understood.

He would have to make his way back to the car before Holly drove it away, drive into Susice and call the consulate, then the police. He had little hope of justice or of enthusiastic co-operation. Those men down at the big house were trained and armed. There might be private armies roaming this land, but private armies put the police in their pockets before they engaged in warfare.

Jago cursed as he skirted the grove in hope of finding Paul somewhere on the fringe of the forest, for he did not suppose that they would have dumped him on the main track.

He held out little hope. That cliff's import seemed unequivocal. The car had been very deliberately and unhesitatingly driven here. It had remained for no more than fifteen minutes – time for no more than the deed itself and the crudest obsequies.

Jago trudged back, slower now, down the long straight track. He must think now how to retrieve Holly without falling into the hands of those men. He must think how to deal with the inevitable enquiries and still to get back to Pardubice as soon as he could. 'Damn it, Paul,' he said out loud to the sky, 'you are a pain in the arse, you know?' And he blinked and grinned.

He stopped.

There was still more crashing in the undergrowth on his right, but it was accompanied by another sound which he had not heard before, a droning, lilting sound, like that of gnats many times amplified. He frowned. He called, tentatively at first, 'Paul?' then there came the unmistakeable sound of a cough.

No matter that horses and badgers coughed and that, for all he knew, so did wolves or wild boar. Jago shouted 'Paul!' and plunged into the forest.

Thorns tugged and plucked at his clothes and sewed zips in his skin. Trunks hit his shoulder. Briars detained him like beggars but he tore himself free. 'Paul?' he yelled. The sound swarmed up the tree trunks and scattered the birds from their tops.

He was in a narrow track little broader than himself which ran parallel to the ride. The droning continued down to Jago's left. 'Paul!' Jago called again. He stretched out his hands at arm's length and walked as fast as he dared down the track.

It was the second time tonight that someone had tripped over Paul. He was just sitting there, legs extended on the grass, gulping air and staring at those tiny eyes ahead of him. He was humming because he had been humming, and it just went on, like a tap when the washer has gone. Jago's right foot caught under Paul's leg. Jago pitched forward. Paul, who was used to being kicked now, said, 'Oh?' rather forlornly.

'Paul?' Jago felt his way up the other man's torso and face. 'God. Are you OK?'

'Jago?' said Paul, only it came out as 'Dragor?'

'Yes. God, man, you get us into scrapes. I thought – crazy, I know – I thought those guys must have bumped you off. Come on. You're off the track. Where did you leave the car?'

'Eyesh,' Paul croaked.

'What?' Jago glanced over his shoulder. Things withered inside him.

He said, 'Oh, Christ,' and he realized that this was not a track made by foresters. It had been made by friends and relatives of the creature who snuffled and stamped not fifteen feet away.

'Back,' he whispered. He pushed Paul, but Paul merely rocked. 'Come on. Back. Out of the way. Quick!' Still Paul did not move. Jago grasped him under the arms and dragged him back into the relative shelter of the trees.

He found that sweat was trickling down his sides and shoulder-blades. 'Come on, man. Walk, will you?' he growled.

'All righ', all righ'.' Paul slapped at Jago's hands. He stood and reeled against Jago. 'God. Headache. Kicked me. Bit woozy.'

'OK.' Jago relented. Behind them, the wild pig, its territory once more unoccupied, lumbered by. Jago put his arm around Paul. 'Come on,' he said, 'and for God's sake, don't hum. I don't think those guys down there like you very much.'

Jago supported Paul down the avenue to the verge of the road. He let him down on the turf. 'Now, listen,' he said precisely. 'Where have you left your car?'

'Down there.' Paul pointed. ''Nother ride, closer to the house. Just few yards up.'

'OK. Give me the keys, then get down and stay down, OK?'

Paul was recovering his senses. He very quickly crawled to the ditch and slid down so that he was invisible from the road. Jago stayed on the road this time. When the engines started and the headlights sprayed, he was ready for it. He scampered for the cover of the trees and remained crouched there as first one, then another car snarled by fast. He waited until their sound had become a mere humming, then returned to the road and ran.

He found Paul's car by walking into it. He rowed himself along the boot and the roof to the driver's door. He unlocked it and breathed a deep sigh of relief as the electric light embraced him.

He took the car down to the junction and briefly considered before turning left. He drove as steadily as he could past the big house. The men's cars were gone. He wound down the window and cocked an ear. Holly was still performing. He was astonished by the strength and range of the fiddle's sound. He drove on. His hire-car remained half propped on the kerb.

Jago nodded. That was OK. So far as he could see, Paul was incapable of driving. Holly could bring the other car on to Plsen when she had taken her bows. He would like to retrieve her now, but Paul was weak and cold, and he needed to get him somewhere warm, fast. Holly could cope.

He turned the car in a gateway and returned to retrieve Paul.

'Some of these are very old,' the old man fingered the vellum pages. 'They might be worth something. No, having spoken to you, I think I'll keep them.'

'They're my family's property, not yours!' Havlik snapped, then, 'OK, OK. You've looked after them, sure. Things've been confused these last fifty years, huh? No, sure, sure, but account books? Housekeeping books? You want those? They're of interest to me, yeah. I mean, like, I see, you know, "to the purchase of the Order of the Knights of St Jude, worked in diamonds", that means something to me. It tells me something about my family history. What's it mean to you?'

Rumlova's long dry hands plucked at the fur of the grey cat in his lap. The cobwebbed eyes slid slyly round. 'So they're worth something to you, hmm?'

'Hell,' Havlik scowled, 'I mean, what are we talking? Sure. You want a hundred dollars, that's fine by me.' He pulled a billfold from his back pocket. 'Here. Two thousand – make it three thousand crowns, OK?' He tossed the money down on the desk by the old man's right hand. 'I mean, seeing as you're, like, a member of the family, knew my dad, all that.'

'Oh, yes,' the old man smiled. 'I knew your father, certainly. That fact alone has cost me a great deal, Mr Havlik.' The smile vanished. The man spat. 'I think you owe me a lot more than three thousand crowns, Mr Havlik. No. I think I will keep these old books. They amuse me. Perhaps they will help me to write my memoirs. I think perhaps five hundred thousand crowns might change my mind.'

'Five hundred thousand?' Havlik laughed. 'Come on, man!

Shit, legally dubious if you even own the things, but, I mean, I'm – you're talking like two hundred thousand dollars! You're crazy!'

'So I'm crazy,' the old man shrugged. 'You want the things, I want the money. This is crazy.'

'I haven't even got that sort of bread, man!' Havlik squealed. He repeatedly wiped his fingertips on his jeans. 'Look. Come on. Let's talk sense.'

'I am talking sense, Mr Havlik. It is you who seems to be talking nonsense. I am offering these old papers to you at a price. You may pay that price or walk away. It doesn't worry me.'

Havlik's face collapsed like something punctured. 'You're a filthy, greedy old peasant!' he yapped. He pulled the oak swivel chair roughly round and lowered his face so that it was mere inches from the old man's. He could see the rose-pink crescents beneath those yellowing eyes. 'Those things are mine!' Suddenly he straightened and raised his hands, palms outward. He turned away. He walked towards the sink beneath the window. 'All right, all right. OK,' he sighed. 'Look, I'll send you the money from New York. I haven't got that sort of cash here, OK? Let's say – shit, let's say fifty thousand dollars. I'll sign something. I mean, that's one hell of a lot of money. Here, I mean, hell, we're talking like a fortune! I mean, for some old account books? Christ!'

'You are a Havlik.' The old man slowly shook his head. 'Your father's son. Dear God. I wanted to know. Had you been like your uncle, I would have given them to you, but you are only like your father. No, Mr Havlik.' Rumlova swivelled around again and examined the papers with increased interest.

He did not see Havlik picking up the dishcloth and doubling it over in his palm.

'If these old papers are worth fifty thousand dollars to you, I would like to know why, and I do not believe your tale nor trust your signature.'

He did not see Havlik plucking the triangular shard of glass from the wooden draining-board, balancing it against the cloth, swivelling it until his grip was sure.

'I know your family. No. I think I will take these up to Prague, to the university, find out just what is so special about them.' His voice wavered and cracked.

He did not see Havlik as he padded towards him, his left hand opening and shutting again and again.

'Then, if I learn that they are, as you say, merely household records, I will write to you and we will make a deal. Perhaps I will go to America. I have never left Czechoslovakia. I have never been able to take a holiday . . .'

His chair was turning. Perhaps he had some intimation that Havlik was behind him. Perhaps the almost unthinkable thought of violence for the sake of account books wriggled into his mind. Perhaps he was turning only to stress a point, to afford Havlik a smile . . .

Havlik rushed at him.

His left hand grasped the man's few remaining hairs and pulled the head hard to one side so that the left cheek rested on the shoulder and the right-hand side of the scrawny neck was taut and exposed.

The old man's right hand rose, too slowly. Dry fingers flapped and fluttered at Havlik's hand, but already the glass had punctured the skin at the throat. Havlik forced it in hard with the padded heel of his hand.

Something burst, and the blood came in a fierce, spraying jet, a flourished cloak of scarlet. The cat squawked and struck, then leaped from the man's lap and ran.

Havlik moved round to the man's left side. The blood pattered on the sink. It toppled the empty milk bottle on the draining-board. It slammed the birthday cards on the chest of drawers hard against the limewashed walls. It spurted upwards too, stippling the ceiling.

A small jet squirted forward in a neat parabola, but Havlik yelped, 'No! No! Don't bleed on those! No! Don't you dare!' and swivelled the chair an inch or two so that the blood squirted harmlessly onto the concrete floor.

Havlik raised his hand and hammered the shard deeper into the flesh. The man in his embrace wriggled and made a strange noise not unlike a bathplug, but did not scream. Havlik held on tight. He waited.

Suddenly the old man's body jerked as though a vast electric shock had passed through him. It was a movement so much more violent than he could voluntarily have made that Havlik leaped back and almost let him go. The body jerked again and again, and, on each occasion, the arms flapped as though the old man were attempting to fly.

There was a hand-pump rhythm now to the flow of the blood. It spurted and stopped, spurted and stopped, and each spurt had less force than the last, until, finally, it dribbled merely, and the twisted body lolled against Havlik's left arm. The eyes stared upwards. The lower jaw sagged onto the chest, revealing jagged brown teeth crammed with amalgam.

Havlik let the body go. The head hit the concrete with a rap like that of a horse's hoof on tarmac. The rest of the body clattered and subsided with a soft hiss. A deep, staccato creaking sound emerged from the throat.

Havlik looked down at the drenched right sleeve of his jerkin, the hand coated with a slick of oily red. He stared with astonishment at the extent of the warmth and the stain. It was everywhere.

Havlik looked down at the old man's body. He said, 'Christ, you are disgusting.' He wanted to kick the corpse, but restrained himself.

He kept his right arm extended as he picked his way from the room, climbed the narrow stairs and found the bathroom. The water that came from the tap was brown. He ran it over his hand and sleeve for over five minutes. It then took him eight basinfuls of water before at last the water remained its original colour.

He looked at the cat-scratches on his wrist and on the back of his hand. He whispered, 'Shit! Fucking evil creature!' He used an old towel to wipe all traces of his fingerprints from the basin and its surround.

He lifted each foot and carefully checked his trainers. They were clean.

He went back down the stairs. He said 'whoops' as he sidestepped the blood on the floor, which already smelled of steel. He was twitching again, bobbing on the balls of his feet. He slid along the wall to the desk. As he passed the body, he did a grotesque imitation of the old man's dying jerks. He giggled.

Using the damp towel, he made sure that no fingerprints lingered on any of the surfaces. Then he gathered together the papers and the books, clutched them to his chest, and sidestepped once again to the door.

Outside, the wind was playing ghosts. Havlik closed the door. He moved quickly to the car outside the gate. He placed the books onto the passenger seat. He swung the door shut and returned to the little garden. He selected a heavy stone from the soil. He flung it hard at the window of the room where the dead man lay. The blithe glass burst into tears.

Paul stirred in the passenger seat. He said, 'God. Bloody hell. Lucky I don't use my head too much. It's singing. There's a musical saw in there.'

'Yup. You've got some pretty bumps, and serve you right,' Jago said cheerfully. 'No pedal steel, then?'

'Oh, Jerry Garcia's doing his worst and all.'

Jago flicked him a look, then realized. Of course. When Paul was a lad about town, Jerry Garcia was almost as big a name as now. The men had grown old. The music remained the newest thing around.

'I'll be pissing blood for weeks too.' Paul spoke with the assurance of one accustomed to injury. 'Lord, should have stuck to taxi-driving. Too old for this stuff.'

'So am I,' said Jago firmly, 'and I'm half your age. So is the world, come to that. Not half your age. Too old, I mean.'

'God. You sound like my esteemed wife.'

'So she was a bright girl.' Jago was merciless. He flicked up the indicator and swerved left to overtake a crawling van. 'So, are you all right, then?'

'Oh, I'll live. What are you doing down here? Where are we? What was that music last night?'

'Somewhere between Susice and Plsen is where we are. The music came from the violin of a nice girl I met on the plane who is still down there, playing her heart out to give you and me covering sound. As for what I am doing here, you ought to be thanking God that I came. You were engaged in dialogue with a wild boar when I found you. You left me a letter, remember?'

'Oh, yes. I remember.' Paul lifted his head from his hands. 'But I put . . .'

'You put "not to be opened unless I'm dead" or something. You really expected me to pay any attention?'

'Well, yes, actually.' Paul may not have pouted, but he sounded as if he had. 'I mean, gosh, if you can't trust a pal . . .'

'Sod off, Paul,' Jago said smoothly. 'Have you the least idea what you dragged us into tonight? Men with guns, hidden "treasure", so called . . .'

'There was!' Paul protested. 'Well, there was something in there, I can tell you. Sort of box or something. I felt it.' He gave a huge yawn.

'I don't suppose it ever crossed your mind that it could have been drugs, forged money, hot money in the box. Oh, no. It had to be a king's ransom in baubles. What did he tell you? Charlemagne's crown or something? That's been found, actually, I saw it today – yesterday. God!'

'No. He told me, there's a river of emeralds presented to someone by Richelieu, a brooch presented by Maximilian . . . I don't know. I think you're being a little unfair, Jago, old chap.' Paul was rueful. 'I mean, OK, you think I'm an old idiot, but I don't believe in thinking the worst of everyone. I don't see the premium in it. All right, sometimes that means people make fun of me. God, I can cope with that. But if someone from a family I know says, "the family jewels are there, they're mine, can you help?" Well, I don't know. You only live once is what I say. I mean, we had family jewels, and the Pickerings are no princes, and one would have hidden them when the commies came in . . .'

'Sure. I'll buy that,' Jago nodded. 'So what's to stop young Havlik claiming the things legally?'

'He says there's a lot of corruption. The things would just

vanish. Even if they didn't, it would take years of court cases and so on. I mean, it's going to hurt no one if I help him to get the stuff out, is it? I don't know. Everyone's so bloody cautious, so – well, middle-class – these days.'

'Yeah, well, it seems to pay,' said Jago. 'No one has ever shot at me, and until tonight I've never had to have a close-quarters chat with a wild boar. You've taken a beating . . . What did they take you out there for anyhow?'

'Chuck me over the cliff if they got the go-ahead, I suppose.' Paul shrugged. 'I don't know. What I gather, they should have let me dig the stuff up, then nabbed me. Instead, they charge in, don't find anything because I've led them away, and they're left with a problem. What do you do with an Englishman whom you've beaten up? Their boss was steaming.'

'I'll bet he was,' Jago hummed, then, 'their boss? What do you mean, their boss?'

'Chap talked to them and me on the mobile phone. Gave them a right bollocking. Must have been in touch with the other fellers – chaps rooting around in the house. He was waiting to hear whether they'd found anything. If they had, I reckon I'd have been bunged over the edge. Didn't give them a chance to find out. I flung the telephone over first.'

Jago cocked an approving, if amazed eyebrow. 'They can't have been pleased by that.'

'No. No, that's when they laid into me again. Probably silly of me. Probably he'd just have said, "leave him there, forget him," you know?'

'Have you even thought what being left there would have meant if I hadn't been there?' Jago demanded. 'They'd have been kinder to throw you over. You were woozy as hell, you'd probably have died of exposure, and you were just bloody lucky you ran into the only hippy, Dylan-fan boar in the forest. There are bears out there too, mouflon, I don't know about buffaloes, wolves . . . Those were nasty people, Paul. You wandered into something way, way over your head. And mine, come to that.'

'No, sorry. You're right. Thanks a lot, really, old chap,' Paul drawled through swollen lips. 'But what I want to know is, who were these people? I mean, apparently they'd bugged us last night at the knocking-shop . . .'

'Knocking-shop?'

'Yes. That's where I met up with this Cyril chappy. Lovely bird was helping him.'

'He says.'

'Oh, Jago, stop it now.' Paul spoke firmly. 'Going round mistrusting everyone. Talk about a wet rag. He's not my type, but he's all right, young Cyril. Anyhow, yes. They'd bugged us there, they'd followed Cyril ever since he arrived, they had the manpower for tonight, the cars, the guns . . . I suppose they *were* official?'

'Sounds like it.' Jago nodded. 'That's what so damnably stupid about the whole lark. You don't know any more than I what sort of semi-official bodies there might be in this country. We don't know how bent the police are, or whether some of the old secret police might now be using their skills and resources for a bit of free enterprise. To be absolutely frank, we know fuck all. All I can tell you is that two men apparently entered our hotel after you had left demanding to know where you'd gone and if you'd left any messages. If it hadn't been for a bloody good receptionist, they'd have had no need to follow you. You gave me a Baedeker: "to find long-buried treasure, take the Susice road, observing the splendid pine forests. Keep an eye open for a bloody great fountain and reach down into the stopcock cavity . . ."'

'All *right*, Jago. All *right*. Do give it a rest, will you? I didn't know there'd be people after me, did I? Didn't know you were the sort of chap'd open letters when I'd said strictly not to, come to that.'

'Oh, stop sulking, Paul.' Jago reached for the boiled sweets and passed the bag to Paul. 'I can't stand it. You see things one way, I see them another. Forget it. We're out of it, thank God. No, but listen. If they bugged you last night, they could have come in a lot earlier, except presumably Havlik didn't say where at the hunting lodge you were meant to start digging or whatever.'

'No. He gave me a map, just in case we were being listened to.'

'Right, so they had to stick with you, come in only once you'd identified the spot. They jumped the gun and you were canny. OK. And this afternoon. Same thing. They waited until you'd left the hotel, then came in to see if you'd left any directions. What I don't understand . . .' Jago chewed the skin by a nail. Eventually he sighed, 'God, none of this makes sense.'

'What?' Paul asked. 'What don't you understand . . .?'

'OK. Listen. They're bugging you, right?'

'Seems so.'

'So they know the name of the house, the town. Why did they need to show themselves at the hotel? They just had to take up position back there at that house, wait a while and go in . . .'

'Which they did.'

'Yup. But someone else found it necessary to come to the hotel in Prague, wanting your destination. Which means . . .'

'Two sets of the buggers,' Paul mumbled with dozy enthusiasm. 'Gosh. Maybe you've got a point, Jago . . .'

'Thanks,' said Jago with a twitch of a grin. A minute later, he saw Paul's head dropping onto his right shoulder, his eyelids perfect peeled almonds in the light from an approaching car. 'Silly old bugger,' he said.

Jago too was very tired. His right eyelid flickered. His reactions were slow. He would get to Plsen.

A city seemed a refuge after tonight.

The road back seemed dull. Not just dull as in: it's dark, there's little traffic, you're tired, and driving is a pain; dull as in: they've left the Madonna tape on replay, you will eat McDonald's forever, oh, and you're chained to a radiator with Terry Waite. Serious dull.

But then, Jago supposed, the last few hours had been a trifle stimulating. This was the adrenaline-drained aftermath.

Return journeys usually seemed shorter. Not tonight. The trip to Plsen appeared endless. Again and again, Jago told himself that the town was just over the crest of this hill. Again and again, the crest of this hill gave him views of further darkness.

He wanted a drink. He wanted company. He wanted to sleep. He wanted to watch snooker. He wanted to polish his car and walk the dog every Sunday morning.

He wanted to go home.

The Continental Hotel at Plsen was a grand Victorian edifice which recalled a thousand railway hotels. It boasted an echoing vestibule, patterned marble floors and high marble pillars. To Jago's astonishment, it also boasted an American owner who afforded him, and even the lolling Paul, a warm welcome despite the hour, poured Jago a stiff Johnny Walker Black Label without being asked and showed both men to a plain, comfortable room. Jago asked him to wake them at seven-thirty. The owner left them then, for which Jago was still more grateful, and returned with a plate of ham sandwiches five minutes later when Jago was stretched out fully dressed on the bed and Paul was already snoring in the adjacent bed. Jago could have hugged his host.

The man left once more with quiet good wishes. Jago undressed quickly and flung his filthy clothes on the floor. He munched the sandwiches and drank the whisky. He walked to the bathroom and splashed his face. He longed to brush his teeth, but all his things were in the car with Holly – oh please God that she was all right. He climbed like an old man between the cold cotton sheets. He switched off the bedside lamp.

Paul continued snoring.

The day which had started so auspiciously had ended in farce.

Jago could not sleep for tiredness. He lay in the darkness for a long time, reviewing the indignities of the evening. In the end, he turned on the television for loneliness.

He worried about Holly. He would wait for her. He would not sleep until he knew that she was safe . . .

The telephone was ringing. Jago hated it. He handled it rudely, like a lover's neck. He dropped it and grasped it again, wishing that it were the throat of Alexander Graham Bell. He sighed something like 'Wheeargh?'

'Sorry, Mr van Zeller,' said the American voice in the receiver. 'It's half seven. Miss Byrne left a message. She's in room 357 and don't disturb her till you have to.'

'Oh, glory,' Jago groaned. 'Thanks.'

He replaced the receiver. He looked across at Paul, who still lay fully-dressed and apparently comatose. He decided that Paul too would prefer additional shuteye and a croissant *en route* to early rising and a full breakfast. He rolled from the bed and went naked to the bathroom. His clothes were dirty, but he had no change of clothes or even a sponge bag. He longed to find out how Holly had fared, but was content, for now, to know that she was safe and here.

The bath was hot and heavenly. He had aches and scratches everywhere, but things were looking up again. He still had the girl and he still had the race. Poverty was the worst fate that confronted him, and poverty was a whole lot preferable to death.

He felt positively optimistic as he ran down the grand, curving staircase and scouted around for the restaurant. He was ravenous.

'Ah, Mr van Zeller, good morning to you.' The voice was dulcet.

Jago turned. He but barely remembered his saviour of the previous night. The hotel's owner was a lean man in his late forties or early fifties. He had an amiably creased face and short greying hair.

Jago extended a hand. 'Good morning. Thanks for last night. I was pretty much out of it. Sorry to have kept you up.'

'No, no. Don't mention it. I'm used to it.' He shook Jago's hand firmly. 'And your friend? He looked – the worst for wear . . .?

'Fast asleep. What time did Miss Byrne get in?'

'I don't know exactly. I went to bed at three-thirty when the casino closed, so it must have been after that. A night porter registered her and took the message. Do you want me to find out?'

'No. No, it doesn't matter. Thanks.'

'This way . . .' He led Jago down a high arched corridor and opened a door on a bright, pale green dining-hall with gilt mouldings.

'Hell,' Jago whistled as he looked around. 'This survived communism?'

'Some of it, yeah.' The man shook his head with an ironic grin. 'It's taken a lot of work. Lot more yet to do. Only got it back three years ago.'

'Your family owned this place before '48, then?'

'Yep.' He led the way to a table by the wall.

'You have a problem establishing your claim?'

He pulled out a chair. Jago sat. 'No. Not really. A hell of a lot of forms to fill in. A hell of a lot of waiting. That was all.' He flapped a damask napkin and laid it in Jago's lap.

'Would that be different with sort of – family possessions, pictures, silver, that sort of thing?' Jago tried to make it sound casual.

'Only, I guess, you know, a picture can have had six, seven different owners in forty-five years. Some of them may have bought it in good faith. Maybe even it was voluntarily sold in the first place by, like, a broke younger son, and now you get guys wanting it back. It'd take a lot more research, I guess. Place like this, everyone knows it belonged to my family. There's not so much argument. There's not a lot of that stuff still around, anyhow. Lot of it in Vienna, lot of it in Moscow, lot of it in the States, come to that. Now, sorry, tea or coffee?'

'Um, tea, please.'

'Sure.' He was looking above Jago's head at another table. 'Cereals and fruit juice are over there, Mr van Zeller. I'll see you later.'

All in all, Jago supposed, what he had just heard in essence confirmed Havlik's claim that the legal retrieval of the jewels would be fenced about with bureaucracy and subject to endless delays and counter-claims. It would also, he guessed, cost a fair amount in legal fees, and Havlik was probably broke. You couldn't smuggle out a hotel, and you couldn't come back to live in a Fabergé egg. Havlik was young and hungry. His frustration was understandable.

Jago walked up to the central table to take his pick of Kellogg's variety packs. He also collected two boiled eggs from one basket, two slices of toast from another, and again he heard English spoken at his back, this time in a deep, coarse, clogged voice, a sound like a vampire's coffin at nightfall. The speaker had a strong Czech accent. 'So, you will forgive me, but you are English, yes?'

Jago half turned. At his left, there stood a man three or four inches shorter than he. The man had a glass of grapefruit juice in one hand, an untipped cigarette in the other. His hair was yellowish white. His eyebrows were the same colour. They spurted out, splayed like old bottle-brushes. His face was soft, buffed wrinkled leather, spattered with asterisks and exclamation marks and brackets. Something about him indicated that he was accustomed to being fit, though now a bulging belly strained his pale blue turtleneck. He had bags like walnuts beneath his eyes, and his eyes were as stained as his fingers. He wore a boxy, belted black leather jacket. He left it hanging open.

Jago said, 'Yes,' in his politest, least inviting tone. Breakfast in grand hotels was one of the last great solitary pleasures.

The deterrent tone did not work. 'You wouldn't mind – I don't like to ask it – but talking me a bit? I used to speak English all right. Now I am – I cannot find words.'

'Rusty,' Jago said.

'Ah, yes, rusty. That's it. Like an old car. Rusty. That's what I need. I have forgot the idiots of English.'

'Idioms,' Jago said with a sigh.

'Idioms! Of course!' The man slapped the leather. He punched Jago's arm. 'There you are. Idioms. Of course. This is why I must talk English peoples when I have chance. Please? You talk me with breakfast?'

'Of course, of course!' Jago smiled, and wished that he had been brought up otherwise. 'A pleasure.'

'You are nice.' The man looked around for an ashtray,

gave up, drained his juice and shoved his cigarette into the glass. It hissed. He now had a hand free. He offered it to Jago. 'Novak. Viktor. I am retreated. Before policeman.'

This country seemed to be packed with policemen and 'before policemen'. 'Retired,' Jago corrected over his shoulder as he headed back to the table.

'What?'

'"I am retired", not "retreated". Sorry. I am Jago van Zeller.'

'Van Zeller? This is a German name?'

'No. Flemish.' Jago revived the dead-swan napkin on his chair. He sat. 'English for some generations now.'

Novak made himself comfortable. 'What you do in Czech Republic?'

'I'm riding in the Velka Pardubicka.'

'No. Is not possible! You ride in Velka Pardubicka? I am myself going to Velka Pardubicka! I am never seen him.'

Jago frowned, suspicious. 'Oh?'

'Yes. Of course, I am not jockey. I just go to see.'

'Ah,' Jago said. He tipped Rice Krispies into his bowl.

'I think it was your friend I helped this morning. Holly, yes? I carry her bags. She is most tired. I come from Susice very late. I arrive same time as she.'

'You came up from Susice?' That did it. 'So what was a former policeman who is headed for the Velka Pardubicka doing in Susice?'

Novak leaned over and took one of Jago's eggs. He grinned as he rolled it on the table. He peeled it with nimbly picking fingers. 'Well, truth to tell, I wasn't going to Pardubice until I met your friend. She said she was going there, and I thought, "Why not?" Get away from the wife and family for a day or two, you know?'

Jago munched cereal. 'I rather suspect,' he said quietly, 'that I am being taken for one of "the idiots of English". And that is my egg.'

Novak opened his mouth to bite on the naked egg. His teeth were ragged as the Dolomites. 'Sorry?' he waffled through egg. 'Whashat?'

'"Truth to tell" is an advanced English idiom,' Jago said

smoothly, 'not commonly taught in the schools, I would imagine. Certainly unlikely to be known by someone who speaks of "the idiots of English". You're a plant, aren't you, Novak?'

His eyes twinkled. They were very blue. 'A plant? Like a carrot, you mean?'

'No, I bloody don't,' Jago growled. 'Did you lose a mobile phone last night by any chance?'

Novak chomped. He frowned. 'Ah, yes. Of course! This is the famous English sense of humour, of course!' He tapped out a cigarette. 'Yes, yes. You ask am I a carrot with a mobile phone, and I say, "No, but I have seen a cucumber with a dictaphone", and everyone laughs, but not a lot, right?'

'No.' Jago was stern. It didn't seem to faze the man much. 'You don't know anything about a princely family called Havlik, I suppose?'

'Havlik? Yes. Yes, I know about them. Fascists. My grandfather worked for the Havliks, matter of fact. Gamekeeper.'

'Surprise, surprise. Well, Mr Novak, I must warn you, you are barking up the wrong tree.'

'Nice idiom, that. Thank you.' His voice was still more gravelly now that he had a cigarette dangling from his lips. He narrowed his eyes against the smoke. 'So, you are friends with fascists like the Havliks, huh?'

'Fascists, communists, what the hell? You call them fascists, but the communists were a damned sight more totalitarian and brutal. Anyhow, I thought all that sort of thing was over?'

'Some things are never over, Mr van Zeller.'

'For some people, Mr Novak. Only for some people. But no. In answer to your question, I am not a friend of the Havliks.'

'Hmm.' Novak held his cigarette between finger and thumb as though protecting it from the wind or from a senior officer's sight. 'So, we are to be companions. I look forward to getting to know this humorous Englishman who has no politics and thinks I am a carrot on the phone.'

'Your English is improving,' Jago told him.

Again Novak's eyes flashed up at Jago, the more sparkling for the dull tan of his skin and teeth. 'That's right. That's what I said, Mr van Zeller. Nothing like talking to a native; gets you back into practice.'

'I'm not sure that we will be such close companions, Mr Novak. The old police do not have a particularly pleasant reputation.'

'Ah, history, history. Fuck it. Written by the winners. It's foolish to condemn in retrospect what everyone thought desirable at the time. It's the fashion, now, isn't it? I've read your pseudo-intellectuals. Shakespeare was a racist and a sexist, is that right? Churchill was a jingoist. Crap. You should know. All right, the Nazis occupied this country, yes? Now, everyone looks back and praises the resistance. Collaborators? Ha! Devils, monsters. But lots of nice, law-abiding people simply wanted peace and quiet. They did not want the unpleasantness which happened when Heydrich was killed. All the nice middle classes, many of your precious aristocracy, collaborated for the very best of reasons. They wanted peace and they cared about their children and the Jews had more money. The resistance were mostly criminals, and the sort of young aristocrats who today take drugs or drive cars too fast. They happened to be on the winning side, that's all.

'Me, then, I find myself one of the villains, and all I have been, as far as I can see, is a devoted public servant. Meanwhile you, who ride races, your fascist friends who frequent whorehouses, the mafia, who run those whorehouses, are on the winning side. Lucky you.'

'Your English is very good.' Jago tried to sound bored. 'You plead your cause very fluently.'

'Me?' he snorted. 'Plead my cause? Go to hell, Mr van Zeller. I have no cause to plead. Communism, capitalism, fascism, all that idealistic bullshit – I just do my job and look after the things I like and kick the things I don't.' He shrugged. He sneered. 'No. We will be close companions, I think, Mr van Zeller. I like you. I like your friend, Holly. I look forward to seeing this grand, mad, aristocratic race.'

'And if I don't want you close?'

'One of the nice things about this democracy lark, Mr van Zeller. We are all free to do as we will, isn't that right?'

Jago sighed. 'Have an egg,' he said. He lobbed the remaining egg. Novak snatched it from the air, one-handed. Jago pushed back his chair. He stood and tried to tower over the man. 'Would you mind telling me whom you represent, Mr Novak?'

'Me?' He looked up, and Jago could see the oily crimson moon-slivers beneath his eyes. Novak smiled, a jerky, sudden smile. The eyes narrowed. The crimson vanished. The wrinkles became welts. 'Me? I told you. My grandfather used to be the Havliks' gamekeeper. Old habits die hard, Mr van Zeller. I am a solitary, and I don't like poachers. That's all. And I have infinite patience. Wait and watch. That's me.'

He looked down, and slowly rolled the egg, from his fingertips to the heel of his hand, on the embossed tablecloth. It crunched. He looked up again. 'I'll see you before I leave, I hope?'

'No doubt,' Jago snapped. 'God, this is the only country I've known where people infest you like fleas.'

Novak grinned. 'Don't blame the country for your personal problems, Mr van Zeller. Blame the company you keep.'

And, thought Jago grudgingly as he wove a way through the empty tables, he might be right at that.

Jago called Paul from the lobby. He said, 'Good morning, Paul. Jago.'

'Oh, right. Gosh. Is that the time?'

'Yup. I decided to let you sleep on. You looked bushed.'

'I was. Thanks.'

'We've got to be at the course by two. We'll have to get going soon. We'll grab something to eat on the way. Are you properly awake?'

'Oh, yes. Rather. Be down in fifteen minutes.'

Jago decided to be more merciful to Holly. He took the lift to her floor and tapped lightly at the door. He called, 'Holly? Holly, it's me. Hi. Holly? Holly?'

There was a flap of bedclothes, then padding footfalls. The latch clicked and the door swung inwards. Jago pushed it and peered in. The room was dark and empty. The bed was spread and strewn, like a cornfield after a storm.

'Hello?' Jago called softly as he stepped in, but Plsen's traffic hushed from far below. 'Hi? Holly?' He pushed the door shut behind him.

'Morning,' Holly croaked, only it came out, 'Merny'. To open her mouth was too much effort. To open her eyes was still tougher, it seemed. She stood rocking in the doorway at Jago's right. She wore a man's collarless shirt. Her eyes were sealed, her hair spiky as a splash. She looked glorious.

'Sorry,' she drooled, 'need pee.'

She turned back to the loo, leaving the door open wide. She placed her head in her hands, her elbows on her thighs. The hissing and tinkling started before Jago could move out of view.

The immodesty seemed, to a bachelor, strange, though, on reflection, Jago could not think why. He was in danger of thinking himself peculiarly privileged, then he reminded himself that Holly had lived long with a man. Such carelessness was the product of habit and a cloudy mind. Jago walked over to the window and gazed at the apricot curtains.

The loo-roll rattled. 'God,' she said. 'Call this a holiday?'

'I'm sorry.' Jago faintly smiled. 'That bloody Paul.'

'Paul? Paul – oh, you got him out OK?' The loo flushed. She was in the room now.

'Yup,' Jago said. 'Not without difficulties. You OK?'

She reeled into the room, toppled and sprawled, face down, on the bed.

Jago turned. Whatever modesty meant, that shirt did not serve to preserve it. Holly had her back to him, her knees raised. Her bum was smooth and white as abalone in a single shaft of light from a gap in the curtains. 'Oh, God,' she groaned in a flute's deepest voice, 'I'm fine. Dead, but otherwise fine.' She nestled into the pillow.

Jago strolled across and sat beside her. He caressed the

nape of her neck between his forefinger and his thumb. 'We'll have to be going soon. Tell me, what happened?'

'Happened, when? What happened when?' she mumbled into the pillow.

'When I left you fiddling at the castle,' he prompted.

'Fiddling? Oh, yes, played every tune I knew. Every time I tried to put fiddle away, no, no, encore. Shit. Then the garden, God, it was cold. Cold.' She shuddered.

Jago leaned down and kissed the nape of her neck. He said. 'Poor you. OK, I'll wait to hear the story in full when you feel more up to it. At least we got the idiot Paul out. It got quite hairy in there.'

But Holly didn't seem too interested. 'Mmm.' She raised her hair to give him better access. She said, 'Bite it.'

He did as he was bidden. 'Mmm, yes,' she moaned. She pushed her rump back against him. 'Harder.'

He bit harder. She shuddered. He nibbled her ear, and she reached back her right hand to hold his crown. He was lying behind her now, and his hand roamed along those flanks, stroked her naked buttocks and the backs of her thighs.

'He's here,' she croaked, then 'mmm' again.

'Who?' he murmured.

'Oh, yes. That's nice.' Her hips were shifting rhythmically. 'Do that again. The guy, old guy, helped me.'

'I know,' he growled, and his hands crossed to caress her breasts. 'I met the bugger.'

'I thought he was quite nice.' She was lying languorously back on him now, the shirt raised high. He reached down, and his fingers found the crisp pelt, the heat and moisture beneath. They dipped and stroked, dipped and stroked. She gasped. Her lips met his. Her voice was small as she said, 'Jago?'

'Hmm?'

'What are we doing?'

'I know several words. None of them does it justice.'

'We're making love.'

'That's one of them.'

'We're not meant to be.' She kissed him again.

'Who says?'

'I do. I don't want to.'

'Oh, yes you do.'

'Yes, I do but I don't. Oh, that's so good. No, we mustn't. We've got to go, haven't we?'

'Yes, sod it.'

'Shall we just stay all frustrated like this all day? It's fun.'

'It's hell,' Jago whispered.

'I know, but it's fun. Come on.' Suddenly she spoke aloud. She wriggled from his arms and rolled from the bed. 'Chop chop. Busy busy. Lots to do. God, my legs have gone. What have you done to me?'

Jago lay back and groaned.

'Where's Paul?' She tore at the zip of her grip. Unspecified cotton things burst from it and flounced to the floor. She cursed. Jago slid from the bed. He bent to retrieve things.

'He's getting ready. I called him. He'll meet us down there.'

She said, 'God almighty, it's cold,' though that was fatigue talking. She flung a cream body and a pair of sueded denim leggings on the bed.

The body was easy enough. She didn't bother to fasten the poppers at the crotch, and Jago wasn't offering. The problem came with the leggings. She swayed and blinked down at them, and three times she raised her right foot as though pawing the ground. Jago took them from her. He rolled them back. He knelt at her feet. She put her hands on his shoulders and he eased her feet, one by one, into the soft fabric. He rolled them slowly and carefully up her legs. Temptation proved too much. He leaned forward and nuzzled in there. She held his head for a second, said 'Oh, oh, God,' and shuddered. Then, 'No, Jago. We're going.'

He nodded and gulped, finished pouring the fabric up her thighs. He wrapped her coat around her shoulders, zipped up her grip, plucked up the car keys from the bedside-table and took the fiddle-case and a carrier-bag in the same hand.

He was holding her close, for warmth and for support, as they came down the stairs. Novak was sitting in an armchair in the lobby. Paul was leaning on the reception desk, attending to his bill. He waved. Novak was reading a newspaper. He looked up as they neared him. Holly said 'Oh, hello!'

Jago scowled at him. He said, 'Go away. She's tired. She needs sleep.'

He led Holly out to the car and ensconced her in the passenger seat. He reflected that Novak had had as little sleep as she, but then he was no doubt used to ramshackle living and irregular hours. Jago leaned over Holly to fasten her seatbelt. He briskly kissed her lips because, like Everest, they were there, and because she smelled good. She kissed him sleepily back. He told her softly, 'I'm just going to change and pay the bill. You sleep, OK?'

She said nothing. She made a noise like the distant sea. Jago locked her door and placed the carrier and fiddle in the back seat, the grip in the boot. He took out his own case and carried it back to the hotel.

'So.' Viktor Novak got to his feet. He clumsily folded his newspaper. 'We're off, are we?'

'Oh, go away, Novak, or whatever your name is,' Jago said wearily. He walked over to Paul at the reception desk. He nodded to the girl there. 'My bill, please.' He mimed writing. The girl smiled. 'So, feeling fit?' he asked Paul.

'"Fartin' and fightin, my dear", as my old dad used to say. Don't look too hot. Still, not entering any beauty competitions.'

It was true. Paul boasted a black eye, a swollen purple lip and a large red lump above his right ear. 'Yes, some nasty injuries.' Novak spoke at Jago's shoulder. 'You will be the famous Mr Pickering . . .' He reached past Jago, offering his hand.

'Er, yes . . .' Paul looked curiously up at Jago then down to the hand. He took it. 'Um, sorry . . .?

'Oh, this is a funny fellow who seems to be following us,' Jago told him. 'His name is Viktor Novak and he says he's a former policeman. He seems to be interested in the Havliks.'

'Oh. Oh, I see.'

'Listen, Mr Novak. Save yourself some time and effort,' Jago advised. 'The facts are these. Prince Havlik suggested that Paul might like to have a scout around the old house.

He suggested that there was some family treasure stashed somewhere . . .'

'Under the big hall,' put in Paul.

'But there was nothing there. Holly and I came down with Paul to have a look at Bohemia. We told him it wasn't such a good idea, nosing around private property, but he reckoned it was worth a try. Well, he paid for it. Some people found him there and gave him a clobbering. End of story. No treasure. Hardly surprising. Probably found years ago. So. There's not much point in following us, is there?'

'Oh, I'm not following you, Mr van Zeller.' Novak blew smoke above Jago's head. 'If I were following you, you'd know nothing about it. No. I'm – accompanying – is that the word – yes, accompanying you. Maybe I learn something, maybe I don't. Certainly, I think, I will learn about steeplechases, and the British sense of humour, and the idioms of English. And maybe you think of doing something else stupid, and I can help you. This is what is so good about being retired in a democracy. We can go where we want when we want.'

Jago tried tough, but it didn't come easy. 'And we can punch you on the nose when we want.'

'You can try,' corrected Novak happily.

Jago nodded ruefully and turned away to study his bill. Tough obviously wasn't in his line. People just didn't say things like that to Clint Eastwood.

Novak trilled. He scowled and reached for the telephone in his breast pocket. He growled into the instrument. Jago gave the receptionist a credit card. He turned to Paul. 'Don't let this guy disturb Holly,' he ordered. 'She needs her sleep. I'm nipping into that loo for a quick change of clothes. I reek. Be back in a minute.'

He was walking past Novak, but suddenly stopped. The Czech was gazing down at the telephone in his hand. He was suddenly very pale. His eyes were dull and dead. His jaw had dropped. 'You all right?' Jago asked casually.

'Emil Filip . . .' Novak spoke huskily. He looked up at Jago. He shook himself. 'No . . . Yes, fine, fine. No, just an old friend is dead, that's all. Shit. I have to go.' He glanced down at his watch. 'You will be at Pardubice this afternoon, gentlemen?'

'You're leaving us?' Jago's sarcasm was ponderous. 'We will be desolate. Yes, Mr Novak, we will be there this afternoon. We have come a long way to ride in this race. Despite you, we will be there.'

Novak glanced from one man to the other. He nodded. He said, 'Christ!' and hit the leather at his hip. His eyes were now red and angry. 'Right . . .' he muttered. He made for the door.

Jago changed his filthy shirt and jeans and brushed his teeth as quickly as he could. He shoved his old clothes into his case any old how. He did not shave. He did not trust Novak, and he did not like to let Paul out of his sight.

That was the problem with Paul. He was so damned trustworthy, you could not trust him an inch.

Holly slept for the first hour of the journey. At a sharp corner, she rocked to her left and her head rested against Jago's shoulder. It remained there as they passed Prague and headed across the plain towards Pardubice.

Holly stirred. Her head fell from his shoulder. She said, 'Ma-ba-oh, God, I was . . . Hi. Where are we?'

'About fifteen kilometres past Prague.'

'You've got the fiddle?'

'Of course.' He cocked his head. 'Back there.'

She swivelled and climbed to check. She sighed. 'And the grip and the carrier?'

'Yes. Everything.'

'God, was it a week ago you woke me up?'

'Yup, and at least month ago since you were giving an impromptu cabaret to a shit-scared farmer.'

She grinned. Her eyes swivelled up to look at him, though her head remained turned downwards. 'Hey, you were doing decidedly rude things to me this morning.'

'Sorry.'

'Taking advantage of a poor girl.'

'Bollocks. Just don't pretend it never happened.'

'Do lots of girls do that, then?'

'It has been known. They blame it on the drink or something. That way they remain eternal virgins and still get laid.'

'Sixteen-year-old stuff.'

'Yup. Right, come on. Tell me. What happened last night?'

'What happened to *you*?'

'Me, well,' Jago mused, 'to tell you the truth, I'm not quite sure. I skulked around the house while you supplied the backing track, and didn't see Paul until it was too late. The cars arrived, and there were all these men shouting and firing guns. Paul got caught, and the less heroic Brer Fox, he jes' lay low. They gave Paul a bit of a pummelling, trying to find out where this precious treasure was, then they drove him off up into the woods. They went off with him, came back without him. I was bloody scared then. I really thought Paul was a goner. I went up there. Didn't take the car. Didn't want to leave you stranded. There was this bloody cliff. I was convinced they'd chucked Paul off it. I was wandering back when I stumbled over him. He was only a few yards away from a bloody great wild pig.'

'God,' she shuddered. 'What were they doing with him up there?'

'Scaring the hell out of him. Interrogating him. Some guy on a mobile phone. Paul says he was furious. These guys had blown it by storming in too soon. All they'd had to do was wait, catch Paul as he came out, catch him at Plsen even, Pardubice, wherever. Paul threw the phone over the cliff.'

'He didn't.'

'Yup. So they kicked him a bit more. I suppose murder was a bit beyond their brief, certainly without authority from on high, so they just dumped him, which came to pretty much the same thing but the post-mortem would have said natural causes. So we can be glad we came down, anyhow.'

'Oh, I am,' Holly gloated, 'I am.'

Jago cast an amused glance at her. 'So. Your version. Oh, and Paul, believe it or not, was bugged by these people up in Prague, so they obviously have resources. I'd lay odds they've searched this car, and you never know, they might even have a listening device in here. Don't incriminate anyone, just in case.'

'OK. Well, so, you dump me, I pull out the fiddle and off we go. And then the good Sadovy bustles out and smiles and claps, and I sort of point to my tummy and say "goulash" and they get the message and bring the poor little waif in, and I give them – well, you heard - a lot of loud fast stuff . . .'

'Paul must have been scared out of his wits up there in the house.'

'House?' She frowned.

Jago winced and pointed urgently at his ears and at the dashboard. She opened her mouth and nodded, 'Ah. Right. So, ten minutes or so in, the cars come racing up and screech to a halt. God, you should have seen the Sadovys.' Her eyes sparkled. 'I suppose, Nazis, secret police, everything this country's been through, it's like a reflex. They hear authority arriving. They look at me. They must have put two and two together. Anyhow, they bustle me upstairs and under the bed. I heard the guns and I almost screamed, but I ran to the window and peered through the crack and I saw Paul being arrested or whatever, but you weren't there, so I went back into my hiding-place. Some guy did knock at the door about half an hour later, but I reckon Sadovy just did the innocent bit. So anyhow, the cars are gone, I am everyone's favourite renegade daughter. I had to play and play, and I didn't like to argue. I wanted to leave them laughing, not calling the police or whatever.'

'So what time did you eventually manage to escape?'

'About two-thirty. I played a lot of adagio pieces and suggested a lot of drinks to send them to sleep. You see, I couldn't think of a way to leave. I mean, I couldn't tell them I had a car parked up the road, could I? I was meant to be a waif and stray. They showed me to a bed eventually. God, it was tempting, but I waited till everyone was quiet – in fact, until I could hear the old folks' drunken snores – then snuck out.'

'And along the way, you met Viktor Novak.'

'That's right. He was behind me. I missed a signpost or something, found myself in a village in the middle of nowhere. I must have been half asleep. He pulled up. I thought he was a gift from the gods, an English speaker headed my way.'

'Yeah. He was headed your way because he was following you.'

She turned to stare at Jago. 'Are you sure?'

'I'm sure. He's as good as admitted it.'

'You think he's one of them?'

'I don't know,' Jago pondered. 'Actually, no. I think the people who took Paul knew where he was because they'd bugged him. I don't think Novak had that knowledge. I think perhaps he was one of the men who turned up at the Hotel President. He may even have followed us down to Susice. I mean, he knew about you and me. The other guys didn't, or they'd have given us the third degree like Paul . . .' His frown cleared. 'Ah, well. It's someone else's problem. We're well out of it, I reckon. Silly business. I'm sorry to have involved you, love. So much for your relaxed cultural holiday.'

Her hand squeezed his thigh. 'Don't worry about it. It was fun. Well, sort of.'

'It was an adventure,' Jago admitted. 'But from now on, we stick to nice safe steeplechasing and opera, OK?'

'OK . . .' She was hesitant. A little smile twitched the corners of her lips.

'What is it?' He half laughed.

'Oh, nothing,' she sang. 'I just think – I reckon you owe Paul an apology, that's all.'

He stared at her. 'Me? Why, for God's sake? We've just wasted a whole day and night saving his skin, haven't we?'

'Jago! Look out!' she yelped.

Jago jumped. He spun the wheel. A yellow car wailed by just inches away.

Holly was beaming. She was aglow with pride and pleasure. She swivelled round and scrabbled around on the back seat. Her blue-gloved rump was neat and pretty. Jago tried hard to keep his eyes on the road.

'No,' she was saying, 'it's just you're an untrusting old cynic, that's all.'

She giggled. Then swivelled back into the seat. She dropped something which rattled in his lap.

He looked down. The breath caught like hydrochloride at the back of his throat. He squeaked. A sinuous snake of green light crawled across his crotch. Each cabochon stone – a lake suspended in air and fringed with sedge-light from the diamonds – was the size of a man's thumbprint.

It was a river of emeralds greater than he had ever seen in a lifetime of ogling Bond Street windows. It had to be Richelieu's river.

Holly was wriggling with delight, and she grinned like a little girl beneath the Christmas tree. She raised her open hands, and fire dripped from them like gouts of molten glass; string upon string of stones, including one phenomenal necklace of lavender sapphires and giant diamonds. There was amber in there, rubies, amethysts and more sapphires and emeralds. There were pearls and jet and opals, jade, tourmalines and aquamarines.

'Ba . . . ba . . . ba . . .' Jago gulped and grinned.

'"Black sheep" are the words you're looking for,' she said coolly.

His grin was insane and involuntary, but at the same time, terror made a rock barge into his bowels. He groaned, 'Oh, God.'

It had all started again.

He could not deny the gleeful avarice that possessed him at that moment, yet he rued it. He had been happy without this hunger. Life had been simpler then. He did not want this hoard, but he knew that he would kill sooner than let it go.

'I – I . . .' He swallowed yet again. 'I need a pee,' he said at last. 'You could probably do to stretch your legs.'

He turned the wheel sharply and brought the car to a screeching halt in a gateway.

'Yes,' she said, 'I could.'

Lust is never readily conveyed to those who are sated or those who have never known it. Men and women gibber and drool in bed and cringe to hear it recorded or transcribed. If they be old or stupid, they condemn it, because it disgusts them, because it abases their high, mistaken idea as to their species's loftiness. Jago and Holly would always hereafter find it difficult and embarrassing to recall the lust which possessed them in those moments.

A fever was on Jago – a crazy, erotic fever. He was grinning from ear to ear. He seemed to have lost the motor control to get the seatbelt unfastened. He was in a desperate hurry to be out there in the open air, to fill his arms with Holly and then his hands with all that frozen history.

He shoved the emerald river into his pocket and almost fell from the car. He had parked at one end of a long, straight avenue of tall poplars. A steep bank ran down from the roadside to the ploughed fields beneath. He grasped Holly's hand as she came round the back of the car. He pulled her roughly down the bank. They slithered and rolled halfway down, and then, with the Havlik jewels clicking and crunching between them, he clambered on top of her. 'I don't believe it!' he squealed. 'I just don't believe it!'

'There you are,' she grinned wickedly. 'Tinker Bell does exist after all, you old grouch.'

He grasped her hair with one hand, her right buttock with the other. He pulled her head to his, her loins to his. Her tongue lashed and wriggled about his. There were blades of grass in their mouths. Her left leg rose to curl about him. Her hand roved and clutched and stroked with urgency and with total licence. They were panting. Their teeth were fiercely gritted. There was diamantine fire in their eyes and simple greed in their grasp.

Jago kissed her eyebrows and those wide grey eyes. He gnawed at her throat. He sucked her nipples through the cream fabric until there were dark stains about the jutting stalks, then he pulled the neckline down and nibbled at the naked breasts, one by one. He slid down her and kissed and nuzzled at the lycra between her thighs, then, with astonishing strength, she rolled him over and sat astride him, all breathless and flushed and dishevelled.

A deep growl seemed to rise from her belly. She took his

face between her hands and she kissed him ferociously. Her tongue flickered hot as a fuse about his throat and collarbone. She unbuttoned the top buttons of his shirt and sucked hard at each of his paps in turn, releasing each with a little plosive squelch.

'Emeralds!' Her laugh was very deep. She strewed a bracelet across Jago's brow. 'And . . . sapphires!' She laid the great necklace across his throat. 'Mmm, rubies, most definitely rubies!' She coiled a bracelet of rubies and pearls around his left nipple, another of gold and rubies around his right.

She unbuttoned two more buttons. One resisted her, so she simply tore it. 'The Emperor's brooch.' She licked his navel before placing a diamond-ringed gold and black enamel representation of the Hapsburg eagles in the cavity. It was very cold.

'And, for the *pièce de résistance* . . .' she lowered her head to his straining cock and rubbed her nose up the slope in his trousers. She spoke in a voice made low by lust '. . . diamonds. Hard, hard, *diamonds!*' She wrapped two thick bracelets around the wigwam down there, then slowly, gently bit its tip.

Jago lay there panting and laughing. He looked up at her across his absurdly festooned body. Her eyes were evil. They spoke in confidence to his. He could feel the heat and the pulse through the lycra.

It was his turn to growl. He rudely grasped her tits, the left warm and naked, the right damp beneath slick fabric. He rolled her over and again was lost in the vertiginous darkness and the slithery heat of a kiss. His hand found puffiness and dampness through the leggings. Her legs fell apart, then clamped tight when he made to move away.

They were both panting as though they had run a marathon when at last they pulled apart. Her hips were heaving still, rubbing that dampness against the side of his hand. He looked down on her. Sex is the dew on the flower. Holly commonly looked pretty. At the moment, she looked lovely. There were beech leaves and grass-blades in her hair.

'One minute more . . .' Jago panted against her lips. He

nipped her lips with his front teeth. 'One minute more, and we run a serious risk – a risk – of – being – arrested. And not for having illicit jewels. God, woman, I need you so badly.'

'I need you.' She raised her arms and stretched, and still her hips kept working. She smiled. For a bare second, she turned her head to one side so that her cheek rested on the grass. She looked back up at him.

'God, what these things must be worth!' he somehow quietly shrieked. 'You bloody marvel. Even the commission on this . . . How did you do it?'

She shrugged. She pouted up like a nymphing trout to kiss him. 'How do you think? All that fuss and bother and clattering around. When I left, I went hunting. "Fountain" was pretty damned obvious. "Stopcock housing", well, I nearly fell into the thing. Paul had done most of the work. He'd cleared the stopcock cover, lifted the stone. I just reached down. He'd caught it with a hook. I just had to pull a bit. It was in this deep black tin box. This isn't all, you know. There is an amazing egg, and spoons and God knows what. I went back to the Sadovys' kitchen and nicked a couple of carrier bags.'

'But Novak?' Jago shook his head, hoping to induce clarity. 'What about him? Didn't he see these things?'

'Nope. He helped me carry them in. He didn't ask any questions.' She sensed that the madness was over – for the moment, anyway. She snapped the fabric back to cup her left breast. 'When I got to the car, I put one bag in my grip. I padded out this one with knickers and things. He won't have seen them.'

'No points where Novak might have searched your bags?'

'Nope. Honest, Jago. A stranger? Middle of the night? No, I was dopey, but not that . . . I mean, if he'd been really quick, perhaps when I was registering at the hotel he could have had a peek, but nothing more. Anyhow, it's all here.'

She looked sadly at the scattered jewels. She said, 'Oh, hell.'

Jago stood and helped her up. Once again, he had the feeling that they were somehow being set up. Novak had been following Holly because he wanted the Havlik jewels, yet he had not looked in her bags. Of course he had. He was a policeman, retired or otherwise. He would not be deterred by the impropriety of probing amongst Holly's smalls, nor, to judge by his attitude to Jago's boiled egg this morning, was he a profound respecter of feelings or ardent champion of proprietorial rights.

Why, then, had he left Holly with this phenomenal hoard?

As for the other faction, if it was another faction, they had been unaware of Jago's and Holly's existence. They might, for now, swallow Paul's protestations of outraged ignorance and innocence, but, if they had any sort of intelligence system, they would know by now of the other two English people seen asking idiot questions in a Susice bar. They might not know the precise details of the car, but they would be waiting for Jago and Holly at Pardubice. They had not scrupled to use violence last night. They would not scruple to use it again. Somehow, then, the car must be empty of jewels before it arrived at the racecourse.

'Listen,' Jago said. He still had hold of her hands. 'Maybe they haven't got a bug in the car, but we can't risk that. We also can't risk them not having attached some sort of transmitter so that they can monitor our stops. We're going to have to be quick. Did you cover up the hole again?'

'Nope. Just shoved the box back down. God, it was freezing.'

'So they're going to work out what happened. They're all going to be very interested in us by the time we get to Pardubice. So what do we do with – all this?'

'Post it?' Holly suggested.

'Yeah, but where? We can't post it to ourselves or to Havlik or to Clay or to anyone at Pardubice, anyone associated with us. We could try sending it back to London, but customs'll open anything with that much metal in it.'

'Bank, then?'

'We come back to the same problem. First, I don't know if a bank would take a mysterious consignment from foreigners and total strangers, otherwise drug-smugglers would have an easy career. Second, we'd have to use our passports, which would be like firing flares.'

'I could go straight back to Prague on my own, get on the first flight back to London.' Holly was wide-eyed.

'No.' Jago shook his head. He pulled her to him. 'No. We do this together. You might make it, but there are the metal-detectors there, and our friends are not pleasant. If they get hold of you . . . No. We'll get rid of the things if necessary.'

She looked sadly down at the glistening scars and scabs in the grass. She turned up to him. 'Or bury them again?'

'Yes. We might have to. Oh, God. I hope not. Havlik seems to think he can get them out if we can get them to him. That's got to be our best chance. Not much of one, but we can try it. Let's get back to the car, get the stuff together, see how much space they take up.'

She nodded. They felt foolish now, scrabbling about in the grass for the gems, buttoning buttons, zipping up zips, flapping off grass and dirt.

They straightened. Her hands dribbled jewels. Jago's pockets bulged. 'Listen, Holly.' He gave an encouraging grin.

'Yes?'

'Whatever happens, thank you. It's been one hell of a jaunt.'

'Say that in a week or two, OK?' Her mouth was suddenly sullen. Those little kinks had reappeared at its corners.

He knew that there was no point in trying to cheer her, to recover that high, heady freedom. They were back to quotidian business and to separate, complex identities.

'I don't want to let them go, Jago.' She looked desperately down at the gems in and on her arms.

'I know,' he nodded. 'It's terrifying, the power they have.'

She looked up at him. Her eyes were filmed with tears. She looked irritably away. 'Well, then. Is that the lot?'

'Yup. We've got them all.'

'Come on, then.'

'Hang on. Let me just have a quick look . . .' Jago scrambled up the bank. He looked to right and to left for waiting cars. There was only a tractor on the avenue. A scarlet coupe' miaowed by, travelling far too fast for the driver to be on the lookout for suspicious characters. Jago beckoned to Holly. 'We'll have to write everything from now on,' he said as he helped her up the bank, 'just in case.'

'Yeah. OK.'

Back in the car, Jago tipped out the contents of his big duty free bag. He loaded in the contents of his pockets and of the plain white carrier-bag from Holly's grip. First, the necklaces and brooches and bracelets, then, gently, an egg, presumably Fabergé – a delicious confection of rosy rhodochrosite with a belt of diamonds. You flicked it open to find a perfect lining of nacre, a pierced ivory division and a tiny enamelled bird at the centre which chirruped and flapped enamel wings at the push of a catch.

Then came two salts of some extraordinarily thin and lustrous wood, encased in tendrils of filigree gold and resting on stalks of twisting gold. The wood was pimpled with stones. Then two cased watches, one of gold, one of platinum and enamel, one Geneva, one London made, two silver snuff-boxes, one with a huge garnet at its centre, the other adorned with a scene of Fragonard-style lovers on a rustic bench, two card-cases, in tortoiseshell and gold, bearing crests in gold and diamonds, and several crosses, stars and other orders, including a huge emblem of St George and the dragon, still attached to a threadbare red ribbon. There was a complete cased set of diamond studs, each of them one carat at least. There were two shoe buckles, presumably of French paste.

That was all.

All told, the bag was strained, but not to bursting, when the last of the jewels had been dropped in and various pieces of Holly's underwear crammed in on top and down the sides.

'Jesus,' Jago whispered reverentially. 'Some Christmas stocking.'

Holly nodded. Her tearful eyes were fixed on the bag.

Jago ran a finger down her cheek. He said, 'Come on. How many people ever get to touch that sort of boodle?'

She nodded again, and took a long look upwards at the sheer grey sky as she walked round to the offside of the car. 'Oh,' she sniffed, 'Oh. Sorry. I forgot.' She started to unscrew the studs in her ears.

Jago gaped, then laughed. She had walked past Novak this morning with two studs, each of them diamonds of at least two carats, in her earlobes. He had been beside her all morning – damn it, he had licked and nibbled those studs – and he had not noticed that they were instinct with fire. He noticed now.

'No,' he told her. 'No. Leave them. They're yours, no matter what.'

She stopped her twiddling. She looked across at him, questioning.

'Go on.' He winked. 'I'll tell the man. He objects, I'll hit him. They're yours. God knows, you deserve them. If they have to come out of Paul's percentage, so be it. He'd say the same.'

She mustered a smile. She blew an ardent kiss across the car's roof.

'OK?' he asked.

She nodded.

'Let's go.'

They made a lot of small-talk over the next few miles.

Occasionally, Holly passed him a note, written on a sheet of Snoopy writing-paper which she had pulled from somewhere. '*Canal?*' she wrote once.

When he had cause to slow, he scrawled as best he could, using the hub of the steering-wheel as a rest. '*Bottom deep mud? You scuba?*'

She shook her head.

Again she wrote, '*Should be near Pardowhatsisname. We'll need to be close to retrieve it.*'

He wrote, '*How near? Every mile leaves us with fewer options*

She nodded.

They were on a giant plain now. Again there were distant misty mountains and occasional high outcrops on which castles perched, but otherwise they seemed to drift over a terrain of purple soil flat as a lake. There was the occasional town, too – dourer now, less whimsical than in southern Bohemia – and regular spick-and-span farmsteads.

That was the distinctive feature of the landscape. Whilst Jago was accustomed to British and Irish farms in relative states of disrepair, these farms might have passed for small factories on industrial estates. Hedgerows were few. Barns gleamed. Furrows ran as though dug by torpedoes. Animals were rare, or, at least, rarely visible. No rats scampered across the road. No pigs or sheep grazed in the fields. They were in a child's model farmland, marred only by the occasional birdshit splotches of Friesian cattle, the occasional peppering of plovers or doodle of rooks about the treetops.

The signposts told of the approach of Pardubice – 36 km passed, 24 km, 16 km . . . Jago looked about him with ever increasing concern. They had millions of pounds' worth of trinkets back there. Not only did he want the things for themselves; he felt sure that, even if the commission on such a hoard were split three ways, it could represent, amongst other things, the future of Zellers, the livelihoods of his friends, some comforts for Paul, a boost for Holly – a squall, maybe a monsoon, in time of drought. He had to think of something, but he did not know who his enemies were, nor what they said when they spoke. He did not know how customs worked, nor what the laws were in these parts, nor what Havlik's intentions might be. He knew nothing of the technology of pursuit, monitoring or bugging.

He was, quite simply, at sea. Doldrums at the moment, but the glass was rising with every kilometre.

He checked the road in both directions. A lorry was about to overtake. A beet truck approached slowly. That was all. He reached for the scrap of paper in Holly's lap. He turned it over. He clicked his ballpoint. He wrote, '*Row.*'

'*Row???*' she sent back. 'As in boat?' she said out loud.

'No,' retorted Jago crossly, and scribbled, '*Argue.*'

She nodded pensively. Her lips twitched. She made a

Jewish excuse with her hands. She scribbled fast. '*What about?*'

Jago shrugged.

She rose to the occasion. 'Can't you go slower?' she snapped.

'For God's sake, I want to get there. I've been delayed by Novak, by you, by those guys last night, by bloody Havlik above all . . .'

'By me?' she shrilled. 'Oh, that is really rich. Who was it persuaded me to go down there in the first place? I was here for a holiday! You – "Let's go down on a *Boy's Own* adventure. Please, Holly, it won't take long." And I went along with it. And *I* held *you* up?'

'All right. All right.' Jago glared at her. 'I'm sorry. I just want to get there as soon as possible. That's fair enough, isn't it?'

'I want, I want,' she mimicked with astounding ferocity. 'Little boy. Mummy, I want. Oh, fine. Do you ever consider anyone else? I'm feeling sick, but that doesn't matter, of course.'

'Come on, Holly. I left you to sleep this morning, didn't I? I'm doing the driving. The road is as near as damn it empty. Anyhow, if it hadn't been for your antics last night . . .'

'My antics?' she stared. 'Oh, that's great, Jago. That's just great. Who was it that wanted to go off on some fucking little boy's fucking treasure hunt? Paul, that's who. Your *chum* . . .'

'You . . .'

'I what?'

'You encouraged me. You wanted me to do it.'

'Oh, sure. Pass the buck. Jesus, do – can you hear yourself? "I want a treasure - hunt," "I want to get there," "It's not my fault. You encouraged me." You're stuck at ten years old, you know that? Christ! Look out!' She shouted and pointed at nothing, but so convincingly that Jago braked nonetheless. 'Right,' she pulled herself upright, 'that's it. Are you going to slow down or not?'

'Look, woman! There's no need, is there?'

'Right.' She made the Mussolini moue. 'Right, stop the car.'

'What?'

'You heard me. Stop the car.'

'Oh, don't be silly . . .'

'Stop the car stop the car stop the car!' She built up to a shriek: 'Stop the fucking car!'

Jago pulled in at the roadside. 'Oh, for God's sake,' he sighed, 'this is just bloody silly.'

'No, you go on on your own. Please. I don't care.' Holly opened the door. 'You're a self-centred, oh, so macho little shit. I've had you up to here.'

She gathered up the duty-free bag. Jago kept gabbling in order to disguise any telltale clinks. 'Look, don't be ridiculous, Holly. We're in the middle of nowhere in a country you don't even know . . .'

'Fuck off,' she said. She slammed the door.

'Holly!' he shouted, then, 'Oh, for Christ's sakes, what is wrong with bloody women?' He unfastened his seatbelt and pushed open the door. He slammed it so hard that the car rocked. He set off after Holly. She was running back down the road. 'Holly!' he roared. 'Come back here! Don't be ridiculous, OK. OK. I'll drive slower . . .'

He sprinted.

He caught up with her some fifty yards from the car. He laid a hand on her shoulder. Her shoulder ducked out from under. He took a deep breath, and said, slow and deep, 'Thank you, love. All right, so what do we do now?'

'You drive on.' She stared straight ahead. 'Forget me . . .'

'Whoa, there,' he croaked. 'I'm not whatever his name was. Jago, remember? We've got to think fast. Ideas?'

She leaned back against him. She sighed. 'Sorry. Going crazy.' They looked out over the great flat expanse on their side of the road. There was no landmark, no stray tree, to mark a cache. It was useless.

As one, they turned and crossed the road. Again, the territory was featureless save for a wire fence which streaked like a jetstream to the nearest horizon, which was many miles away.

Jago shrugged. 'It'll have to be here. Use one of the fence-posts.'

'We'd be seen, for God's sake.' She spoke irritably, as to an argumentative child. 'Look.' She pointed out through the smoky dust at a white house a good two miles away. Further off, at their left, a tractor pulled a plough, pursued by a Mexican wave of gulls.

She was right. The inhabitants or the driver might see two furtive strangers crouched in a field, and might come over to investigate, or wait till the car had moved on, search the ground, find evidence of digging . . .

'Oh, shit,' he sighed. 'What can we do?'

'We've got to keep them near us, Jago.'

'Sure, but how? Novak will be waiting for us. These other guys'll be waiting for us . . .'

'Where?'

He shrugged. 'Hotel, racecourse . . . They'll know we're coming.'

'OK, so we split. I don't think they've bugged us or anything. It's too – well, it's silly.'

'They bugged Havlik and Paul in Prague.'

'OK. We assume they have, anyway. So I left you here. We keep up the charade. Listen. We drive on. I don't say a word. They think, they're listening, we split up here, right? We get to Pardubice. I mean, it's a town, isn't it?'

Jago nodded.

'Fine. There'll be traffic, noises, trams, whatever. We find the right spot, the right moment, you say, "stupid bastard" or something, like someone's done something really dangerous. Then you sound the horn, open the door to shout some abuse, only you don't. I open my door, you shout abuse, I slam my door. I – I don't know what I do. I go somewhere, find a hiding-place. Maybe I call Cora, see if she can help. She's not materialist and she'd love the chance to do these totalitarian buggers down.'

'You'll not try to get out on your own with the stuff?'

She hesitated. 'No.'

'Holly, I'm serious. I won't go along with this unless I have your word. I don't mind playing the game as far as it goes, but I'll not die for it and I won't have you endangered for it. We get caught, we say, "OK, take the baubles. Sorry, we were trying to help a friend." It can't be a capital offence.'

'God, I hate this.' She was speaking to the air. 'I couldn't bear to let all that go.'

'I know, but we will if necessary. We won't go to war over some bangles which Havlik will eventually get anyhow. Agreed?'

She shook her head fast as though trying to wake up. 'Yes. Yes, of course.'

'So you promise? You'll not try to go it alone?'

'I promise. OK.'

Jago took a deep breath and tried to practise what he was preaching. 'We have to face the fact that the odds are very, very long against our holding onto this little lot. You know that?'

She nodded.

Moments later, a rough plan in place, they climbed back into the car simultaneously. Jago shut his door, then said, 'Bloody seatbelts.' Holly worked the handle on her door and slammed it hard.

He fumed a bit about women in general, about their ingratitude and their stupidity and their lack of backbone. He watched Holly out of the corner of his eye. He brought some sort of smile to her face when he got to the subject of her in particular – 'neurotic little nobody, didn't even put out, God, how could I have been such a fool . . .'

He relapsed into broody silence. She laid a hand on his thigh. He drove on. It was peaceful now, but they were both wondering how it had happened, that fierce frenzy which had exposed them and bonded them as effectively as sex itself, and left them desolate when it was gone.

Neither of them, Jago thought, was dedicatedly materialistic. Both of them had proved it, he by his calm and contentment at loss, she by her calling. They were self-sufficient. They both got by. So why was it so hard in this case to say, 'Easy come, easy go.' They had never expected such a bonanza. Why then should they so fear its loss?

Why? Because they never wanted to lose that carefree, childlike jubilation which had been its gift, that joy which, contrary to the puritans' inane mumblings, was so much headier when the good fortune was unearned.

Oh, there was pleasure enough in wealth acquired by hard work, but the pleasure of a big win on the turn of the wheel was unalloyed by responsibility. You could account for every penny earned, so, as Miss Sniffy would tell you, you *must* account for every penny earned. Each pound had cost you minutes or hours. It was justly yours and demanded to be valued. Money won, however, was mad money. The pools winner had the happy sense that he was the favoured son of the gods and, godlike, could share his good fortune without a whisper of guilt – with, on the contrary, the godlike sense of self-righteousness which comes of making his world conform to his whim.

No wonder pools winners so often blued the lot. For a while, they had nigh limitless power without responsibility, the prerogative of the harlot.

But more than anything, Holly and he had been infected by a passion which was, in the loosest sense, aesthetic. The jewels were beautiful, certainly, but to their inexpert eyes, glass would have served as well as sapphires. No, just as a collector would pay millions for an original but would scorn a perfect reproduction, so these trinkets were principally desirable as relics. Those stones had lain in the earth before any human passion, before any Christ or Caesar, before life or desire. They had been mined, polished and set by skilled hands long stripped of flesh. The finished jewels had been handled by the great, cherished by the gallant, coveted by women in chemises and camisoles, crinolines and farthingales, mantuas, dominos and periwigs. They had even, no doubt, bought such women. They had been the motive for a lot of sex and death.

And perhaps it was the very intimacy of jewels which made them so potent. They had lain on the downy arms or the smooth breasts of beautiful women – and ugly ones – long dead. They had, each one of them, been loved and desired. They were charged with all that erotic intensity, or, perhaps more accurately, Holly and he charged them with it, and they reflected and intensified it, even as the diamonds transmuted light.

They were *premier cru*, château-bottled poison.

Jago knew a little about Pardubice from his reading and from other riders. It was an industrial town of medium size, sprawling, unfocused, as industrial towns are. It possessed the dubious distinction of being the home of Semtex, which was manufactured at a plant in its suburbs. Its principal export was death.

It proved predictable and predictably dreary. There were rows of working men's houses; there were factories; there were grey tower-blocks with balconies caparisoned with laundry. Children kicked balls on the scuffed and welted waste land beneath. The road on which the car entered was a broad boulevard. Trams clanked and clanged above it.

Holly already had the carrier-bag in her lap. She had been right. There was noise and traffic aplenty. The car was nearing traffic lights. They showed green. Jago glanced to right and left. No one was evidently watching. He nodded to Holly. She winked and grinned, assuring. He braked at the junction.

It took about ten seconds before the first horn sounded behind them. Jago muttered, 'Bloody fool. You blind or what?'

Holly did not move. She sat still, smiling and waiting. When three or four horns were blaring in chorus, she nodded and opened the door. Jago bellowed, 'Get out of the bloody way!' The door clunked shut. Holly was off, trotting and weaving to the far pavement.

Jago sighed, and looked up at the lights. They had turned red. The horns continued their protests. A face appeared at his window. It resembled a punctured football. The hair was black, sparse and wiry. The man's scalp looked like Sean Connery's shoulders. He was shouting something. Jago could guess what it was. A lorry driver on the A303 had once told him that the only difference between him and a bucket of shit was the bucket. He assumed that Czech lorry drivers thought along similar lines. He shrugged. He wound down the window. He said, 'Sorry. English.'

The man threw his arms high in the air and rolled his eyes heavenwards, as though that explained everything. He nodded and talked to himself as he strode back to his lorry and climbed into the cab.

Jago drove on. The buildings grew heavier, more Victorian in style. He pulled up outside a bank to shout, 'Velka Pardubicka?' at a woman with a pushchair. She pointed. He waved and drove on.

There was no mistaking the racecourse. There was already a deal of activity in the car park. Dust flew as at a rodeo as horseboxes and cars trundled to and fro over dry turf. He caught a glimpse of the tall Lombardy poplars behind the stands. Everywhere there were pairs of uniformed policemen, some of them with Alsatians. Jago jolted in and out of the tyre ruts and leaned forward to see his way through the rising dust. Two policemen turned towards him. They approached at the trot. One of them tapped on the windscreen as he parked. He saw shiny black belts, brass buttons, and again those stubby black machine-pistols which he had seen last night.

'Hello,' he smiled as he unwound the window, 'do you want me?'

'You come. Papers,' said the absurdly young and glossy face that appeared at his window. Jago reached for his coat. He pulled the envelope containing his passport, accreditation papers and invitations from the inside pocket. He handed it over. The young man handed it in turn to his partner, an emaciated hawk of a man, with cheeks smudged grey by stubble. Jago was directed to pull his car over to the side. Then he opened the door, stepped out and stretched, all very casually.

The hawk perused his documents very carefully, even holding them, one by one, up to the light to squint through them. 'Good,' he said at last. 'You come.'

Jago locked the car. He went. The crowd parted to make way for the men as they crossed the car park. Policemen held barriers open for them. They were at the back of the stand.

Jago's escorts swung to the right. They shepherded him into a shed directly beneath the stand. They were in a narrow corridor in which men smoked and waited for things. There were offices at either end. The policemen led the way into that on the right, where a small woman with short blonde hair and very pink cheeks stood behind a desk piled with papers. She looked flustered. Three or four men in overcoats were gabbling at her simultaneously. She lifted and lowered piles of papers, hunting.

The hawk-like policeman spoke three or four words. The woman pushed the hair at her brow so that it stood upright. She turned to the waiting men and spoke to them briskly. They objected. The hawk snapped something. Their shoulders drooped. The hawk bustled them out. His partner shut the door behind them.

The woman sank into the only chair, puffed out air and slid downwards. She sprawled.

The hawk spoke some forty clipped words, which included 'van Zeller'.

The woman roused herself. She leaned forwards on the desk. She snapped a few sentences back. It sounded like someone playing the penny-whistle on a switchback. The policemen looked affronted. They looked at one another, then long and hard at Jago, before marching out in step.

The smile that the woman turned to him was bleary, uncertain. 'Mr van Zeller.' She held out her hand. 'We have spoked on the telephone. I Pavla.'

'Ah, yes. Thank you so much for organizing everything.'

'Nothing.' She flapped away his gratitude. 'Is your first time to Czech Republic?'

'Yes,' Jago grinned. He borrowed a leaf from the Country-singers' book. 'I love it. It is a beautiful country.'

'You are staying at Hotel Sport, yes?'

'Yes.'

'So are we, the organizers. I will see you this evening. However, first, these polices say is senior officer wants to see you. I tell them senior officer can talk with me. You are honoured guest. Not to be nuisanced. They nuisance you, is become garbage mens.'

'Thank you so much,' Jago said sincerely. He wondered if she could deal with all his nuisances so efficiently. 'Has my friend Paul Pickering been here yet?'

'Pickering . . .' She frowned. 'No, I have not seen. You will wish to walk through the fences, yes?'

'Very much,' Jago said when he had worked out what she meant.

'You have someone to walk with?'

'Yes,' he told her, 'two people who are with me. Mr Clement Levine and Miss Holly Byrne.'

She pushed pen and paper over to him. 'You write, please?'

He wrote the two names. She copied them laboriously onto card badges. She scanned a chart on the wall. 'So. You have ceremony at two o'clock. You are ready to read?'

Jago had forgotten this additional duty which she had asked him to perform in her letter. 'I suppose,' he shrugged.

'So, you walk three o'clock?'

'Fine.'

He spent another few minutes with this heroine of the Revolution, during which she equipped him with two posters, two car-stickers and two impressive little brass and enamel badges.

Jago emerged from the shed to find Novak waiting for him. The sun had emerged. It made Novak look mortally pallid. He was sweating and smoking. 'Ah,' he croaked at Jago. 'Good. Where's the girl?'

'I don't know,' Jago said truthfully. He strode past the smaller man. 'Leave me be, would you, Novak?'

'Nope.' He stayed at Jago's heel, though he had to scurry. A plume of cigarette-smoke waved over his shoulder. 'I think I'll stay close to you all the way, Mr van Zeller. I told you. I am learning all the time. And I like you, despite your politics.'

'I'm flattered,' Jago told him, 'but you're wasting your time, Novak. Why are there so many policemen around, anyhow?'

'Security,' Novak hummed, 'for the race.'

Jago did not want Novak's company at thc moment. He

wanted no one's company at the moment. He was walking through a dark tunnel beneath the stands, and ahead, in an ever expanding square of bright green and bright blue, was the racecourse of which he had dreamed for so long.

He stepped out onto the grass before the stands. He stopped and he smiled. He breathed it all in. A light, cool breeze tugged the hair back off his brow. He scanned the great park. It took him seconds, by reference to the two gleaming water-jumps down at his right, to identify the start. His eye followed the course, over the first, down to that giant strip of water . . .

Then here, slap bang in front of the stands, horses and riders would swing around and gallop to that fence straight ahead.

The Taxis.

It did not look so bad. Not from here. A large fence, no more, no less, and a natural hedge at that. In theory, then, you could plough through the top third without injury.

If only you weren't on top of a precipice.

He did not like the fact that they would jump it with their backs to the stands, almost as if the scene on landing were unsuitable for children or for those of a nervous disposition. An X certificate fence.

His eyes continued to follow the course round, over the dusty plough, over the giant Irish bank and on, round the corner, into the shelter of the wood. Then the runners would become invisible to the crowd. When they re-emerged, out there to Jago's right, it was to tie a tortuous knot with their trail, doubling back again and again. There were no running rails here. According to Jago's cherished video, there were twenty-five points at which they might run or jump into stragglers or fallers.

You never jumped any obstacle twice in this race. Jago prayed with all his heart that he might jump every obstacle just once. Winning was a pipe-dream, best kept to the last few furlongs. He hated only the idea that his race, as so many before, might end at fence number four, because this course was beautiful and fascinating, a three-day-event cross-country course squeezed into a formal garden.

And they would take it racing.

It looked terrifying.

It looked something like heaven.

'I've never sat on a horse.' Novak spoke at his side. 'I suppose it's easy enough.'

Jago glanced at him. Novak's chin was thrust deep down against his roll-neck as though he were about to belch. His rheumy eyes stared at the vista. Jago wondered what they saw. 'Oh, yes,' he said, 'easy enough.'

'All you'd need is balance and familiarity with the horse and a completely irresponsible lack of concern for your welfare or that of your dependants.'

'Yup. That'll do it,' Jago agreed. 'Oh, and passion, of course.'

'Like the passion of the mercenary soldier.'

Jago considered. 'Yes. Very similar, I suppose. Not that we make any money, but yes. I knew a chap once, nice, gentle, sensitive, perceptive. He became a mercenary helicopter pilot. I think – it's something to do with that sensitivity. He was very feminine, I think, very self-critical. He didn't like the warrior in him. He was able to keep control only because he had that release. In battle, in a race, that sort of thing, you're free of all those nasty, petty restraints and responsibilities. It's very hard to give up that sort of freedom. What it feels like – it's the world's biggest joke. You know what a joke is, Novak?'

'We have jokes, Mr van Zeller.'

'I'll bet you do. But what is a joke? You ever ask yourself that?' Jago still studied the course as he spoke. 'I'll tell you. You spend the whole of your life expecting to have to answer sensible, responsible questions sensibly and responsibly. Your schoolteacher says, "What's two and two?" You're meant to say "four", not "apple-sauce", right? But a joke – someone says to you, "Why did the chicken cross the road?" By trained reflex, you consider. You're under pressure to be right, it's a complicated question. But then comes the blessed answer, "because it wanted to get to the other side," and we laugh. Tension has been created, then released. No one expects anything of you after all. That's joke type one.'

'Hysterical.' Novak's lips jerked downwards.

'Joke type two is much the same,' Jago persisted. 'It deals with serious matters, pomp, circumstance, religion, death. Again, we expect to respond in a certain way, but we're let off the hook. The Pope farts or the fat man slips on a banana skin. Same thing. Release.'

'You find these things funny.' Novak made a statement of it, like a psychiatrist taking notes.

'Well, it's like that out there,' Jago said, his enthusiasm just a little muted by Novak's scorn. 'We're brought up looking after ourselves and behaving with decorum and propriety. Suddenly we're free of all such concerns. We kick on. We laugh. Morality, the rest of it, forgotten. We're on our own. No debts, no dependants, no constraints. It's very wonderful.'

'Very aristocratic.' Novak made the word sound foul-tasting. His lighter clicked.

'Oh, damn it, Novak. Go away, will you? You're a killjoy. It's like explaining *Chant d'Aromes* to a billy-goat. I've got things to do.'

As he set off across the lawn, Novak beeped. He reached into his coat pocket. He snapped open his mobile phone. 'Ah,' he said, and his eyes swivelled, gloating, towards Jago. He chewed words from off a sticky block and spat them out. Jago knew what he would tell him. 'It appears Miss Byrne has shown up,' he said. 'She will be searched.'

'I'd be very, very careful, Novak,' Jago told him. 'I don't think you're as powerful as you believe. The British consulate would not like any unpleasantness, you know. The tourist board might object too if visitors to Pardubice are going to be abused by clapped-out old commies.'

'Oh, I am terrified.' Novak's tone was pitying. 'No, I am sure that no abuse will be necessary. Ah . . .' his eyes narrowed as he looked up into the grandstand, 'our noble prince.'

Jago could not contain his curiosity. 'Which one?'

Novak nodded and pointed with his cigarette. Jago took in the slight, fidgety frame, the sandy hair, the bulging eyes. Havlik sat perched on a rail halfway up the stand. One leg, enveloped in pale denim, swung from the knee. He chatted with evident disinterest to a florid young man with crimson cheeks, dark brown sidewhiskers and slicked-back dark brown hair. The stranger had that truculent look of one who called spades spades and was uninterested in explanations or refinements, thank *you.*

Eight or nine other young or youngish men sat or stood slouched up there. They were all awesomely laid-back. These were the riders. Once, such ease had made Jago feel alien and inadequate. Then he had noticed that he was doing the same things as the rest of them – guffawing, for example, clasping his hands about his knee or the back of his neck, crossing his legs or allowing them to fall nonchalantly open – banishing nervousness by feigning ease.

Paul Pickering arrived at the foot of the stands even as Jago did. He was looking up at the younger riders, faintly grinning. He climbed wearily up the stand. He sat on a step, slightly apart from the other riders. He leaned forward as though already racing. His hands were clasped on his knees. Those pale eyes flickered this way and that about the course. That white hair gleamed.

Jago strolled up the steps towards him. Novak remained at heel.

Jago felt, then saw, Havlik's glare. He ignored it. He said, 'Paul. Good. Everything OK?'

Paul looked up. He blinked away the reverie. 'Jago!' he grinned. 'Oh, bloody marvellous. Just look at all this . . .' Those long fingers flickered like shuffled cards. 'Brilliant stuff. Got turned over when I arrived at the stables. Funny little chap sticking like a burr. Where is he? Oh, that's the fellow. Look.' He indicated a tall, thin, stooping man with a studious air and glasses like ice-cubes who stood at the foot of the steps. 'Absurd. Still, it's their time they're wasting. Just arrived, have you?'

'Yup.' Jago turned to watch the course with him. 'Have you arranged to walk the course yet?'

'Nope. Went to the stables first. Didn't know how to go about it. Only problem here, all this security, rules and regulations. God, you'd have thought it was Fort Knox. You need accreditation to go to the lavvy.'

Jago nodded. The only figures that he could see out there were in military khaki or police black. 'What's it all about?'

'I don't know. Habit, I should think. Clay's still on good form. Horses fine.'

'Good, I didn't even have a chance to get down there.' Jago looked at his watch. 'It's only five minutes till this prayers number.'

'Ah, Mr Pickering.' Novak appeared on the step beneath them.

Paul looked down at him. He said, 'Oh, jolly good. You here?' He raised his eyebrows quizzically at Jago. 'Place is full of burrs, eh?'

'Yes, so it seems,' Jago snapped. 'I have picked up Mr Novak rather as one picks up a tick on the moors. He suspects me of something or other. He has appointed himself my guardian.'

'Still got some bloody funny ways over here, haven't they?' Paul said, wondering.

'Paul.' The voice at Jago's shoulder was hard. A staccato trumpet.

Paul looked up. 'Ah, Prince Havlik.' He was affable. Jago too looked up. Looking into Havlik's eyes was like peering at the sea through slashed canvas. 'Jago van Zeller, this is Prince Cyril Havlik.'

Havlik nodded. 'What's this guy doing here?' He indicated Novak.

'Following us, actually,' Paul said amiably. 'Why? Do you know him?'

'I've seen a lot of him,' Havlik scowled. 'He's one of the guys been dogging me. Who is he?'

'A retired policeman, actually,' Jago said. 'His name is Viktor Novak. Apparently the privilege of his company is now to be mine. I cannot think why.'

'Which does not mean, *Mister* Havlik, that you will be unsupervised.' Novak was unembarrassed. He smiled that lopsided smile as though he were sharing a dirty joke with Havlik.

'Look, just who are you guys?' Havlik yelped.

Novak shrugged.

'I rather fancy that this former policeman is now engaged on unofficial business,' Jago droned. 'We met at or near the Zichy place near Susice. Paul and I took your suggestion. Fascinating place. Nothing under the floorboards, I fear. Mr Novak objected to Paul's being there.'

'Nothing under the floorboards,' Novak said slowly. His lips crackled. 'No. But a large manhole in the garden cleared, its cover raised and a box found close by. I wonder how that came about. Subsidence, perhaps?'

Jago was all innocence. 'How would I know?' Out of the corner of his eye, he saw Havlik turn and look at him.

Paul started and stared at Novak for a second. He was suddenly pale. 'Gosh . . . Box? Lord, I don't know . . .' He regained his composure. He shrugged. 'Maybe I was just a decoy. Maybe when I was looking under that big room, someone else was having a go – in the garden, you say? Well, well . . .'

'I know nothing of all this.' Havlik drew himself upright, a shop-soiled aristo, trying to dissociate himself from the others' lowly world, though he, Jago suspected, was more at home with the lowly than, at any rate, Paul or himself.

'But I know much of you, Mr Havlik,' Novak said. 'My grandfather, and my father in his youth, worked for your family. I was denied that privilege.'

'Your English really has improved, Novak.' Jago slowly smiled.

Novak caught his eye. The Czech's eyes glittered. Perhaps he enjoyed a joke after all. He chewed nothing with a slow, churning motion of the jaw and a long, low growl. 'I spent some time in your amusing country, Mr van Zeller.'

'In Notting Hill?' Jago asked, thinking of the Czech Embassy where he'd had to go for his visa, just a quarter of a mile from his new home.

'Not far, not far.' Novak puffed smoke skywards. He spat

tobacco onto the step. He pestled it into a smear with his toe.

'Paul.' Havlik drew close. He was one of those people who have no understanding of the proper body distance. He drew altogether too close. Paul's teeth made to grind. 'Listen, can we talk? Away from all these . . . people?'

He may have been a politically correct New Yorker, but his tone, and that pause, gave away the habits of generations. He disliked . . . 'people'. Paul was elevated above that base category simply by Havlik's whim.

A tannoy farted. A man beneath spoke into a microphone on the lawn. His voice was unamplified. He did not stop speaking, but he looked about, seeking assistance. Someone close by said 'Sh!'

Another amplified raspberry then. The man's voice rattled at the riders' eardrums and rang in the roof of the stand. Every hand rose to cover an ear. The microphone shrieked. A blond man in a white T-shirt scurried, bent as though the scene were on television, to the mike. He fiddled and twiddled a bit, never rising from his crouch. The volume sank. There was a lot of sighing. The man in the T-shirt ducked down and slunk off, below the conjectural line of sight.

The man at the mike clattered away in Czech – a sort of Welsh German, so far as Jago could tell – for three or four minutes. His face was astonishingly rectangular, and white save for the vast blotches of crimson on either side. His black hair had been unsteadily painted on his brow and his temples.

'What's he saying?' Paul murmured to Havlik.

'How the fuck should I know? Listen, can we go somewhere . . .?'

'Not now, obviously, old chap.'

Novak spoke. 'He is inviting you to be honourable. He is reminding you of Captain Rudolf Popler, who won this race in 1926 and 1930 and broke his silly neck here in 1931.'

'Good of him to remind us,' Havlik drawled.

'He is talking a heap of dung,' said Novak in cheery conclusion.

Jago heard the man at the microphone speak his name, or at least, he heard 'Iago Fan Tsellair', then silence. Heads turned towards him. Some of the young men nodded at him and made dumbshow. He got the message. He was meant to do something.

He jumped down the steps. The stout, sweat-soaked man at the microphone held out a sticky, heavy hand. His tight, metallic-blue suit-coat, in some man-made stuff which aped mohair had all three buttons fastened. The collar was turned up. He reached forward, beaming. 'Otto Svoboda,' he said. If you blew gently down a kettle's spout, you'd get a similar sound.

'Hi.' Jago smiled back. There was desultory applause from the watching civilians. A few policemen and soldiers stopped their patrolling and now stood watching with that calculated air of scorn which such men adopt for fear that they might seem impressed.

Mr Svoboda mopped his gleaming brow, then looked down at the paper with which he had mopped it. 'Oh,' he said sorrowfully. He handed the crumpled and damp square of paper to Jago.

Jago took his place at the microphone. He said 'Er . . .' just testing levels. He then read in tones which he gauged to be at once sensitive and manly, clear yet unassertive, '"We dedicate this race to the memory of Captain Rudolf Popler, and declare that we will contest it in a just and sporting manner worthy of that gallant officer."'

Again there was applause like the patter of melting ice-cream on a pavement. He handed back the sweat-streaked scrap of paper. Svoboda shook his hand again. Jago gratefully leaped back up the steps.

'Jolly good.' Paul blinked. 'Super.'

'Ridiculous.' Novak tossed his head. 'Like saying you'll cut someone's throat nicely.'

Svoboda struggled up the steps to shake more hands and to present the jockeys with maps of the course. He introduced Jago to his wife, Zdena Svoboda, whose cheeks were sunken and whose eyes were wild. Fake tan had turned her skin copper. Her hair was brilliant orange. Her smile showed teeth which had plainly been made before the ban on African ivory. 'Try not to fall your horse,' she croaked earnestly, if superfluously. 'The animal rights persons do not like.'

'Nor do I,' Jago told her, but she was already clasping Havlik's hand and, no doubt, giving the same excellent advice.

'Is that it, then?' Jago asked.

'Seems so.' Paul stretched and yawned.

'Tell you what. Why don't you dash down to the shed by the gate and get your accreditation papers? Then you can string along with us. We're walking the course shortly.'

'Really?' He was delighted. 'I say, that's bloody good of you, Jago. Really.'

'Go sort it out. Ask Pavla. She's having a breakdown under all the pressure, but she's nice and she speaks English.'

'Give her a bit of the old Pickering pulling-power, you mean? I know. Right. Is that where you got that natty little badge?' He eyed the glinting horseshoe in Jago's lapel.

'Yup.'

'Don't suppose they'd let me have one, do you?' His Adam's apple bobbed. 'Probably – old crock, bit of a joke, not worth it.'

'Bollocks, man.'

'It's just – well, I mean, Clare – you know, my daughter – would love one. Wouldn't mind one myself, come to that. Bit dead smart.'

'So go and see Pavla!' Jago almost howled. 'She'll shower you with gifts! Badges, posters, pennants, God knows. Just go and ask her!'

'It's just, you know, go back with nothing but a broken neck for a souvenir . . .'

'Go!' Jago pushed him. Paul set off at a sprightly trot. His bespectacled pursuer walked after him, just keeping him in view.

Novak sat on the step at Jago's feet. He too watched Paul go. 'This is part of the great joke, is it?' he croaked. 'Old men falling off horses? Subtle, this humour.'

'Jago . . .' Havlik was again at Jago's shoulder.

'Ah, Mr Havlik.' Novak looked up at the American. 'Of

course. You want to talk to Mr van Zeller about his little escapade last night. Good idea. Let's talk about it. An empty tin box, Mr Havlik. Curious. And Mr Pickering has not got its contents. Mr van Zeller's car has been searched, but there is nothing there. And Mr van Zeller's young friend has been searched, and I'll warrant they'll find nothing on her.' Jago felt Havlik's eyes swivelling round to watch him. Novak nodded and slyly smiled. 'If they have any sense, they'd have buried whatever it was somewhere else. A few months later, they send a friend to dig it up again. What claim would you have then, Mr Havlik?'

Havlik gazed scornfully down at him. 'Don't you get kinda bored with all these little intrigues, man? I mean, wise up. Those days are gone, you know? Time for the pipe and the pushchair.'

Novak spat again. He looked out across the course. 'It's a game I've played all my life, Mr Havlik. No reason for me to give it up now. I can still play as well as any young "amateur", I reckon. And I do like to win. However, you needn't worry. I will try to – what was it? – contest in a just and sporting manner.' He snorted at his own joke. A large gout of smoke burst from him. He coughed – or rather, for there was nothing active about his role, a cough happened to him. It jerked him. It punched him. It doubled him up. It made his eyes water and his hand flap for support. At last he gave a sort of jubilant roar, as though the whole experience had been a pleasure.

'No.' He blinked. 'No. I don't give up, Mr Havlik. Give up and I'd die.'

'Don't give up, same thing could happen,' Havlik snapped. 'OK. See you later, Jago. Good to meet you. I got things to do.' He set off down the steps, shaking excess energy from his fingertips.

'Not a very gracious exemplar of our precious aristocracy,' said Novak with raised eyebrows.

'Maybe not. But in the new regime, rights aren't only afforded to the gracious. Tell me something, Novak.'

'Hmm?'

'What's the purpose of all this? Normally, if you want to

watch someone, you stalk, you stay in the background, play the cat. That way, the subject is careless, he does what you hope he'll do. You, your approach is that of the bull-terrier. Bite and hold. You think any of us is going to do anything stupid with you right here?'

'Ah, Mr van Zeller, as the greatest Englishman who never was would say, "I have my methods." Now. Look. Isn't that Miss Byrne?' He pointed.

Jago was already waving and walking down the stand. Holly ambled across the lawn down to the left. Clay walked backwards in front of her, arms held wide. He bumped into some white railings, stood back with a flourish to allow her to pass through.

She looked irritated but not, Jago was glad to see, disconsolate. The sparkle had gone from her earlobes.

Clay saw Jago first. He called, 'Hey, J! Good to see you, mate!'

Holly looked up. She gave Jago a resigned little smile, then came into his arms as though they had been doing it for years. Jago took Clay's hand as he hugged her. 'All well?' he whispered.

She nodded. 'Fine.'

'Clay. Gather all's well with Burly?'

'Ace. Could not be better.'

'And how's the casino?'

'Yeah, well, last night wasn't the best ever, I'll grant . . .'

'You lost.'

'Yeah, yeah, but, you know, tonight, tomorrow . . .' Holly leaned back against Jago. They watched like parents as Clay expostulated and shuffled. 'Anyway, stuff that. Nice, this girl. Damn sight more oomph than most of your flash floozies, I'll tell you that. Listen, doll. This guy, grey little man, right? Nine to fiver. Sure. Leave him a couple of days in Czechoslovakia, he comes back with a bit of cuff like you, begging your pardon, ma'am, and policemen buzzing around. So what you been up to this time, then, J?'

'Me? Nothing.' Jago grinned. 'Listen, we're about to walk the course. Here's your accreditation, Clay, and yours, love.'

Novak stepped forward. 'Where did you get those?'

'Mind your own damn business,' Jago said cheerfully.

'Who's this, then?'

'Viktor Novak, our pet pain in the arse. A sort of policeman. He's the one who's been causing all the trouble.'

'Oh, yeah?' Clay swaggered towards Novak. They were of the same height, much the same age and build. Clay was broader in the shoulders and deeper in the girth. He was less fit than the Czech. His hair was grey in comparison to Novak's discoloured white, his eyebrows black and straight, where Novak's were white and arched. 'What's with you, Vic, boy?' Clay poked Novak's chest with his finger. '"Sort of policeman" sounds pretty darned iffy to me. You give the orders for Miss Byrne here to be searched, did you? More like a bleeding assault from what she says . . .'

'Is that true, Holly?

'Oh, all above board,' she shuddered slightly. 'Woman, you know. Bull dyke with a moustache. Looked like Leo McKern in drag.'

'Right, Vic, son. So Miss Byrne is going to be having a little word with the British Embassy, isn't she? Then we'll see what sort of power you got to chuck around.'

Novak looked past Clay's shoulder at Holly. 'I do not think so,' he said softly.

'Yeah? Whassat supposed to mean, then?'

'I just don't think that Miss Byrne will be lodging a complaint, that's all.' Novak shrugged. He smiled that smug one-sided smile. His voice was suddenly harsh. 'It's no use playing the innocent little tourist with me, Miss Byrne.'

Holly flushed. She said, 'I don't know what you're talking about.'

It seemed that everyone ended up saying that to Novak.

'Don't you, Miss Byrne.' Again, Novak spoke a syntactical question like a grave fact. 'I know your purpose here. If you go to your consulate, you will find fuck all sympathy, if you'll pardon the expression.'

'I will not pardon it.' Clay had reddened. 'You look at a British passport lately, Vicky boy?' Clay pulled the blue and gold document from his raincoat pocket. 'See?' He pointed. 'Royal coat of arms, right? Not your tuppenny 'a'penny nineteen to the dozen Ruritanian prince. No, Her Britannic Majesty, see? "Requests and requires" – get that? *Requires* – "all those whom it may concern" – that's you, kartoffel-stuffer – "to allow the bearer to pass freely without let or hindrance." Get it? That does not mean, "give my subjects eighteen compulsory rounds with a mud-wrestler with a dildo", does it? Remember Jenkins, Vicky boy, and that was only his ear.'

Jago sighed and smiled fondly. The Britons, it had been said, conquered the world as much by their diplomacy as by Tommy's doggedness. This was Tommy trying diplomacy. It was magnificent, but it was not pacific.

Novak's smile grew ever more patronizing. 'Strange friends you keep, Mr van Zeller.' He brushed aside Clay's arm. 'This Jenkins, I take it, was a Briton?'

'Too right,' Clay sneered, 'and his ear.'

'But Miss Byrne is Irish and therefore carries an Irish passport.'

'So?' Clay was not for a moment discomfited. Jago had often heard him rant about the bleeding Irish pig-ignorant fuckpigs bombing our boys what they need is a taste of cold steel. Now, what he said was, 'So? English? Irish? All the same to us, mate, and don't you forget it. Odd little tiff, sure, like in all the best-regulated families, but you fuck with a Paddy, son, you fuck with me.'

Novak was shaking his head in amusement and amazement. Jago shared a bit of both emotions, but he was not letting on. 'I'd leave Miss Byrne alone, Novak,' he agreed. 'I met her on the aeroplane coming over. She's a musician touring your country, that's all. If you have a problem, it's with me, and I'm prepared to bet that, as a guest-rider in this race, I have a whole lot more clout than you have the balls to confront.'

'Ah, yes. Of course. I am amongst sporting gentlemen. And I will have a bet with you. I will bet that I will hear not a word from Miss Byrne's consulate, whatever I may do.'

Holly raised her head. Her voice was high and quavering. 'The man is absurd,' she said. It was an uncharacteristic remark, and Jago looked down on her curiously where she stood in the crook of his arm. She was tight and trembling as a column of neon.

Paul now half loped, half skipped over the lawn towards them, Groucho on tin-tacks. He had rolled posters beneath his right arm. A badge twinkled in his lapel.

'Hello, Jago. Hello, Clay, old chap.' He turned his gaze to Holly. His smile became one-sided. His right eyebrow rose. 'Hel-lo,' he drawled. 'So, gosh, Jago, is this your fiddler friend? I say. How do you do? Sorry. Paul Pickering.'

'Holly.'

'The holly bears the crown, eh? And quite right too. Yes, well, Jago. Yes. Pavla. Marvellous. My des. gent's res. is going to be overflowing with proof that I've been here. You were absolutely right. Posters, badges . . . And the tour of the course. Thank you. Made my day.'

Jago glanced at his watch. 'We'd better be on our way. They'll be waiting for us.'

The four of them marched down to the gate immediately beneath the stands. Two policemen, both armed with dogs, stood like caryatids on either side. They examined the passes and nodded them through.

Behind them, Novak gabbled. Palms were held upright before him. The policemen spread their legs. Novak gabbled some more. He reached into a pocket for something. The policemen shook their heads.

Novak dropped his cigarette and raised his voice. He pointed at the party on the course and stamped. The policemen shook their heads again and slouched now. They had made up their minds.

Novak was not accredited. He was PNG.

Clay chuckled and waved. Novak hopped from foot to foot. He looked like an orchestral conductor on a bed of coals.

'They have their orders, and they do not include Novak, it seems,' Jago laughed. 'He can't believe there's anywhere he can't go. Phew, I do believe we have a bit of privacy at last.'

'Strange chappy, that,' Paul mused. His eyes were skittering everywhere.

'Listen,' Jago said quietly but urgently. He retained the smile on his face. 'I'm not happy to talk too loud even here. They could have those bloody snooping long-range microphone things. Paul. Whilst you were blundering around last night, guess what Holly here was up to.'

'Oh, I don't think "blundering" is fair, I must say . . .'

Jago ignored him. 'She was creeping down to your stopcock and filling a couple of carrier bags with what she found there, and I owe you an apology for one thing at least. It's not drugs and it's not bent money. It's baubles such as you have never seen outside the Tower of London. You were right, damn you! There's a bloody fortune there! All of which,' he said more soberly, 'poses quite serious problems.'

Paul stopped in his tracks. He beamed. 'I say, well done! I knew it would be all right with Havlik. Gosh! Well! That's more like it. Well done, Holly. If we can get the stuff over to Cyril, you should be jolly well off.'

'Nonsense,' Holly smiled. 'No, I'd never have got near it if you hadn't been such a nutter, and neither of us would have got away with it if Jago hadn't insisted on chasing you. I reckon we split it three ways. If we ever get it to him.'

'Damned good of you. Well, so I was right all along. See, Jago? These things do happen.'

'To you,' Jago nodded.

'So, where is it now?' Paul was rubbing his hands, all smiles.

Holly looked down at her feet as she walked. 'In a haynet. In one of the racecourse stables.'

'What?' Jago stopped short.

'Well, security's good at racecourse stables, isn't it?' she shrugged. 'Only people involved in the race can get in. Seemed sensible.'

'Yeah, she was brilliant,' Clay almost shouted. Jago hushed him. 'OK. Yeah. I mean, I don't know what the fuck's going down here, but listen, this girl was brilliant. Tell you, she walks in, tweed cap, covered in straw, hair all tucked away beneath the cap, chewing gum, dirt on her face. I thought she was a boy. Honest, doll. No offence. No, seems she found the box with the British number plates in the horsebox car park, right? Finds a haynet, loads up whatever it is. Comes to the security guards, cool as cool, says, "this is for Mr Levine." I get called out, say, you know, "so who the fuck are you?" begging your pardon and all, but, see, I thought she was a boy, didn't I? Maybe a nobbler or something. She says, "Jago sent me. Take this into the stables and get it hidden or at least unobtrusive. See you back at the horsebox." Bloody good thing the security boys didn't speak English.'

'I'd already checked,' Holly said.

'Where'd you get the gear?' Jago asked her.

'Bought it. Well, the cap, the shirt. That was all there was to it. So Clay's standing there gawping, so I just strolled off, went back to your box, took off the cap and the shirt, combed out my hair, cleaned up and so on. They'd obviously said "look out for this fairish girl." The policeman and policewoman were onto me almost as soon as I appeared in the main car-park.'

'Like flies on a cowpat,' Clay sniffed. 'Bloody lucky I was there. Now, would someone care to tell us just what this is all about? Baubles, you said. You mean like jewels?'

Jago and Holly grinned at one another. 'We mean like jewels,' Holly said.

'Sorry, Clay.' Jago smiled reassuringly. 'We'll put you in the picture, but wait till we're out in the country.'

They were approaching the nearest fence. Two soldiers in khaki stood at one wing, four policemen at the other. Two Alsatians lay at their feet. They sighted down their forepaws at the British party. Their hindquarters were higher than their shoulders. They were not relaxed dogs.

'So,' Paul hummed, 'this is it.'

Jago started. He looked around, getting his bearings.

Of course. This was IT.

The nearest fence to the stands was the Taxis, the most terrifying single obstacle in steeplechasing. Jago looked over the hedge, then realized that, on foot at least, you could not look over it. Its enormous width meant that you could not see the turf on the landing side for ten yards or more.

So they walked around it.

Jago said, 'Jesus Christ Almighty.'

Paul said, 'Hell's teeth.'

Clay croaked, 'Bloody Nora.'

Holly said, 'Oh, God, no.'

It was like that, the Taxis. The Pope could not see it for the first time without blaspheming.

For once, the reality exceeded an awesome reputation. Paul clambered down into the ditch. You could have stood his twin on his shoulders and Holly on top of both of them and she might just have caught a glimpse of the other side. Technically, of course, you should clear the ditch, so its depth need not concern you. From level ground on one side to level ground on the other was a distance of twenty-one-and-a-half foot. Allow, say, eight foot for take off and you were asking for a thirty-foot long-jump. If you were not to clip the hedge and so pivot downwards, in which case the depth of the ditch would suddenly become a very pressing concern, you also had to attain a high jump of five foot six or more.

Of course, between the vertical plunge and the perfect parabola, there were all sorts of in-between courses on the menu. The far bank of the ditch sloped at forty-five degrees. It was therefore conjecturally possible to land halfway up the slope, find a foothold and scrabble up to level ground. All in all, Jago did not favour this course. What with the combined effects of a prodigious long-jump and the force of gravity, you'd hit that bank – or it would hit you – with a brain-rattling, teeth-crunching, arse-lifting thump. Even if you stayed in the saddle and the horse did not somersault or sink back, footholds looked scarce.

He sideslipped down the bank to join Paul. The two men giggled nervously. 'Um . . . why are we doing this?' Jago asked him.

Paul shook his head, bemused. 'Insanity?'

'You can't expect a horse to jump this,' Holly called down to them.

'Many have,' Jago shouted up. 'Horse called Zeleznik, for example, has won four times. He still sets off with a will. He likes it. Before that, an animal called Sagar won it three times in a row. They're like us, horses. They like to confront their fears, practise for the hard times. Everyone today. Nice, civilized, hate contention. Sure, sure. Only their idea of entertainment is sit down and watch other people killing one another – OK, fake, but you don't believe that when you're watching – on the television. If I'm honest, you give me a choice between watching Audie Murphy or fighting the battle, I'd take the battle every time. You give Burly the choice between this and a nice warm box and a six-pack of linseed mash, he'd be out here in a flash.'

'You can't know that!' Holly was exasperated.

Paul and Jago clambered up towards her. 'Oh, yes, we can,' Jago grinned. 'We know our animals.'

He caught a glimpse of two men and a girl walking towards them. He said, 'Uh oh.'

Holly turned. 'What? What is it?'

'Bloody television,' said Paul.

The man at the front held a large video camera at his right shoulder. Just behind him, a quiffed, blond man in a leather bomber-jacket combed his hair. The girl carried a clipboard. She looked very fierce.

'Hah-low.' The blond man was unctuous, his smile a freshly painted picket-fence. 'You are English, yes?'

'That's right,' said Paul proudly. 'And you?'

'We are Dutch, from television,' said the blond. The camera moved from Jago's face to Paul's.

'Oh, jolly good. Splendid,' said Paul without conviction.

'What do you think, then, of this fence?' The blond was directing the question at Jago, and the camera followed.

He shrugged. 'It's big, but it's fair.'

'It's a very nice fence,' put in Paul. The interviewer gawped. The camera swung instantly back to Paul. Even the lens looked astonished.

The Taxis had been called many things in its time. 'Very nice' was surely not amongst them. It looked positively affronted.

The Dutchman struggled to recover professional cool. 'You do not think it is cruel?' he persisted.

'Course not. Wouldn't be here if we did, would we? Damn tough, sure, but then, so's running the marathon. Don't be silly.'

And Paul, having significantly contributed to the myth of the Englishman as unfeeling lunatic, strode on.

'What about you, miss?' the Dutchman called after Holly, but she muttered, 'No comment,' ducked, and trotted to catch up with Paul.

'Bloody puritan killjoys.' Paul was spitting like pine-needles when Jago reached them. 'Everyone so bloody responsible all the time. No foie gras, no steeplechasing, no fast cars, no proper sex, no conspicuous waste . . . God, what is this world coming to?'

Clay and Jago grinned at one another. Holly looked studious and dour.

'You know what the best things are?' Paul demanded over his shoulder. 'Whisky, fucking and hunting. And the worst things? Shandy, sodomy and . . .' he clenched his teeth to speak the word, '*dressage*.'

The tension had been building. On hearing this walking anachronism being still more anachronistic, Clay and Jago briefly looked as though they were about to burst into tears. Then the hysteria got the better of them, and simultaneously blew. They whooped like country-music fans, they clapped Paul and one another on the back, they chortled like loons.

And Holly still looked studious and dour.

And angry.

Paul made it worse. He forgot his anger and laughed too. He said meekly, 'Silly old bugger, eh? But it *was* better, you know? You *had friends*. Sorry, Holly. Silly nonsense. All boys together stuff. Silly. Sorry. Still. I stand by it. Prejudice. Damn sight better than legislation, you know? Oh, God, I don't speak today's language. Sorry. Damn it. I am who I am. *Bloody* killjoys!'

They walked on.

Holly looked studious and dour.

The next fence, the Irish bank, posed no particular problem – if, that was, your mount knew about banks. One notorious Czech rider in recent years had ridden his horse at it as if at a fence. A horse that hit a seven-foot-high earthwork amidships was not going to see his pension schemes maturing.

From there on, turf made way for plough. Provided that it remained dry, this was a reasonable galloping surface. If there should be a downpour tonight, it would be weary, heavy-hooved and unrecognizably filthy animals that staggered past the post.

Fence number six was the mini-Taxis, almost as high but considerably narrower, with a landing-side ditch only five feet wide. A good sort of fence, Jago reckoned, which gave your mount plenty of room in which to straighten his forelegs for a clean landing. The problem here was that it was on a sharp dogleg. You had to swerve sharply to the right in the stride away. You'd have to look out for over-enthusiastic horses crowding you, cutting the legs out from under you as you swung for the shelter of the trees.

Because now the stands were out of sight, with a band of thick pine forest at their right. The next fence looked, Paul and Jago agreed, rather worse than it was. It was a double – two four-foot-high obstacles with a ditch in between – an overall span of twenty foot or so, but the hedges looked soft and forgiving enough. Next came a combination – an in-and-out – then an open ditch. They were back out in the open then, and heading back towards the stands.

'Right, Clay,' Jago said when they were a reasonable distance from the nearest patrolling policeman. 'We're going to need your savvy on this one. Let me put you in the picture.'

He briefly recounted the tale of last night's adventures. Clay whistled and said things like, 'Gawd!' and ''at's my boy!' and 'Just let that Vic bugger get in my way.'

'So,' Jago concluded, 'we're going to be watched all the way. God knows by whom. Novak is the only enemy who's declared himself. I think there has to be another. The first crowd – the lot who attacked Paul – knew in advance where he was going. Novak didn't. Equally, he knew about

Holly. The other guys didn't, or they'd have had her within minutes.'

'Yes, but hold on.' Paul winced with the pain of thinking. His lips were drawn back in a rictus. 'That could have been just a delay in intelligence, you know. They could have been in the same team, just Novak had different sources.'

'Sure. They both had mobile phones. It's possible,' Jago agreed. 'The things you've got to look at: yes, the guy you talked to on the telephone could easily have sent to have Holly picked up. Maybe he did. Maybe Novak and he are in the same team. God, maybe he *was* Novak, but I don't think so. Why would he have been so secretive then and so overt just minutes later? Also, we're talking different styles. Those guys up in the mountains were pretty ruthless. They took you up there with the intention of disposing of you if ordered. I know it sounds melodramatic, but there really can have been no other reason for the clifftop. It can't have been just to scare you. They were armed. Damn it, they used those arms. Just warning shots, I reckon, but all the same . . . If they'd known about Holly, they'd not have picked her up and given her a lift like Novak did, they'd have grabbed her, searched her, intimidated her. I think Novak *must* have looked in those bags. The other guys would have taken them straight off. Novak's playing some slower, cuter sort of game.'

'Maybe right.' Paul watched his stride. His usual cabochon toe-caps were sheathed in black galoshes. 'So who's official and who isn't? That's what bothers me.'

'I know. The first crowd had the resources to bug a Prague whorehouse, they had the guns, the manpower. Novak – well, he seems to have policemen at his disposal, but not the whole bloody police force, or he'd be here now. His car – did you see it this morning?'

'*En passant*.' Paul shrugged.

'Well, you saw the cars last night all right. Neat and tidy?'

'Oh, yes. Spick and span. Everything clean and shiny.'

'Exactly. Novak's car, on the other hand, is scratched. One of the brake lights is broken. The interior is littered with sweet-wrappers and old cigarettes and crumpled polystyrene mugs. It's his car, not a car from a pool.'

'So Novak's what he says.' Clay used his usual rhetorical gestures. He spread his arms, he pounded the air. 'He's an ex-cop, 'e's got friends in the firm. 'E can't make waves, but this is his 'obby. You said. 'Is family worked for this rich family. 'E's read books about it, checked the computers, all those commie years. The other guys are official, like.'

'So why an interview in pitch darkness on a hillside while Novak is prepared to be seen in public with us?' Jago demanded as they examined the Drop, a simple five-foot slither and pop over a narrow ditch.

'Gawd.' Clay played a windmill, just once, then his shoulders slumped. 'It's like this bleeding country. Whole thing's crazy.'

'Yes,' said Paul, only he gave it three syllables. 'All right. We don't know who the enemy is, but, whoever he is, we've got to keep this stuff safe until Havlik can take it off our hands. He seems to think he can get it out safely. Once we get it to him, our part in the business is done.'

'Problem's gonna be telling 'im the good news and making the transfer, innit?' Clay mused. 'All these buggers running around us all the time, it's going to be bloody difficult.'

'Damn difficult for them too, though,' Jago pointed out. 'I mean, this is a public place and we're pretty high profile here. The security at the stables is tight, and we're surrounded by police. They can't all be in on the plot – unless the people we're up against are the government, in which case we can kiss the lot goodbye anyhow. Somehow – no, it doesn't make sense, but . . . Somehow I don't think they can be entirely official. First, they don't behave official. Second, why haven't they pulled the boxes and the stables to pieces by now?'

'Perhaps they have,' suggested Paul.

'Yes, perhaps they have . . . No . . . Paul says the first mob – the crowd that got him – got a right royal bollocking for jumping the gun, so they've backed off now. They don't want a public scene. I think whoever's involved wants to stash the jewels away for himself. I think we've got a bit of freebooting here.'

'Could be,' Clay nodded, 'or it's just, now you're in a public place. They got to be a little more careful, so they keep an eye on you, they know where the things are, they wait till you get to the border, plant a load of drugs in the horseboxes or something and – gotcha!'

'You've got a nasty mind, Clay.'

'Yeah. It helps.'

'But from now on, the horsebox must be kept locked at all times. We've each got a key. Otherwise it would be too easy for something to be planted by any official or semi-official. That way they'd be sure they'd got us for a good long time. But first they're giving us rope. They might not know whether we've reburied the stuff or what.'

'Yes . . .' It was amazing how many flat syllables Paul could get into that word. 'But then we've got this funny little chap Novak who's being anything but subtle. He's clinging like a shadow. So he's either hoping to hustle us into doing something stupid . . .'

'Or he's trying to deter the other crowd,' said Jago.

'Come on,' Clay chided, 'we can play "what if?" till the cows come 'ome. What it comes down to is, one of us is going to have to tell this Havlik we got the stuff, then somehow we got to get the things to wherever he wants 'em. From there on, it's his problem.'

'It seems to me, the only useful thing we can do is keep them distracted and busy.' Paul shook his head and inhaled through pursed lips. 'As long as we're all acting vaguely suspiciously, one of us should get the chance to have a word with Havlik, perhaps act as decoys or something when he comes to fetch the things. I only hope his plan is good. He's going to have to do something before the race. That's for sure. The security will be relaxed after it's over.'

'Yup.' Jago nodded. 'It's really up to him from now on.'

Fence number seventeen was one of the four water-jumps. At fifteen foot, it was the broadest that Jago had ever seen. Whereas English waters are shallow, a horse could sink breast-deep in this one. At least, however, the take-off side was three foot higher than the landing side. It was the next obstacle, another snake-ditch, which drew gasps and groans from both Jago and Paul. It was narrower – just thirteen-and-a-half foot – but this was the flat one.

Rivers habitually have banks. This would be one huge, stretching, galloping stride. Misjudge it and you could find yourself hitting the far lip with spine-crunching force.

'That,' said Paul, 'is a bit of a sod.'

They walked on. 'Listen. We'll just have to see how it goes,' Jago said, suddenly cheerful. 'There's no point in making any fixed plans now. We're in the hands of the fates. *Dolce far niente* and probably wiser *far niente*. Basically, we're in with the faintest chance of a share in a fortune, and I'd sooner have a ticket than not when there's a lottery like this one on.' He looked round at the faces surrounding him. 'Come on,' he cheered, 'it's a game, that's all. It's not a disaster if we lose.'

'Depends what stakes these guys is prepared to pay,' Clay brooded. 'Just remember that, J. For you, OK, a million or two's to be played for. No big deal. For a lot of people, a million can be killed for. Likes of Novak may play playful, but I'd guess 'e could fight real dirty.'

'Oh, dear,' Paul sighed. 'Just what I was saying, you see? There's no river today without netsmen and no game without professionals.'

''Sright,' Clay nodded, 'and professionals can justify anything in the name of their children or their paymasters. And when I say anything, I mean anything. I should know. I came from those streets, mate. At least when we played 'ard ball it was to keep our lot above the breadline.'

'Mmm. Now the same principles are invoked to keep the fourth car and the house in the South of France.' Paul too was nodding.

'God, what a double act!' Jago tried a chortle. 'Job and Jeremiah, the gruesome twosome. Shut up, will you? I'm enjoying the game. Don't spoil it.'

Clay caught Jago's eye. He grinned wickedly. His hand clasped Jago's shoulder. 'All right. Play on, J. Just don't say we didn't warn you is all.'

'Shut up,' Jago said again, but there were suddenly a lot of sax *glissandi* sounding down there in his bowels.

The racecourse had alarmed but not scared him. In the battle between man and nature, the odds weren't good, but at least you knew the extent of the threat.

When men who called themselves 'professionals' entered the arena, the risks became as incalculable as human evil.

He had yet to hear of boundaries there.

Novak was waiting for them when they returned to the racegoers' enclosure. They set off for the racecourse stables with a police escort. The hawk-like policeman was at Clay's right hand, the younger, scrubbed one at Paul's left. Novak walked between Holly and Jago. Only the two riders and Clay were permitted into the immediate area of the stables.

Jago greeted Burly, who looked magnificent but stared disdainfully back, as though he considered Jago to be in pretty poor condition. He looked up at the haynet, which Clay had slung high up in the corner. He nodded and winked at Clay.

He attached a lead-rein to Burly's headcollar and led him out into the sunshine to examine him. Holly stroked Burly's snip very tentatively. Jago noticed that neither of the two younger policemen was anxious to come within a length of the horse.

Holly and Jago returned to the car to find that, in searching it, the policemen had tidied it. They had laid the maps and the log-book and the rental agreement in a neat pile. They had set the suitcases upright where previously they had lain flat. Holly examined her violin. It was undamaged. All in all, a fair free valeting job.

This morning's hysteria seemed long gone, implausible as a drunken dare. Holly's shoulders were defensively hunched. She too was a long way away. She did not speak on the ten-minute drive. Jago tried to tell her how clever she had been. She just said 'Hm' and studied the roadside.

She was thinking of the race.

Whilst Jago was trying hard not to.

*

The Hotel Sport was an oblong cement block, a big brick with windows. It obviously owed its name not, as Jago had hoped when he made the reservation, to the racecourse, but to the soccer pitch opposite.

They ignored Novak, who remained on their tail. They just parked, fetched out their luggage and walked into the hotel. They registered and collected the keys whilst Novak leaned on the plate-glass door. There was no point in Jago's even asking for a separate room for Holly. Tomorrow was the town's big day. There would be no room at the least of inns.

They left Novak downstairs. The room was sanitized Lego. They'd called in a Swissair designer and asked him to design a monastic cell. It was furnished entirely with shiny white oblongs – a shiny white bed with drawers beneath it, a shiny white headboard, a shiny white mirror-frame and a shiny white dressing-table. There were neither flowers nor pictures. The walls were of pale pimpled caramel. The carpet was cappuccino. It was a sunbleached skeleton of a room.

Holly was brisk. She walked in ahead of him. She dumped her holdall and her fiddle case on the bed. She said, 'So, what's the routine, then?'

'I don't know,' Jago admitted, though in truth he had hoped that the afternoon would include, inter alia, the shedding of clothes, a deal of caressing and some homemade earthquakes on that sterile bed. 'We're bidden to a soiree by the organizers at six, then . . .' He shrugged. The ensuing silence was pregnant. At least it got lucky. 'Do you want a bit of a rest?'

'Maybe . . .'

She had strolled over to the large steel-framed window. Now she stretched. Her buttocks were very tight and round. Her long hands mimed flowering. The white light tangled in her hair, casting a halo about her head.

Jago stepped forward. He wrapped his arms gently about her waist. She did not lean back. She stood very still, as though the slightest movement might alarm the goalposts on which her gaze was fixed.

He kissed her hair, the nape of her neck. She laid her hands lightly on his. That was all.

'Jago . . .' That little piping voice again.

'Mmm?'

'Listen. I like you.'

'I like you,' he murmured in her ear.

'I know. No, but listen.' She pulled her head to one side. 'No, it's just . . .' She drew away from him. She sat heavily in the chair by the dressing-table. She looked down at the backs of her hands, quickly up at Jago, then down again. She swivelled. She told the mirror, 'I just wish that you weren't you, that's all. Oh, I don't bloody know.' She laid her forehead on her hand so that the hair spurted out above her fingers.

Jago hunkered down beside her chair. He said, 'What do you mean, you wish I wasn't me? Wherefore art thou Jago?'

'No. Oh, I don't know.' She screwed up her face in frustration. 'I mean, steeplechase-jockey, hunting, businessman – it's just not me.'

'You mean you have an idea and I don't conform to it?'

'No!' she protested, then, 'Well, yes, I suppose. All this hearty, sporting, macho stuff. You guys out there . . .'

'I'm not hearty,' Jago said softly. 'Sporting? Well, I hope so, but I don't exactly spend my life in a jock-strap working up a sweat. As for macho – well, that's an image you've projected onto me. I don't think it's me. OK, so you wouldn't have picked me out of a catalogue. That's the way it usually works, you know.'

'I know, but, God, all the bloody mistakes I've made. I don't want to make another.'

He laid his arms on her thigh, his head on his arms. 'You're not the only one around here to have got turned, you know.'

'Oh, come on. I couldn't hurt *you*.'

'Oh? What makes you think that, pray?'

'Oh, God, I mean, look at you. Friends, big cars, money, probably thousands of bimbettes throwing themselves at you.'

'God in heaven, woman.' It was his turn to be exasperated. 'What do you think I am? A rock star or something? Talk about lack of self-esteem! You look like you, and you see me as more captivating and secure? Christ. Listen. I'm a small-time businessman with a failing business and a slightly unusual hobby which I can't afford after tomorrow. Some men fly model aeroplanes, some dress up as Cavaliers and Roundheads and fire caps at one another, some dress up as women, some keep mistresses, some jump off bridges on rubber bands. I ride horses over fences.'

'You don't need me,' she said suddenly.

If she was looking for an argument, she was looking in the right quarter. 'Too bloody right I don't need you,' Jago snapped. 'I can live without you. I'd sooner not, but sure I can. But that's the whole point, isn't it, love? You need to be needed, so you've always picked the weak little bastards who end up possessive and jealous and bullying. I have my life just as you have yours. I have no intention of altering that. I'd quite like them to move in tandem, that's all.'

But a Roman road is an affront to a woman. Byways lead to nicer gardens. 'God, that fence,' she suddenly shuddered. She covered her face with her hands. She pulled her legs away from him. 'I'm sorry, Jago. I know your arguments, but it just must be cruel to race a horse over that. I mean, he trusts you. He can't know what's on the other side.'

Jago sighed deeply and stood. The mizzen and the main were gone, but she'd not be striking her colours this afternoon. 'You call it cruel, I call it life,' he said sadly. 'It's cruel that people die. It's cruel that relationships break up. It's cruel that animals must eat other animals. Earthquakes and diseases are cruel, but to complain about those things is to blaspheme, and to give yourself a nervous breakdown into the bargain. I try to avoid ugliness – bullying, rape, unjust imprisonment, that sort of thing. Pigs in batteries again. A man's relationship with a dog or a horse, co-operating in competition, seems to me a beautiful thing, not an ugly one. That's man working with a fellow being – mutual aid, not domination and submission.'

And yes. Somehow, that byway had led back to her original thoroughfare. She was staring at, not through, the window now. She was slowly shaking her head and sucking her lower lip. 'I don't know. There are just so many contradictions . . .' She spoke like a robot. 'I'm not . . . Someone's got to be able to resolve them.'

'Nope,' he told her. 'No one. There's nobility in the vilest and vileness in the noblest. You can only love what is, with all its contradictions, not judge everything, see everything as somehow flawed because it doesn't match up to a fairy tale. You – it's like looking at a greyhound, saying, "He's no good because he hasn't got a nose like a spaniel's," then looking at a spaniel, and he's no good because he's not as fast as a greyhound. Oh, Christ, Holly, I don't know the answers. All I know is, God seems to be a hell of a generous host, and most generous hosts like a guest to eat with relish, drink deep, belch loudly and say "thank you." That's as near as I can get to a philosophy. Others – the Coras of this world no less than the sniffy middle classes – pick fastidiously. "That's not nice," "that's not good for you," "I'm on a diet, actually." The hell with them.'

'No.' Holly stood. She walked to the bed and picked up her shoulder bag. Her eyes were slippery stone. 'No, it's got to be tougher than that. Sorry, Jago. That can't be enough. I'm going for a walk. Sorry. Do you mind?'

'Of course I mind,' he grinned. 'I'd like to be building up a steam on these double-glazed windows, but if you want a walk, a walk you shall have.'

'No.' She set the bag down again. 'Go on, then. All right.'

'All right what?'

'You want to fuck me. All right. Let's get on with it.' She shrugged.

He stared at her, bemused. He had been here before, but still did not understand what triggered such cold ferocity and self-despite in a woman. He kicked off his shoes. He said, 'Sod off, Holly.'

She said, 'No. Come on. Why? You've earned it, haven't you? Hotel room, diamond earrings? Come on.'

Jago stretched out on the bed, which was too short for him. He rolled onto his side. He mumbled into the pillow, 'Sod off.'

She breathed a bit. Noisily. Deliberate, like.

She sodded off.

'Right,' said Paul Ward. He strode into Havlik's room as though into a stiff gale. 'My name's Andrew Hayward. Andy to you. What the fuck's going on?'

Havlik stood at the basin, stripped to the waist. His hair stood upright, flecked with foam like a tussock with cuckoo-spit. As he heard the voice, his hand jerked, and the shower-head sprayed water on the wallpaper. Blinded, Havlik laid it down in the basin and fumbled for a towel. The water spurted upwards now. Havlik said, 'Shit! What are you doing here, man?'

'Cleaning up, as usual.' Ward sat on the candlewick bedspread. He picked fastidiously at the white ridges, flicked invisible blemishes away. 'Knocking some sense into dick-heads. Making sure I get what's due. Fuck, this is – what's happening here?'

'I don't know!' Havlik mopped his eyes. 'I done what I said. Everything. I got old man Pickering, he got all hyped up like I said. Jumped at it. You guys heard that. Goes down there, doing it, getting the stuff, what I gather, some guys come storming in, scare him off, Christ's sakes. Now this guy calls himself Novak, following me everywhere I go – shit, why I got the Pickering to do it – says someone's got the stuff. I mean, were those your guys?'

'They were associates.' Ward dropped the words as if down a well. 'Fucking Czech associates. Even they couldn't fuck up, simple job like that, what I reckon. Follow the guy, don't get seen, keep people off his back. Take the stuff, there's any danger. Otherwise, we go along with your plan, shove it in your mare, go that way. Hell, they can't fuck up. These geeks'll fuck up, shit, kid's building bricks, two plus two. They gotta be the big heroes. Well, they's big heroes can't walk just now. They can, they'll be shining hookers' shoes, cleaning the johns some dive in Bratislava. Shit.'

'So they didn't get it?' Havlik reached for his shirt. He averted his eyes from Ward. He tried to keep all trace of hopefulness from his voice. 'They're not trying anything?'

'That I can guarantee. They're dumb, but they ain't that dumb. What's this?'

'What?' Havlik's head jerked round fast. His jaw dropped.

'This stuff.' Ward did not see the fear on Havlik's face. He fingered through the sheets of yellowed paper and vellum. 'Old papers . . .'

'Oh, yeah. Oh, yeah, some old guy, used to work for my granddad, he says. He sees in the papers I'm here, drops this stuff off. Old account books, ledgers, household things, you know? See, that's the Havlik coat of arms, right?' Havlik reached over Ward's shoulder to pick up one sheaf of papers, revealing the tall ledgers beneath. 'I might, you know, one day, get it translated, find out where the family fortunes went.' His laugh came out as a nervous snigger. 'Maybe some museum, you know, some library, be interested . . . So.' He turned away. He pulled open a drawer and slid the papers casually in. 'If your guys haven't got them, it's got to be Pickering or van Zeller. They were both down there. Pickering gets scared off, van Zeller goes in, something.'

'You mean you haven't seen these guys? They got your millions, my millions, you ain't so much bought them a drink, checked like what they done with it?'

'Sure.' Havlik extended his hands to catch invisible cannonballs. 'Sure, I see them. Just now, this afternoon. They got Novak and his pet heat with them watching them every inch. I just say, "Oh, how do you do. Which one of you got my family jewels and where you got them stashed?" Sure. Come on. All I know, they were playing it cool with this Novak, giving nothing away, so I reckon they got the things somewhere. You ask them. You got as good a chance as me. Listen. It comes down to, it's easy. Pickering's got them or van Zeller's got them. No one else has had a chance, except the geniuses you use for muscle, and you say no. I mean, I come to you with a good – my plan's working, right? You guys fuck up, I'm not paying. I done my bit. You can't turn it around, blame me. You say, get these guys go down, pick up the stuff, bring it back. I done just that, man. You guys decide to have all-out war, the cops get it back, I paid my debt.'

'Sure, sure,' Ward said amiably. He flicked the ledger shut with his thumb. 'You paid your debt. You ever hear of someone being murdered just for practice? Just 'cos the guy with the gun gets annoyed? It happens. It's unfair, but it happens.' He stood and stretched with much creaking. 'You find out where the things are,' he said. 'That way, I stay happy, OK?'

'OK,' Havlik sulked. 'Yeah, OK. But keep them gorillas under control, Ward.'

'Hayward.' Ward turned from the door and growled. 'Andy Hayward, and I work for *Newsweek*. Don't forget it.' He ducked beneath the doorframe. He left the door open behind him.

Havlik sank onto the bed. 'Oh, Jesus Christ,' he murmured, 'Him I don't need . . .'

Jago awoke feeling stiff, cold and gloomy. It was pouring with rain.

He heard the frenzied dancing of the water, the lapping and chuckling as it ran away. He thought of the sucking, hock-deep mud through which Burly and he would have to wade tomorrow. He groaned.

He opened his eyes on clear blue sky.

He blinked. He rolled over and sat up. The puddering and splashing came from the corner by the room's door. He called 'Hello? Hello, Holly?' Only then did he feel a little foolish.

'Hi!' Her voice was strong and clear now. 'You were sleeping like a baby!' The water was suddenly cut off. Jago wondered if she was rapidly snatching up towels for fear that he might venture in.

'I needed it.' He stretched. He shook the clouds from his head. 'So, how was fair Pardubice?'

'Foul!' she shouted happily. She walked out, trailing a cloak of steam. She wore a blue towel in a sort of plumed turban. She wore another wrapped about her in a pareu, like a Gauguin girl. She came straight over to the bed and knelt beside him. She said, 'I'm sorry,' and her arms rose to encompass his neck. She kissed his eyes and his cheeks. She was very warm and damp. Her skin juddered against his. Her tongue was cool and slick by contrast. 'I'm sorry sorry sorry.' She laid her turbanned head against his collarbone. 'I just get all nervous and confused, and this sex business . . . It's so easily done, but . . . It's like, you know, your filthy fence. You're out of control, your horse is running up to it, why not just go for it? But you've got to think about the other side, the consequences, the drop . . .'

'I know, I know.' His hand stroked her bare back. He kissed her crown. 'Don't worry. I understand.'

She leaned back. Their teeth collided, then her open lips met his, and her tongue was quick as a startled trout. Her hand pressed hard at the back of his neck. The towel fell from her head as she slid back down into his lap. The tendrils of wet hair were cool against her warm skin.

The frustrations of the day were telling. His hand was moving urgently now and of its own volition towards the central source of heat. Her legs fell readily apart. Her moan was muffled in his mouth. The blue lava-lava somehow slipped from her breasts. The warm air rapidly made her naked skin soft and smooth. Her breasts were small but full. Her body was light and limber. The white bikini marks were very distinct.

He was on top of her then, nibbling and flicking with his tongue at those pale pink nipples. Her crotch moved against his thigh like she was riding at a slow hack canter. Little groans and whimpers and gasps pushed their way up from her belly. Her fingers were everywhere, pulling, fluttering, scrabbling, squeezing.

Jago raised his head and looked down on her. With her hair splashed on the white quilt, her eyes wide and glistening with excitement, her lips flushed and gleaming, she looked utterly beautiful. Sex is the dew on the flower, he had said. Holly had been no dandelion to start with.

And after the initial heat and fervour, there was stillness, tenderness, awe. Her hands slipped slowly, appreciatively down over the muscles of his back and clasped his buttocks. Suddenly from the room next door there came a sound all too familiar to Jago – a series of retching, woofing coughs, a deep sigh, a male voice pom-pomming the tune of *The Man Who Broke the Bank at Monte Carlo*. A lavatory seat clattered. The cistern flushed. 'Oh, for Christ's sakes,' Jago breathed. 'Clay . . .'

Holly giggled huskily. 'And paper walls. Come on. It's time for your soiree.'

'Bugger my soiree,' he breathed.

She shook her head many times. She giggled. 'No. Come on. You've got to go. Let's get it over with, then . . . Well, we can go somewhere else. Somewhere a little more private.'

His stomach whined its protest. His balls thrummed. Nonetheless, he nodded and flung himself back on the bed. 'All right, all right!' he sang. 'Oh, God, I do want you.'

'I got that message, thanks.' She clambered up to kiss him. 'I want you too, God help me.'

Before she could change her mind, she swung her legs from the bed. She walked unsteadily but gracefully to the chair where she had laid her clothes. 'God,' she giggled, 'you've done it again! My knees are gone.'

She was uninhibited, unashamed. She enjoyed his gaze as she sat and pulled on black stockings, one by one. Her eyes caught his and wickedly gleamed. 'Come on,' she said, brisk as a school prefect. She stood. She stepped into knickers. White cotton cupped. Elastic snapped. 'Come along. It's after six already.'

Jago groaned and rolled from the bed. His legs too were weak. 'Do you think friend Novak is listening to all this, getting off on it?' he asked.

'Give a poor warped old man his kicks.' Naked to the waist, she wrapped that Lauren plaid mini-skirt about her hips. 'Listen, yup.' Now that she was nigh decent, she turned her back on him. Her arms hooked like lobster claws to fasten her bra. 'Tomorrow. Do you think – if I've got to watch this, I'd rather be involved. Do you think I could be out there, in the middle, taking photographs? It's funny, you know, but a camera sort of distances you . . .'

Jago threw back his suitcase's lid. He selected a shirt. 'I can't see why not,' he told her. 'Good idea. You can cradle my head and croon sweet words as I breathe my last, like Barbara Allen or whoever it was in the song.'

'Please, Jago. Don't.'

'Sorry, sorry.' He shrugged on the shirt. It was very cool and crisp. 'No, but I'd like a good shot of the Taxis. I'll ask if it can be arranged.'

'Great.' She padded quickly past him. She peered into the dressing-table mirror. 'No, it's just – it'll be something to do. I might even get a shot good enough to sell. You never know. Oh, and Jago?'

'Hmm?'

'Let's not spend too long at this thing, OK? We've got better things to do.'

Jago smiled over his shoulder at the tight, shady calves, the fringed skirt, the swoop of her back beneath clinging black wool. He wondered whether his body would let him down again, but said, 'We do indeed,' and found it easier, just at that moment, to sit down.

Bars, in the West, habitually essay an illusion. They attempt to persuade us that we are in a country mansion, a country cottage, a conservatory or an ocean liner. Decor therefore ranges from flock and veneer to frills and velveteen, from glass and ferns to chrome and pine. Bars here, it seemed, were mere rooms in which drinks were served, and decorated, if such a word served at all, like milk bars back home. The walls were white, the floor of linoleum which would not show the blood, the tables topped with yellow formica.

Novak sat with another man at a table beneath the room's only window. Jago saw them through smears of smoke. Novak's new companion had an Armenian look. His oval face was smooth and tight over the cheekbones. He had a steep black widow's peak and thin, straight lips. He wore oblong steel-rimmed glasses. Novak pointed. The lenses flashed as the man looked up at Jago and Holly. Both men wore dark suits of a stuff which owed its origins more to oil fields than to pasture. Both wore plain ties. Novak's was plain red, his friend's plain blue.

Holly and Jago pointedly ignored them. They walked to the bar and perched on high stools. Jago ordered white wine by pointing. Both looked around.

Down at their right, the race's organizers conferred. Otto Svoboda had loosened his tie. His brow, the colour of campions, was once more spangled as he sorted papers and supped beer. His wife's hair had staged a mass breakout. Autumnal tendrils straggled everywhere over her oaken skin. Pavla sat in the far corner with her notebook and pencil. She looked calmer than before, but still confused as the Svobodas bickered.

Further to their right, behind Holly, a young blond man held court. His hair was golden, flat and shiny. It was parted right of centre, and flowed down to his dark right eyebrow. His eyes wore heavy helmets. He must have been twenty-eight, twenty-nine. He had long, beautiful hands which he used expressively as he talked. He wore a green sweatshirt with a picture of a jumping horse and the legend 'Grand National' on the chest. An attractive girl with long blonde hair sat at his right, a startlingly beautiful girl with long dark hair at his left, and, to make up a complete set, a small, mignonne girl with cropped hennaed hair faced him across the table. All four wore blue jeans.

Jago caught his eye or the blond man's his. Jago smiled. The younger man was at once out of his seat and extending a hand across the table. Jago jumped down and took it. He said, 'Hi. Jago van Zeller.'

The other's grin was a hundred candlepower. Life had not argued with this man. ''Allo. I see you this afternoon. Jean François de Roquebrune.' Jago felt the wide-eyed upward gaze of the small girl beneath him, but his gaze was fixed on this remarkably beautiful young man with his dazzling, lopsided smile. He was a friend. They both knew it. Jago did not release his hand as he drew Holly in and introduced her.

There were a whole lot of introductions then, and a lot of scraping of chairs as the English couple were admitted to the circle. Jean François made much of Holly. He insisted that she sit at his right. His eyes lazily appraised her, lazily lingered on the most heavily covered parts of her, as though in time his gaze might penetrate the fabric. She looked happy. She struck up a conversation with the blonde girl in English.

'So,' Jago said at last, 'have you ridden in the National?'

'No. You 'ave?'

'Twice. Once, I fell at the Chair. Once I finished, but I never troubled the judges.'

'Troubled . . .?' He considered. 'Ah. Yes. I like it. Troubled the judges. Good. Ah, no, but next year, I ride. Wait and see. I 'ave the 'orse. He is . . .' He joined fingertip and thumb. He kissed the air. 'This year, I tell you, I win Pardubice. Next year, the Grand National.' The girls at Jago's either side nodded as though they had made the reservations for the winners' enclosures. 'Come. You go to this *emmerdant* party tonight?'

'I reckon so,' Jago nodded.

'You 'ave *place* in your *bagnol*?'

'Not for all of you, no.'

'No. Just me and Corinne.' He cocked his head towards the dark girl. 'We go to this party for two seconds only, then, the others, they meet with us chez Maxim.'

'Maxim?'

'*Oui, oui*. There is a restaurant here in Pardubice which calls itself Maxim. *Incroyable, mais quand même* . . .' He shrugged. 'Holly. That is right?'

'That's right, yes.' Holly grinned.

'You come for dinner, Hol-ly. It is a charming name and I like to say it and you have very nice *genoux*. I forget him now, what is *genoux*?'

'Knees,' supplied Corinne and Jago.

'*Exacte*. Ker-nees. No. These are not ker-nees. Ker-nees are bumpy and lumpy. These are smooth. They are *genoux*. So. You come have dinner with us later?'

Holly's glance at Jago was amused. A smile lingered on her lips. She said, 'Look. Can we leave it open? It would be fun . . .'

'Of course, of course!' Jean François stood. 'So. We go?'

Jago glanced over his shoulder. Novak and his companion

were already up and walking towards them. Jago sighed and pushed back his chair. 'We go,' he agreed.

The two Svobodas and the blessed Pavla were already in the hotel foyer. Jago touched Pavla's shoulder. She mustered a smile for him despite her fatigue. 'Excuse me,' Jago murmured, 'but where is this do – this soiree?'

'At the university,' she said. Clasping her notebook in her hand, she added, 'If perhaps you wish to follow us?'

'Good idea. Look, just one more favour. Do you think it will be possible for Holly here to go into the centre of the course tomorrow, to take photographs?'

Pavla winced. She was apologetic and intimate with Holly. 'No, no, impossible. All the permissions have been granted. No more.'

'It's just – it'll be horrid watching it,' Holly explained passionately, 'and if I were involved in some way . . .'

'Yes, yes. I understand.' Pavla glanced over Holly's shoulder at the Svobodas, who were moving towards the glass doors. 'But there are only forty photograph passes, and all granted. Security is important, strict.'

'Yes, but my friend, surely . . .'

'I will see what I can do.' Pavla nodded. Her hand touched Holly's forearm. 'I will try. You come see me at ten o'clock tomorrow, yes?'

'Yes.' Holly was keen, grateful. 'Thank you so much. It'll make such a difference.'

'I no promise, I do not think possible.' Pavla was backing towards the doors. 'I do what I can. Is very, very difficult. I can only try.'

'Yes. Thank you,' Jago said, but she gave no indication that she had heard him. She was gazing enviously, admiringly, almost greedily at Holly. He had the feeling that Pavla had instantly fallen a little bit in love with Holly. He wondered if Holly always had that effect on susceptible women, and what, if anything, it signified. He held the door open for the pair of them. The French couple followed. Novak and his friend stood behind Jago. The new man carried a neatly folded grey raincoat over his arm. 'Come along, gentlemen,' Jago beckoned impatiently, 'I'm not standing here all night.'

Novak smiled. The other man glowered. He had eyes like almonds behind those flashing glasses. The two men whooshed past. Their feet chomped on the gravel. Car doors clunked. Engines shuddered as they started up.

They arrived at the high wooden hall as though in a cortège. Women in black thrust trays of brandy glasses at them. Zdena Svoboda had already grasped a glass and drained it in one gulp. Jago and Jean François waved the drinks away. '*Vin,*' Jean François ordered, 'Wine, *wein*, OK?'

The woman shook her head. Svoboda hustled over. He puffed heavily. His rosy fingers fluttered. He begged, high speed. The woman sneered but laid down the tray and slouched off in search of wine.

'Jago, a word.' His arm was grabbed. Havlik was jiggling from foot to foot at his side.

Jago pulled his arm free. 'Ah, Havlik. Holly, you haven't met Prince Cyril Havlik. Holly Byrne.'

'Yeah. Hi.' Havlik nodded absently. 'Listen, Jago, Christ's sakes, tell me what gives, will you?'

'That's a nice blazer,' Jago said.

'What?' Havlik shook his head fast.

'You never had that made in America.'

'What? I mean, no. It was my father's. Huntsman's.'

'Uncommon, that, seven showing six, buttonhole cuffs – nicely built.'

'Look, are you trying to pull a fast one, Jago? Is it true what that guy said, you're bust? Because if you try to rip me off, Jago, let me tell you . . .'

His boyish face was ugly now. Those bulging eyes were narrowed, the nose wrinkled, those thin lips twisted.

'I don't know what you're talking about,' Jago told him, then had to raise his voice as, in the far corner, a five-piece band set up a militaristic honking and bashing. 'Everything is under control. Everything, that is, except you.'

Havlik glared. He perceptibly shook with frustration. His gaze flickered from Jago's left eye to his right, as though in one eye he might find evidence of deviousness invisible in the other. He pointed over Jago's shoulder. 'Christ, man, he can't hear us!'

Jago swivelled his head. Novak and his friend were watching them, but were surely out of earshot amidst all this music and burble. 'That's what worries me, Havlik. Why isn't he listening to our every word? And I don't think he's the only one after us, either. All is well. That's all you need to know. If Paul or I find a chance to speak, we will.'

'Yeah, but . . .'

Jago had turned away from him. He wasn't going to give Havlik the chance to blurt out his fears and suspicions. Clay and Paul were standing by a long table beneath the bandstand. Jago took Holly's elbow and steered her towards them.

Clay wore a quite beautiful midnight-blue single-breasted cutaway frock-coat, an elegant affectation for an ex-teddy boy. Paul was in an off-the-peg grey chalk-stripe worsted flannel suit with four-inch lapels and trouser-cuffs which must have been all of twenty inches. A crimson handkerchief of Macclesfield silk billowed from his breast pocket.

They were talking to an incongruous creature. His head came from a nineteenth-century sporting-print. His nose was bent and bulbous. He sported prodigious sideburns and whiskers on his cheekbones. They made his head seem enormous, yet the body beneath was slim and slight and all twentieth-century in open-necked check shirt worn over a T-shirt, cream blouson, cream chinos, ornately worked cowboy boots.

'Ah, Jago,' Paul shouted above the oom-pahs, 'and Holly. My dear, you look perfectly gorgeous. This is another of our competitors tomorrow, Chiko Novotny. Used to work as a whipper-in with the Pytchley, didn't you, Chiko?'

'Ass right, I did, sure thing,' Chiko chortled. 'I a goer and thruster in the shires. I see you win Melton Ride. Give me five, yeah.'

Jago gave him his hand. Chiko did his very best to crush it. He then turned to Holly. 'You are also a goer?'

'Oh, definitely,' Holly giggled.

'Is good. There is womens are great goers and thrusters, yes, Jago. Sideways, yes? Not with pussy on saddle?' His mime was expressive and completely uninhibited.

Jago nodded sagely.

'You got good horse. Big arse go pretty quick like shit off shovel I think.'

'He's a good animal,' Jago agreed. 'Which is yours, then?'

'The one ahead of you!' Chiko brayed. 'Name Slovenic. He little horse bay or brown but he got me and I kick ass. You watch out. They say, all old fashion like you this afternoon, we all ride sporting and et cetera, but me, I know what is capitalism. Anyone get in my way, I do them proper. This is spirit of democracy, right?'

'Not exactly, old boy,' Paul said.

'Yes.' Chiko swept on as though Paul had not spoken. He picked up a piece of toast with a roll of ham upon it. He threw it into his open mouth and chewed as he spoke. 'No fooling me. I know. Democracy is best man win, devil take the hindmost. Me, I need monies.'

'Yeah, Chiko wants to get married,' Clay explained.

''Sright. Is lovely big fat chick name Sharon. Wooh, has hots for me. Big titties.' Again he mimed. 'I winning, I have half million crowns, I go back to Melton Mowbray. Easy street.'

Jago refrained from pointing out to him that twelve thousand pounds was hardly going to buy him a dog-kennel in Melton Mowbray. He simply said, 'Well, good luck.'

Jean François and Corinne turned up with two bottles of white wine. Introductions were general. Jago took the opportunity to murmur to Paul, 'Your friend is impatient.'

'God, don't I know it?' Paul sighed. 'Doesn't think to check who speaks English, just charges up – "So where is it?" I don't know. Don't think much of his manners to be frank. Still, will you tell him if you get the chance? It would calm him down, OK?'

'Sure,' Jago nodded. He took Holly's hand then. 'What do you reckon?' he asked softly. 'We tag along for dinner?'

'Might as well.' She was smiling as she answered. 'I'm starving, and I can't eat this stuff.' She gestured at the expanse of ham, sausages and hard-boiled eggs.

'OK,' Jago agreed, only a little ruefully, because whilst those parts of him which the Gaelic calls 'the angry place' were seething, his stomach was also clamouring, not, perhaps, so insistently, but he had to concede that it had a claim.

The party which left the university as soon as they deemed it polite was a large one. Chiko, the novice capitalist, had appointed himself one of them. His assumption of familiarity was vaguely alarming. He slapped Jago's back a lot. He slung his arms around Jean François's and Clay's shoulders. He said things like, 'We rider boys after eat go find nice Czech pussy for bonk, yes?' Clay found him fantastically funny. He found Jago's English embarrassment still funnier. Havlik, accompanied by a brown-suited American, attached himself, uninvited, to their party. His hyperthyroid eyes lingered constantly on Paul or on Jago. His jaw remained tight-set in resentful petulance. His arms and legs jiggled. When he spoke, it was in sullen monosyllables.

It was dark when Jago parked the car in Pardubice's main square. Jean François led the girls into the restaurant. Jago was locking up when Novak and his friend strolled up the pavement towards them. The lean, dark man with the raincoat looked as though a joke would have much the same effect on him as a bucket of water on basalt.

'So,' Novak said, 'dinner, is it?'

'Ah, I can see you were a detective, Novak,' Jago grinned. 'Evening, a restaurant marked "restaurant", people going in – from little clues like this, he builds a case. Acute, Novak.'

He chuckled – a sound like an old car refusing to start. 'You'll learn soon enough how good a detective I can be, Mr van Zeller. My – my friend here – is about as much fun as a maggot in a corpse. Do you mind if we join you?'

'Frankly, I think I'd prefer it,' Jago admitted. 'I don't like looking over my shoulder every few minutes. I hope the others won't mind.' He led the way to the restaurant's door. 'Why don't you just give up, Novak?'

'I told you. I grip. I never give up. And don't you see, Mr van Zeller? You have to return to England, don't you? Your friends must return to France, to America . . . I know every step that you have taken. I have searched your rooms, your cars, your persons. Nothing. What does that indicate to an acute detective, hmm?'

'Tell me. Astound me.' Jago pushed the glass door inwards.

'It tells me that Mr Havlik's toys are still in the Czech Republic, doesn't it?' They stood side by side and watched as the dark man meticulously hung his raincoat on a peg and smoothed it down. 'So you have found a hiding place. I must merely prevent you from getting to that hiding place or, better still, find it myself. Once you leave the country – and do not suppose that anyone with whom you have associated will pass the border unsearched – once you leave the country, I have plenty of time to retrace your steps and find any little hiding place.'

'Come along, Novak.' Jago pushed open the inner door. Conversation clattered at them. 'Stop gibbering. Let's eat.'

There were thirteen in the party, and Jago, coming in last, had to take an isolated and rather ignominious seat at the foot of the table. At the far end, girls alternated with men. Holly was installed between Jean François and Paul. Jago had to content himself with Anick, Jean François's blonde friend, at his left, Novak at his right. Novak's dark colleague, whom he had mentally christened the maggot, hovered with a disapproving air until Novak ordered him, in English, to pull up a chair. His name seemed to consist of the last five letters of the alphabet. It sounded like the nose-trick.

Havlik leaped to his feet as soon as Novak sat at the table. 'Now, look, Jago, what's going down here?' he demanded. 'I'm not sitting down with this guy.'

'So leave,' Jago said sternly. 'If you can't behave with common courtesy, we don't want you here. OK, so this fellow's watching us, for whatever insane reason, and there's damn all we can do to stop him. We either make it easy for all concerned or we make it bloody unpleasant. Personally, I'm here for fun. Ease up or get lost – and take *your* friend with you.'

Havlik looked from Jago to Novak and back again, evidently torn between the impulse to flounce out and the terror of missing something. At length, he slumped into his chair with a snarl. 'Christ,' he spat, 'if I'd known what I was letting myself in for . . .'

'Ah, that is so often the trouble, isn't it, Mr Havlik?' Novak flapped his napkin and stubbed his cigarette on a side-plate. 'As the poet says, "*all that glisters is not gold.*" Such true words, I'm sure you will agree.'

Havlik gulped and scowled and turned away.

'Hello, Czech bloodhound!' Clay bellowed down the table.

'Hello, Cockney person!' Novak waved.

'Hi, Jago, right?' Havlik's new companion leaned across Anick to offer Jago a thick hand adorned with thick rings. 'Andy Hayward. From New York. *Newsweek*. Good to know you.'

Jago had to stop crushing a bread roll in order to take the big man's hand. It was plush and strong. The rings were slabs of polished stone set in burly gold shanks. The hair was very black on the backs of the hands as on the man's head. His teeth were alarmingly small and white and perfect – a string of graded cultured pearls.

'Hi.' Jago for some reason found himself wiping the shaken hand on his trousers. 'Maybe you can help Holly. We're trying to get her a photographer's pass for the race. Your lot haven't got any spare, have you?'

'I can ask, Jago, I can ask.' Hayward was expansive. 'I doubt it, but I'll try. Best I can do.'

'Of course. Thanks.'

'You haven't come all the way out here just for the race?' Paul asked.

'No, no. A lot of stories coming from, like, Eastern Europe right now, as you'd imagine. No, I just figured, Prince Havlik, you know, returning to do this – this crazy steeple-chase. Colour piece, you know? Thought I'd just tag along, see how it all pans out. Old world meets the new kind of thing. You and me, Paul, perhaps we could have a talk some time? Get the all-round view, just what sorts of different guys feel drawn to risk their necks in a thing like this?'

Paul shrugged. 'Oh, dear. I shouldn't think I could

enlighten you much. Frankly, I'm not sure I understand it too well myself. It's just – well, fun, I suppose. You don't think about the risk. I mean, you're aware of it, course you are, but you sort of push it to the back of your mind. Unfortunate but necessary part of the whole shebang. No, but of course, if you think you can dig out some deep-seated self-destructive trait in us, feel free to have a crack. Don't think you'll get very far.'

'These English.' Hayward guffawed, sharing his admiration and amusement with Anick, Novak and whoever else might be interested. 'Fun, the guy says! I don't know. Sorry.' He half stood to lean over Anick and Jago in order to reach Novak. 'Didn't catch your name. Andy Hayward. *Newsweek.*'

'Viktor Novak.'

'Czech, right? So,' Hayward sank back into his chair, 'what's with you and the prince, then, Viktor? You know one another from way back or something?'

'No, no.' Novak spoke slowly. 'Barely acquainted at all. Isn't that right, Prince? We have a few interests in common, that's all.'

'Oh, yeah?' Hayward was jovial. 'Such as?'

Havlik sneered and was about to answer when Novak said in that deep, rusty creak, 'Oh, archaeology, for instance. Particularly with reference to Troy, isn't that right, Havlik?'

Above, by the head of the table, Jean François was showing off, filling glasses, pouring the wine from a height. Everyone was on that anticipatory high. Chiko was woofing and roaring. Holly was chaffing and chiding. The girls shouted and giggled. Food was being ordered.

Down here, things were not so relaxed.

Havlik had frowned and snarled, 'Ridiculous little . . .' but the bread roll had fallen from his hands and the colour had fled from his cheeks and his eyes were like flies in a bottle. His fingers clawed at one another as if to pull off invisible, skintight gloves. Novak just smugly smiled, and kept smiling as he raised his head to give his order to the waitress. Jago did not know what was happening here.

Then Havlik was up and his chair toppling backwards.

'Paul . . .?' He jerked his head sideways like a pimp beckoning. 'Quick. A quiet word . . .'

Hayward was already standing, but Novak reached across and eased him back into his seat. Paul frowned, uncertain as to what he should do. He cast an imploring glance at Jago. He gestured with his thumb. Jago nodded. He tossed his napkin onto the table. He said, 'Yes, OK. A quick word. Novak, order steak for me, please, or its nearest equivalent. Medium rare.' He pushed back his chair, winked at Paul and headed for the rear of the restaurant.

Behind him, Hayward called, 'Hey, Prince, 'n I be of help here?' He mopped his lips and threw down his napkin. He pushed himself up into a standing position, but by the time he had straightened, Novak and the maggot were blocking his path, soothing, as though explaining that this was a lovers' tiff, that he should keep out of it. Hayward puffed out his cheeks like a bullfrog, even at one point tried to straight-arm Novak out of his way, but the two men stood firm.

'For Christ's sake, Havlik,' Jago sighed as they reached the dark corner and a door with a cutout figure of a man upon it. Jago pushed open the door and quickly scanned the loo. It was empty. He didn't like that. He came back out into the twilight of the restaurant, where his words were smothered by the chatter all around and he could keep an eye on any pursuers. He muttered down to his shoes. 'You're going to blow this whole bloody thing. Calm down, will you? Do you realize what we had to go through last night on your little mission? Paul bloody nearly got killed. These people, whoever they are, are well-equipped and they play rough. One chance, one loose word, you'll have lost the lot. The things are here. They're not entirely safe, but they're as safe as they're going to be anywhere until you pick them up by whatever means you've planned.'

'I can't, man. There's Novak, all his cronies around. It's just too much of a risk . . .'

'Sure, it's a risk. You wanted it that way. You wanted to do it the quick and easy way, and the only quick and easy way I've ever known of making a fortune is to gamble. I don't reckon it's a bad bet, as things stand. Up to you how you make the transfer, how you get it out of the country. You were confident enough before. We've done our bit. We've taken all the risks up to now.'

'Novak *knows*, Jago. You hear what he said about Troy? That was the whole idea. Ship the stuff out in this mare. You got to help me.'

'I have helped, Havlik. So has Holly, so has Paul. We've all been bloody scared, and Paul has been shot at and interrogated for his pains. Come on. You chose it this way. Novak is probably just guessing anyhow.'

'No. No, he *knows*. Listen, and didn't Father Hacha talk to you back in London, huh? You don't – I mean, that don't mean nothing to you?'

'You mean this was what *that* was all about?' Jago stared.

'Yeah, like, bona fides. I mean, you think a Catholic priest is involved in anything shady?'

'No. I don't know.' Jago shook his head. 'No. Look, I don't object to what you're doing. If I were in your position, I'd probably try to do the same, but I'm not going to blow everything for the sake of a few trinkets, I'm sorry. Neither is Paul. I also promised I'd try to keep him out of trouble. Anyhow, how the hell can I help? We've done everything you asked. We're going to be as suspect as you . . .'

'Oh, shit, and there's this race . . . I don't know if I can do it . . .'

'This is no time for a sports-psychology lecture. Listen. The things are safe. What do you want us to do with them?'

'Won't you take them out, Jago? Please?'

'I wouldn't know how or where to start,' Jago said. 'None of us is going to cross the border without having our cars and boxes taken apart. I reckon we've done all we can. Now. Let's go back and act as though we were innocent jockeys and gentlemen. The only thing you need to know now is that the things are safe in a haynet in the racecourse-stables. No reason why you shouldn't stroll into Burly's stable for a chat with me or Clay, go in with one haynet, out with another. Just look for your moment.'

He turned and led the way quickly back to the table. Havlik followed in a sort of parody of casualness, fingertips in pockets, legs swinging slowly one about the other. Jago smiled up at Holly, but she was engrossed in some story of Jean François's. She did not see him.

'So,' said Novak cheerfully, 'we are all settled, yes?'

'Yes, yes. Pre-race nerves, that's all,' Jago announced. 'We all get a bit uptight.' He sipped from his glass of purple wine.

'So,' Novak was croaking in Jago's ear. He had been served some sort of stew in the two men's absence. His left hand held his glass of wine, his right a cigarette and a charged fork. His napkin spurted from his collar. 'Tell me. Motivation. What does make you do things like this?'

'What I want to know,' Hayward boomed, 'just what I want to know, Viktor. It is Viktor, isn't it?'

'Do things like what?' Jago asked, all innocence.

'Sitting on horses. Projecting them at ridiculous fences.'

'Like Paul said, fun, I suppose,' Jago said simply. He leaned sideways to allow the waitress to deposit his plate before him. 'Companionship, adrenalin, I don't know. What makes anyone do anything?'

'Yes, but it has no purpose!' Novak objected.

'Nor has fornication really, nor has having babies, nor has gardening or painting or playing music. They just make life worthwhile.'

'Get scared?' Novak chomped.

'Of course, but I can enjoy fear. God, I'd be scared driving fast, scared going into battle – I'd sure as hell be scared if I were going to have a baby, but I'd not be denied the experience. I could never sleep again if I walked away.' He cut his steak, which might once have belonged to a relative of Burly's, but was at least medium rare.

'Ah, the English . . .' Novak stirred his stew a bit, then dropped his fork with a clang. 'The dirty little soldier, whining about his boots, talking about his woman as I would not talk of a pig; he picks his nose and eats it, then he gets up and performs deeds of heroic savagery and gallantry. Then it's back to whining and picking his nose.'

'Well, what would you?' Jago grinned. 'Heroes can't be heroic full-time. Rather exhausting, that would be.'

'There you are! Just listen to you – "rather exhausting". You meet Venus Aphrodite arising from the sea, you say, "Your appearance is quite acceptable, old girl.' Someone saves your family from a fire, you say, "Jolly good. Anyone heard the cricket score?" I don't mind that. It's the self-delusion that gets me. You not only project it, you actually believe it.'

Novak's cheeks bulged as he rinsed his teeth with wine. He swallowed and rolled his lips back and forth over those jagged teeth.

'What self-delusion's that?' Jago asked.

'Oh, you know, niceness, respectability, civilized behaviour, restraint, all that. You talk about the weather, you drink tea, your cleverest men pretend to be buffoons. You mistrust excellence and idealism and grandeur. You dislike passion.'

Jago acknowledged it. 'So? It's true. Idealism's a killer, and passion's usually just a generous word for self-indulgence and cowardice. Real passion, sure, but that's a private thing.'

'Exactly! It's private, so you pretend it doesn't exist, just like you're so civilized and restrained, only in fact you're the most warlike race in the history of the world.'

'He's got a point, Jago,' put in Hayward, who appeared to have regained his bonhomie. 'We Americans, now . . .'

'Ah, the Americans,' Novak chomped. His blue eyes twinkled. 'The Americans are as much use at fighting as Abelard at fucking. You ask me who are the typical Americans? John Wayne? Ha. Another curious delusion. No. Laurel and Hardy, Charlie Chaplin, strutting, put upon, inept – and two of them were born in Europe. So, for that matter, was Wayne. In that, too, they were typical.'

Hayward coloured and looked nigh apoplectic. 'Now see here . . .' he began, and Novak grinned happily as he lit another cigarette.

Jago too sat back content. Novak and Clay, he thought, should at once be posted to the United Nations.

They couldn't make things worse.

*

'Almost everything here is mafia-controlled these days,' said the lugubrious Scot who managed Pardubice's casino.

Paul had retired to bed. Havlik had vanished with Hayward in his wake. Jean François, Clay, Chiko and the girls, however, had wanted to come on here. Holly had pressed Jago to accompany them. 'Come on,' she said, 'you had a good rest this afternoon and it's not late yet. Please. Just for a short while.'

Adolescent jealousy and unfulfilled lust made Jago sour, but he had done his best to repress them. Holly was nervous, that was all, and glad of carefree youthful company. Jago's isolation at dinner, however, left him still more isolated now. She and the French crowd had in-jokes. They knew one another's foibles and nicknames. He was way behind them. He had staked her, therefore, lost a thousand crowns on the blackjack table, then retired for a chat with the manager.

He was short and chubby. He had twin ticks for a moustache. He droned in broad Glasgow. 'The velvet revolution, oh, sure, sure, but what about the aftermath, eh? You get rid of the keepers, bloody maggot-pies take over, right? Everyone has a gun here. Ex-Russian, military stuff. They sell 'em to you – Christ, they force 'em on you – on the streets. Brothels – you should see the fourteenth floor here. Of course, that's why, casinos opening up everywhere, they all have British managers. We're known to run a tight ship, see. We're straight. Jeez, I mean, you just look at the taxis. You get a hotel cab, you'll pay a fair price. You hail one of the mafia cabs, you'll pay twice, three times the fare and you better not argue.

'Average weekly wage these parts'd be – what? Fifteen hundred crowns, right? What? Not far over thirty pound. You'd never know it, not from the way these guys spend in here. Och, I'm not talking your real high-rollers, but a lot of these people, they'd seem to have money to burn, you know? D'ye know this is where they make Semtex?'

Jago nodded. He knew. A sudden burst of cheers and laughter from the Pardubice party over by the roulette table made the man's head jerk round. Jago was glad when the man strolled away to supervise. He was altogether too much of a Jeremiah for tonight. Jago was a strangely empty vessel this evening. Jean François's ebullience or this man's gloom could possess him in equal measure.

Five minutes later, trying very hard to sound neither ardent nor persistent, he murmured in Holly's ear, 'Can we be going soon?'

'Yup, OK,' she said in a high, tight voice. She did not turn. 'Just a second. I'm on a roll.'

'Come on, Mr van Zeller,' Novak growled. 'Why don't you let me buy you a beer . . .'

'So,' Ward aka Hayward asked Havlik in the taxi, 'What's he say? Jeez, my jaw's achin', all this nice guy stuff. Yeah. So, what's the guy say?'

'He's got the stuff.' Havlik nodded, then realized that, in the darkness, there was no point. 'No, like he was afraid, bugs, so on. He says the stuff's somewhere in the racecourse-stables. A haynet, guy says, but he'll not tell me more.'

'So we go in tonight, get it safe.'

'Christ, you crazy? You seen the security down there? Fuck. Mix with these guys . . . You haven't had enough? Last night, you got warfare down Susice, tonight we get the gunfight at the OK Corral at Pardubice. You guys crazy or what?'

The car stopped at red lights. A square of yellow light swung about the car's interior. Ward growled, 'I ain't seen it. So tell me.'

'Armed security guards everyfucking where. I mean, we are talking – the race is tomorrow, Christ's sakes – we're talking pros, guns, probably got bets on the race. Everyone goes in or out, you get frisked. Stuff's safe, why not leave it? Tomorrow, sure, race is over, even next day, everyone's leaving, sure. I thought – the idea was, get the things out of the country, right? Nothing criminal once we're over the border. So these guys, they're allowed to move around in there. No one freaks they transfer a haynet, their loosebox to mine. I put the stuff in the mare, get over the border, you're away.'

'OK, OK.' Ward's glowing cigar-butt nosed at the door. It missed the ashtray and suddenly went dark. 'But I want to know it's there. It's there, OK. We can watch, make sure no one moves it. You can go in this time of night?'

'Sure.' Havlik shrugged and sighed heavily. 'Why not? I wanna see my horse, I'm worried about its breathing, something.'

'Yeah, but you're going into the wrong stable . . .'

'So I made a mistake, anyone notices. They search me anyhow when I go in. Check, you know, no hypodermics, no sugar, things . . . Shit, we give it a try, we foul up, no harm done. Let's go.'

Ward leaned forward and tapped the glass partition. He said, 'Racecourse.'

The driver leaned back and released a brief rivulet of Czech.

'Velka Pardubicka,' Havlik called, and clip-clopped with his tongue, just in case there should be any misunderstanding.

Holly's 'roll' lasted a further half hour. Even then, she eked it out, reducing her stake, borrowing chips from Jean François, who was winning, or giving a good impression of doing so. Then there were cheery farewells and fond embraces which took another ten minutes.

Novak was the last to wish Holly and Jago goodnight. He caught them at the doorway. He yawned, making no effort to cover his mouth, then went cha-cha-cha with his palate and his tongue. 'Yes,' he said, 'yes, I think I'll go to bed too. Long day tomorrow. I'll leave my friend to see you home, make sure you don't get lost.' Behind him, the dark man nodded. His sandworm lips wriggled. His glasses flashed. He pulled on his raincoat, which rattled and whooshed like a heating kettle.

'We'll miss you,' Jago told him. 'Well, see you in the morning . . .' and suddenly he had problems in remembering his name – 'er, thingy,' he mumbled. 'Sorry, I'm . . . Bit groggy. Must be the smoke or . . .'

Jago could hear himself slurring and gibbering, yet still could not resume control. Perhaps that Czech red was more powerful than he had thought.

The fresh air did something to awaken him. He breathed it in deep and shook the fuzzy edges from his perception. Somewhere a car roared and screeched. Somewhere a bell clanged as he unlocked the car. Jago climbed in and reached across to unlock Holly's door. The car woofed as she opened the door and climbed in. Her door thumped shut. Seatbelts clicked. Holly sighed. Jago said something like 'phew'. He turned the key in the ignition. The car laid down a rhythm in preparation for song.

'I'm glad to be out of there,' he said. 'The smoke was beginning to get to me.'

'I really enjoyed it.'

'Good. No, nice crowd.'

'Yup.'

'So, where to?'

'Well,' she shrugged, 'you wanted to get to bed, didn't you?'

'Don't you?'

Again she shrugged.

'Fine,' Jago said as equably as he could contrive. 'Look, if you want to stay on here, that's fine. I'm sure Jean François or Clay will see you safely back. I've got to get to bed. I have things to do tomorrow. Sorry.'

She was silent. She did not move.

'Holly?'

'Oh, God.' It was two quick strokes with the heel of the hand on a tom-tom.

'It's OK, for Christ's sake!' Jago lied. 'I'm not a love-sick swain who'll die for unrequited love . . .'

'Don't say that. God, that race tomorrow.'

'. . . and although I'm not in the least chivalrous or politically correct, and believe some sort of pressure to be part of the game, we've long since reached that point and passed it. If I put pressure on you now, it'd be no fun anyway. So let's leave it at that. I enjoy your company, OK? I'll make another pass at you tomorrow evening and every evening thereafter, just for form's sake. All right? But I do have to go to bed now, so either you go back and play some more or we return to the hotel and place a sword between us.'

'So I'll feel guilty if I do and I'll feel guilty if I don't,' she said on a monotone.

'So don't, for my sake. I don't want to feel lousy in the morning, thanks.'

'Not that sort of guilt. You don't understand.'

'Probably not,' Jago said softly. Something was pushing his eyelids hard down. All this business seemed irrelevant and irritating. He touched her arm. 'Look, let's leave it be. We've got a race tomorrow and a date at the opera the next day, and if you do a bunk, I'll have a quest. King Pellinore will look like a quitter next to me.'

The seat beside him creaked. There was another click from a seatbelt, then her clothes were gasping and her breath was warm on his ears, his cheeks. Her throat clicked. She said, 'Jago . . .' and a shrill like crystal seeped from her before her lips met his and blessed darkness and warmth engulfed him.

He found himself shaking as he grasped her to him, and when at last he spoke, his throat seemed full of gravel. 'You're sure?'

'I'm sure. Not the hotel, though.'

'No,' Jago nodded, 'Clay's nocturnal sound-effects I can do without. OK. Where, then?'

'There's the horsebox,' she murmured. 'Have you ever used that before?'

'No,' Jago said truthfully, 'never.'

'Come on, then,' she whispered. 'What are we waiting for?'

Jago released the handbrake.

Ward tapped the driver's shoulder. 'Stop here,' he ordered. The driver looked up into the mirror to see the upraised hand. He nodded and braked.

'Right.' Ward tossed his cigar out into the car park. It rolled end over end, trailing a flush of sparks. 'Get in there, find it, bring me something back.'

'I'll try,' said Havlik. He opened the door.

'Hold it,' Ward sighed. He too opened his door and stepped from the car. He walked around the rear. 'Just a double-check, OK?'

By reflex, Havlik raised his arms as Ward's big hands searched his collar and lapels, then patted down his body and up and down his legs. 'Right.' Ward puffed as he stood. 'You're clean. Get on with it.'

Havlik lowered his arms and set off across the car park at a trot. There was not a cloud in the sky, and the moonlight was bright. At the perimeter fence, two uniformed guards stepped forward to stop him. The buttons on their tunics glittered. The leather belts which ran diagonally across their chests softly shone at the shoulders. Behind them, two more pairs of guards who sat with their dogs between the stable doors sat up and took notice. Havlik fished the accreditation documents and his passport from the inside pocket of his blazer. The guards flicked on torches. They examined the documents, then Havlik's face. One essayed a question in Czech, but Havlik smiled and shrugged. 'Amerikaner,' he said.

The documents were handed back. Havlik held them in his right hand as they patted him down. One even raised his feet, one by one, to examine his heels. The other called something to his colleagues by the stables. He nodded Havlik through.

Havlik headed directly for the box where he had seen Clay Levine and the big brown horse this morning. He waved to the men at his right as he unbolted the lower door and ducked into the darkness. Something heavy rustled and thumped in there. Havlik turned round and reached for the light switch at the side of the door. The something heavy snorted, inches behind him. Something hard pushed at his arse, forcing him staggering against the wall. 'Get away, damn you!' Havlik breathed. He flapped at the darkness. His open hand hit mane. 'Go on. Shit. Fucking horses!'

He fumbled for the other side of the door and found the switch. He turned it. He snarled at the horse, who looked enormous. He held out a halting hand as he made his way to the back of the box where the two haynets hung. One hung at head-height in the corner, the other high above it, secured by a short string to the same hook.

Havlik scrambled up onto the manger. He reached across at full-stretch and grasped the string. It took him three or four attempts to work it off the hook.

He jumped down into the straw and, keeping a wary eye on the horse above him, crouched over the net. He tugged the drawstrings apart and reached down into the hay. He felt the coldness of metal. He heard the rattle of stones.

A torchbeam flickered over him. He pulled the net together and turned towards the door. He raised an arm against the starburst in the doorway. 'OK?' asked a deep voice.

'*Ja, ja . . .*' Havlik nodded. He pointed at the haynet. '*Ja. Alles ist OK. Danke.*'

The torch receded. Footfalls crunched. Havlik hunched his shoulders now about the haynet. He picked through its contents. He found what he was looking for. He pulled it out, forced it into the pocket of his jeans, then drew the net together and once more clambered up onto the manger. He hung it up again and jumped down.

Quickly now, he unzipped his jeans and reached into the front of his jockey-shorts. He pulled the thing from his pocket and slid it beneath his scrotum. He zipped up his flies again. He was still adjusting the thing as he reached up to switch off the light. He ducked under the top door and stepped out into the cool wind.

'*Alles in ordnung.*' He recalled the words from war movies. He spoke them with a wave as he bolted the door.

The search at the gate was a cursory formality. Havlik waved and grinned as he made his way back to the headlights. He stepped into the car. He shut the door.

'All there?' asked Ward.

'Every last piece,' Havlik crowed. 'Come on. Get us out of here.'

Ward knocked on the partition. The car started to move. Ward held out a hand. Havlik glanced up at the driver, then reached down for his zipper. Ward said, 'Christ!'

*

Holly was urgent now. She had not refastened her seatbelt, but leaned across to nibble and tongue Jago's ear. Her hand fumbled at shirt-buttons, then slipped down, stroking his nipples and stomach. Headlight beams followed all the way. They were smudged in his sight. He picked out his horsebox and drove towards it. The headlight beams lurched as they bounced on the turf. Another car complained as it bounced across the grass from the direction of the stables. Jago parked. The car behind drew up alongside. The other car reached the road and shouted as it turned for the town. Neither Holly nor Jago cared; Jago because he was not sure where he was or what was happening, Holly because, her mind now made up, she seemed possessed of an uninhibited frenzy.

Under the doubtless disapproving eye of the dark man, now double-glazed behind his dirty windscreen and those tablet glasses, they staggered like drunkards to the side-door of the box, which Jago unlocked with fumbling fingers. He pulled her up behind him, and they were in darkness. He switched on the dull light and they stumbled into one of the two compartments which was laid with straw.

Little light crept in here; just enough to gild Holly's shoulders and nipples as buttons spat beneath his fingers. In silence, they sank to their knees on the straw, and her hands pushed back his unbuttoned shirt so that she could kiss his neck and his shoulders. Then her breasts were cold against his chest as their tongues again intertwined and spun threads of saliva. The saliva dried on Jago's face and throat. She bent to suck on his nipples. Her tongue flickered, lighting a cool fuse over his chest and sides as her hands tugged at his trousers. The air was cool on his buttocks then, and her hands cool on his balls. Again she pressed close up against him, and he pulled her to him and kissed her eyes and ears and throat.

The clasp on that little skirt gave. The fabric fell to the straw. Jago pushed her back onto the deep, crunching straw, and it was his turn to fill his nose and mouth with the scent and the taste of her.

Then came that caesura again, when their eyes locked

into one another and, for a moment, they returned to themselves. She panted. Her hand rose, tentative and wondering, to push the hair back above his left ear. For a second she looked as though she must cry, then she released a sound which started as a keening and ended as a suppressed roar as she rolled him over and dived back into the oblivion of sensation. She was biting now, and working fiercely at his body, licking, squeezing, pulling, sucking. Jago knew where she was, or, at least, where she wanted to be. Cytherea would do, and innocent, fearless love, but, since that was not to be found, 'Anywhere Out of This World'.

He lay back as she panted and snuffled and growled. Once he looked down, just checking.

The flesh was willing this time. It was the spirit that was weak. He was seeing through ill-adjusted binoculars. Blackness masked the upper half of his view. His eyelids trembled and sank. His veins, save that one which seemed steel, were full of molten lead.

'Jago . . .' she urged next, maybe five minutes later, 'Jago?'

He said 'Mmm?' He was bobbing on a jet-ski off Cadaques. The sun was hot and heavy.

'Jago?' A plaint, maybe five minutes on. She was shaking him.

'Mmm?' Straw and hair were indistinguishable.

'Oh, God, Jago, listen, will you?'

'Um list'ning. Um list'ning.' And eating red mullet at a seaside bistro in Piran. He was getting about tonight.

'Oh, fuck it.' She punched the straw by his head. 'Damn you, Jago. All right, sleep. Just remember. I'll always be grateful for the fun we've had and – well, I really care for you . . . I . . . Just remember that, OK?'

Her words were distant and strange, but he was still somehow able to make the association. 'Steerforth,' he mumbled. Then her warmth was gone, and Jago sank from twilight into the brilliance of dreams.

In the dark lounge of the Hotel Novotna, Paul Ward tilted

his head to pour back his brandy, then returned to a study of the thing in his hand. 'You say – you want me to believe? Shit, you saying this was a gift from a fucking Emperor of Mexico, some dame your family?' Ward turned the brooch over in his hands. He went 'Hoo,' falsetto.

'Yeah. 1863. Maximilian, they say, you wanna be Emperor of Mexico, right? He says – what you say? Huh? Younger brother? All that shit? You say no? But my great-great-grandma, she's his mistress, OK? And she don't think a whole lot, like, to this New World. You wanna have the thing checked out? It's in the books. Not a jeweller in the world won't tell you it's the real thing. So. Now you satisfied?' Havlik looked smug as he picked his brandy-glass from the low table. He had plugged in the only lamp above them.

'So far, sure.' Ward could not take his eyes from the diamond-encircled plaque. 'Pickering got it from the place you said. It looks the business. OK, so, fuck, we talking fifty years underground. Crazy, you think. These stones, the gold, come from underground, then, eighteen – shit, sixty . . .'

'Sixty-three,' supplied Havlik.

'Sure. Sixty-three. Hundred years before JFK croaks, right? Thousands of years underground, few years everyone says, like, amazing, makes nuns roundheeled, then fifty years underground again, here it is. Shit. So what's this worth, you reckon?'

Havlik shrugged. 'Sky's the limit. I mean, this one, maybe fifteen, twenty grand, just the diamonds, enamel, so on. I stand up, say it's mine, give the provenance, shit, what's a Mexican millionaire give? Chunk of history, right? Or a museum? Or a Hapsburg, huh? All these guys bidding it up, Christ. Name it.'

Ward kept turning the thing over and over. 'Maybe I hold on to this. Souvenir,' he purred almost lovingly. 'This is what it's meant to be, we leave the stuff there for now, pick it up we get the chance.'

'You do the fuck you like.' Havlik strutted whilst sitting. 'Just so's you don't go screwing up with the heavy artillery shit. I worked this one, man, and it's working ... You screw up, I don't pay.'

'I heard this song, Prince. You think I don't know it? Yeah, yeah. You bought yourself twenty-four hours with this ...' Ward tucked the brooch into his handkerchief-pocket. 'So far, it's all I want. My people watch the stables. Anyone moves from that stall with a haynet, we have your fuckin' war, OK?'

'OK,' Havlik nodded. 'Yeah, OK. Let it run. Keep watching.'

'And now,' said Ward, 'I want to make some calls. I need to find out just who this Novak is. He's getting in our way.'

Holly cursed and hit the straw a few times. She shook her head, incredulous. She said, 'God!' in a voice which shook. '*Bloody* man! Christ, self-esteem? Thanks a million, Jago ...' She shook her fist in his face, then smiled and struck him a glancing blow on the upper arm.

She drew her knees up to her chest and sat there for a while, hugging herself and wondering just how she contrived to make such a mess of things. At length, she stood and pulled the knickers and the sweater on again. It was going to be a cold night.

She remembered that horses have blankets. By the light which trickled from the box in which Jago snored, she walked in tiny, cautious steps along the narrow corridor. She peered into another dark cubicle, but could see nothing and suddenly visualized rats. She felt her way up to the cab. She fumbled above the windscreen for a courtesy-light.

Her hand never reached it.

It was a hateful memory from schooldays which leaped from the darkness behind her: the strange male hand pressed hard about her nose and mouth, the strange male arm about her waist, the strange male body against her back, the stillborn screams, the twisting and kicking and flailing, to no avail, as she was dragged backwards.

There was fresh air then, on her skin, her naked legs, but in her lungs only the smells of flesh and tobacco. She lashed and jackknifed, but the arms held her firm. There was cold metal against her calves. She was pulled backwards through the car door into musty warmth. The car seat puffed beneath her weight and that of the man who held her. The door was slammed. The car rocked. Another door on the other side also shut. Dark things flew towards her, landed on her kicking, outstretched legs and wrapped about them. Her clothes.

The ignition gave its whooping coughs, then roared. Still the hand remained clamped about her mouth. She writhed and squealed, but only when the car was out on the road was she permitted to take in two lungsful of air.

She at once expelled them again in a scream like a saw shearing steel.

'Gor, what a sight!' Clay's voice made the partitions buzz then hum. 'Jane Russell you ain't, J.'

A bucket clanked. Footfalls thudded.

Jago said, 'Jesus, where . . .?'

He rolled over. He opened his eyes, which were dry and smarting. He looked to either side.

Holly . . .?

She was gone.

He groaned and rolled back. He covered his eyes, as though that might blind memory. He could not believe – and yet, strangely, his memory was horribly intact and precise – that he had nodded off *in medias res*, yet that was unquestionably what had happened. But why? Was this a new form of impotence which ensured as much pain to others as to himself? A sort of sexual catalepsy which caused him to pass out just as crisis point was reached? Of one thing he was certain: it could not have been the drink. He had drunk one glass of white wine at the university and two-and-a-half of red at the restaurant, then a glass of beer at the casino. Barely enough to make a toy poodle stagger, and certainly not enough to distract it in the presence of a well-turned table-leg. Anyhow, in his limited experience of alcoholic stupor, he remembered not a single moment of the final hour or so before absolute oblivion set in. On this occasion, he remembered every ghastly detail, right up to that final, mumbled 'Steerforth.'

For now, anyhow, whys and wherefores were unimportant. The shameful, staggering fact was not that he could not get it up – so much, as he understood it, was commonplace – but that, with a beautiful, naked girl clambering over him, giving her all at his behest and request, and doing so, furthermore, for the first time, he had preferred to sink into sleep. Somehow, he did not think that 'Regard it as a compliment. It means that I'm so relaxed with you' would salve that wound.

He could not, on balance, blame her for bolting.

'Oh, my God,' he moaned.

'Whassup, mate?' Clay strolled into the box, 'Everything OK? What yer doin' down 'ere?'

Jago blinked and reached for his boxer-shorts. He sat up to pull them on. 'Yes. Everything's fine.'

'Glad you did that.' Clay nodded at the underpants. 'Gawd, that sort of thing before breakfast. I'll not be ordering bangers, I can tell you.'

'Jesus, today's the day.' It suddenly struck Jago. The thought did not entirely banish shame, but it afforded enough adrenalin to get him to his feet.

'That's right.' Clay had wandered out again. 'It's half seven. Thought you could exercise 'is lordship, then get back to the 'otel for a bite to eat. He's been fed and watered. I make some coffee for the bold equestrian?'

'Yup. That'd be good. Thanks.' Jago picked up his suit trousers. 'Oh, shit, I can't ride in these.'

'Thought of that,' Clay called from the cab. 'Here. What would you do without your old batman, eh, general?' A folded pair of Levis hit the straw, then a pair of jodhpur boots. 'Nah, banged on your door at six, only everything's quiet as a tomb, isn't it? Put two and two together. Got a key from Reception. I was frisked both ends – of the journey, that is.'

'Friend Novak?' Jago shouted.

'Holly's bearded policewoman at the hotel, Vicky boy this end.'

'Oh, he's back on duty, is he?'

'Looked to me as if 'e'd been on all night. Eyes like piss'oles in the snow and white as Queen's Velvet, but yeah, 'e's back again.'

'Good. I didn't much like the look of last night's recruit. Strange. There only seem to be three or four people who do all his dirty work.'

'Yup. Vic seems to have 'is own fan club.'

'Yes . . .' Jago considered. 'Yes, he does, doesn't he?' He sauntered through to the little driver's section, where a kettle sputtered and rattled on a primus. It whistled, and Clay snatched up a gingham cloth to protect his hands from the heat. He poured steaming water into two mugs. 'So,' Jago tried to make it casual, 'any sign of Holly this morning?'

'Not a trace. She's moved 'er stuff out of the room, though.' Clay handed Jago a mug as though in meagre consolation. 'Bit of a tiff, was there, J?'

'No, no. Nothing like that.' He fancied, though, that she was lost to him for good. Again he winced at the memory of the night. 'Probably just – you know. She doesn't like the idea of this race. I'll catch up with her somewhere along the line.'

'Sure. Nice girl, that.'

'Yes. So . . .'

It was much the same sort of 'so' as that in which Cora specialized. It meant nothing. It was a capital blank, indicating that a new sentence had started, though there was nothing to say.

'Paul's gone off to do a bit of sightseeing out west of 'ere,' Clay said with a wink. He tipped in his habitual three spoonsful of sugar. 'Thought I might 'ead out that way an' all.'

'Good idea,' Jago said. 'You should visit Petrovice. I passed through it yesterday. Nice spot.' He spoke for Novak's benefit, should he be listening. He would know that Petrovice no more merited that description than did the Taxis.

'Right. What are your plans?'

'Dunno,' Jago said, resolved to enjoy this day for which

he had waited so long. Endorphins were suddenly squirting everywhere. 'Might drive around a bit, but the first race is at twelve-fifteen. I'd like to be there, see the competition, absorb a bit of the atmosphere. Might even pick up a stray ride. You never know.'

'Sheesh!' Clay knocked back his coffee with much noisy gulping. He gasped. 'Sooner you'n me, mate, all I can say. The nags they got 'ere, most of 'em are ratty little creatures. Oh, sure, Paul was ever so snooty, I suggested training Burly at flat-out racing pace. I din't know different, did I? And the guys out 'ere, they all do it that way. Shit, their idea of training, go like the clappers and fling the poor bugger at the nearest wall that's 'andy.'

'Ah, well,' Jago grinned. The coffee and those endorphins were hitting the right spots. 'We'll see.'

He switched off the gas and drained his now lukewarm coffee. The hell with Novak, the hell, even, with Holly. She'd probably run back to Cora: good luck to them. This was his day, his and Burly's. They were going to enjoy it. 'Right,' he said. He picked up his heavy saddle. 'Let's see if I can remember how to ride.'

The morning was not as he had expected it. The sky was Sèvres blue, just barely smeared in cleaning by high cloud. The air was still and cool. It felt firm and fissile. Tinny music bounced from over there, where the racecourse was.

Novak was waiting. He stood leaning on his car's open door. He was buffing his throat with a buzzing Remington. He wished Jago good morning whilst looking at the sky. He said, with no trace of a leer, 'I hope you had a good night, Mr van Zeller.'

'Fine,' Jago told him in a bored, dismissive tone. 'You?'

'Busy, very busy.' He snapped off the razor. He peered down into the grille as though his severed bristles might include some gold-dust.

'You need a good night's sleep.' Jago strove to appear chirpy. 'I'm going to exercise my horse, if that's OK with you.'

'OK? Of course it's OK!' That impish grin returned. 'I'm

here to look after you, Mr van Zeller! You know that, don't you?'

'Of course, nanny. Don't know how I coped without you these last twenty years,' Jago sang. 'Come along, then.'

'Vicky boy, I tell you,' Clay slung his arm around Novak's shoulders as they followed Jago down to the stables, 'you're a sticker, whatever else you may be. Amusement value low – ticks, burrs, Geoff Boycott, that sort of thing springs to mind – but you got to admire the ability to hold on.'

'It has its virtues.' Novak hawked and spat. 'The principle is simple enough, you see. It seems, you see, that there is something very attractive about this little English party. Now, if you have a very alluring wife, then a bad case of lice, say, or a weeping sore is more effective a deterrent than any chastity belt. I am your weeping sore.'

'You mean you're on our side or what?'

'I'm on the side of . . .' Novak considered. 'D'ye know? I haven't a clue whose side I'm on. I just know who's side I'm not on. Best I can do.'

Jago and Clay were frisked as they entered the stable-area. They left Novak at the gate. Jago entered the loose-box and spoke the usual soothing nonsense to his horse. Burly was carrying what, in any other animal, he would have called too much condition and was in frolicsome mood – 'gassy as all get-out', as Clay put it.

'You check out the things?' Jago breathed as he felt Burly's legs. 'I'll stand guard.'

Clay clambered up onto the manger and poked fingers through the net and the hay. 'Still all there,' he announced.

Jago shook his head. 'I still don't get Novak's game,' he said. He eased the bit into Burly's mouth and pulled the bridle up over the head-collar.

'Me neither,' Clay growled.

'Why hasn't he taken the bloody place by storm, for God's sake? Why hasn't he torn this box, our box out there, to pieces? It doesn't make sense.'

'I tell you this, J.,' Clay lifted the saddle off the door with a grunt, 'that feller, whatever he's up to, it ain't stupid. 'E looks like an amateur, it's 'cause 'e wants to look like an amateur. 'E's a grafter and 'e's no fool. I know a good poker player when I see one.'

'I've given up worrying, Clay,' Jago said contentedly. He led Burly out onto the cobbles. 'It's Havlik's worry now. I've seen the things and I don't want to see them again. They're dangerous. Bloody dangerous. Sooner they're gone, the better as far as I'm concerned.'

Burly played up as Jago saddled him. His hooves slithered and clattered. He raised his head skywards as though to tug the reins from his hand. He tapped a frantic tattoo with his forefeet. Jago led him out of the stable area before mounting. Burly's rump swung round, narrowly missing a skittering Novak. Jago knew the horse well enough and just laughed, told him that he was an old fool and a poser. 'Pay no attention,' he told Novak. 'He's just like a middle-aged man who buys a sports car and starts wearing a medallion. There's no malice in him.'

'Maybe not.' Novak eyed him suspiciously. 'But he's big, too big for me to want to romp with him.'

Burly danced sideways as Jago mounted. He raised his head and sniffed the air, then bored low in a bid to be free of restraint. He farted with every stride.

Jago steered him onto the training-ground – no more than a headland around a three-acre field. He leaned forward, sat into him and clicked his tongue. Burly pounced.

He did not like his gangling burden. He shook his head. He snorted his protests. He even put in a couple of small bucks. It was all show. He was too old a hand to seek to bolt. He knew there was a race in the offing. He wanted to get at it.

Jago crouched forward circumspectly, because the crowns on his front teeth were expensive, and Burly, with all this head-tossing, could smash them as efficiently as Mike Tyson. He kept him rocking at a contained hack-canter. It would take a deal more than this to get his back down, but Jago was not too worried. True, this boisterousness could cost them dear this afternoon, but it could also give an edge to his performance. Sooner such exuberance – the consequence, Jago thought gratefully, of Paul's restraint – than lacklustre torpor or complacency. He must trust to the horse's unparalleled experience to bear them through.

He asked Burly a question – and none too taxing a question – only in the final two furlongs. Burly opened his stride, lowered his head, and suddenly his mane was whipped back and his hoofbeats became a roll.

He felt full to bursting with life.

Jago prayed sincerely, as he pulled him up and patted his neck, that they would both be so this evening.

Burly didn't care either way. His ancestors had been at Zama, the Boyne and Waterloo. It was his turn. He was born for battle. He wanted to try himself.

Jago couldn't explain to Holly and the others who judged by reference to words and principles just how clearly a horse like this could tell him of such desires. If they could feel what Jago could feel, their arguments would founder, but the anti-hunting, anti-meat, anti-steeplechasing brigade came, to a man, from the towns. They were Mr Pooter's direct descendants. There was 'nice' and 'not nice'. Blood and sweat and mud and contention were not nice, and there was an end on it.

Novak reached up tentatively to touch Burly's snip as Jago rode back into the yard. 'I think perhaps I'll have a bet on this brute.'

'You do that,' Jago laughed as he dismounted. 'You might yet see a profit from this jaunt.'

'Oh,' said Novak ponderously, 'of that, I make no doubt.'

Holly was not at the hotel.

That did not stop Jago from looking for her, nor raising his head at every girl's voice.

In what had last night been the bar, Clay and he breakfasted on *schwinken mit ei*, as ever, and gritty coffee. Novak watched from beneath the window. He chain-smoked and slurped coffee noisily.

There was a lot of silence in that room, interrupted by sudden bursts of chatter and clatter which seemed disproportionate to the number of people there.

Pardubice was nervous.

The Svobodas and Pavla were once more in their corner. Svoboda bent low over his runny fried eggs to scoop them up with his fork. The thick fingers of his left hand drummed stiffly on a pile of papers. His wife contented herself with cup after cup of coffee, which she drank with a shaking hand and an extended pinky. Pavla gave Jago her faint, weary smile. On her way out, she came over to say, 'I saw Holly this morning.'

'You did?' Jago frowned. 'What time was that?'

'She come to the hotel very early. Seven maybe. I tell her there is forty accreditations for photographing. Two have not yet been taken. If I have one still at eleven, I will have it leaved here at Reception for Holly. She is very nice girl.'

'Yes,' Jago nodded. 'Thank you so much, Pavla. That is really very kind.' He was genuinely touched and grateful to this woman who had somehow, despite her manifold and solitary duties, found time to oblige one troublesome foreign rider. There was something very sad in the way she basked for a moment in his grateful smile before her shoulders sank, the frosted glass doors slammed shut and she turned back to her exigent masters. He had no need to look at her ring-finger to know that it was unadorned. It was in her voice, her bearing. Sweet, competent, pleasant-looking Pavla had been spoon-fed fairy-tales, he reckoned, and found the world void of handsome princes.

Three other riders whom Jago had seen yesterday on the stands were breakfasting here with trainers, friends and hangers-on. They ate, for the most part, in moody silence. When they spoke, it was with forced smiles.

Jean François's two friends, Anick and Agnes, strolled in halfway through the Englishmen's breakfast, all smiles and bright, tight jeans. They greeted Jago with waves and grins. They gabbled briefly to one another before they too were immersed in the sombre atmosphere, and they also fell quiet.

It was after half-past nine when Jean François and Corinne put in an appearance. She looked great. His eyes were opaque as snails and their shells heavier than ever. His skin was pale. He laid a hand on Jago's shoulder as he passed. 'Jago,' he gasped.

Jago remembered, just in time, that Frenchmen expected their hands to be shaken at every meeting. He stood. 'Jean François. Heavy night?'

''Alf-past four we are leaving the casino.'

'You win?'

'Not bad, not bad.'

Jago sat again and spoke over his shoulder. 'Not tucked up in bed like a good little pro, then?'

'Nah. Bof.' He shrugged. '*C'est normale, hein?*'

'*Anesthésie pour la journée?*' Jago ventured.

'*Exacte,*' he said. He reached over Jago's shoulder. He grabbed and gulped his black coffee. Then he slapped his forehead and sighed, '*Oh, nom de dieu.*'

Jago liked Jean Francçis, a madman with a lot of the woman about him. He liked his cavalier attitude, his disdain for precaution.

He didn't like the look of his chances today.

It was a long, long way from Royal Ascot.

Giants were smoking underground. Dust swirled everywhere. There must have been a hundred stalls back here behind the stands. They sold books, toys, lottery-tickets, beer, sausages, soup and sauerkraut. Jago made his way past chomping punters to the main gate. He flashed his accreditation card at the policemen there. Their Alsatian, mistrusting documents, sniffed at his crotch. All of them seemed satisfied that he was *persona grata.*

Outside the shed where yesterday Pavla had been besieged, three men were arguing in Czech and semaphore. Hayward ran forward and again proffered his hand. He also clouted Jago's back and called him a lucky dog. 'That Holly is something, hey? Listen, Jago, I got a whole load of things I want to ask you about. Your chances, how you feel, are you scared of that Taxis thing and what about these rumours that the Czechs are out to get you?'

Jago answered, pretty good, I reckon, fine, thanks, not a lot, and what rumours?

He was apologetic. 'Hey, I don't want to worry you. No, it's just there's a whisper going the rounds. Because you're the favourite, I guess.'

'I am?'

'Oh, yeah. And they say – I don't know if it's true – they say you should be on your own as you approach this Taxis.'

That undammed a chilly rivulet in Jago's stomach. His mouth seemed suddenly dry. He recalled, however, that Hayward was a pressman. 'There are always silly rumours like that. I'm sure the Czechs will be true sportsmen,' he said with more hope than certainty. Chiko's interpretation of capitalism had alarmed him, and if the casino manager was to be believed, the first prize of 500,000 crowns represented more than a year's income. Coupled with enduring glory throughout Central Europe, that could constitute a hell of an inducement for rough riding. Jago was the biggest rider in the race, and he'd lay odds on Burly's being the biggest horse, but he didn't want so much as a rabbit crowding them as they approached the Taxis.

He walked through to the lawns in front of the stands. Soldiers in silvered dark glasses strode through the already considerable crowd. More patrolled at the centre of the course. A helicopter puddered above, its engines barely audible above the music of Queen which blared from loudspeakers on the rails.

Jago scanned the crowd for Holly. He found Chiko. The Czech bounded towards him and hit his left shoulder hard. 'Good morning, Jago old bugger. Is cracking day for go like fuck, no?'

'Absolutely,' Jago agreed. It was indeed good riding weather, cool, clear and sunny. The plough would bog the runners down as little as tan. The ground would be firm for take-off. It would also be very hard to fall on.

'That Holly some crumpet. Me, I go find fat chick for bonk.'

'Jolly good,' Jago said vaguely.

'You want to ride very good horse in hurdle?' Chiko held his racecard up in front of Jago. He hit it with a stubby finger. 'Jockey go smash up in car, silly bastard, no can ride.

Me, I ride Kosmos, see? Trainer say find me fine rider goes like shit. I think friend Jago. He thruster. You say yes I tell it.'

Jago frowned at the card. Chiko appeared to be indicating a horse named Labirint in the 1.15. 'He's a good animal, you say?'

'Sure! Fine! See, he winned Cene Slovenska. He go like buggery. You wish?'

Jago shrugged. 'OK. Why not? Yes, OK.'

Chiko was delighted. 'I go tell Mr Pineva, say my very good friend Jago say yes. You be at weighing-room for twelve forty-five for meet him, yes?'

'Fine.' Jago nodded. Chiko bounced off. Too late now, Jago was beginning to wonder whether accepting a ride on his recommendation was exactly wise.

He climbed the stands to the sponsors' hospitality suite. Again his accreditation card had to be checked before he was permitted to enter this glass-fronted eyrie. Pretty girls in blue uniform stepped forward with trays of brandy and sherry. He said 'No. Coffee, please.' A minute later, one of them stepped forward with a cup and saucer. The tables were laden with canapés, predictably composed in large measure of cured or cooked pig. Sonja Svoboda was gushing at various fat dignitaries. Her husband, sweating profusely, scurried back and forth with plates of canapés for them. A couple of British journalists hailed Jago from the ranked seats beneath.

At that moment, he saw Holly.

She stood on the lawn by the rails. She wore jeans tucked into boots and a white angora sweater. Above these she wore a bright orange sleeveless waterproof which was obviously standard issue for accredited photographers. The official photographers already gathered at the Taxis were similarly dressed. So she had got the pass; he was glad. She was talking to a young man in green cords and a checked shirt.

Jago pulled his binoculars from their case. He focused on the pair. They wavered, then sprang forward into his view. That mouth was talking. That hand was pointing. That hair was scooped up in readiness for action. The camera with its telefoto lens hung about her neck.

The young man had short honey-coloured hair severely cut in a pudding-basin fringe. His face was sallow, his chin weak. He looked like a bit-player in a miracle-play.

As Jago watched, Holly finished what she was saying and turned away. She walked quickly, head down, to the gate in the rails. Four policemen barred her way. She held out her arm, showing some form of wire bracelet on her wrist. Still they were not satisfied. She fished into the pocket of the waterproof for her accreditation and her passport. There were nods then. She was allowed to pass. Jago thought at first that she would join the group at the Taxis, but she veered to her right and walked down towards fence number 3, the first water in the big race.

A study of his racecard told Jago why. The crowd at the Taxis were merely setting up their shots for the big race, placing fisheyes in the ditch, no doubt, for the standard dramatic shot. They, too, had telefotos five times as powerful as Holly's. They could catch dramatic events anywhere on the course. The Taxis, however, was jumped just once a year, in the Velka Pardubicka itself. In the first, a 3,600 metre steeplechase, the horses would jump just sixteen of the obstacles. Of these, fence number three in the big race would, in fact, be the eleventh.

'Hello, old chap.' Paul appeared at his shoulder. He smoothed back the already smooth ivory hair at his temple. 'All well?'

'Fine. I've gone and landed myself with an outside ride, God help me, in the hurdle.'

'Lucky old you. Well, this is it, eh?' He spoke with satisfaction. 'At last.'

'At last,' Jago nodded.

'Never forget this. Perfect. Lovely day, beautiful course – God. To think that I'd have missed this if I'd been sensible. I'm damn glad I never was.'

'So am I,' Jago mused. He felt a sudden upsurge of affection for this man – a figure of fun, no doubt, to many, but Jago would be well-pleased if he were as clear-eyed, as brave, as fit and as kind as Paul twenty years on. He reminded Jago to be happy. Havlik's jewels could go hang. Holly's unpredictable behaviour and his own body's strange responses were transitory problems. He was about to ride in the world's greatest remaining steeplechase on a lovely sunny day. A daft grin suddenly spread across his face. 'Goddamn it,' he murmured, 'you're right. This is the big day. I should be relishing every minute.'

Paul raised a canapé to his mouth. 'Damn good tucker,' he drawled. 'Super spread.'

Jago could have hugged him.

There was a stir then as, from down at their left, a carriage bedecked with the Czech red, white and blue crept onto the course. There were no longer twelve in hand as on Jago's well-worn video. Six blackers towed the catafalque down the straight, and Elvis was replaced on the tannoys by something ponderous and militaristic. As soon as the heavy horses had passed, the music stopped and a woman's amplified voice droned. She needed no interpreter. She was welcoming everyone to another running of the Velka Pardubicka. She listed the sponsors. Then, as the runners in the first cantered to post, she identified them one by one.

Jago looked down at the list of past winners of the race. He saw that a man named Sayers had ridden the winner of the first running, back in 1874. He was followed by Herbert, Phillips, Harraway, Geoghehan, Moore, Fletcher, Williamson and Westlake among several others. All in all, seventeen British or Irish riders had taken the prize before the outbreak of the Great War. Jago remembered Count Charles Kinsky, whose family's palace he had seen in Prague's Old Town. He must have ridden here. He rode a Grand National winner at the back end of the last century, and died of a broken heart when he was recalled to fight the Kaiser's war against his beloved British.

He pointed the names out to Paul. 'I never realized that us lot had so much to do with this part of the world.'

'Oh, yes, yes. Absolutely. Cousins, really,' Paul grinned. 'I've got a daft sort of theory about that.'

'Shoot,' said Jago, who was glad of anything to keep his

mind off the risks of falling, however much he looked forward to the race.

'Well, the thing is, the Cold War never really seemed convincing to me. I mean, the Yanks, charming chaps, so on, always seemed odder and more alien than the Russians and Germans. Equally, the marriage twixt north and south in the Common Market had always felt – I don't know – uncomfortable, an arranged marriage only, between incompatible partners, for political and economic advantage. East is east and west is west, and the twain can not only meet but get on famously. North and south, however, remain essentially irreconcilable.'

'Characterize north and south,' Jago smiled.

'Well, we northerners like solitude. Southerners like company. Northerners like sado-masochistic sex, southerners go in for all that unguent amour. Northerners like war, southerners like murder . . .'

'We have working animals, they have pets.' Jago joined in the game.

'Exactly. We go in for ritual hypocrisy and empiricism, they like self-expression and bombast and revelation.'

'We sleep on hard beds and keep the windows open . . .'

'Yup. Whilst they have soft beds and heating. We like black ironies, they have jokes about wee-wees. Northerners are deeply pragmatist. When we drill, it is to kill. When we kill, it is in pursuit of a considered end. Southerners are opportunist. When they drill, it is because they look nice in ravens' feathers. When they kill, it is because they are cross.'

Jago laughed. 'I like it,' he said, 'but don't spout your theory in North London. They don't acknowledge cultural constants round there. So, what do you put this distinction down to?'

Paul shrugged. 'Climate, genes – food and drink, probably. We all eat tons of meat and drink beer and spirits. They're all wine-bibbers and cereal eaters. That'll do it.' He raised his binoculars. The race was about to start.

Jago too adjusted the focus on his glasses. Fatuous though Paul's theory might be, he thought, sitting here, watching young men joyously hurtling over vertiginous obstacles, all for a prize of £1,000, all aware of the tradition which they aspired to maintain and fulfil, it all seemed quite self-evident.

A matador would have declared the lot of them stark, staring mad.

Jago felt quite at home.

The weighing-room proved to be yet another wooden shed tucked away beneath the stands. By pointing at his racecard and then at himself, repeatedly speaking his name in the German style – 'Fan Tsellair' – Jago at length acquired a set of colours: yellow, red sash, red cap. They were too small for him. If he so much as raised his elbows to chest level, a gap opened up between the hem of his sweater and the waist-band of his breeches.

The cap, too, for some strange reason equipped with a hat-band and strangely flat in shape, like an Australian cricketer's cap, was stretched to splitting over Jago's helmet. He was forced to lodge it on the very back of his head so that it covered only the crown. The peak pointed upwards. His face was in the maws of a laughing duck.

Sartorially, then, he ill matched the Sartorius which his imagination had painted. He was a scarecrow jockey, straw extruding at the head.

He removed the cap and donned his tweed coat to wander out and watch the next race, a five-thousand-metre chase which took in a set of fences entirely different from those in the first. He stood on the lawn and watched the horses cantering to the start. He said, 'Heaven help us.'

'Getting nervous?' Novak did his materializing act at Jago's left shoulder.

'Oh, sure, a little. I always do.'

'So why the prayer?'

'Because there are horses out there which I wouldn't run in a pony-club gymkhana,' Jago told him. 'Ratty little bastards with ribs like draining-boards and arses like rent-boys. If they don't get smashed up, I reckon they'll have twisted guts by the end of five kilometres.' He looked them up on the racecard. 'One of them's Russian, one Hungarian. Watch them. They shouldn't be here.'

'All right, Nostradamus.' Novak chewed dead skin from an orange finger. He spat. 'Make a prediction that'll pay. What do I back in this race?'

'Ah, that's quite another thing. I can tell you when I see a bad horse. I can tell you when I see a fit horse. I can tell you very roughly if a horse has good conformation. Given two or three fit horses with more or less classic conformation, however, I'm as much at sea as you. Still, all right. I know nothing about his form, his ancestry or his character, but if you want a hunch, I'd favour number three, the bay.'

Novak nodded. He rolled his racecard and forced it into an already bulging pocket. 'I'll take your advice,' he said as though surprised at himself. 'God knows why,' he added graciously. He drew apart an approaching family with a gesture like opening curtains. Now they flopped naturally together again. Novak had disappeared.

Number three duly obliged. He skewed over the last and he reeled in the straight, erring from the stands side to the opposite rail, but his nearest opponent, though gaining, was still six lengths back as he passed the post.

As for the Russian and Hungarian horses, the Russian, flung at his fences with a recklessness which gave amateurism a bad name, ploughed through what Jago thought of as fence number twelve and just kept on diving downwards. He landed with his head on one side and his arse in the air like a child going to sleep. He slid a bit and his rider went for an airborne run. The horse did not get up.

The Hungarian animal battled on to fence number eighteen, the big snake ditch. He castled it. He took off almost vertically, like a child in wellies trying to make the maximum splash in a puddle. He never had a chance. Jago winced as he jumped, inhaled with a hiss as he descended. He could imagine the thudding of the other horses' feet all around, the jaunty tinkle of harness, the sucking, swirling and splashing as the horse depth-charged the stream, the thud as he hit the opposite bank.

He could imagine too what Holly saw through her lens where she stood by the side of the ditch. He saw her there, legs set wide, weight now on one, now on the other. Her face was a black pout. She never lowered the camera. She just kept on shooting, now crouching, now straightening.

Jago understood. Without the camera, she would have been sobbing or screaming or rushing vainly forward to offer assistance or to push back the hands of the clock. Whilst she continued to shoot, however, she was merely a component of a perceiving machine. The camera was an isolated module, a locked cell from which she could view the world but never touch it. She had to stay inside.

The horse dragged himself out. He looked down at his curled-up rider. He cropped grass.

It was the condemned man's hearty breakfast. His off fore was kinked at the knee. Pastern and hoof lay flat on the turf. The white blood-wagon bounced towards him where he grazed.

All in all, Jago thought grimly as he returned to the weighing-room, Novak should be pretty impressed by his precognitive powers, though in truth he had to avow that fortune had attended his hunches better than was her wont.

Chiko, bare barrel-chested, with skin which had never known a summer holiday and a typhoon of hair about his flat orange paps, greeted Jago effusively. 'You see me go for get buried at Anglicky Skok?' he chortled proudly. 'Bitch buggery horse go uparse like at doctor's adopt the position, right?'

'No harm done?'

'No, no. Horse go bouncy bouncy, me chewing grass, but OK, fine. Now you.'

'Me?'

'Yes,' he said gleefully, 'now you. My good friend Jago, hunter and goer, ride first time in Czech Republic. Me, I watch you, maybe, like they say, do you, yes?'

'No, please . . .' Jago very much wanted to compete in the big race before he was crippled. 'Please, Chiko. No games.'

'We see. Your horse here, he like much go like shit off

shovel. He start up front, he finish in front. He go like buggery. He not likes jockeys.' He spoke happily. He held up his green sweater and frowned at it as though working out just how so complex an artefact might work. 'Still, you hold him back, yes?'

'Oh, God,' Jago whispered sadly, 'you mean you've got me on one that pulls like a train?'

''Sright! 'Sright!' The words were muffled. Chiko's whiskered face emerged, crimson and beaming. 'Is good, no? He run like wild pig nothing stop go through stone wall. He goer bugger, like you.'

'Thank you, Chiko,' Jago sighed. He slipped out of the jacket and pointlessly tucked in his sweater. 'Thanks a bloody million.'

The good news – the amazing news – was that Jago reached the start without mishap. This owed more to the animal's refusal to be left behind than to Jago's horsemanship. They started late, and the animal wanted to be up there with the others. Jago did nothing much to restrain him.

A showy flame chestnut, this horse would, had he been human, have been a great gawky redheaded adolescent of Celtic origin, talking up a storm in his cups, picking fights, occasionally winning them by default, but easily flattened by anyone with a cooler eye and a deeper girth. He had a firm conviction that he was intended to walk on two legs. On water, if possible.

Jago had watched him in the paddock. He had touch-typed in the dust, head held high and aloof save when he lowered it as though myopically and scornfully to check his text. His gaunt quarters were lower than his withers. They slithered sideways. They suddenly bunched forwards. As Jago had watched him, his own quarters had similarly bunched and remained so. It was going to be like riding a caterpillar on speed, at speed.

Chiko had presented Jago to the trainer, who in turn had proudly shown him to the owners. Chiko had laughed as though at a great joke – the sinking of the *Titanic*, say – slapped Jago's bum painfully with his whip and moved off.

The trainer, stubby as a tor, with a hugging copse of hair atop and cheeks the colour of heather, had had as little English as Jago had Czech. 'Gall-op,' he had essayed, whilst apparently simulating intercourse with a dwarf. 'Yes?'

If this was advice, Jago considered it superfluous. He smiled, however, and keenly nodded.

'Grant Nazi On Al,' added the owner's wife. She was an attenuated chicken, a broiler, with dry white skin and a wobbly crop and a dyed blonde comb with brown roots. She described undulations with her hand. She cackled. Her husband laughed. The trainer laughed. Jago laughed. They loved one another, and they didn't make jokes like that any more.

This was the sum of Jago's instructions. He was heaved into the saddle. The dust in the paddock laid a coarse gauze film over everything.

Beneath him, the horse's rump suddenly dropped away. It reappeared three yards to the right. This time, it jerked upwards whilst the forefeet were firmly planted in the turf. If Jago's testicles had not been ellipsoidal to start off with, they sure as hell were now.

The real problem was that there was nothing to this horse, he thought, as now he skittered and slithered and danced towards the start, shooting forwards at the very sight of another of his kind, stopping dead at a sound from the tannoy or the crowd. He had no neck to speak of. If Jago leaned – or was jolted – forwards, he had an uninterrupted view of chipped turf. As to that rump, it continued to do its disappearing-here-and-reappearing-somewhere trick.

He was riding a nerve.

'Very fine horse, yes?' Chiko greeted Jago as they drew up beneath a row of poplars. Jago's mount contracted to a single cell, then burst back into solidity five yards forward.

'Very bloody hateful Araby case of sausage-meat,' Jago panted and tried to snarl. He dared to take his hand from the reins for just long enough to wipe sweat from his eyes. The horse played the minute-waltz on the turf. In ten seconds. His hand returned fast.

Chiko roared with jubilant, triumphant laughter, a sound

sufficient to alarm several of the horses milling about. It caused Jago's mount briefly to squirm, then to dissolve and reconstitute itself, almost instantly, ten yards away. Finding Jago lying on his back, he did some sideslipping exercises.

Jago turned him and coaxed him to the very back of the field.

He looked up at the sheer blue sky. He looked over to the stands where, he was convinced, his friends gleefully observed every undignified moment. He glanced over to his left, where he had last seen Holly. She had vanished.

He had not thought to die like this.

Still, if die he must, he might as well – well, not enjoy it, exactly – but at least put a bold face on it.

Chiko was still laughing. Normally Jago liked a cheery disposition.

His views were changing.

The off was a sort of relief. At least it brought the end that little bit closer. The other riders leaned forward. Their mounts too bent their necks studiously to their business. Jago saw them doing it, for the barest split second.

Then he was squirted out into the middle of the track and saw them no more.

He was not sedately bent over his horse's non-existent neck. He was leaned backwards, his seat very firmly in the saddle. He was tugging hard. As for the horse, he was no longer watching his forefeet. He was addressing the tops of the poplars and wondering at just what speed he might take off.

He was now nearing that speed.

Jago was being definitively, unquestionably, right royally carted.

There were other terms for it. 'Run away with' would do, but was definitely pony-club. On the gallops, they laconically observed, 'he's gone to fetch the papers'. Whatever they called it, it was amongst the world's nastier experiences. Jago was astride twelve hundred pounds of muscle and bone possessed of self-induced terror, and his efforts to check the rush were not dissimilar to Canute's erosion-prevention scheme.

Jago tried to turn the beast's head to the offside. The horse was having none of it. Jago tugged all the more resolutely. The course remained a blur of blue and green. His cheeks were whipped by the wind, though the trees were still.

There was an obstacle in their way.

Then there wasn't.

Jago was still wondering what to do about that obstacle five strides after they had cleared it or smashed through it or whatever it was that they had done. The horse had not broken his stride. He had, very slightly perhaps, left the ground. Basically, he had gobbled the hurdle, absent-mindedly, *en passant*.

Jago risked a glance over his shoulder. The field was fifteen, twenty lengths back.

It was lonely out there.

Jago recalled the serenity prayer. 'God grant me,' he found himself murmuring, 'the serenity to accept the things I cannot change, the courage to change the things I can, and the wisdom to know the difference . . .'

There was only one thing about his present situation, he concluded as they flew through the next hedge, that he could change; not the speed, nor the likelihood that they would hit a hurdle and execute a double somersault in sudden silence. These were beyond his control. He could, however, influence the direction that they took.

He did not want this horse taking an unscheduled crack at the Taxis, just for fun.

He crouched forward. What he had said to Novak about the irresponsibility of jokes came back to him. Here was the biggest, blackest joke. He was about to die in some corner of a foreign field on a mad bastard of a nag which he did not know in order to earn money and pride for some Czechs who did not speak English and whom he had never met before.

So he grinned. He growled, 'Go on, you old bugger.'

He urged him on.

He was never to know precisely what happened from there on, because, in a sense, when you abandoned responsibility, you abandoned too all those conscious faculties with which you named and counted and estimated. Somewhere in his head there must have remained the memory of the course because he steered the beast around it. He shouted quite a lot. He may even have called 'Whee!' or something suitably epigrammatic as they approached yet another obstacle which, if the animal took it too low or too hard, would unquestionably constitute his last problem on earth. Sympathy between horse and rider was a wonderful thing. This horse was mad. His rider – his passenger, rather, with a midriff gap and a cap like a snood – was madder still. Hollering, gibbering, gabbling, screeching mad.

He also, for some strange physiological reason, had a hard-on like a railroad spike.

'There's the secret, Julie girl,' he thought as he urged the brute down to the final bend. The animals behind them at last became audible. 'Forget your blue movies and your blandishments. Take from a man every care in the world, and what was dead in him will rise again.'

They were in the straight now, and racing. Chiko's whiskers bobbed at Jago's offside. Chiko had stopped smiling. His mouth was a razorshell. His jaw jutted. Jago laughed. Chiko's face for a second jerked towards him. A grey head worked like a piston at Jago's near heel.

They never had a chance. To his credit, Jago's demented rat of a mount did not give up. He was blown, but still he struck forward with that telltale flap of the knee, still his head nodded and that scrawny neck stretched. This animal very much disliked being headed.

Jago did not pick up his stick. There was no point. The horse foundered through the last two hurdles, stumbled at the last and nearly fell for sheer exhaustion. Jago gave him what help he could by pushing him out with hands and heels, but Chiko passed the post a good six lengths ahead. He stood in his irons and punched the air like a soccer player. A grey came in a length behind him. Snorts and footfalls at Jago's back meant that others were drawing in the rope, but they lurched into the safe haven beyond the post in a third place which would ever hereafter look more distinguished than now.

Chiko lingered until Jago drew upsides. He pulled down his goggles. He wiped his nose on his sleeve. He clapped Jago between the shoulders. 'You still alive, then, my good friend? You lucky man.'

'You mean you expected me to break my neck?'

Chiko shrugged. 'Is possible.'

'No bloody rider had a car-crash, did they, Chiko? You set me up on this pig, didn't you? You hoped I'd come a cropper.'

'Is possible,' Chiko admitted again. 'Anything is possible in free society, yes? Democracy is good.'

Jago gritted his teeth and thought nostalgically of the good old days when tanks rumbled about Wenceslas Square and free enterprise was rewarded by a spell in the salt-mines.

He would have liked to collectivize Chiko just then.

It was building, always building. There were three more races before the big one, always picturesque, sometimes exciting, but somehow trivial distractions in relation to what was to come. You could hear it in the buzzing of the crowd, the deep, conspiratorial rumble beneath sudden, nervous barks. Money was invested here. Necks were at stake. They had had the soft core; now they were waiting for the real thing. They had had the simulation; now the gladiators waited in the wings, the lions in their cages, and both tridents and teeth were sharp.

And Jago, incredibly, was to be one of the gladiators.

He felt like a fraud. Gladiators lived, surely, on a diet of raw meat, bull's blood and helots' quims. They swore and they sang and they told tales of bloodshed. They never, surely, suffered from a fear of moths, as did he, nor measured inside-legs nor counted Lapsang Suchong as a favourite beverage.

And yet, as they sat in that sweaty, cramped little shed and almost at once found reason to stand, performing little, meaningless rituals (why did he remove the collar-stiffeners, for example, or fold his shirt so carefully, or arrange his loose change in separate piles, one for each denomination?)

he reflected that precious few of them fitted the gladiatorial mould.

Paul looked leaner than ever in his green and yellow sweater and his wafer-thin breeches. He sat talking to himself, urging himself on. His loosely clenched fist beat time upon his knee. His eyes glittered – a glimpse of Adriatic through venetian blinds. He vaguely smiled at anyone who passed, as though afraid of causing offence.

Chiko, now, was nearer the mark. His body might not have encouraged underwriters about the Circus Maximus, but his mind seemed of the right sort. He guffawed. He slapped his fellow Czechs. He teased and chaffed and bellowed. Everyone whom he addressed moved away, save one boy with a face so new that it must have been bought, not inherited, who strove to echo Chiko's bravado but contrived only a trickle of sound and some nervous giggling.

As for Jean François, he was far too beautiful for a gladiator, with that palomino forelock and those capuchin eyes and those expressive velvet lips. He sat with his legs extended and his head thrown back against the wall. His eyes were closed. He was enjoying what he saw there. A conjuror's thread tugged his lips into small, sudden, sensuous smiles.

Havlik was the last to join the company. He stormed in, frowning deeply. His bulging eyes swung at once to Paul, then to Jago, then away again. He changed as though in the Arctic, fumbling and tearing at buttons and zips, hopping from foot to foot and cursing. He banged things, yet started angrily whenever anyone behind him so much as coughed. His cheeks were drained of all colour.

At last he was dressed and weighed in. He marched back into the changing-room and slumped down on the bench between Paul and Jago. 'Oh, Jesus, guys.' It started as a belch and ended as a whimper. 'This – you've got to help me.'

Paul frowned. 'You've moved the things, I trust, old chap?'

'I – no. No, I couldn't.' Havlik gulped.

'Well, I must say . . .' Paul objected. 'All we've done. It

seems bloody rotten to leave us lumbered and taking all the risks. I've involved Jago quite enough. It won't do. Come along. Buck up.'

'I told you, Havlik,' Jago said firmly, 'we've already helped you. We've had enough of the business. If your plan doesn't work, you'll just have to go through the official procedure. That's hardly the end of the world.'

'Christ, what do you know about it?' he blurted. Jago suddenly realized that he had been drinking. 'No, no. No, sorry, Jago. No, I mean . . . this race . . .' His fingers plucked at Jago's sleeve. 'Jesus, risking my neck for nothing. It's crazy!'

'You'll be OK,' Paul said with a degree of assurance that he did not feel. 'Come on.'

Jago voiced an incredulous suspicion. 'You've ridden races before, haven't you?'

'Not . . . Oh, dear God, like, sure, I did a refresher course last month, practised in an indoor school, that sort of thing, but you know, real thing, shit, we're talking five fucking years.'

'Then you're a damned fool, and you need your wits about you even more,' Paul snapped. 'For Christ's sake, man, how much have you had to drink?'

'Three or four brandies's all.'

'Well, steer clear of me,' Jago told him uncharitably. 'Just cling onto your neckstrap or the mane and hope for the best.'

'Oh, God, oh, God, oh, *God*!' Havlik hugged himself. He started the litany with a murmur and ended it with a little scream. 'This is crazy. This is suicide. And all . . . He *knows*, guys. That Novak guy. He's playing with us. You hear what he said about Troy, Paul?'

'Yes.'

'You see, he *knows*! It's all fucking pointless . . .'

'Oh,' Paul said slowly, 'I see. The mare.'

'Yeah, I reckoned, you know, most people are scared of horses. They stop the trailer, sexually abuse my horse, it's, like, diplomatic suicide. But they can't X-ray, 'cause X-rays there'd cause sterility, right?'

Paul nodded. It was not so bad a plan. There was room enough in a mare's uterus for twice the hoard that Havlik wished to conceal. It was a method which, legend had it, had been used before. It was true that the average customs man would hardly be in a hurry to approach the rear of a race-mare, still less to goose her, but Novak was a countryman, and, for all that he did not know horses, might have experience of bovine obstetrics at the least.

'You'll just have to decide,' Paul said. 'Either you hope that he didn't mean that and try for it, or you give up and declare the things. I'd help you if I could, but it's Jago's box, not mine. I'd declare it myself. You might have a long wait, but you'd get it all in the end.'

'Oh, shit, shit . . .' Havlik blinked smarting eyes. He stared at the opposite wall as though at a vision of hell.

The man at the door summoned the riders. Havlik's eyes opened still wider. A shudder shook him. A whine escaped him. 'Come on.' Jago stood. 'You'll be fine. Dismount at the first or something.'

Paul and Jago left him to his terror and walked out side by side. They blinked at the bright light and the bright clothes all around. They could stop dragging their feet now. They were on the downward slope.

Here, at last, it was.

The paddock was a cowboy corral surrounded by banked tiers of seats. The dust kicked up by the horses' hooves made both men raise their arms as though somehow to sweep aside the net curtain which masked their view. Madonna was hiccoughing on the PA system. They saw Clay standing with a fair-haired woman at the centre of the ring. They strolled over, saluted him with their whips, then turned to greet the woman.

She smiled.

Jago said 'Er . . .' He said 'I . . .' He said 'But . . .' He actually staggered two steps backwards as though he had been shoved.

She just continued smiling.

'What the hell are you doing here?' Jago yelped to Diana Osborne, and he gathered her to him, pressed her to him hard, so her feet left the ground. 'What in God's name are you doing here?'

She squeaked in his hug. He let her down but did not let her go. 'Come to see you off, didn't I?' she mumbled into his chest. 'Only just arrived in time. Look behind you.'

Jago swivelled round, and suddenly his throat was tight and his eyes were brimming. Cindy was waggling fingers at him. Neil and John were grinning and giving the thumbs up. The entire staff of Zellers was there, looking insufferably smug at Jago's surprise.

He said 'But . . .' a few more times. He allowed a washy bay to saunter past him on the tan, then scampered across to the rails to take hands, to hug, to ask asinine questions such as 'How did you get here?' and 'What are you doing here?' and 'How did you pay for it, you madmen?'

From the various giggled and gabbled answers, he gathered that they were here because they were damned if they could see why he should have all the fun and they reckoned that, be it for death or glory that he was bound, they had a right to be involved in either. They had flown in this morning. As to the finance, they had earned their fares by moonlighting, and then Miss Sniffy had come up trumps, decided that five hundred pounds could be deemed bona fide promotional expenses . . .

Madonna had given way to Freddy Mercury again. 'Bohemian Rhapsody', perhaps unsurprisingly, was big in these parts. Beneath the plaintive '*I don't wanna die*', which must have been striking chords in poor Havlik, Jago heard Clay calling, 'Come on, J, mate! Race to be run!'

Jago turned. The horses had been turned inwards. It was time to go. Jago waved to the gang. He called, 'God, I am glad to see you guys,' and meant it with all his heart. There was a chorus of 'Good luck!' and 'Hold on tight!'

He returned to Clay and Diana. Paul had already mounted and was grinning more broadly than Jago had ever seen him grin. Burly was playing it cool. He appeared to be almost asleep on his feet. He gave a laconic greeting by placing his forehead against Jago's chest. He then suddenly raised his head, shoving him reeling backwards. Clay caught Jago, steadied him.

'Trainer's advice,' Clay said as he bent. Jago gulped nervously. He raised his shin. Clay grasped it and flicked him up.

'Go on?'

'Don't fall off.'

Jago reached down to take Diana's hand for a quick squeeze, then turned Burly to follow Paul and Avocet towards the gateway onto the course.

Burly suddenly picked up. If he had impressed with his composure, he now reckoned that the crowd should gasp at his magnificence. He arched his neck and raised his tail and trotted as though on sponge. Jago sat upright, reins crossed beneath his crotch. The arrival of the Zellers crowd had much the same effect as the sunshine on his shoulders. He felt warm and very happy.

As they moved out onto the course to parade, he gazed out at the Taxis where the photographers were gathered. He could not see Holly amongst them. He looked back over his shoulder to where last he had seen her, over at the course's perimeter fence by the giant water.

He saw the orange waterproof, the flash given off by her hair.

What was she doing? Every sports photographer in the world would welcome the opportunity to be here, on the course at Pardubice, and every one of them would be stationed very firmly beneath the Taxis. Holly had already had plenty of opportunity to snap horses and riders as they took that big stream. Perhaps she was hiding, then, from the horrors which she foresaw at the giant fence?

But she was not standing still. She was running, stumbling along the perimeter rail, her hair bobbing behind her. The woods behind her were deep and dark.

'What the hell . . .?' Jago murmured, but then they were before the stands and applause crashed over them like a great breaker. Jago grinned at the excitement of it all. He said, 'What the hell.' Burly pricked his ears and pranced. Ahead of him, Paul, in white with red crossbelts, was scanning the course and grinning. Ahead of him, Jean

François, in black and yellow wasp hoops, slouched in the saddle. Ahead of him again, Chiko was scooping up the cheers with his big hands, milking it for all he was worth. He sat down then, leaned forward, swung his big orange bay round and cantered past at Jago's offside.

Burly tossed his head and snorted. Showing off was fun, of course, but that running lark looked better.

Jean François too turned and set off for the start. He was bunched up, neat and aerodynamic as an American on the flat.

It was Paul's turn, then Jago's. Even as Jago eased Burly around, even as the horse took a hold, the crowd's cheering and clapping turned to jeers and groans. A moment's affronted paranoia afflicted Jago, then, between Burly's ears, he saw the reason.

Suddenly, there was a whole lot going on on the course.

Policemen were running in pairs in the same direction as the horses and riders were cantering. Mounted policemen, again in pairs, wheeled and cantered at Jago's nearside. Their long night-sticks hung from their wrists. They were grinning.

Jago moaned 'No . . .?' as the chill pain of betrayal spread through his veins. 'No, no, no!'

He kicked on, and Burly, mildly surprised, obliged.

Ahead, a man with a flag indicated that Jago was to steer his mount in to the right, where the other horses and riders had already taken shelter behind a wall of soldiers.

Beyond that man, a hundred, two hundred people in jeans and T-shirts and suede boots streamed across the racecourse. Some held placards. One read *Stop the Slaughter!*, another, *Blood Sports are Murder!* Other slogans were emblazoned in German. The protestors' destination was the Taxis. They came from a small gate in the perimeter rails, just where Jago had last seen Holly.

You could not miss her, in the bright orange waterproof waistcoat which had bought her protection and trust. You could not miss her, running there, up front, urging her *confrères* on.

The police and the army were about and upon them now. Jago pulled Burly up, but remained at the centre of the track, watching. The demonstrators' progress to the Taxis was cut off, so those to the fore, including Holly, dived to their right and sat beneath fence number thirty-two. The remainder who were still running were dragged or clubbed down. The big batons flashed. Dust spurted. The helicopter grumbled angrily above.

The crowd groaned again. Another wave of demonstrators broke from the western end of the course, again bound for the Taxis. The mounted police wheeled like hussars. A pair of them set their mounts at one of the race's big hedges and leaped it upsides, to roars of approval from the stands. More footsoldiers, policemen and dogs gathered about the protestors like antibodies about germs. Again the dust sprouted from the dry ground. Again the course was rapidly littered with little heaps of colour which had just now been running men and women.

Jago's mind raced. This was no coincidence. It had all been a set-up. They must have known from the racing-press and from their intelligence that Jago was bound here. He was easy enough to recognize. On Cora's instructions, no doubt, Holly had picked him up and made herself charming, with this in mind, had winsomely kissed him, with this in mind, had been willing to allow him to plunder her body, with this in mind.

For a cause, she would say; for the sake of the poor little animals. Omelettes. Eggs. The hateful and specious justification of idealists throughout the ages. And Jago was just an egg to be broken. He had allowed himself to believe in a human being and in human affections, in spite of theory. She had allowed herself to believe in a theory in spite of human beings and human affections.

In both instances, they had sought a passion to fill a vacuum. She had chosen this. He, like a fool, had chosen her.

Almost unconsciously, Jago was letting Burly wander towards the fight. He heard the thuds and cracks as batons hit flesh or bone, the gasps and squeals as blows went home. He saw the stocks of automatic weapons hooked in crotches, then jerked hard upwards. Men screamed.

He was torn. As a good little Western liberal, of course, he was shocked by such techniques. As a pragmatist, he could not but admire the ruthless skill and efficiency with which police and soldiers worked to contain and subdue a force which far outnumbered them.

An orange and white coach had bobbed across the turf. More police leaped from it and shoved the staggering, coughing, moaning men and women inside.

A smaller group of demonstrators emerged from beneath the stands. They had a shorter distance to cover. They jinked like soccer-players about their stretching, unbalanced challengers. They sprinted for the Taxis. The mounted police pursued. Their horses, Jago noted with interest, had been trained to strike with their forelegs. They drove the protestors thus until they fell or were cornered against the fence, then the men on foot fell upon them, and the batons flashed and swished.

A warning shout from the crowd. All heads and hands swung round. Jago looked back to the fence beneath which Holly had sought refuge. There had been a breakout. Some twelve of them, taking advantage of the distractions, had resumed their run for the Taxis.

Holly was amongst them. Her cheeks were red. Her mouth was open. Each protestor had been marked by a pursuing soldier. The soldiers were fitter and had not run so far. They were inexorably gaining. Their batons were raised high.

Burly was cantering.

Behind him, someone yelled, 'Jago!'

Burly snorted. He was mildly disappointed to find that no flames emerged.

Holly was beneath him, still running. She did not turn, but raised an arm behind her to protect herself. The policeman behind her lunged and dived, but Jago grabbed the extended wrist, and pulled. The man fell forward. He yelled something in Czech.

He tried to tug Holly up across the saddle-bow, but she resisted. 'You sluttish little bitch,' he snarled down at her, and he wrenched Burly around so savagely that he had to go back on his hocks. 'I got you in on trust . . .'

She rolled over. Her eyes were neon bars. Her upper lip curled upwards in a snarl. She laughed.

She was not Holly.

The shock was so great, the metamorphosis so nightmarish, that he let her go and released a little shriek. Cora Sanderson slid from the saddle, but she landed, bounced on the balls of her feet and swivelled round. 'Bastard!' she shrieked above the thudding of hooves and of clubs on bodies. She grasped Jago's thigh. She heaved herself upwards again. Heat seared through his lower body as her teeth sank into the flesh through the fabric of his breeches. He raised the whip high. He brought it down in a deep, savage arc. Had it been a cavalry sabre, it would have cloven her head. As it was, it lit a fierce red fuse across her forehead. Flames of blood burst from it. She yelped and fell back, both hands now covering her face, and the man behind her was on her. His baton descended, and saliva sprayed from her head. His baton then gesticulated quite plainly that Jago should move away, back to where the others were milling about.

Jago was confused as he rode back towards them. Initially he was relieved that it had not been Holly out there, but then he wondered exactly how she had been involved. He felt hope, then. Perhaps she had not been insincere. Perhaps she had been used by Cora. Then he realized that the whole thing would have had to have been planned well in advance. At what point had it been arranged that Cora would have her hair highlighted and cut to the length of Holly's? Yesterday afternoon, as he had waited in silly, solitary frustration whilst Holly had supposedly wandered about Pardubice? Or last night, as he had lain in a stupor, having promised to try and obtain accreditation for her? Or was it always a component of their plan as they and their colleagues giggled and plotted back in London?

He had been a means to an end. And the end was this, this devastation, this squalid, sad, absurd 'mopping up'. The ignorant and anthropomorphic had made their point before the world. Blood had been shed. Holly and her friends were content. Another good day had been ruined.

That was all.

The holiday was done, then. The illusion had proved just that. Jago had thought to find a better life, a greater equality, a truer, more indulgent trust between friends. He had discovered only what he had always been taught – that better lives were the creations of good painters, good writers, good liars.

Then a freezing fury burst in upon his thoughts. There might be another reason for which Holly had eschewed martyrdom here. Animal Rights demonstrators liked and needed money. She was one of only five people who knew where those jewels were hidden. The remaining four were on the racecourse.

Havlik would have little claim on those stones if they were to turn up on the black market in Antwerp or London.

Suddenly Jago's avowed disinterest in the jewels evaporated. They represented the hopes of his friends back there in the stands as much as those of Cyril Havlik. The passion was back. He hoped that Holly had not twice betrayed him, not least for her sake.

Horses and riders were at last allowed to move up to the start. Even then, they were kept milling around, just waiting, whilst the demonstrators were bundled into buses and driven away.

'Already a most stimulating day,' Jean François languidly observed.

'What was all that about, then, Jago?' asked Paul. 'Gosh, you're bleeding.'

'Bitch bit me.' Jago looked down at the crimson patch on his breeches. 'Forgot her vegetarian principles, it seems.'

'Wasn't Holly, was it?' Paul asked gently.

'What? No. No, it was a friend of hers,' Jago said, shaking his head. 'She was one of them, I'm afraid. She set me up. God, Paul, what is it about men that makes us such suckers when it comes to women?'

'No good asking me.' Paul shook his head. 'They always saw me coming a mile off. I'm sorry, old chap.'

'Ah, well.' Jago made a conscious effort to pull himself up in the saddle and to smile. 'Easy come . . .' He checked himself, realizing that he might have phrased it better.

'Jesus, Jago, what's the matter with this goddamn horse?' Havlik was shaking as he drew up alongside Burly. 'She doped or what? I don't think she can run, man.'

His mount was a handsome, iron-grey creature with lop ears. She had an honest head, but she was not behaving honestly at the moment. Her eye rolled. Her neck and her belly were darkened by sweat. She skittered and tittupped and leered. She was plainly distressed. The world, for her, was full of unseen terrors.

Maybe it was just the confusion of the past few minutes which had agitated her. Jago did not think so.

'Fear travels down the reins,' they say.

She was getting an overdose.

'She's fine,' Jago lied. 'Stop jagging her in the mouth. She's a steeplechaser, not a cowboy's nag. And try to relax. Give her a pat. Tell her she's lovely. Tell her you're going to help her to win. Visualize her winning. Give her that thought as a present.'

Havlik nodded. 'Sure. OK.' But the fingers of his right hand still raked the fabric at his thigh and his eyes still swivelled and stared. 'Oh, shit, man. I got gutrot. I can't do this.'

'So don't start. Let us go without you.'

'I can't, man!' he wailed, and his eyes were now filled with tears. 'That Novak knows! I don't start . . . Jesus, all that bread just sitting there, and . . . I'm fucked, I don't get it home. It's all I got, you know? I just stand here, they'll be on me like vultures. Oh, shit, man, this is crazy. Why'd I get myself talked into this? Those guys, they said they'd stop the race! I mean, you guys . . .'

'You mean,' Paul drawled menacingly, 'that you had some contact with those people?'

'No!' Havlik's inhalation was a honked chord. 'Just, like, I heard they were coming. Six hundred people, they said. Six hundred wimps, they can't do better . . . They were gonna stop it. They guaranteed . . .'

Paul wheeled his horse away. His disappointment was more palpable than his disdain.

Jago shared a little of the disdain, but Havlik was plainly suffering and Jago pitied him. He suffered from vertigo. He knew what it was to be frozen by terror. He knew the agony of fear so intense, so unceasingly urgent that you'd sooner fall than keep fearing falling. Havlik should not be here. It was potentially lethal, not merely for him, but for those who must ride with him.

'So stay at the back,' Jago advised. 'Just hack round as best you can. That's a legitimate strategy in a race like this one. Come on. Your ancestors did this. There's a lot of nostalgic Czechs out there rooting for you. There's a lot of resentful commies wanting to see you fall. You show 'em.'

Havlik sniffed. He drooled, 'Right, yeah,' but the shakes had a hold of his shoulders. Tears dripped heavy from his jawbone. He was in fugue. 'Yeah, right,' he croaked. 'Yeah, show 'em, right, right, yeah . . .'

The field was moving forwards now, forming up in line. Havlik's grey went with them like flotsam. Havlik was blindly borne into the battle lines, murmuring, 'Right . . . show 'em . . .'

The flag was up and flapping. There was a sudden stillness all about the course. You could hear the breeze.

Just ahead of Jago at his right, Paul turned and flashed him a grin of pure happiness. 'G'luck, Jago, old boy,' he whispered.

'Good luck, mate,' Jago smiled, and rather wanted to cry.

They asked him why he did it.

This was why.

Because it was clean and straightforward and simple. Because, in the midst of it all, there was nothing else. The petty ambitions and betrayals, the affections, ideals and disillusions, all dropped away.

There was only now.

It was not a trance. You were aware – God, more aware than ever in quotidian doings – of each sound, each movement ahead, to either side, behind, aware of your position in relation to the rest of them, of the nature of the ground, of the peculiar dangers inherent in every fence. You were aware of the sunlight leaning, aware of the plucking of the fine wool at your skin, aware of the twittering of the birds in the woods, the glittering of the ribbons of water . . .

This was the *eau de vie* of awareness, distilled many times to a purity, clarity and heady potency many times greater than those of everyday perception. All the cloudy maybes, all the whatifs, all the habitual preferences and memories were left behind in the mash.

Here was the great joke, the great prayer.

The riders no longer – with the exception of poor, gibbering Havlik – cared about themselves.

So they asserted that something greater existed.

Even as Burly put his head down and charged like a bull from the line, Jago took a pull.

For the moment, at least, they were eventing, not racing.

Burly objected, but then Burly would. Jago crooned to him, he soothed him, he held him hard. Ahead of them, the attenuated keyhole of Paul's lean arse and legs was right up there in the midst of the charging Czechs and Russians. Chiko crouched at their outside, already pushing and urging. Jean François's wasp colours had swung over to the inside rail just a length or two ahead of Jago. He rode beautifully, as though on springs, legs clinging tightly, head well down.

Jago was at the rear of the field, which was fine by him.

He had only one problem. Cyril Havlik appeared to have adopted him as his talisman.

Maybe it had nothing to do with Havlik. Maybe, whilst he had been reproving and encouraging him, his mare had been quietly making up to Burly. Either way, they clung to his offside.

Havlik was not happy. He whimpered and sang and muttered strange, high-pitched imprecations. His mare had caught his misery and his insecurity. She was leaning on Burly. Jago had his stick in his right hand. Burly was hard against the nearside running-rail. Jago could still feel the heat of her against his right knee.

Jago wanted room. He wanted freedom of movement. He had expected that he would be hampered by Chiko or one of his countrymen, but Havlik was doing their job for them, and inadvertently.

They took the first, a simple, yielding hedge, but Jago wanted Burly to respect these fences from the outset. He made him put in a short one, go back on his hocks and clear it as though it were a post and rails.

Havlik's mare veered away from them and smashed through the fence's crest. Havlik yelped. He landed back in the saddle with a thump and rocked forward, clinging to the mare's neck for dear life. With no help from her pilot, the mare relied on big reliable Burly and big reliable Jago. She was back at their side.

There were no casualties there, nor at the second. Burly had readily sussed the ditch on the landing side. He stood off and took it in a perfect flat parabola. His belly scraped the top of the fence. His hooves cleaved the turf a good metre beyond the ditch.

Havlik was all over the place, flopping like a stringless puppet, but his mare was doing her best, and he was still in the saddle.

Now the first of the waters – a flat three metres. Burly watched the horses ahead. So did Jago.

The leading pack took off and landed at the same moment. There were two or three little bullet splashes as hind feet clipped the water, but they were all over safely. Jean François and the two horses which had dropped back to join him constituted the second group. They too took it without problems. Jean François was all verve and style. Where Jago sat sedately in the middle, the Frenchman kept a forward seat and flung the reins at his horse's ears as they jumped, gathered them briskly as they landed.

Both Havlik's horse and Jago's had hunted. They had no problems with dykes and rivers. Burly's quarters bunched. He stretched. They were over. Havlik's mare negotiated it with similar ease, but her rider was leaning back, his weight on her mouth. It made her peck on landing, but she rapidly recovered and raced to resume her position upsides.

Her lop ears were stiff and flat on the top of her head. She was hating every minute of this.

Jago pitied her, but he very much did not want her hard at his side just now.

The next fence was the Taxis.

He pulled in a reef and steadied Burly, as if to say, 'Watch this one, lad.' He tried to project a telepathic picture of the drop, the fallers that they could expect in their path.

The leaders had unforeseen problems. As they turned into the straight, a redheaded girl in green flung herself down just a yard or so ahead of Chiko's horse.

If she had hoped to be a martyr, she was to be disappointed. A three-year-old at full stretch in the Derby straight is very different from a steeplechaser at half-pace. By nature, a horse is capable of dance routines to worry Gene Kelly, simply in order to avoid obstacles. Chiko's mount jinked to one side. Two of the soldiers posted along the rails grabbed the girl, one of them by the hair, and pulled her back.

Two more idiots rolled before the leaders. The horses treated them as disdainfully, the soldiers as roughly and efficiently.

However high-minded their half-baked principles, the protestors' actions attained precisely that which they deplored. The riders were all trying to soothe and steady their mounts as they approached that precipice. The sudden appearance of would-be suicides in their path served merely to alarm and unbalance them. If horses died at the Taxis today, the blame would lie, at least in part, with the demonstrators.

Their consciences, of course, Jago thought, would not be troubled.

Omelettes. Eggs.

They were in front of the stands now, and swinging right-handed towards the Taxis.

The field split. Paul and four other jockeys swung out wide and galloped towards the left-hand side of the fence. Chiko and five or six others stayed on the right. Jean François and his two outriders were behind them.

There was likely to be a bit of a mess over there, so Jago

too let Burly take the bend wide. Havlik's mare leaned on them all the way.

'All right, my boy,' Jago breathed in Burly's ear, 'this is the big one . . .'

Burly's ear flipped back, then forward again. Jago clicked on, as much in hope of getting clear of Havlik and his tremulous keening as to encourage Burly to take this at full stretch. The mare stayed with them.

Up ahead, they were taking off. Jockeys' arms were rising. Dust spat. Plates flashed. Horses and riders vanished completely as if into a void. There were thuds and grunts and yells. Paul appeared to have met it first and to have risen to it perfectly. Chiko was the only rider to remain crouched forward, sitting into his mount as it rose.

Jean François never had the pace. His animal lolloped up to the fence and barely rose. He was lucky to miss the guard-rail. Jago saw the hind legs reach the vertical, and move onward.

Havlik was pushing Jago hard against the left wing. Burly had had enough. He barged Kalliope to one side. Jago shouted, 'Garn!' They were airborne.

For a moment, then, Jago was atop a chasm filled with dust and twisted, straining bodies.

Jago would not later know how much of the data he had dredged from his memory, how much reconstructed from videos. What he saw in that split second, consciously or unconsciously, was this:

Paul, still in the saddle, flapping at his horse's neck with the rein.

Two other horses, also up and running.

Chiko, still in the saddle, his mount on its knees but lurching upwards.

Three horses with their noses or brows to the ground and their riders curling up on the turf, ten or twelve feet on. Another horse, a bay, on his side, his rider's leg trapped beneath him.

Jean François, spreadeagled like St Andrew crucified as he flew forward and crashed with sickening force onto the turf. His mount was stuck in the ditch down at the right.

And right beneath them, a chestnut, lying on his front like a dog, dazed and struggling to rise, as his rider made a run for the rails.

Then they were down, and in the thick of it.

Burly made a deep sound as though someone had punched him low. Down at Jago's right, someone shouted. Jago was lying almost flat back on Burly's quarters one moment, jolted forward and mouthing mane the next. He choked up dust. Burly's neck hit his jaw and clunked his teeth together. They were on top of that sprawling chestnut. They could have sidestepped, but Havlik's mare was plummeting vertically, hard at their right, and Havlik flailing, flapping and yelling as he flew forward like a human cannonball. There was no room.

Burly did the only thing possible. He had just made the biggest leap of his life. Now, in the next stride, he must jump again. He contracted like a spring. It felt as though his hind legs and his forelegs were a bare inch apart.

He leaped.

And at that moment, the groggy chestnut found his forefeet and lurched upwards.

They hit him amidships. They stopped dead in a crazy tangle of equine limbs. The chestnut went down with an 'ouff', his head somewhere in the region of Burly's stifle. Jago was projected slowly but inexorably forward before Burly's reproachful eye. He hung like that, bunched up over Burly's head. He was slipping downwards.

He groaned. He was aware for the first time of the clicking and whirring of the cameras. He did not cut an heroic figure. But suddenly the head and neck beneath him shoved hard upwards. He slithered sideways now, but his hands had a firm grip of mane, and Burly was moving forward. Jago was back in the saddle. He had lost his cap and must kick for his missing right iron, but he was back in the saddle again.

He kicked and steered Burly clear of the animal beneath him, who looked as if he had decided that getting up was a bad idea in this strange new world where the ground opened from time to time and other horses jumped on top of one.

As he heaved himself back upright, Jago vaguely noticed that all the jockeys were up, save Havlik, who was groaning, and Jean François, who lay alarmingly straight and still. He vaguely noticed too that Havlik's grey mare lay very unequivocally dead in the ditch.

She had deserved a better fate.

Jago gathered up the reins. He growled, 'Get on, lad,' and gave Burly a quick slap just to wake him up.

Burly went.

He went soberly and sensibly, at a stiff eventing pace.

Paul, Chiko and the rest of them were already over the Irish bank and kicking up a cloud of dust in the dry plough as Jago and Burly set off in pursuit, but Burly was unharmed by his experience. He knew what he had to do. He reckoned that he could do it.

The bank was a formality – a prance to the top and a slithering leap downward. Then came the two longest uninterrupted runs in the race, to the fence on the bend (which Burly popped with such ease that Jago felt he was disappointed to be denied what, by now, he was sure, he would have characterized as 'a proper drop') and on, behind the woods, out of sight now of the stands, to number seven, the two, metre-high hedges separated by a metre-wide channel. It was a twenty-four-foot-long jump from take-off to landing, but Burly sailed over it and was so quick away that Jago rocked backwards and had to flap to regain the reins.

Burly was in command, which was fine by Jago. The horse knew his business better than he.

Fences eight and nine were two identical thick hedges separated by only eight metres. Such doubles were meat and drink to Burly, and the hedges were forgiving. At the Anglicky Skok, or English open ditch, however, at which Chiko had come a cropper earlier, Burly blundered.

It was a good ditch and a paltry fence, and, as usual, it was the small fence which caused Burly problems. He was cocky. He took it on the forehand, too fast and too flat. They smashed through the hedge. No problem there save a few staggering strides on the other side, but if he tried such tricks later, at Popler's, for example, the low standing post and rails, or at the small stone wall known as the Zed, their race would be very uncomfortably cut short.

Perhaps Jago had his uses after all.

They swung to the right now, once more in the open and heading back towards the stands. The bulk of the remaining eight horses was still a fence away as they re-emerged, but fences now came thick and fast. They were gaining.

They were gaining still as he streaked across the centre of the course and, still right-handed, described a large loop over eleven, twelve, thirteen, fourteen – Popler's – and back to fifteen, the big drop at the centre of the track.

They caught their first stragglers at the Zed, which Burly took as respectfully as if it were six foot, not four. Others were coming back to them. Paul and Chiko were well up front, perhaps twenty lengths up on them.

The two big snake-ditches, then, the huge number seventeen and the almost as broad and twice as tricky eighteen. Two lengths up on Burly, at his nearside, another weary straggler teetered momentarily on the edge, then leaped. There was a terrible swirling and sucking sound as the animal broke the water and slid backwards. His rider, however, rolled like a woodlouse on the opposite bank and appeared completely dry. They both looked ruefully up at Jago as Burly flashed by.

Compared with the rapid rough-and-tumble, the close infighting of British steeplechasing, such a race might seem dull. It was anything but. Each obstacle was an end in itself. Each demanded intuition, skill and experience. Each had its perils. It was as different from, say, the Grand National as épée from sabre, yet the skills required here included those needed at Aintree and many more.

And they were going to win. Jago was confident of that now. Burly was the best horse here. He was chomping up the powdery plough. His ears were pricked and he was full of verve and running. They were fifteen lengths back now, twelve . . .

Fences twenty and twenty-one constituted another double, this time with both ditches on the inside of the combination. A bay in fifth place staggered up to it whilst Jago and Burly were still five strides off. He was well to their right. Jago maintained their position, hugging the nearside rail. His scarlet jacketed rider gave him a slap as he got too close. The bay made a desperate, futile attempt to climb the hedge. He ploughed through it. The rider's hands rose in the air. Other, invisible hands grasped his buttocks and heaved him upwards. For a moment, he stood, unsupported on the air, then he swung forwards and downwards. Jago heard the thud as he hit the ground, the hiss as the wind was driven from his body. The bay had also disappeared.

Alarm bells screamed, too late; far, far too late.

Burly was airborne.

And beneath them in the road, a tired, confused horse with no intention of jumping out of the combination, careered back towards them like a clumsy puppy.

They landed bare inches from the loose horse's nose. He planted his forefeet and whinnied in protest. Burly swerved left so sharply that Jago only stayed in place by clinging to the saddle tree. Burly screamed something unsuitable for the ears of two-year-olds and under. Jago pulled himself upright again. The bay swung round and galloped off fast in the opposite direction.

The damage was done. Burly was out on the grassy perimeter. There was no room for a run-up to the second element.

Jago forced the word 'Shit' out between gritted teeth. He jagged Burly's mouth and wheeled him round. They cantered back, ten precious yards. He turned him again, roared, 'Come on!' and gave him a quick one down the shoulder. Burly plunged forwards, took the first, then gathered himself for the second and projected himself over with a prodigious leap.

They were going to have to do it Burly's way after all.

For the second time in a day, Jago entrusted his life to a horse.

There was a bitch of an open ditch at twenty-five. Burly flew it. There was the fattest fence that Jago had ever seen at twenty-seven as they galloped out into the country again. Again Burly flew it. He took them both like hurdles. Jago just sat still.

They were doubling back behind the woods again, parallel to their original outward route. Burly kicked up spurts of dust as though strafed. He swung round the bend at a motorcycle's angle and set off downhill on the long, long, run in, once more on turf.

He was damned if he was going to be denied his place in the history books by a bloody tailor.

There were four animals still ahead of them: two anonymous Eastern or Central Europeans, and, once more ten or fifteen lengths ahead of them, Paul and Chiko.

Burly did it, Jago would later swear, not he. Fatigue filled Jago's veins with something warm and clogged like porridge. Sweat blurred his vision. Every muscle in his body was hot and hurting. Burly caught the two strangers and swept past them. Burly flung himself over the plain fence in the back straight as though he thought himself a swallow. Jago could merely push him out and pray. His prayers were probably more effective than his pushing.

They jumped the last just two lengths behind the two leaders, who were shoulder to shoulder.

Paul sat down, crouched low, and rode.

Chiko raised his whip in a sort of ornate flourish and brought it smacking down on his mount's quarters.

Jago was grinning as he leaned forward and did his impersonation of a jockey.

The crowd roared and thumped. The stand's roof rang. The divots flew like clays. Chiko, at Jago's offside now, was shouting at his animal, thrashing him with an ungainliness which must have lost him lengths. Jago rode as a drunkard drives, essentially unaware, but going through the motions. The Irish training told. He kept low. He thrusted forward. He forced his aching limbs to hurt still more. Chiko dropped back. The colours of the crowd were scattered like a confetti shower.

Burly had forgotten his years. They had not forgotten him. He was reeling, leaning hard to the left. Paul was still up there, no more than a length ahead. Burly might have caught him, given a hundred yards more.

A hundred yards was not on offer.

They passed the post amidst throbbing and singing like the echo of a disco.

Jago pulled Burly up, to a trot, then to a walk. He rocked forward and hugged Burly's neck. He just needed that moment's darkness and warmth. He could not catch a decent breath. There was a hand on his shoulder. Jago looked up. Paul's cheeks were red. His eyes were shining so brightly that they seemed white. He offered his hand. 'Bloody well done, Jago. Bloody brilliant! Two of us! We did it!'

Jago smiled at his generosity and ebullience.

The joke had reached its punchline. The irresponsibility was past.

Everything suddenly crashed in on him.

He covered his face with his hands, and he cried like a blasted baby.

It was ridiculous, of course.

It was just the finality. The last race, for Burly and for him, was run.

It was Holly, and the sense not simply that he had been mocked but that the very currency of their dealings – the intimacy, the laughter, the hopes – had been abused and devalued.

It was a valediction to so much that he had loved.

'Golly, Jago. You OK?' Paul's hand was back on his shoulder.

Jago lowered his hands and raised his head. He blinked up at the sky. He laughed. 'Just being bloody silly.' He sat up straight. 'Not bad, hey? A British one-two.'

'I can't really believe it.' Paul shook his head. He could not stop patting his horse's neck. His eyes too were misty. 'It's not really happening. I mean, me . . .'

'Believe it, Paul,' Jago grinned. 'This is one they can't take away from you. Not women, not lawyers, not children, not even the taxman. It's yours, forever. Pickering P., victor in the Velka Pardubicka.'

Paul was still shaking his head, but a broad grin creased his face. Those eyes studied a distant angel. 'It's not possible,' he muttered, 'not possible . . .'

The crowd engulfed them then. Newsmen shouted. Officials gabbled and grasped their reins. As they left the track, well-wishers patted their horses and them. Clay was down there in amongst them, and Cindy, jumping up and down and clapping, and Diana, crying, of course.

Novak appeared at Jago's knee, chewing a burned-out match. 'Well, well,' he growled, 'demigods now, are we?' Then he was swept away like flotsam on the tide of people.

'Filthy English fuckpig bastards,' Chiko called above the crowd, but his gap-toothed grin was broad. 'I think I turn over this Pickling, but I honour his white hairs. I am nice born. I am stupid is what.'

The riders weighed in and were at once bustled out again to be photographed with their horses. Paul's and Jago's backs were slapped, their hands shaken. They were placed upon a podium like Olympic medallists whilst a brass band played what sounded like an underwater rendition of 'God Save the Queen'. A laurel wreath was slung about Avocet's neck, commemorative medals about Jago's and Burly's. Journalists shouted leading questions at Paul.

'Do you see this as a triumph for the senior citizen as much as for Great Britain?'

'No,' said Paul without hesitation.

'Would you say you feel as fit today as twenty years ago?'

'No. Good heavens, no.'

Then, from a Czech girl, in faltering English, 'How think you of the demonstratings?'

'Um, I think they're jolly silly, really. There's plenty to protest about; real things like nuclear-testing, hmm? And pollution? How about the extinction of hundreds of species every year? All these silly, boring killjoys can concentrate on is something beautiful, innocent. Sod the lot of them, I say.'

Chiko whooped and led the applause which greeted this astounding burst of heretical eloquence. Paul flushed and was suddenly shy. He said, 'Sorry. You know. But.'

Paul Pickering, gentleman and taxi-driver, could now retire, showered with honours and privilege, provided, of course, that he was prepared to move his mobile home to Bohemia. He was a national hero.

Jago wasn't doing too badly either, come to that. He was kissed by three girls on his way back to the weighing-room. His hand was pumped countless times. 'Fan Tsellair' was not essayed by Czech tongues quite as frequently, perhaps, as 'Pick-airing', 'Pick-a-ring', 'Pickling' and 'Picking', but, in this part of the world at least, the name would always henceforth educe a flicker at least of doubtful recognition.

The bad news came in as they stripped and changed back into civvies. Jean François was still unconscious. He had *une commotion cérébrale*. They could not tell how serious it was. Havlik had broken a collarbone and had done something unspecified but nasty to one of his wrists. His mount, Kalliope, was the only fatality. She had broken her neck at the moment of impact.

Jago had fastened his cuff-links and was reaching for his coat when the full significance of this intelligence penetrated his dull brain. 'God,' he said, 'that puts the lid on that.'

'Howzat, old chap?' Paul looked up at him with raised eyebrows. His compulsive grin dug deep furrows in his either cheek.

'That mare. She was meant to be the transporter.' Jago sank gapelegged on the bench beside him.

'What? Oh, gosh, yes. Of course. Blimey O'Reilly, that's gone and blown it. Silly damned fool. Didn't give the poor animal an earthly. Nice beast, too.'

'Yes, all right, but what the hell do we do about the – you know?'

He shrugged. 'Bury it again, I reckon.'

'Hmm. Well, how d'ye feel now?'

'Very, very odd,' Paul admitted. 'I still don't believe it, and somehow I don't think I ever will. Not properly. You know, go home, back to normal. I won the Pardubice. The what? Jolly good. Old boy's rambling. Some donkey derby out east. It'll only ever be real once a year, like that Scottish thing, you know? Brigadoon. Amazing. Change my life not a jot.'

'Except with us,' Jago said, 'those like us – damn few.'

They completed the Pickering toast in chorus.

'Yes,' Paul mused, 'yes, that's nice. Can't wait to tell the girls. Silly of me, I know.'

'The girls?'

'The dogs. So you think you're quick? You should have seen your lord and master . . .'

Jago watched him as he sat there, as ever crouched forward, as ever gazing out at some point which Jago could not see. He dry-washed his hands. A rueful smile now jerked the corner of his lips. He was battling with elation, confronting the paradox of solitary triumph.

'We'll tie one on tonight,' Jago said. He slapped his thighs and stood.

'Don't think so, Jago. Bit tired, all that.'

'Bollocks.' Jago was brisk. 'I've got a whole gang out there who will want to toast you and sing your praises to the echo. I'll not have you creep back to your hotel like a troglodyte scuttling back to his cave. You're a hero. You're coming out with us and we're going to make it a night to remember but will probably forget.'

'Really?' Paul blinked up at him. 'You think so?'

'I know so.'

'Thanks, Jago.' He too stood. 'For all this. Couldn't have done it without you.' He held out a long and beautiful hand.

Jago took it. He drew Paul to him and hugged him. 'What friends are for,' he said platitudinously, but he reckoned that Paul would not count himself a friend unless given explicit sanction.

When Jago stood back, Paul looked bashful. His eyes were once more wet. He looked down at the backs of his hands. 'Sorry about Holly, old fellow.'

Jago nodded, shrugged. 'Well . . .'

'Not her fault really. Not really. Beastly, though, feel you've been used, all that. Best intentions, though.'

'Oh, sure. Lots of those. The Bolshevik revolution had

them too. Know what they say about the road to hell? Ah, well. Let it go. Come on, mate. Let's go and meet our public.'

'No, it's my job, mate,' Clay protested, but Clay's cheeks were red and his stance unsteady, and Jago very much wanted to bed Burly down.

'No. I insist,' Jago grinned round at the Zeller's crowd. 'No. I'm going to take the boy back, and, for the first time since I've known him, give him everything he feels like. What do you think, Paul? Bran mash? Linseed? Molasses? Polos? Mars Bars?'

'The lot,' said Paul, 'and buckets full of Black Velvet. God, I *still* don't believe it! Me. Me!'

So the two men and their horses had trudged, anonymous now, across the car park where the boxes were parked and, after congratulations from the security guards, into the stable-area.

Jago hugged his horse, kissed his snip, even, then sang to him as he wisped him down. He could hear Paul doing much the same with the laureate of Pardubice next door. He longed to climb up on the manger and to investigate the contents of the haynet, but Burly deserved his pampering. Only when Jago was content that that manger was well-filled and Burly breathing steadily, only then did he climb up and peer down into the haynet.

He pulled the hay apart.

The jewels were still there.

He sighed. It was strange but, having hoped that, by this afternoon, they would be gone, he now found their presence consoling. He pulled out the thing which fitted most readily into his hand. He gazed down upon it with something like love. The river of emeralds smiled back at him.

'The things are still there,' he told Paul as they wandered back towards the racecourse.

'Leave 'em there. You were right, Jago,' Paul sighed, 'Havlik's not worth the candle. Damn him. Nice things, I'm sure, but who needs people like that little shit? I was conned. Sad, but true. Sorry to drag you in. Solemn promise,

OK? Next Mephistopheles, I'll say, "Sod off," all right? Today – best day of my life . . . I don't want the likes of Havlik hanging around. If he doesn't want to collect them, that's his business. We'll drive off and leave the damned things hanging there if necessary.'

'We are agreed, then?'

'Course we are. He can play his own bloody games. I have no time for him. Little shit. Hope he's OK after the fall, but . . .'

'Right,' said Jago, but he was concerned by what was happening. Dashing, reckless Paul was content to forswear this adventure. Sober, sensible Jago glanced wistfully back at the stable. He did not like to admit it to himself, but he was already trying to think of places where he might hide the jewels.

He reproved himself. Of course Paul was right. He needed no more trouble. The day after tomorrow, he would be back in the office, back to normal. Perhaps it was only because the landscape of the future appeared featureless without his races that he even considered so absurd and unfeasible a scheme.

He considered it, all the same.

Waking up to uncertainty, as that morning a mere three days ago in London, was a joy. Waking up to cold, prosaic certainty after vivid dreams could be very hell. So, after the hopes of the past days, were the wearisome facts of life.

It had been, God knew, an ambitious menu of dreams. Love, wealth and glory in one weekend constituted a tall order. Love had been cruelly mocked. Jago had compromised with glory. As to wealth, though there was a remote chance that Havlik might yet escape the country with some few of his baubles, Jago frankly doubted, after the man's behaviour today, that his helpers would ever receive their shares. Anyway, it would not have been enough, not really enough to save Zeller's.

The gods were giggling over their dice.

Oh, they spun out the dreaming that night. They drank and they danced. They feted Paul. The Zeller's crowd had just one night in which to create Bohemian memories. They were not going to waste a minute in sleeping – even if, as Jago doubted, they had managed to get rooms at the last minute in this town which was overrun with visitors.

Midnight found the party back in the casino, where Diana, after a series of idiotic calls – twisting to seventeen, splitting a twenty to be dealt two straight aces – found herself six hundred pounds to the good.

And somewhere in there, amidst all the giggling and the swirling of whisky in tumblers and the smoke which burst whenever anyone moved, Havlik stalked in, scowling, with Hayward in tow. Havlik bought the journalist a drink, then, when Novak's back was turned, drew Jago aside. He was subdued now, and whining where formerly he had yapped. A puce turf-burn covered his left cheek. His right arm was in a polka-dotted sling.

'Jago. Hey, listen, what do we do?'

'Christ, man!' Jago snapped, as much in anger at himself as with the American. 'How often do I have to tell you? *We* do nothing. *We've* done our bit. It's your problem now. Have you picked them up?'

'I can't! Shit, where'd I put them? I tell you, they're watching and waiting every goddamn moment. Even if I get the net in the box, what then, huh? You think they're gonna let me pass the border without stripping the thing down?'

'Nope. So, you either have to re-bury the stuff or declare it and go through the courts. Sorry. Nice try.'

'You don't care?'

'Sure, I care. I'd like some of that money, but that's the state of play whether I like it or not.'

'Look, Jago.' Havlik laid a lean left hand on Jago's forearm. His protuberant eyes shifted this way and that. 'Look, Jago. Right. I got it wrong. I fouled up. I was – you know, the race and things. I'm no fucking jockey. I was – you know, my head was screwed up, right? It's just . . . You're good at this kind of thing. Me, I'm . . . It's not my . . . Come on, man, I mean, I'm sorry. You take it over for me, huh? We meet in Frankfurt. You stay cool. Me, I get all wound up . . .'

'I'm flying back on Tuesday morning,' Jago said firmly.

'Yeah, but – I mean, you can change plans, can't you? You drive back. Paul or that guy of yours can take the plane. Where's the problem?'

'Where's your problem?' Jago demanded. 'I mean, I'm grateful for your faith in my abilities, but my box is going to get stripped down as surely as yours. So we've lost. Accept it. Declare the stuff. You'll still get it, or at least a good chunk of its value.'

'I can't do that!' Havlik pouted. 'Come on, man, you'll think of things. You're that sort.'

It was true that Jago had thought of some things, most of them wholly impracticable. He had thought of gluing gems to Bohemian glass and letting all the Zeller's staff carry back plausible souvenirs. The problem with that was that, in this case at least, the jewels' settings were more crucial to their value than their clarity or caratage. He had, of course, thought of stitching them into any number of garments, horse-blankets, rollers and so on, but, aside from the saddle, nothing was so thick and so sturdy as to deceive the assiduous searcher. He could swallow the odd stone. He could even force a few down Burly's gullet, but again the problems of the settings remained. Gold filigree would be converted to nuggets by the chomping of a horse's gut.

'Please, Jago . . .' Havlik was now plucking at Jago's sleeve. He was a toucher. That was not the least of Jago's reasons for disliking him. 'I'll up your commission. I agreed fifteen per with Paul. Make it twenty.'

Jago considered. 'Of anything I get out?'

'Yeah.' Havlik frowned as though such irritating details were beneath his attention. 'Yeah, I guess. OK.'

'Why the hurry?'

'What?'

'You want me to take the risks. I need to know. Why not take the legal route, or bury the things and recover them piecemeal? Why go for broke? I don't get it.'

'I . . .' he started. He shrugged. His eyes once more swivelled. He leaned close. 'I guess – I kind of shot my mouth off a bit, you know? Gambling, that kind of thing. I – they gave me credit, lent me money. Now they want to know where the stuff is. These guys, they're OK, generally, you know, but they're not pussycats. They want the stuff bad now. They were going to come in themselves, but you give a secret like this to guys like that? Shit. I – I got a friend, pay for the horse, this trip . . .'

'Oh, Christ,' Jago sighed. So Havlik was in hock to the mob. They must have seen the young prince coming a mile off and reeled him in with girls and booze and flattery. 'How long have you been living off them?'

He shrugged again. 'Six, seven years. Hell, if I go back empty-handed . . .'

He did not need to complete the sentence. So the amassed wealth of a great dynasty was destined to end up in the hands of some cheap Brooklyn hoods because the last of the line was a shiftless shit.

There was still something wrong, something which did not fit. Jago wanted to think, but this was neither the time nor the place. The noise was great, the air too thick for clear thought. He told Havlik, 'I've got to have time. I'll see you tomorrow morning.'

'What time you leaving?'

'No later than nine. Be at the hotel first thing.'

Havlik was pathetically grateful. He even fondled Jago's lapel. 'Sure, Jago. You think about it. And, like I say, sorry, you know . . .'

Jago barely concealed his sneer as he stalked away.

He made his excuses amidst groans from the Zellers' crew. He was tired, he said. It was all very well, but they hadn't ridden seven kilometres cross-country today. He would see them all back in London. He was going to ask Paul to come with him, but there was no need. He too wanted to call it a day. Diana kissed Paul very warmly and made him promise to call her.

At last the two men were allowed to leave, both with a deal of moisture on their cheeks. Novak, as usual, was waiting for them at the door. He had his bespectacled friend with him again. Novak scampered to the door and gave a deep ironic bow as he pushed it open. 'I think it's time that we all had a little chat,' he said.

Jago ignored him. He had not brought the car out tonight. He said, 'Taxi, Paul?'

'Mmm? Yes. Good idea.'

'Bad idea,' Novak droned at their backs. 'The taxis are owned by the mafia.'

'Ah, yes, they told me that,' Paul mused, 'and I have no desire to put money in those buggers' pockets, but I don't see . . .'

'I see,' Jago said morosely. He shuddered. 'And I suppose the mafia would be able to listen in on Prague brothels as well, Novak?'

'For certain.' Novak dropped in at Jago's left, his colleague at Paul's right. They all four strolled very slowly along the pavement towards the lights of the main square. All of them, save the bespectacled one, had their hands in their pockets. All of them looked down at their shoes. 'That is where Havlik gave you your instructions, hmm, Mr Pickering? In that knocking-shop?'

Paul cast a quizzical glance at Jago. Jago shrugged. 'Oh, damn it all,' he said, 'the man seems to know everything, or, at least, a damned sight more than we do.'

'All right.' Paul sighed. 'Yup. The Club André.'

'Where he knew that the mafia could easily set up a listening device,' Novak hummed. He shook his head fast.

'Hold it,' Paul winced. 'You mean he – Havlik – wanted the conversation bugged?'

'Of course. He had to get you to risk your neck and satisfy his employers that he was doing everything to retrieve the jewels. At the same time, he didn't want to specify where at the Zichy house the things were, otherwise they might have shot straight down there and got them for themselves. They had to wait for you to start digging. Problem was, they got greedy and went in too soon. You managed to fool them, and they didn't know about you, Mr van Zeller, or that clever Byrne girl.'

'Sorry,' Paul said languorously, 'but I'm in the dark here. Who's doing all this bugging and chasing? Who are Havlik's employers?'

'The mafia,' Jago told him, '*cosa nostra*, the mob or whatever you call the people who run the casinos and whorehouses and protection rackets in New York and Prague and everywhere else. Havlik told me. He's been living on credit from the mob on the strength of his famous treasure. He's under pressure to get the stuff out, fast.'

'Silly damn young fool.'

'Did he tell you how much he owed?' Novak's voice was charged with scorn.

'No.' Jago was tired and showed it. 'He said he'd been living on credit for six or seven years.'

'Since his twentieth birthday,' Novak croaked. He hawked and spat a glistening gob before Jago's feet. 'He frequents whorehouses a great deal. He likes cocaine and Cointreau. He entertains his insalubrious friends at night clubs. He does not roll from his bed until mid-afternoon. None of this has cost the mafia a great deal, of course, but one of those girls can set you back two grand a night, and Havlik likes more than one at a time. He used to gamble a lot. All in all, I understand, they claim that he owes them more than four million dollars. Their accounting may not be good, but it's unwise to dispute the bill.'

'Four million . . .?' Paul and Jago stared at one another. Both whistled.

'So he won't tell them where this supposed treasure is, but says he'll come and get it. He knows they're going to watch him all the way. He doesn't want them thinking maybe he's outlived his usefulness once he's got the things, and anyhow, he's being very obviously watched by me, so he pseudo-secretly recruits you, Mr Pickering, to do his dirty work.'

'Why me, for God's sake?'

Novak leered at him. 'Was he so wrong? He convinced you that it was nasty commies after him, and you are – romantic, shall we say? Strange, really. You are romantic, so you end up working for the mob. Still, you are English.

You have a very simplistic attitude towards history. I think it comes from imperialism rather than simple stupidity.'

'I say, steady on . . .' Paul murmured.

'No. Our friend Havlik did not want to take the risks himself. His plan to place the jewels in the mare is perhaps hackneyed but it works. The mobsters, I assume, are happy enough with that. The racecourse stables are secure. They are watching them. They will continue to watch until the jewels are safely over the border, then, presumably, they will take them to an auction house. To do this, they need to keep Havlik sweet. They go along with his plan. They will pay him some small share in exchange for his provenance, knowing that he will pay it back to them for girls and drugs. So they think, at least. Did he offer you some sort of payment for your help?'

'He offered me fifteen per,' Paul said.

'He's upped it to twenty now,' Jago told him.

'Ha!' Novak barked. 'You know what Havlik has in his suitcase? A false passport and a one-way ticket from Frankfurt to Paraguay. He intends to vanish off the face of the earth.'

'With the mafia behind him?' Paul hissed. 'No easy trick, I'd have thought.'

'Impossible. He is a silly, silly man. I think perhaps his brain is fucked.'

'Filthy little *crook*!' Jago spat between lips suddenly thin.

'So that's why you've been making your presence felt.' Paul nodded. 'Yes. I see.'

'Precisely. I have been – choreographing things. These mafia people are impatient. They might just take it into their heads to dispense with Havlik's provenance, dispose of him and sell the loot on the black market. Equally, when they did not know where you had put the things, they might have decided to torture you two, say. As long as I or my assistants were very obviously around, they had to be circumspect. When you arrived here, for example, they would have searched you at once. Maybe something still worse. I had to do it for them.'

'I'm still not with you,' Jago frowned. 'You have to tell us who you are, Novak, whom you represent. We can't believe you otherwise.'

'No?' Novak sourly grinned. 'You think Havlik honest? You think I have done all this for fun?'

'No . . .' Jago started hesitantly, 'no, but how come . . .? Twice now you've allowed Havlik to talk to me in privacy.'

'Indeed. Last night at the restaurant, because I had deliberately made my remark about Troy. I wanted to scare these people into asking you to take the things on. I did not know, of course, that the mare would be killed. Then tonight, they had no choice but to ask you again.'

'Why on earth did you *want* him to do that?'

'Because tomorrow there are only two options. The mobsters take the things, probably with violence, and we lose sight of them, or we convince them that they can safely be taken over the border and the game goes on.'

'Game?' Jago blinked. 'Look, just who are you, Novak?'

'I told you. I am an ex-policeman who was born on Havlik's estate. I have made a speciality of the Havlik treasure. I know more about it than almost any man alive. I am, shall we say, on a special assignment.'

'So why don't you just take the things, for God's sake?' Jago asked. 'Why didn't you take them when you were helping Holly on the way to Plsen? And – oh, yes. How did you know she was there?'

'I knew because I was telephoned from the bar in Susice. I was only informed at two o'clock that afternoon that Havlik had been in the brothel at the same time as a mysterious English rider. I had to find you fast. I put out an alert for stray Englishmen. Names on the list of riders were obviously high on my list. You, Mr Pickering, stopped at Plsen for a drink and a piss, so I go to Plsen. I hear nothing more till my informant tells me that Mr van Zeller and Miss Byrne are in Susice asking about the Zichy place. I was late for the party, but I saw you two leaving that benighted house. I hung around for the missing member of the group. She was my ace in the hole. It was obvious they knew nothing about her.'

'Don't tell me you didn't look inside the bag,' Jago sighed.

'What do you take me for? A gentleman? Of course I bloody did,' Novak cackled. 'Miss Byrne – I do like Miss Byrne – stopped for a piss en route for Plsen. She also left me at Reception in our Plsen hotel. I had plenty of time.'

'I don't get it.' Jago gazed at him. 'So why not take the lot?'

'Ah. There we have a problem. It might take a minute to explain. I need to talk to you, both of you. Shall we sit?' He pointed down the dark, grassy bank at their right. There was a river down there, only it appeared to be mostly mud with just a trickle at the centre. Novak was pointing at a concrete bench on the towpath.

Jago looked at Paul. Paul shrugged. A lorry rumbled and roared as it swept past. 'All right,' Jago called above its wake, 'we'll sit.'

They clattered down the steep white steps cut in the bank. The air had a silver border to it now. Rain was on its way. Jago sat at the far end of the bench and gazed out over the mudflats. Novak sat at his side, Paul at the other end. The rustling of their clothes and the rasping of their shoes on the path seemed very loud. The man with glasses made no move to sit, nor was there room for him. He walked briskly one hundred yards upstream. He stopped, cocked an ear, looked around, then wheeled and marched one hundred yards downstream.

'Are they following us, then?' Paul asked.

'Sure to be.' Novak tapped out a cigarette. He called to the man in Czech. The cigarette wagged between his lips.

He had it lit by the time the man came close and quietly spoke his answer. Novak nodded. The man straightened and marched off again. 'Yes. They're there.' Novak blew smoke. He looked heavenwards and blinked those rheumy eyes. 'See? They're trying to be unobtrusive.'

'Not your style, it seems?' Paul was just mildly sarcastic.

'Ah, Mr Pickering, there are times when you do not want your prey to know that you are there. There are others when you want to drive him from his cover into the open, give him your wind.'

'So you've been giving us your wind, have you?'

'You and Havlik.' Novak was proud. 'And these very, very unpleasant people. Now. Listen. First, these jewels – the so-called Havlik treasure – is neither legally nor morally Havlik's property.' He pulled a rolled-up magazine from his coat pocket.

'Says you,' Paul said bullishly. 'Where we come from, if something is honestly earned . . .'

'Ah, shit. Shut up, would you?' Novak snarled. 'You really are a bloody fool, Mr Pickering.'

'I say . . .' Paul started vaguely.

'It's all right, Paul,' Jago told him. 'Let's hear the man out. All right, Novak. Say your piece.'

'I don't know why I like your countrymen.' Novak was leaning forward, elbows on thighs, shaking his head, bemused. 'I suppose because you cling so fiercely to your illusions, and because somehow, despite them, you cope. Listen, gentlemen.' He sat back with a grunt. 'Prague was liberated in May 1945. The Russians arrived in February 1948. A communist government was elected in 1946. Why do you think that was? Because Havlik and his kind were gentlemen with nice castles, happy peasantry and nice manners? Balls. Because Czechoslovakia had been under Nazi rule for eight years, that's why, chucked away like so much embarrassing garbage by Neville Chamberlain and his chums. Ah, but all the aristos were gallant partisans, battling up in the hills, weren't they? Like hell they were. Oh, some of them, sure, but others . . . Listen. During the war, where did all the top Nazis take their holidays? In the protectorate, of course. Nice girls, nice chocolates, nice castles, a sympathetic population that spoke German, best fucking standard of living in Europe. And many of your precious aristos, they had family in Germany, friends in Germany – Christ, Sudetenland was crammed with Germans – and they hated Jews and gypsies and commies too. Some just collaborated. Others were downright fanatical supporters. Prince Havlik flew a Nazi flag on his fucking schloss, man. He thought Heydrich was too liberal. His son Vaclav, this little bastard's father, wore the uniform of the Hitler Youth, then that of the SS. So that's your precious fucking romantic aristocrat hero, son.'

The grating voice drove the coarse words into Jago's dull mind. They rang in there long after Novak had stopped speaking in order to release a stupendous sigh of scorn. He leaned forward again. He flicked his cigarette in a great arc towards the water. Jago sorted the impressionistic sum of words into distinct facts. He said, 'No, Novak. It can't be true. You'd have told us before.'

'I had my reasons. If I'd told you, you'd have taken the things to the nearest police station. I didn't want that.' Novak looked back at Jago over his shoulder. The breeze which came up the river puffed the hair at his brow into floss. The breeze smelled of rubber. 'Here.' He opened out the magazine. He slapped a pen-torch down on its curling pages. 'Look at that. You might recognize a few things.'

'God,' said Paul, 'if this is true . . . but Pavel . . .'

'Pavel Havlik, your father's friend and this Havlik's uncle, was a gentleman and a liberal. He was a playboy, an amateur rider. He therefore travelled to Britain, to France. He had friends there. He valued democracy. He was not a parochial, bigoted lout like his brother. I knew them both. They were chalk and cheese. Read it, Mr Pickering.' Novak stood so that Paul too could see the pages.

Jago flicked on the torch. The magazine was *The Connoisseur*. It was almost exactly two years old. The article was entitled, '*Lost Treasures in Bohemia and Moravia*' and subtitled, '*Objets d'Art Lost or Hidden under Nazi and Communist Occupation*'. The first paragraphs dealt with the history of a reliquary from the days of Rudolf II, a thing richly embossed with Romanesque panels and jewels, buried by a Nazi nobleman as the communists approached, and recently unearthed. It rehearsed the history of Hitler's annexation, the protectorates of von Neurath and Heydrich, Heydrich's well-deserved assassination, the terrible reprisals, the arrival of the Russians in 1948. It went on to list further liturgical treasures – manuscripts, chalices and plate – then paintings, sculptures, glass and, finally, jewellery and metalwork.

Inevitably, for a town which was at many times the social and cultural capital of Europe and boasted such close links at once with the Russias on the one hand and with Germany and France on the other, Prague attracted some famous bijouterie. Many of the great jewels, of course, came from distant courts and households as gifts or in marriage-portions. Notable amongst these is a river of emeralds (see Figure 8) presented by Richelieu to Viktor von Rothschild and a brooch depicting the Hapsburg Arms, given by Maximilian to the same house. The Nazis compelled the von Rothschilds to 'sell' their diverse property and art treasures in Bohemia, a sale which has since been deemed invalid. The bulk of the Rothschild legacy has been returned to the family by the Czech government, but these two historic artefacts have not been seen since 1944.

It is difficult to separate fact from legend, particularly where precious stones are concerned. As the most portable and easily concealed form of currency, it is likely that many were smuggled out of Czechoslovakia by exiles and their households or by invaders. Others, no doubt, have been found and broken up by unscrupulous hunters. Given, however, the quantity of fine jewels recorded in pre-war Czechoslovakia and the preponderance of Jews, aristocrats and clergy who possessed or dealt in fine jewels, we can confidently surmise that there are yet many more to be discovered.

'The bastard!' Pickering squeaked. 'He told me that Maximilian and Richelieu had presented those things to his family.'

'Of course he did. No. The Havliks were nobodies. They had great lands, but they were drunken country louts to a man from the mid seventeenth century onwards – except for one younger brother who invented scientific instruments and drew maps of the heavens. A Richelieu would barely have nodded to a Havlik. No. The Havliks won those jewels in a poker-game. On one side of the table was Vaclav Havlik, an armed SS officer. All around the room were his friends, also armed. On the other side was an unarmed, devout Jew who had never been known to gamble. Unsurprisingly, the Jew lost. He was quite a collector, Havlik. Of the things left at the Zichy house, his family might barely claim a tenth. The rest were taken by brute force and blackmail between 1937 and 1945.'

'So some of them are rightfully theirs?' Paul asked, hoping at least for some ambivalence.

'Not one. Oh, they have some claim to that egg, for example. That was made for a wedding between a Menchikoff and a Havlik, but the rules are strict. There will be no reparations to known collaborators. The Havliks' every possession in this country is forfeit. Those jewels belong to the State, or to the Museum of World Jewry which is to be established in Prague, or to the families from whom they were taken.'

Neither Paul nor Jago for a moment doubted Novak. Everything – Havlik's furtive behaviour, the violence and resources of the men in the woods, Novak's single-minded dedication – suddenly made sense.

Not, then, after all, a tale with which to bore the grandchildren. Just a shameful tale of overgrown schoolboys who very nearly abetted a theft.

'OK, OK.' Paul stood. His illusions had received their biggest knock yet from the modern world. 'I've been a damned fool. You're right. You were right too, Jago. God! I just thought of it as an adventure, a bit of fun . . .'

'A joke, Mr van Zeller?' Novak's eyebrows shot up. He was smiling.

'Yes, I suppose. God, wherever we've gone, we've been conned, haven't we? What about the priest I met in London? Father Bernard, was it?'

'Ah. Bernard Hacha. An old acquaintance of mine. Yes. He was their priest, and as rabid a Nazi as the rest of them. Did you notice if he had any teeth left?'

'Not a lot, anyway.'

'Good.' Novak's smile crackled. 'I kidnapped and interrogated him once. I personally removed five of them.'

'All right, Novak,' Jago sighed. 'I'm convinced. You, Paul?'

'Oh, absolutely. No question. You don't fake a whole edition of *The Connoisseur*. God, that little bastard!' he seethed. It hurt him very much to see his adventure fouled by such men, such motives.

'So let's just go get the things.' Jago was businesslike. 'They're yours. You should have taken them before.'

Novak raised his hands before his chest in a halting gesture. His head turned to right and to left. 'Sh! No, damn it. Sit down again. If we went in there and started fiddling around, we'd be mown down and so would any security guards that got in the way. Listen. I want to talk to you.'

Paul sat once more. This time, Novak squatted down at the Englishmen's feet. 'Listen,' he murmured, 'all right. At first I was annoyed at your meddling in things which didn't concern you. Now, I reckon you can be useful. You've done bloody well, both of you – all of you. You've kept them in the dark and you've given me a hell of a lot to do.'

'Crap,' Jago said brusquely, because he had a vague suspicion that he was being set up again. Holly had flattered him. He hoped that now he was flattery-proof. 'At any time, from the outset, you could have taken the things.'

'And I'd instantly have been shot for my pains. No, it's worked out well their way. I've been able to keep an eye on the things and we've avoided confrontation. They've had to move cautiously, but so have I. You have to understand. Look. I grew up on what had been the Havliks' lands. I saw young Vaclav strutting around in his black uniform. I saw the Nazi flag. Goering, I am told, once gave me a chocolate bar when he came to stay. I was taught Latin by young Bernard Hacha. I went to church in the family chapel. Then, when the war was over, the Havliks spent more and more time away, and, when they knew there was no hope, fled the country. The house soon started to crumble. It became my playground. I hunted for treasure. I found quite a lot of it. I still have the biggest moufflon head that I have ever seen which used to hang in the hall. I have a gold and tortoiseshell comb which I found in the gardens. I found coins, including an English gold spade guinea. I found a punt-gun, and gave myself lifelong water-on-the knee firing it. My father told me about the treasure, and I was sure that I would find it.

'Then, as you know, I became a policeman. I went to England. I became an expert on the Havlik jewels. I continued to seek information regarding them. I hunted down people who might have known about them, including Father fucking Bernard. Then I had some power. I had Havlik senior watched. I had this little shit watched.

'Now, for better or worse, things have changed. I no longer have power in this country. I belong to the bad old days. The new police may be riddled by the mafia and easily bribed, but they are democratic, so that's all right. At least two of the men who beat you up, Mr Pickering, were policemen working for criminals. Many of the people who have been watching you and Havlik are also policemen, but they are not working for the police.'

'God almighty,' Paul breathed. 'Maybe democracy's not such a good wheeze after all.'

'He thinks!' Novak mocked. 'No, it's not all black and white, Mr Pickering. So I think, if I find the jewels, all these mafiosi are watching. Those fuckers would shoot me for the drippings from my nose. For a few million, they'd shoot everyone in Pardubice. Their network is widespread. They reach throughout our society. Even if I could get as far as the police or Prague Castle, I have no guarantee that the jewels will reach their rightful owners. You, however, you go back to England. I escort you in the Czech Republic. You are famous now. Afterwards, I organize a triumphal procession. Schoolchildren, the mayors of the towns you pass through, that sort of thing. When you return to London, you call the editor of *The Times*, the head of the British Museum, the head of the V and A. You organize a meeting. You announce to the world, "We have found these jewels. We take great pleasure in returning them to their owners." Perhaps you even get some money from the newspapers for your story. Perhaps, even, you share it with me. Certainly you get much kudos with Central Europeans and with Jews worldwide, including Rothschilds, which is always very good for business, hmmm?'

His voice had dropped to a low, caressing growl, like the deepest notes of a bowed cello. He was appeasing.

'It's a damned good idea, Jago,' Paul drawled.

Jago cleared his throat. 'For us to take the jewels out is a damned suicidal idea,' he announced. 'We'd be in a lumbering great horsebox in the mountains with armed mobsters on our tails. No. I'm sorry, Novak. *You* do what you suggest. Call the editor of your *Times*, the boss of Prague Castle, the President . . .'

'It won't work.' Novak shook his head. 'They'll never let me take the things from the stables in the first place, and we haven't got a *Times*, a seagreen incorruptible newspaper. No. This is the game we have been playing. As soon as I move, they move, and they have more firepower than I. It is warfare here. Internecine war. The barriers are down in the henhouse, so it's time to sort out the pecking order. I'm an old man, for Christ's sake . . .'

'Oh, come on, Novak,' Jago grinned down at him, 'you're fit, you're trained, you're sharp and you're devious. You wanted us to do this from the outset. That remark about Troy, the way you allowed Havlik to talk to me in the restaurant, the way you've needled me. They've all worked towards this end. You're doing just what Havlik did. You want someone else to take the risks. You've got men at your disposal . . .'

'They will be at your disposal, Mr van Zeller. I swear it. They are my son, Karol,' he indicated the man in glasses, who was now one hundred yards up at their right, 'my son Jan, whom you met in the car park at the racecourse, my sister's son, Klaus, who was also there in the car park, my wife, whom your friend, rather perceptively, I thought, likened to Leo McKern, and one or two others, veterans, old friends, whom I can co-opt as and when they are available. Police uniforms are not so hard to obtain. Don't you see? I'm pretty much alone in this! I am not even technically allowed to carry a gun, for Christ's sake. Come on. I've trusted you. Trust me. I'll get you out of here. If you will not take them, Havlik's friends will, and they will vanish for good. Come. You are gentlemen. Are you going to subsidize a nasty little man like Havlik? You are sportsmen. You have shown today that you have courage. Please.'

'We should try, Jago,' said Paul. 'We don't want all that money to end up in the hands of some nasty little druggy, nor these villains. And it'll do your business some good, that's for sure. And – oh, I don't know. This is really quite good fun. I don't want it just to be all over. And if they catch us . . .'

'*If?*' Jago cast his eyes heavenwards. No stars were visible. '*When*, you should say. The customs guys'll take us to pieces.'

'Yes, well, when they do, we don't have to take it to the death, do we? I mean, OK. They take the darned things. We hand them over, then call the police and hope for the best. I'm sure Viktor here has a plan, haven't you, old chap?'

'I have a plan.' Novak rewarded Paul with a grin. 'And you are the best people to execute it.'

'Oh, God,' Jago groaned. 'And you are going to tell us that there is no risk?'

'Minimal.' Novak shrugged.

'Here we go again,' Jago sighed. 'All right, you horrible little leprechaun. Talk.'

Novak talked.

And the apology for a river giggled at them all.

'What's he say, then, this van Zeller guy?' asked Ward. He swung the door of Havlik's hotel room closed behind him.

'He'll take the stuff. I'm sure of it.' Havlik cautiously shook his coat off his left arm and onto the bed. 'He's leaving before nine. Might as well let them take it to the border. Once it's over, it's legal. They have to go through the courts, they want to dispute our claim.'

'I want to see it transferred, Prince.' Ward walked to the window. He pulled the curtain to one side to peer down into the street. 'And I'm not letting them out of my sight. That brooch thing, it's the real McCoy. So far, you done what you said.'

'I told you, didn't I?' Havlik snarled. 'Shit, like I say, where's the profit trying to screw you guys? Sure. You watch 'em. There's any hassle, you move in. Otherwise, soon as we're in Germany, they hand the things over nice and peaceful and my debt's paid, right?'

'That Novak'll still be sniffing around.'

'So? You can't deal with him? He's not heat, is he?'

'No. He's out of a job, far as I can see. Used to be a policeman back in the commie days. He'll have a network, but he's got no clout. Yeah. We can deal with him. It's OK.'

'Course it's OK. I told you.' Havlik sank onto the bed. 'Shee-it, what a bitch of a day.'

'You got a drink up here?' Ward was tetchy. He swept about the room, opening cupboards and slamming them shut.

'Nope. Get one downstairs in the bar. Come on, man. Leave me sleep. I'm beat.'

'What you done with them book things? Accounts, them old things?'

'Ah, binned them.' Havlik lay back and closed his eyes. 'I thought about it. I mean, how much's it cost, get things like that translated? Mixture of – what they say – French, Bohemian, Christ! Spend all that dough, you find your great-granddad bought twenty dollars' worth of coal, something? Fuck it. I'm out of this, I got better things to do. Hey, I'm going to be at this auction you're holding. I'm gonna have to look the part, right? Maybe I get van Zeller to make me some suits. Oh, shit. Uh uh. Not if he's after his percentage. Maybe I better leave van Zeller alone.'

'I advise it, Prince,' Ward said dourly. 'You get us off your backs, OK, but you got something of a gift for making enemies.'

'Yeah.' Havlik frowned without opening his eyes. 'I wonder why that is?'

Jago lay awake, reviewing the day's triumphs and disasters. On the credit side of the ledger, he had completed the Pardubice, and knew that the vertiginous chasm beneath the Taxis would feature in his dreams tonight and on many other nights to come. He counted Paul's victory a profit too. On reflection, the result had been the best that he could have hoped for – better, even, than a reversal of the placings. Paul was a blessed find, and if, as Novak insisted, his impulsive innocence marked him as stupid, Jago could wish a lot of people stupider.

On the deficit side, he recorded Holly's treachery and the death of Havlik's mare. The more he thought about Holly, however, the more he became convinced that she had acted as she had with genuine regret. She had placed her principles above her feelings, which was, he supposed, praiseworthy, but he flattered himself that those feelings had nonetheless been affectionate and sincere. Guilt or embarrassment might keep her away, but Jago knew the schools which she had attended, the orchestra with which she played. He would track her down.

And so his thoughts turned to tomorrow's adventure. Novak had argued that there would be no danger. 'Look,' he had said, 'we'll be with you all the way. They're not going to want to take them inside the Czech Republic, because you're running the border for them, and anyway, they're going to see the police in attendance. As far as they're concerned, you're going to hand them over to Havlik in Germany, so they'll leave it at that. Once you're outside Czech jurisdiction, that's when they'll move, and I'll do my best to make it fucking difficult for them. I've got friends in Germany who'll give police protection there. But OK. Say the worst comes to the worst, they catch up with you, all right, you just roll over and let them have them. These guys are pros. They don't murder people unless they have to. It's messy.'

'You're sure about that?' Jago had asked. It had seemed an important point.

'You have my word on it. Christ, can you imagine what sort of problems you'd have with a dead Englishman, a hero of the Velka Pardubicka, on German soil? And if you kill that Englishman, you re going to have to run very fast and very far, but what they want's the jewels. Really, you have nothing to worry about.'

'I still don't understand . . .' Jago had started that sentence over and over.

'Just look at the options,' Novak had insisted. 'I try and get the stuff from the stables – there's war. You refuse to take the jewels, Havlik's creditors grab them and they turn up broken up all over the world. You say you will take them, Havlik and Ward are happy.'

'Ward . . .?' Paul got in first.

'Hayward, Ward, whatever he calls himself. He's Havlik's master. He's the one who's extended all this credit. New York hood, pimp, dope-dealer, what you will. He doesn't trust his brethren over here, with good reason, as it happens. Sure, if necessary, he'll seize the things, but then he has the problem of getting them out without entrusting them to someone else who just might betray him for that sort of money. He's far happier with Englishmen who have shown themselves to be honest and crazy. He can keep you under his eye. You can take the risks. He keeps Havlik sweet. From our point of view, whilst you have them, we've a chance of saving them . . .'

Jago remembered his pledge to Paul's daughter, but Novak's pledge was absolute, and the appeal of the jewels was strong. He had said, 'OK. If Paul agrees . . .'

'Oh, absolutely, absolutely . . .' Paul had nodded. 'No question, our duty, I think . . .'

'On one condition,' Jago had warned. 'No. Two. One is that, if you drop out of sight, Novak, I'm going to throw the things out onto the roadside. The other – and this concerns you, Paul, more than anyone – is that heroism is strictly banned. I've been given a hard time for being the meek and mild practical businessman. OK, but I haven't been shot at and beaten up on this trip, so, on balance, I think that my philosophy works. By their fruits ye shall know them. No heroism of any sort, OK?'

'OK,' Paul had said meekly.

'Right.' Jago had stood and offered his hand to Novak. 'You've got a deal. I'll lay odds we won't get through, but we'll give it a go.'

He wondered now if Novak's specious arguments were more than specious. Certainly, the mobsters would be reluctant to kill. So much was consoling. Certainly too, Hayward or whatever he called himself would hesitate to order an attack within the Czech Republic, where the gangsters would be forced to take on Novak and his friends, and where the law would be against them.

Jago was not entirely happy about tomorrow, but he thought that at least he had installed safety-nets.

He did not normally take such risks, play such games.

But then, he did not normally fall in love with haynets, nor ride his last race.

He understood now where Paul chose to live.

He would quite like to live there too.

Jago woke Clay the following morning early to tell him of the change of plan. Clay was sleepy, but not so sleepy that he could not work out the costs involved. 'Sure, J.! Sure! No probs. I'll fly back tomorrow. Only thing is, of course, it'll cost. We're talking, hold on – don't want to get stranded – what? I take your hire-car back. How much is that the day?'

Jago told him.

'Yeah, yeah, but that's only – I mean, accidents, things like that.'

'You've got my credit card numbers in case of emergency.'

'Yeah, but hold on, J, mate. There's the hotel, and I got to eat.'

'You can't eat in the hotel?'

'Gawd, you're a tight bastard. I forget to eat, don't I? Have to be here between seven and nine, that sort of bull. Nah. Best thing, you lend me – what? Five thousand crowns? That'll cover it.'

'I'll make a bet.' Jago raised an eyebrow.

'Go on,' Clay jeered. 'Try everything once.'

'I'll bet that four thousand of these . . .' he tossed the notes onto the bed, 'end up in the hands of that casino. Do your worst, mate.'

'Thanks, J,' Clay grinned. 'Been fun, eh?'

'Yes.' Jago groaned and grinned. 'Yes, it's been bloody marvellous. I'm glad you pushed me, Clay.'

'You ain't 'eard nothing yet!' Clay croaked. 'You OK to load the nags up, then?'

Jago said, 'Sure. Paul's doing that. You stay in bed. Make the most of it. We'll manage.'

'Yeah. Could do with a lie-in. Great. See you back in the smoke then, J.' He rolled over and pulled the sheets over his head.

Novak was leaning on the reception desk, chatting in a desultory sort of way to the girl there as Jago descended the staircase. The usual cigarette with its hook of ash jutted from his orange fingers. He turned those wet, sagging eyes towards Jago. 'Ah, Mr van Zeller! Our last day.'

'Yes,' Jago told him loudly, 'I've decided to go back in the box, take it easy. Clay will fly back tomorrow.'

'Good, good. So we will see a lot of our fair country today, hmm?'

'We really do not need an escort, Novak.'

'Oh, it's no trouble, honestly. My pleasure.'

Jago wheeled away from him. 'This is boring. I need breakfast. Morning.' He nodded to Ward as he emerged from the restaurant.

'Good morning, Jago!' Ward slapped Jago's shoulder. He wore a yellow shirt, a red tie, a peculiarly noxious brown suit. 'So, did I hear you say you were driving back today?'

'That's right. Paul and I.'

'Yup, I'm heading back that way myself. Can't spend my whole life having fun, eh?'

He laughed. Jago shuddered but smiled politely as he moved on into the dining-room. Havlik was in there, pouring black coffee with a shaking hand, his left leg jiggling. He called, 'Jago! Hi!' He waved and made to stand, but Jago was already at the table where Agnes and Corinne sat.

'What's the news of Jean François?' I asked.

Corinne looked up. There were dark half-moons beneath her eyes. 'He is still not conscious,' she said, 'but they think he will be all right. I was there until six this morning. Now Anick is there.'

'God,' Jago said, 'I'm sorry.'

She shrugged. Her smile was faint. "We will take him back to France as soon as he can travel.'

'Yes. Listen, I'll call here to get the news, but will you give me a number where I can get hold of you when you get back?'

'Jago, hi,' said Havlik's voice at Jago's back. Jago did not bother to turn.

Corinne took the pen that he offered her. She wrote on a paper napkin. 'This is my home address and telephone number,' she said. 'Perhaps if you come to France, you will come to see us.'

'I'd love to,' he told her, and he meant it. No less than by battle, friendships were quickly forged by the shared experience of a race like the Pardubice.

'Jago . . .' Havlik whined.

'Good luck.' Jago squeezed Corinne's shoulder. 'I'm sure he'll be OK. I'll see you before we go.'

The two girls nodded and smiled. He turned to Havlik. 'Now,' he said briskly, 'Havlik. Yes. Paul and I are taking the horses home. What's your arrangement?'

'Hey, that's great, Jago!' he grinned, and his head bobbed like a boxer's. 'No, really. Thanks, Jago. No, me, yeah, I'm – I'm going to Frankfurt tonight, drop off the horse-trailer, then – fly back to New York tomorrow. Guy I bought the horse from is sending a lad to pick up the box there. Er, you know, might see you there, hey?' He whispered, then, 'Hotel Landesmann.'

'Sure,' Jago said as he sat at a table. 'Good idea. Should be there by eight. We can have a drink.'

Havlik beamed as he bounced back to his table. He did not sit, but downed his coffee in two gulps, then set off, presumably in search of Ward.

Of one thing, Jago was certain. He was going nowhere near Frankfurt tonight.

Paul arrived as Jago polished off his eggs. He was excited. He looked scrubbed. His eyes and his teeth glittered. He wore a crisp cream shirt, cream cords and tan boots. His hand was taken and shaken five times between the door and Jago's table.

'All loaded up,' he announced with a wink, 'and ready to roll.'

'No one's going to fuss about a haynet,' Novak had said, *'and even if they did, they're not going to do anything in the middle of Pardubice racecourse . . .'*

Then there were emotional farewells and Gallic embraces, bills to be paid, and a surprising hug from Pavla, who came trotting from the organizers' offices at the back. It was after nine when at last Paul and Jago climbed into the cab of the horsebox. Paul took the wheel with one hand, but the other was busily engaged in waving at the crowd on the pavement. They set off westward. Jago watched in the wing-mirror. A maroon Volvo bounced out of the car park behind them. Novak's car was already two cars ahead.

'Who's that in the Volvo, then?' Paul nodded at the mirror.

'Ward's men, I reckon,' Jago shrugged. 'Look like heavies.'

'Lots of spectators for the loading?' Jago asked.

'Oh, lots,' Paul laughed. 'Two girls wanted me to sign their bosoms. Couldn't believe it. No, Hayward or whatever he was called turned up, half of Novak's friends and relations. Lots of clapping and stuff. Rather embarrassing, really. Gosh, Jago. Stole a peek. Fantastic stuff in there.'

'I know.' Jago shook his head. 'Vonnegut somewhere has a money tree which fertilizes itself with the bodies of the human beings who kill one another round its roots. You can understand it when you see things like that.'

Jago waited until they were some twenty minutes outside Pardubice. 'I'll just check back there.' He winked. Paul nodded. Jago staggered through to the back of the box.

'Never tell anyone else what to do if you can't show them how it should be done.' His father's words had tormented him in childhood, but, since the alternative was a lecture and a gym-shoe to the buttocks, Jago had heeded them.

He never travelled without his kit – the needles, shears and chalk which were the tools of his trade. He addressed himself first to the hessian quilting which lined Burly's section of the box. He unpicked the stitching in seconds. He lifted down the haynet from the empty stall.

This was where his advantage told. Anyone could restitch the fabric. Jago could do it fast, and he could do it invisibly to every eye save that of an expert. He slid the jewels into the padding, then stitched with the speed and precision of long years of practice.

He moved on to Avocet's stall. Again, the whole process took him mere minutes. He then took the two saddles. He slipped a few of the jewels – those that he deemed most desirable – into the bodies of both his and Paul's saddles, Again he 'invisibly mended'.

It would not deter a maniac, nor one whose life depended on recovering the Havlik jewels. It would, however, fool a professional, a Customs man, for example. It was all that he could do.

'Well, prince, you're almost home and dry.' Ward held open the passenger door of the German horsebox as Havlik clambered in. 'You won't mind a little escort, will you?' He clicked his fingers to a man on the pavement. The man walked around the front of the vehicle and clambered in beside Havlik. 'Hans here will stay with you until everything's sorted. He's your chauffeur. And if I've forgotten anything, I can just give Hans a call, right?'

Havlik nodded. He did not welcome this squat dark stranger in his cab, but he had expected some such encumbrance.

'So, we meet at Frankfurt, Prince.'

'You will wait this time?' Havlik eyed the suspicious bulge beneath his passenger's armpit. 'Till we get to Frankfurt, do it all peaceful?'

'You know me, Prince.' Ward smiled and expansively gestured. 'I like peaceful. No one messes with me, I'm a pussy-cat. No. See you in Frankfurt, you're in the clear. We'll need you back in New York – what? Couple of months' time? Set up the auction of the decade, right? Take care of him, Hans. The prince wants foot massage, whatever it's called, you start licking. OK?'

The door slammed shut. Hans started up the engine. The horsebox shuddered. Havlik did his best not to smile too broadly as he waved to Ward. He did not believe for a moment that Ward would wait until Jago handed over the jewels in Frankfurt tonight, but that was no concern of his. He was on his way to freedom at last.

He gave it just fifteen minutes. They were out in the country, and apparently unfollowed. He felt like he used to feel, when his father was out of the apartment, and he could get his hands on the *Playboys* in the den, light a cigarette, have fun.

For the past thirty-six hours, since Ward had come crashing in, Havlik had been longing for a gloat, but Ward had sharp eyes. To his lieutenants, old papers and ledgers were just that. You lit fires with them, wiped your arse. Ward might just have guessed that these were something more. Havlik had stashed them, ledgers and loose sheets, in the cavity beneath the seat, locked the horsebox and very deliberately not returned until this morning.

He tried to keep it casual. He even hummed as he half stood and raised the vinyl-covered cushion. Hans afforded him a glance, no more.

Havlik picked out the road map which lay there.

Everything drained downwards. The blood left his head and shoulders. The stuff in his gut put on a spurt and wanted out, now. He whispered, 'No!' He patted the boards there. 'No?' he keened. Then he screamed, 'No! No! Fuck, no! Christ, what's . . .? No no no no no. No, it can't be. Jesus, no. No!'

He dropped to his knees and feverishly patted the floor. Again and again he raised the seat and peered inside the cavity. Hans braked. His eyebrows rose, questioning. '*Was ist* . . .'

'No!' Havlik screamed in his face. He hit him on the shoulder. Tears now filled his eyes. 'Nooo!'

Hans shrugged stupidly.

'Go back!' Havlik yelled. He pointed backwards. 'Back! Go back to Pardubice.' He grasped the steering wheel and turned it. 'Back! Now! Quickly!'

Hans frowned. He pulled out the telephone and mumbled something about 'Herr Ward'. 'No!' Havlik grabbed the instrument. 'No, just fucking go back, right?'

Hans growled and eyed the telephone, but obeyed.

Havlik looked down at the telephone. He thought of ringing Ward himself, telling him – telling him what? He had to think. He clasped his hands in his crotch and rocked back and forth. Shrill squeaks of anguish seeped from his lips. He had to think, he had to think . . .

'Nice girl, that Diana, I must say,' Paul mused.

Jago, once more at the wheel, cast him a fleeting glance. 'One of the best. Hasn't always had it easy, but she's gutsy and she's fun. Bounces back. I hope you will call her.'

'Well, yes, maybe, just to say hello or something.'

'Why not, "hello, how about dinner one night?"'

'Oh, no. No, I think I'm past all that sort of thing. Old crock. Anyhow. No. Haven't got the money for girls and things.'

'Oh, yes, you have. You've got five hundred thousand Czech crowns, remember? That's quite a lot of decent dinners and country weekends. And forget the "old crock" stuff, will you? If you can get yourself into the kind of trouble you got yourself into on Friday night, then ride and win the Pardubice, you're man enough for the likes of Diana.'

'You really think she'd be interested in dinner or something?'

'Man, I've known Diana Osborne since we were both in short pants. She'd be interested. I give you my word on it.'

'Gosh.' Paul examined the backs of his hands. 'Best thing I ever did, coming on this trip. Everyone thought I was crazy, but there you are. It can pay.'

'It can indeed. And when I am venerable like you, I'll remember your example and do precisely the opposite of what my children, doctors and well-meaning friends advise,' Jago laughed.

'You're sure you're happy driving?'

'Certain. I'll take us past Prague, then we'll stop somewhere to water the horses, get a bite of lunch. Our friend still there?' He looked up into the rear-view mirror.

'Yup.' Paul swivelled round. 'About five hundred yards back now.'

'Hey, what's Novak up to?'

'Hmm?' Paul faced front and narrowed his eyes. 'Stopping for petrol,' he said. 'Oh, very smooth.'

For as Novak swung into the petrol-station forecourt, the driver of a pale blue car saluted and the car nosed into the traffic. The two young Novaks sat in the front.

'Yup,' said Jago. 'So far, it's all going to plan . . .'

'Nothing suspicious either end,' Ward nodded. He held his left finger against his left ear against the sound of the passing traffic. 'That's good. I'll be on my way.'

He switched off the telephone and slid into the silver Mercedes. 'Right,' he said, 'they given me someone speaks English, just for a change?'

'Sure did, Mr Hayward.' The chauffeur turned with a dazzling smile. He was very young and tanned. 'Mark Barrow, at your service.'

'You a Texan?' Ward demanded.

'Sure am. Out here learnin' the casino business.'

'Christ,' Ward sighed. 'Oh, well, it's one better than a fucking Czech, I guess. You don't talk a lot, do you?'

'Not if you don't want it, Mr Ward.'

'Yeah, well, I don't. You know where we're going?'

'Waldsassen, Germany,' said Barrow enthusiastically.

'Round there, yeah. Just the other side of the border. I'll tell you when we reach the spot. It's gonna be a long journey. Just so's you know, I'm allergic to cattle and oil. The very mention of either makes me behave like manic. Let's go.'

'Yes, sir,' Barrow nodded.

'Here.' Ward reached forward. 'Put this on. It's Mozart. You like Mozart?'

'Sure,' the boy shrugged.

'You like Mozart, you don't say "sure" like that. You say, "yeah, Christ, I love Mozart." You say "sure" like that, means you never listened to a note in your life. Come on. Put it on. I've had enough of this dump for a lifetime.'

Mark Barrow did as he was instructed. As he turned onto the street, however, and Papageno started singing, Ward leaned forward and snapped, 'Stop!'

Barrow braked hard. Ward breathed, 'What the fuck?'

He opened his door and stepped out into the street. He waved down the approaching horsebox. He sidestepped through the traffic and climbed onto the box's running-board. 'What the fuck you doing back here?' he shouted into the cab.

Havlik was white. He gabbled, 'Listen, I've got to talk to you. You've got to change plans. The whole thing'll be fucked up, I just realized, you don't . . . Wait. Listen.'

He opened his door and jumped down from the cab. He carried the road-map. Ward joined him on the pavement. 'What's this all about, damn it?' Ward demanded. 'What's gone wrong?'

'Listen. You haven't taken nothing from here – this box, have you?'

'What you talking about? There was something to take?'

'No, no. Don't worry. Just a map is gone. No. Listen. I been thinking. Last night, I hear van Zeller, talking to Novak, right? He says, "The police get it by arse." First I think he's saying, "my arse", but Novak repeats it – "by arse", and I think, OK, these English, they speak weird. Maybe this is like an English expression. The police don't get it, sort of thing. Then I'm looking at a map, and I see this place right on the border, this side of the border – "As", see? Novak's got to them. They're trying to screw us. We got – we thought, easy, do it the other side. They're setting it up here. The heat here's gonna do a big raid, something. Long way out in the country, long way from, like – I mean, this looks pretty wild country, right? We got to get those things from them before they get to this place As. We got to get moving.' It was the best he had been able to come up with in the last fifteen minutes. It would have to do.

'Hold it, hold it . . .' Ward looked down at the map. 'You're sure of this?'

'Sure I'm sure! I stand to gain, coming back, telling you, like, take the things while they're still in the country? You want – Novak and half the fucking Czech police arrive at this place with guns and . . . shit, man. Let's go!'

Ward considered. He was suddenly brisk. 'OK. We play it safe. We do it before the border. Hans, you come too.' The three men crossed the road and climbed into the Mercedes. Ward was already tapping out a number on the mobile as he climbed in. He slammed his door. 'Barrow?' he said to the driver.

'Yes, sir?'

'You ever had a Czech speeding-ticket?'

'No, sir.'

'Earn some today,' he ordered. 'Move!'

Jago remembered from school how Baudelaire used to get all hot and bothered about the landscape of his mulatto mistress's body, and particularly the fragrant forest of her hair in which he could wander and sleep. Driving through the forests that afternoon was like being a flea in Jimi Hendrix's parting. The woods were relentless, endless, dark, oppressive.

Paul was driving again. The horsebox climbed in third gear, moved up to fourth for a hundred yards, then shifted down to third again, engine groaning as if at a bad joke, or to second as it hit some of the paper-clip bends on the steep descents. And always there were trees, crowding them, gasping as they passed.

It was like a birth dream, seeing all that blurred darkness pulled back about them. Sometimes, at the crest of a hill, there was light at the end, where trees had been felled or where a clearing had been cut for a boar-hide. Then there were views of more forest, dabbed by light like the white in an old negro's hair. As ever, there were castles and mansions, always unexpected, on the distant hills, peeking up above the trees on stocky outcrops of stone. They looked like barely sharpened pencil-stubs with their erasers neatly laid alongside.

Somewhere around midday, Paul and Jago had stopped

at a town named Rakovnik to water the horses. Some twenty miles further on, Paul had jumped down to buy Coke and sandwiches. He had been recognized. Newspapers were produced so that the shopkeepers could compare the photographs with the original.

A small crowd had gathered to shake his hand. He had signed autographs, then pointed Jago out.

Jago too had had his hand pumped. He too had signed newspapers, books, even a packet of cornflakes. He had taken over the driving.

'Your celebrity is going to be an advantage, Shit, they can't kidnap or beat a national hero, especially a foreigner. For as long as there are people around, you'll be OK . . .'

But there were no people now. Not here in these endless wooded mountains as they drew nearer and nearer the German border. Novak and his nephew, the young, fresh-faced boy, were ahead now. The maroon Volvo had been joined by the younger Novaks in their pale blue car which obviously stayed on its tail. Jago identified it as the same car which had previously led them.

'. . . As soon as you enter Germany, you'll have the protection of the police. I'm going to alert them, tell them that you're carrying a valuable consignment and that you've been threatened . . .'

They had driven down into Marianske Lazne, or Marienbad, around three-thirty. The great spa town, like so many spa towns, had seemed to have no centre. It sprawled, made up of thousands of grand villas built for rich bathers and scattered about the hills for miles around. The rich bathers had gone. There was something sad and sterile about the faded grandeur.

The horsebox had strained and grumbled in traffic-jams there, then started the climb up into still higher hills. There had been occasional cars in both directions. From time to time, so narrow were the roads and so broad the vehicle, they had had two or three cars mixed up in the four-vehicle cortège, but the interlopers had overtaken whenever the road was wide enough, and were soon out of sight.

Now they were at the top of a very deep pass with a long

lake or reservoir scintillating down at their right. Within fifteen minutes, they would be in Germany.

It all happened very suddenly. Suddenly three dark and powerful cars appeared below. They crept, it seemed, along the snaking road, vanished at a hairpin bend, and then they were wailing as they climbed the straight, headed straight for the horse-box.

Paul and Jago saw the four dark figures in each car. Jago said, 'Whoops, miscalculation.'

'Yup,' said Paul, 'this is it.'

Novak braked. Paul followed suit. The maroon car behind slewed at a diagonal across the road. The first of the cars from beneath mounted the verge in order to career past the horsebox. It made an arrowhead with the Volvo. The second car skewed to a halt in front of the horsebox. Even as it rocked, men were out and running. It was an intimidating cliché, and it worked. The third of the cars, either by accident or design, sideswiped Novak's car before spinning to a halt.

The horse-box was very thoroughly bent.

Neither Paul nor Jago noticed the big silver car which pulled up smoothly behind the blue car at the rear. They were too busy looking at the guns. Two guns pointed down at Novak and his nephew, Klaus, who had not moved from their seats. The Englishmen assumed that another two guns were covering Karol and Jan Novak, because that left four, and four muzzles pouted unwavering towards them.

'Here we go,' Jago sighed.

'Ah, well.' Paul unfastened his seatbelt. 'Oh, by the way, did you know that I won the Pardubice?'

'I had heard.' Jago grinned.

Paul flashed him a smile of fellowship. 'Let's get this done.'

They opened their doors and jumped down. That made it two guns apiece, which did not feel twice as good.

Novak and Klaus were ushered from their car. Novak was frowning deeply. He caught Jago's eye. He shrugged.

There was silence, then, save for breathing, the hushing of the trees as they bobbed their lower branches, the twittering of the birds. Someone coughed behind the horsebox. Several eyes swivelled in that direction as though it had been a fart at a funeral.

The door of the car back there slammed shut. Footfalls crunched. Ward strolled up at Jago's right. Havlik followed, eyes swivelling everywhere, hands fluttering. A solid-looking dark man increased the offensive arsenal by one handgun.

'Ah, Mr van Zeller,' Ward said robustly, almost jovially, 'Mr Pickering – and Novak. Good. Frisk them, please.'

Jago and Paul found themselves leaning up against the side of the horsebox as inexpert hands patted and groped. Jago straightened and turned to see a pistol removed from Novak's pocket and flung onto the verge.

'So. Now what?' Paul dusted himself down.

'Up to you,' Ward smiled. 'How you want to do it.'

'Do what, exactly?'

'You got some things here Prince Havlik asked you to look after. Now he wants them back. Isn't that right, Prince?'

'That's right,' Havlik strutted. 'You try to shaft me? Shit. Hand 'em over right now.'

'We are, fairly obviously, going to have to search your vehicle.'

'Search away,' Jago shrugged.

'Ah, no. There ain't no need, is there?' Ward smiled. 'Tell you what. You force us to search this vehicle, we search the straw, the saddles, the horses, but we do those last. First we rip open the seats, then we pull up the floors, then we search your asses. Alternatively, you simply tell us where the things are, I say, "thank you very much, goodbye," and you go on your way. Your decision.'

The breeze brushed the trees. It had a sharp, chill edge to it which made Jago shiver. Birds chimed in the forest. The Gatling rattle as a pigeon burst from the woods made the hawk-like policeman start. His head swivelled. Novak half crouched, then straightened. He shook out another cigarette.

'I suppose,' Jago said, 'that it's no use my saying, "this is a gross breach of my rights and I demand to see the ambassador"?'

Ward slowly shook his head. His eyes met Jago's. He smiled and inaudibly enunciated, 'None – at – all.'

Jago looked across at Paul. Paul shook his head. 'This is intolerable,' he said. 'For God's sake, are we amongst bloody savages or what? I think we should jolly well . . .'

But Jago had recalled his promise to Clare and had appraised the odds. He turned away and puffed air in resignation. 'OK,' he said, 'come with me.'

'Wait!' Ward barked. He leaned out to call around the horsebox. 'Barrow? Get over here! I want someone speaks English and has a name!'

The tall blond Texan sidestepped between cars to the ring of vehicles. His jeans were tight. He said, 'What's goin' on here?'

'You gonna help here. Take one of these guns. You. Give this man your gun. Right. Two of you – you and you – stand by the door. Come on, Mr van Zeller. Let's do this nice.'

Jago led the way up into the horsebox through the door behind the cab. Ward heaved himself up behind him. Barrow, who did not appear happy with the gun, sprang up lithely. Two men took up their positions on either side of the door.

The men outside heard the thudding of footfalls, the rumble of voices. They heard one of the horses snorting and stamping. The solitary sun shimmered as though through water, just ten degrees above the German horizon. The lake far below seemed to creep and climb like tinsel in a breeze. Paul leaned back against the horsebox.

Havlik stalked over to Novak. 'Right, shithead fucking Czech peasant bastard,' he spat the words from between gritted teeth, 'where'd you put those papers? You tell me or I get these guys to shoot you right now.'

'I don't think so,' Novak croaked. 'And anyhow, I don't know what the fuck you're talking about, Mr Havlik.'

'You know. Oh, you know OK. Christ! I'll tear your car, this box, everything apart, you hear?'

'Off you go,' said Novak.

'Don't you *talk* to me like that,' Havlik danced, and, on 'talk', drove his fist hard into Novak's lower stomach. Novak bent, and reached for support on his nephew's shoulder, but did not go down. Havlik danced back with a single bark of laughter.

'OK. You.' He spun on his heel and stalked over to Paul. 'Mr gallant jockey. Fucking mobile home. You try to screw me, you end up dead. Where are they?'

'You are a filthy little man,' Paul said quietly. 'A disgusting, crooked, corrupt little lout. You make me sick. Go away.'

'Oh, yeah?' Havlik yelped. 'Oh, yeah? You know what's gonna happen, you talk to me like that? You know who . . .'

'You come up here, Prince?' Ward's voice was a muffled boom.

Havlik turned his head. His snarl remained on his face. 'You know what's going to happen to you?' he muttered at Paul. 'You treat me like shit, you fucking mobile-home fucking nobody? Right.'

He twice punched his own thigh, then turned away and jumped up into the horsebox.

Paul once more relaxed.

'In here, Prince,' Ward's voice called from a stall ahead. Havlik was shaking. He nodded to himself as though encouraging himself. His arms twitched. He made his way to the stall where Avocet stood.

Ward had spread a New Zealand blanket on the straw. He was squatting, picking through sparkling ribbons of gems. 'This the lot, then?'

'No, it fucking isn't,' Havlik twanged without even examining the things. 'You not gonna strip this fucking box apart?'

'Oh, I don't think that is necessary.' Ward pulled a sheet of paper from his pocket. 'Mr van Zeller is being co-operative, aren't you, Mr van Zeller? You tell us what's missing, Prince.'

Havlik turned his attention to the jewels. 'Shit, try the two big necklaces, the emeralds and the sapphires.'

Jago sighed. 'Oh, yes. In the saddles.' He led the way. The other men followed.

'You see?' Havlik squealed. 'He's – they're trying to shaft you! You should – shit, kill the fuckers, rip the whole thing in pieces! And that Novak's car. Come on, man!'

Jago smoothly and swiftly unstitched the saddle. The sapphires and diamonds slithered into his hand. He passed them on to Ward.

'Seems to me, Prince,' Ward stared down, 'your list here. We got the Maximilian brooch already . . . Twenty-eight items . . . Mr van Zeller gives me an egg, a river of emeralds, some diamond studs, that should be the whole shebang.'

'How do you know?' Havlik whimpered. 'How do you know? Maybe – maybe they got – maybe they found more stuff? Maybe I didn't know it all! Maybe – my dad said there was other things – gold, gold plates . . . Loose stones . . .'

'Prince,' said Ward happily as Jago passed him the emeralds and the egg, 'we're obstructing a thoroughfare. We want to get out fast. We got what we came for. You can stay if you like. Thank you, Mr van Zeller. The studs?'

'Haven't a clue,' Jago shrugged. 'Sorry. That's all we got. If you're talking just solitaires, they'd have got lost that night when we were chasing round the countryside. They could be in the straw here, I suppose . . .'

'Shit. Forget it. You get your souvenirs too. Why not? Barrow, bring that blanket, and don't drop nothing.'

'No!' Havlik snatched the saddle from Jago. He plunged his hand into the opened seam. He groped, found nothing, and flung the saddle at Jago's head. He stooped down to examine the other saddle. Jago walked past him, weary now. He followed the two big men ahead of him towards the daylight.

Jago ducked to step down through the door. Footfalls thudded fast behind him. Havlik released a sort of sob, close at hand. Something swished. Jago jumped down onto the tarmac. He turned. There was nothing in the door-frame.

'Everything OK?' Paul droned where he lounged against the box.

'Fine,' Jago nodded.

'Right, thank you.' Ward waved contentedly. 'Let's get the hell out. Everyone, scatter. Thank you!' He jogged towards his car.

Paul was watching him go. He said, 'Is all this melodrama over, then?'

The moment was to remain frozen in Jago's memory as though God had taken a Polaroid.

The man beside Paul was turning away. Car engines were coughing. Novak was moving forward.

There was a flash of steel in the horsebox doorway, a swift glimmer, no more. It could almost have been a reflection from a mirror. Paul raised his right hand. His head rocked back. His knees gave. His shoulders slumped. He very suddenly dropped.

'You don't ever talk to me like that!' Havlik jumped down from the doorway with a stirrup-leather dangling from his hand. 'You don't fucking talk to me like that . . .'

He swung the iron back and would have brought it down again on Paul's unprotected, lolling head. Jago yelled, 'No!' and threw himself forward. He grasped the stirrup in his right hand, shoved at Havlik's back with his left. Havlik fell forward into the doorway. All around them now cars were starting up and reversing.

'All right, then. Where are they?' Havlik stood and turned. 'Come on. Quick. Speak up. Come on.'

Jago grabbed him by the shirt front and simply flung him out of the way. He knelt at Paul's head. He reached for the wound at the left temple. It was nothing dramatic, just a neat, moist contusion covered with matted hair. He turned Paul's head towards him.

Those eyes were still fixed upon something distant.

'God . . .' Jago felt with trembling fingers for a pulse. There was only stillness and flaccidity.

'No. It can't be–' Jago was puzzled. 'Paul?' He raised the head in the crook of his arm. 'For Christ's sake. Someone come here! Someone help!'

'He's dead,' thudded a croaking voice above him.

'Don't be silly,' Jago panted. 'A stirrup can't bloody kill him. Someone do artificial respiration or something.'

A hand clasped his shoulder even as Paul's had clasped it the afternoon before. 'He's dead,' said Novak. 'I'm so sorry. I don't . . . Oh, God, it's madness . . .'

'No?' Jago was straining for breath. An invisible giant was shaking him violently. 'For Christ's sake, what's happening?'

Novak was cursing in Czech. He struck the horsebox again and again with a clenched fist. He blinked and shook his head, incredulous. He called to his sons. They answered from either side.

Jago stared down at Paul. The dead man lay elegantly sprawled as though sunbathing, his arms outflung, his head turned to one side, one leg slightly raised at the knee. 'No . . .?' Jago sobbed, and he did not know whether pity, terror or anger were greatest in him at that moment. 'You said we'd be fine. All for some bloody pebbles . . .'

Novak released a long, low grunt. Again he consulted in murmurs with his sons. They shook their heads. He nodded. Nothing more could be done.

Somewhere behind the horsebox, car doors thumped. For a moment or two, voices were raised. Someone yelped in protest. There was more movement between the cars. A door opened.

Havlik's voice wailed, 'Shit, you can't!'

The door shut again. The cars vroomed backwards. The brakes whined. The big silver car bounced onto the scrub and made noises like a weightlifter.

It bounced back onto the road, and was gone, howling, down the hill towards the border.

Another car roared off towards Prague. Someone was whimpering out there in the road, crouched behind the pale blue car.

Jago knew who it would be.

'Havlik!' Jago roared. He let Paul's head down upon the road. 'He's dead! Come here, you disgusting little *shit*!

'You shouldn't have double-crossed me, Jago. I told you!' His tone was cocky, but his voice quavered.

'I, double-cross you?' Jago squealed indignantly.

'Yeah,' Havlik shouted. 'You and Paul and that Novak

guy. You were all in it together, weren't you? You had my jewels, OK, but you and Novak found my papers and you cut a deal, right? Shit, and there was I trusting you. "Please, Jago, help me to carry them out." Christ. I get to the horsebox this morning, find the papers and books gone as well, I thought I'd die. You shouldn't have done that, Jago. You kept your part of the bargain, you'd have had your share.'

'Oh, yeah? From Paraguay, was it?' Jago shouted.

'Oh.' That gave him pause. 'Yeah, well, yeah, sure. I keep my word. Anyhow, that was only, you know, if things didn't pan out. You guys hadn't stolen those things, we might be free and clear in Frankfurt now. Shit, girls, good booze, good times . . . I found them gone, what the fuck's I to do? I needed those papers to get my tit out of the wringer. Come on, Jago. You – we make a deal, right? Fifty-fifty. Shit, bet you don't even know what they are!'

Jago understood barely half of what Havlik was shouting. What he did understand was that Havlik had attempted some further bit of jiggery-pokery involving papers, and that, when he found them gone, he had sought the help of his mafia creditors. In consequence, Paul lay dead on this road.

That was enough.

'I'm going to kill you, Havlik!' Jago yelled. The words rang in the hills. Jago meant them, too, in so far as he was aware of their actual meaning at that moment. Terror and grief constituted a bleak vacuum. Nature and he agreed in abhorring such a state. Blind, disdainful fury stormed in to fill it.

'You know what they are? The papers? Must be worth – shit, tens of thousands, yeah? We split . . .'

Jago had pulled himself to his feet and stepped forward from the shelter of the horsebox. He did not know whether Havlik was armed. At that moment, he did not much care. He screamed above the prattling. 'Do you hear me, Havlik?' he screamed. 'You're a filthy, self-indulgent, cowardly little jerk and you've killed a good man and a good mare, so I intend to kill you . . .'

'Hey, Jago, come on. You tried to rip me off, what was I meant to do, huh?' The man was incredible. Jago thought perhaps that Havlik believed himself.

Havlik was just a car's width away from Jago now, crouched down below the level of the windows. Jago could even see the top of his head through the car's rear window. The head was rocking. The man seemed to be humming.

'Stay still, Havlik,' Jago ordered. He worked his way round the back of the car.

Havlik's head appeared for a split second over the car's roof. Those bulbous eyes were plaintive. His right hand clasped his left arm. He raised his jaw. His upper lip rose in a punk sneer. His eyes were hard now. All plaintiveness was gone. He had been a hurt child for a second. Now he was the decayed adult once more, and perversely proud.

He ran.

He headed downhill. Jago lunged at him across the bonnet of the car, but Havlik jinked with a high-pitched giggle and sprinted. Perhaps he still thought that those people who had abandoned him were really his kind, his friends. Perhaps he believed that they were waiting for him down there, like loving parents who have driven on as a reproving 'joke'.

Jago started to pursue him, but the horse-box was in his way, and his heart was no longer in it. He was too pathetic, too human to warrant his anger.

The Novaks did not move as Havlik scampered by.

Viktor Novak grinned his sour, jagged grin. He held a gun in his right hand.

It was not much of a gun. It was small and black and glazed.

Novak raised his left hand to his mouth. It held a cigarette between finger and thumb. He inhaled deep. He pulled the cigarette from his lips with a 'pht'. His thumb flicked it away. His eyes became narrower and narrower. His smile never faded. He said, 'Look away, little liberal. You're about to see murder done.'

He sighted. Jago yelled, 'No, please . . .'

The gun spat once.

Havlik was perhaps fifteen yards away, and nearing a

bend, and there was no sound save the dwindling patter of his footfalls and Novak's long, old-dog growl of satisfaction.

The bullet hit Havlik just above the nape of his neck. His arms spread. He staggered for some five paces, his whole back crescent, then he went down. It was not an actor's fall. His hands did not protect his head, nor did he turn to protect his face. It hit the tarmac hard.

'So.' Novak dusted off his hands. 'That is the end of a lot of bad blood.'

Jago stared down the road at where Havlik lay. 'You mean . . .' he gulped. 'You mean he's dead?'

'I should hope so.' Novak was already reaching for another cigarette. He passed the gun to his bespectacled son. 'Go and make sure, Karol.' He turned back to Jago. 'He was a skid-mark on life's bottom-sheet. Anyhow, they'd have got him if we hadn't.'

'What is happening here?' Jago wailed.

'Well, you wanted him dead, didn't you?'

'Well, in theory, maybe, Novak, but . . .'

'You see? You English. You'd have done it if you'd had the gun, but now that it's done, you'd sooner pretend that you're above such things. Fuck it, I don't know.'

Down the road, Karol was kneeling over Havlik's body. He pulled back the eyelids with his thumbs. He gave his father a thumbs-up sign.

'Everything's gone mad.' Jago stared and licked his lips.

'No. We had a murder victim, we had to have a murderer,' Novak explained simply. 'I'm a law officer, which makes it almost all right. This is the man who killed my friend and teacher, Emil Filip. He also killed a nasty, crooked man called Robinson back in New York, but that nasty, crooked man trusted him. He killed Mr Pickering, too. He would have turned up at your door one day. Three murders was enough, I think.'

Novak barked orders in Czech. Karol grabbed Havlik under the shoulders and dragged him up towards the vehicles.

Jago walked over to where Paul lay. He knelt. He smoothed back the white hair. There was a trickle of dark blood over his left ear, but the face was as in life. Jago closed Paul's eyes. Paul seemed quietly amused by the turn of events. Jago could imagine his version: 'Jolly exciting life you lead, Jago, must say. Great gas. Look after the girls for us, won't you . . .'

Simple shock, for the moment, banished grief. It was so impossible – so unnatural – that one state should be so instantly exchanged for another. There should be evolution, transition, whether to genesis or to extinction. Life took nine months to create, a man like this, many years. It was beyond belief that all that could so totally be wiped out in a moment. It was wrong. It challenged the foundations of perception and emotion. It could not be.

Later, Jago would murmur the epitaph which Paul would have liked to hear. 'A very gallant English gentleman,' and his eyes would fill and his voice would crack, but that would be many hours and many miles away. For now, there was only this bewilderment and incredulity. Jago reached down to empty Paul's coat pockets. He found a passport, a diary, a tube of mints. He swallowed and turned his head away. His breath still came too fast.

'Leave the passport and drive on, Mr van Zeller.' Novak stood above him. He sagged. He was at last very tired. 'I'll clean up this mess. I'm used to it. Don't worry. Paul will have a proper Christian burial. I am so, so sorry. I would never . . . The professionals were professional, like I said. Havlik was a vengeful amateur. There was no point to what he did. He saw his last chance going away from him. Even if the mob got the jewels, he'd have seen one hell of a profit. He was desperate.'

'I still don't understand.' Jago frowned. 'What's all this about some papers?'

'Climb into the box, Mr van Zeller. I don't want anyone coming along and seeing you here. We'll have a story sorted out for the Press. I'll travel with you to the frontier.'

He gave more orders. The car in front of the box was driven onto the verge. Paul's body was dragged onto the grass verge. Jago climbed up into the cab. 'Move over,' Novak commanded. 'I'll drive you.'

Jago nodded. Just – what? Ten, fifteen minutes ago, Paul had been vital, strong and happy in this seat. Now Jago was leaving him to chill on alien turf. It would not sink in for some time. When it did, it would hurt like hell.

Novak knew that. He wasn't giving Jago time to think. He turned the key. The engine started first time. The box rolled forward.

'You're just letting me go on?' Jago said, bemused.

'Yes, yes. No point in anything else. Or did you want to stay here and be interrogated by the police and the press?'

'No, but . . .' Jago winced. He had objections, but he could not remember what they were.

'Listen. It's confusing,' Novak acknowledged. 'Yes. Havlik was tricky. He knew that he'd be followed. He had to. Incidentally, I work for the Metropolitan Museum.'

'The New York Met?' Jago yapped and stared.

'Yep. Oh, dear, where do I start? Well, you see, Prague Castle received the jewels eighteen months ago.'

'What jewels?' Jago blinked. 'You're not making sense, Novak.'

'The so-called Havlik jewels. Havlik came here looking for them as soon as the communists fell, but I was on his tail full-time. He couldn't do a thing. A couple of months later, a peasant girl named Novotna found them under her father's bed when he died. He'd found them in that fountain some thirty years back. She had the sense to deliver them to the right authorities. I got called in to broker the whole business. OK. We made a deal with the Met. The Met gets to hold the exhibition, *Lost Treasures of Bohemia*. The exhibition travels, London, Milan, Tokyo, ends up back here, where the Met will have paid for a magnificent gallery for their permanent exhibition. Right?'

'Sure.' Jago shook the clamouring shock waves from his head. 'But . . .'

'You know how long it takes to get an exhibition like that together? Provenances, cleaning, restoration, security, cataloguing, all done in strict secrecy? The exhibition won't open for another eighteen months as it is. Right. Security's my business, these jewels my hobby. I know about Havlik. I know he's been living on the credit of the jewels. What I didn't know was that one of our master jewellers, a man named Robinson, had also met Havlik. What I think must have happened is that Robinson went to Havlik and told him that the things had been found. Havlik thinks, Christ, that's me fucked. What do I do? So they cook up this plan. Robinson makes replicas – hell, he's living with the things day in, day out. It's expensive, sure, but he stands to make millions. He comes over – why not? He was a Czech by birth. He slips them into the fountain stopcock, checks out these documents Havlik's told him about. What they've got to do then is satisfy Ward and his friends that they've got the jewels for as long as it takes for them to get the documents, get out and vanish in South America. That's what this charade has been about. Havlik wanted you guys to hold onto the things right up to the last minute, so there would be as little time as possible for their authentification. They think he wants his share and therefore won't do a bunk. They'll take them off you, be happy as Larry, couldn't really give a damn about Havlik. What they don't know is that he couldn't give a damn about the so-called jewels. He'd be flying off to Paraguay tonight.'

'You're saying . . .' Jago was still shaking his head. The information would not lodge. 'You're saying those were fakes?'

'Yup.'

Jago thought back to the passion which those things had engendered in him and Holly. It seemed apt that they were counterfeit.

Novak read his thought. 'Yup. The idea was good. Jewels have that effect. They blind people to everything else. He had one piece – the Maximilian brooch – which was genuine. His grandmother had smuggled it out, but of course, Havlik couldn't sell it because it was stolen property, so he threw that in as a tester. Ward swallowed the bait. That was genuine, so the rest must be. I'm telling this like I knew it all from the outset. I didn't. All I knew was that Havlik had suddenly been riding a lot, that he was heading for the

Czech Republic and that his car had mowed down Robinson.'

'He killed him?'

Novak nodded. 'The night before he flew out. Don't mourn little Prince Havlik. So I came out too, engaged my family to help as best they could. Then Holly dug up these jewels. I thought, what the hell is going on here? But I take a look when she's checking in, dead beat, at the hotel in Plsen. They're fakes. Then the mob muscles in. I'm working it out as I go along. What I know is – if there are fakes that good going around, and the mob's involved, I want to know what's happening. I want to keep them under my eyes full-time.'

'Which is why you conned us into carrying them.' Jago nodded.

'Right. That was one of my reasons.'

'So Paul d-d-died for fakes?' Jago blurted.

'No. Paul died because of a violent, desperate little man. Ward did it the accepted way. I didn't know – oh, God, maybe I should have guessed – I didn't know Havlik would look for those papers. I didn't know he'd react that way. Christ. I have to live with that.'

'Papers?' Jago was irritated. 'What is all this about bloody papers?'

'There was another treasure. Again, it had Havlik connections, but it was not Havlik's. He'd been told about it by his father. It wasn't a treasure back in '48. It had been given away without a thought. I think he asked Robinson to find out if it was still where it was meant to be, in the house of a man named Filip, a man I have known all my life, my teacher at school. I knew there had to be something that Havlik stood to gain, something that would persuade Robinson to do all this work, something that made it worthwhile to kill Robinson. I only discovered it the night before last. I, in common with everyone else, was looking for glittering stuff. It was dirty old sheets of vellum. God knows what it is, but it must be very important. Havlik killed Filip, not that I can necessarily prove it, whilst all of us were watching you and Pickering and Holly down in Susice. His hire-car tyres drove up to Filip's gate. There were no fingerprints, but forensic will dig something up.'

'Christ!' Jago moaned. 'This is all too much.'

'Oh, he was a very desperate man, Mr van Zeller. And he wasn't stable, of course. He kept a lot of white powder in a toothpaste tube in his room. I think he'll have snorted a lot of that today. So what should have been a simple hold-up on a country road becomes a murderous attack. I'll not forgive myself for that.'

Jago was shaking his head again as he spoke. 'I just don't believe it,' he said. 'Paul dead. I don't believe it . . .'

'Like I said, I am very, very sorry.' Novak spoke gently for the first time since Jago had met him. 'He was a very fine man. And he did not die for fakes. He died to save the real treasure, whatever it may be, and, strangely enough, to save Holly. I think that would have pleased him.'

'Holly?' Jago gulped. 'What the hell are you talking about, Novak?' Novak braked. At that moment, the frontier post loomed up.

'That's right, Mr van Zeller. All will be made clear. Send my love to her, won't you?'

Jago nodded without thinking.

'Goodbye, Mr van Zeller,' Novak called quickly. He opened the door, jumped down and was gone.

Jago moved across to the driver's seat. He was on automatic pilot. He drove on as if the whole drama had been a dream.

But he drove on alone.

For all the difference that it made to his life, the trip might never have happened. The racing fraternity, of course, knew of the exploits of Pickering and van Zeller in some foreign field, but Jago had little cause to mix with the racing fraternity, at least in his quotidian London life. He returned to a doormat piled with bills, a broken immersion heater and a lonely dinner at his local Italian. One of Ian Johnson's lads had taken over the horsebox at the Robin Hood roundabout, and was taking it on down to Wiltshire.

The following day, Jago awoke to wriggling rain. He

washed in cold water, dressed and made his way to work. There was a three-column, two-inch piece in the *Telegraph* about Paul who '*died just hours after scoring his greatest triumph. On Sunday, he won Czechoslovakia's formidable Velka Pardubicka steeplechase. On Monday, he and fellow rider Cyril Havlik were attacked by mobsters, thought to be German, as they drove homeward.*' The *Life* and the *Post* made the race front-page news, but, frustrated by their absence of information, were forced to consign the deaths to a secondary role.

That morning, Jago broke the news to Clay, who punched the office wall. He also had to tell Diana.

She cried a lot, and, as she cried, she looked very old. She looked a lot like Paul.

And that, Jago thought, was that. He was a businessman and a bachelor. His racing days were done. Ian Johnson had offered honourable retirement to both Burly and Paul's Avocet. The adventure was over.

But it wasn't.

Not yet.

At two o'clock that Wednesday afternoon, Clay came in with a sheaf of papers. The top sheet read: 'Whilst you were on the nest . . .'

Clay had been busy. In between visits to the casino, he had called upon Vanya, manufacturers of a cloth still lighter and more weather-resistant than Loden. Vanya were looking for designs for businesswomen in Prague, Budapest, Berlin and Moscow. At the same time, they believed that their sportswear – characterized by leather braiding – might do well in Britain and America. Clay had suggested a trade. Zellers could have the exclusive rights to the cloth and could make up suits for the East. The Czechs would use Zellers outlets to sell their shooting and country lines. Jago would lend his name and face to the sportswear in Central Europe. No cash would change hands. Jago looked at the projected volume of the first year's orders. It would fill their books, but they could manage it.

Jago examined the documents as though eager to find a flaw. He did not want to allow himself to be excited again. There would be something wrong. There always was.

At last, he called Miss Sniffy and told her the details. If she was not sceptical, no one would be.

She called him back after just twenty minutes. She said, 'If these people are for real, you're back in business, Mr van Zeller.'

Jago allowed himself a grin. He told Clay, 'All right, mate. You're appointed Eastern Europe Liaison Officer, with an expense account. Which means you can spend a lot of time in those bloody casinos. Do the deal, Clay, and let me meet these guys within the fortnight.'

At four o'clock that evening, Jago supervised the replacement of the immersion-heater element, then drove down to Hungerford. Paul's diary had given him Clare Pickering's number. He had rung her from France last night. He had broken the news as gently and as briefly as he could contrive. She had said, 'Oh, God. I had a feeling . . .'

'I know,' Jago had said helplessly. 'I'm sorry. I did my best, but . . .'

'I know, I know. I'm sure you did. Can we meet, but first, would you do me – and dad – a great favour?'

He arranged to meet her in the bar of the Ritz at 9.30 that evening. This, meanwhile, was the favour. He had a vet come out to Paul's mobile home. John, the lad who had been feeding the dogs, took his favourite. Jago took a young brindle bitch. He held and soothed the others as the vet did his business. He buried each one before calling out the next.

He was late for his appointment with Clare. She sat very upright in the Palm Court. Again she was dressed all in black, though not, Jago assumed, in mourning. She greeted him with a little uncertain smile. He said, 'Sorry. I've just got back from Hungerford.'

'Thank you.'

Jago sat opposite her. It was strange to see Paul's eyes once more staring at him from under that swooping black hair. 'No, least I could do. Listen, I really am so sorry. He charged off into this absurd adventure, and I pulled him out once, but then – oh, hell, I got caught up in it too.'

'Yup.' She nodded wisely. 'He had that effect.'

A waiter appeared at Jago's shoulder. Jago said, 'Champagne cocktail for me, please. Same for you?'

She smiled. 'Might as well drink a toast to the old idiot. Yes, please. Good idea.'

Jago gave her a much abridged account of the trip to the Czech Republic, omitting all mention of murders or fakes.

'Poor old bugger,' she said dreamily at the end, 'consistent from start to finish. He couldn't have died in bed – unless it was with a Grand Duchess. I reckon he was a lucky man. Lots of us – we let him down, but he always stuck to his guns. He never grew old and cynical.'

Then she cried a bit.

Jago returned to the flat in splashing, chuckling rain. Despite his umbrella, he was sodden. He flung his steaming jacket on the bed. He pulled off his tie. He turned on the television. He stepped out of his trousers. He strolled through to the bathroom and spun the taps. It was then that the telephone trilled.

He left the taps running. He sat on the bed. He reached for the telephone. 'Hello?'

'Jago. Hi.'

'Sorry . . .'

'It's me. Holly.'

'Oh.' He paused, then decided to play it cool but friendly. 'Hi. How are you?'

'Fine. Listen, I didn't want to bother you or anything, but can I come and see you? Just briefly?'

'Sure, sure. No, be good to see you. When would suit?'

'How about now?'

'Er, sure, fine! Please. Where are you?'

'Bloomsbury. Just up the Central Line from you. I could be with you in twenty minutes or so, half an hour.'

'Good. Look forward to seeing you.'

He laid down the receiver and he wondered how this interview would go off. One thing was for certain. He was not going to get involved in a discussion about animals and their putative rights. He bathed. He dressed in jeans, a fresh shirt and moccasins. He scooped up the dirty clothes flung from his suitcase. He made a pile of newspapers and magazines and hid them in the kitchen cupboard. He switched on the gas-flames. He plumped the cushions.

When the doorbell clanked he was tempted to play it slow, but the rain was slashing down. He could not leave her waiting. He dived at the door. 'Come in,' he said firmly. 'Come in.'

She looked up. Her hair was wet. It clung in looping tendrils to her brow. It coiled in tight springs above her ears. It made her eyes seem very large. A little smile tugged at her mouth for a milli-second, then vanished.

She walked past Jago with a sort of soft flounce. She wore black leggings again, and a maroon polo-neck beneath a Harris tweed jacket. She said, 'I'm soaked.' She laid her shoulder-bag on the floor by the sofa. She shrugged off her jacket.

'Can I get you a towel?' Jago asked.

'No. I'm OK. Just let me warm up by the fire.' She sank to her knees on the kilim.

There was silence then, save for the pipe-smoker popping of the fire, the trickling of the water, the rushing of the traffic up above.

'So, how are you?' Jago tried.

'OK, I suppose.'

He sat on the sofa and instantly stood again. 'Sorry. Let me get you a drink.'

'Thanks.' Again there was a twitch of the lips. 'I'd love one. Tea, please, or whisky. I'm not sure.'

'Try both.'

'Sounds great.'

Jago whistled as he strode into the kitchen. He never whistled. He turned on the kettle. He pulled out a mug and two tumblers.

'I was sorry about Paul,' she called.

'Yes. Yes, it was nasty.'

'Were you there?'

'Yes. And Novak.' Jago did not move back towards the sitting-room. He just stood there, shifting from foot to foot and waiting for the water to boil.

'Was it really gangsters?'

'Yes. It was Havlik who killed him. Ridiculous. Just one crazed blow with a stirrup, for God's sake. But he was with these gangsters. Hayward – remember Hayward? He wasn't a journalist. He was there to watch Havlik. Havlik was into them for millions. He set us all up. And the jewels weren't his anyhow. The Havliks were Nazis. Novak killed Havlik.'

She said nothing. The kettle rattled. The lid clanked. The mounting seashell roar subsided. The water babbled. Steam jetted from the spout. Jago poured the water before he realized that he had forgotten the tea bag. He opened the tin and dunked the bag. He squeezed it against the mug with a teaspoon. He sniffed a milk carton and poured milk.

'So . . .' Jago picked up the mug and the two glasses. He walked briskly through. She lay flat on the rug. He laid the mug on the brassbound seaman's chest. 'The ridiculous thing is, the jewels were fakes anyhow, planted by Havlik in the first place.'

'I know.'

'*You know?*'

'Yup.' She enjoyed his bemusement. She sat up and curled her legs beneath her. She sipped. 'Oh, God, that's good. Yes. Viktor told me.'

'Viktor?' Jago was at the drinks table. 'Novak?'

'Yup.'

Jago slurped two fingers' width of Irish into the glasses. 'When, for God's sake?'

'That last night. He kidnapped me whilst you were very gallantly snoring.'

'Yeah, well, I'm sorry about that.' Jago started. 'He did *what?*'

'Kidnapped me. No, look. This is all arse-about-face. I came here to say sorry to you. I really am, Jago. I know how you must have felt.'

'No. No, come on . . .'

'Hush, Jago. Let me say my piece. I'm sorry because you were good to me, and your self-esteem isn't armour-plated either, and it must hurt like hell to think you were set up, that the whole thing was planned from the start. It's no excuse to say that it was Cora's idea. She had seen you at

Aintree, when she was on a protest. When she saw you at the check-out desk, she got all excited and rushed me through to the departure lounge, primed me, told me to make friends with you. I was keen to do it. I thought you were just a rich, brutal shit who thought he was irresistible, so why not? I was wrong. I think I was wrong about the racing too, but I'm not so sure. I was definitely wrong about you. I realized that. I told Cora no way would I abuse your kindness. And you must know – I mean, I swear – when we – in the horsebox, all that, it was because I really wanted . . . Oh, shit. I meant it.'

'And I fell asleep,' Jago smiled. He handed her the glass. 'God, bloody brilliant.'

'Yeah, talk about my self-esteem. Great. Until Viktor told me.'

'Told you what?'

'About emptying the contents of three of his sleeping-pills in your wine at dinner.' She giggled. 'Didn't he tell you?'

'No, he bloody didn't!' Jago shouted. 'The bugger! But why in God's name did he do that?'

She shrugged. 'Two things. He knew who I was, what I was doing out there. I think he wanted whoever was watching us to think that we barely knew one another, met on a plane, quick screw, but in fact I was your enemy, out there to use you, to protest about the race. That way, maybe they'd not concentrate so hard on me as your ally. The other thing, God, he wanted me to do a whole load of things right then. It was horrid, him coming in, grabbing me, dragging me off. It took a while for me to shut up. He told me about the Havliks being Nazis, about the jewels being fakes, but he'd found these things in Havlik's box. He wanted me to take them out. He said I must go through with it – the protest. He said, "There's a gate in the rails out there by the snake-ditch, but it can only be opened from inside. Go back to Cora and say, OK, I'll get the accreditation to be in the centre of the course, but you'll have to pretend to be me, cut your hair like mine." That way, you know, I took off that orange thing, sneaked off the course after the second race and Cora went out there disguised as me. Of course, she jumped at it. At that distance, no one's going to notice the change. Anyone watching me still thinks I'm out there in the middle. Martina – that's Mrs Novak – the one who searched me, drove me out of the country. She was listening to the race on the radio, translated for me. I wish I'd seen it.'

'You mean, that night, when I was lying there doped, you two were rushing around organizing all this?' Jago stared.

'Yup. Busy night all round. Then we went off to see my friend Pavla, and Novak put some pressure on her to get me the accreditation . . . God, I was beat by the time I got into Martina's car. See, everyone else who met you on that trip will have got well and truly searched on their way out. Not me. I was just another tourist with a respectable Czech friend, and as for the gangsters or whatever they were, far as they were concerned, I was still busy getting beaten up at the racecourse. He's not stupid, that Novak.' She was grinning broadly now. 'So, do you want to know what we preserved for the Czech nation?'

'Havlik said something about papers,' Jago recalled. 'Even after he'd killed Paul, he was trying to make deals with me.'

'Yuk. He was a horror. Right. I have just spent the entire day in the British Library, surrounded by security guards. What we have saved is . . .'

She made the most of it. 'Go on,' Jago grinned.

'Is . . .'

'I might strangle you.'

'A cookery book.'

When Jago had finished mopping the hot tea from his crotch and thighs, Holly pulled him down onto the carpet and leaned back against him. 'Right,' she said. 'History lesson.' She grasped his hand and pulled his arm about her. 'You know who Catherine de Medici was?'

'Daughter of Lorenzo, sixteenth century. Married Henri II of France. Became queen effectively whilst her two sons were too young.'

She looked up. 'How'd you know all that?'

He smiled down at her. 'Van Zeller,' he said. 'Huguenot. Catherine killed a lot of my ancestors at the massacre of St Bartholomew.'

'Did she? Ah. Well, she's making up for it now. She is credited with the invention of haute cuisine, so they say. All these French, swear they invented good food, apparently it's crap. Catherine arrived in Paris and imported her own chefs, and she got them from – guess where?'

Jago shrugged. 'Italy?'

'Wrong. One came from Vienna, two came from Prague. And one of the ones from Prague, as yet nameless, seems to have come from the Havliks' kitchens. And these cooks wrote down their recipes, if you can call them recipes. OK, they're in Hoch Deutsch and French and Lord knows, but even so, they seem to me to be almost in code. There are recipes for bread and for curing and for pickles, recipes for boar and all sorts of other game. There's pasta in there, and the most fantastic patisserie stuff, *and*, believe it or not – well, they're not quite sure, but they're having multiple orgasms about it down there, so I think they're fairly certain – these recipes are annotated by none other than Her Majesty herself! Well, they think what happened is, this chef gets homesick, too old, he goes home. These documents – they're just sheets of vellum tied together – are used a bit in the Havliks' kitchens, but end up in the muniments room, then get given to the schoolmaster when the Havliks are leaving.'

'Good God,' Jago breathed. 'The first ever cookery book annotated by a queen.'

'Yup, so the bibliophiles are swooning, and the sixteenth-century cookery expert they've roped in is wetting himself because apparently it proves that – I don't know – choux pastry had been invented before it should be, that sort of thing.'

'It would fetch an absolute bloody fortune.' Jago nodded. 'And the publishing rights . . . no wonder Havlik – he killed for that book, you know?'

'Yes,' she shuddered. 'A little old man.'

'So he sells the mob a load of fake jewels, and hunts down a far less obtrusive treasure. He flies to Latin America, where, I suppose, he or his friend Robinson have organized a buyer for the papers . . .'

'And it's easy street.'

'Until Ward and Co found him. And they would most certainly have found him, in the end. God,' Jago sighed, 'what a week.'

She nestled in, watching the flickering flames. She said, 'Do you think – I mean, would you ever trust me again?'

'Depends on you,' Jago said sadly. 'I can only trust you if, when you disagree with me, you say so and hear me out, not if you keep secrets, not if you treat human beings as representatives of a class or a cause. I don't mind people hating – I don't know – communism, say, but you can't go round hating every communist you meet.'

'I know. I tried to tell Cora. She . . . I just needed all that certainty. Everything else seemed so chaotic. She – her ideas – were something to cling onto.'

'You don't need that now?'

'Nope, but . . .' She paused. 'I could do with a helping hand. Please, Jago. I've got rid of Cora, all that. Can you forget it ever happened? God, there aren't that many chances on this earth, and I have an infinite talent for blowing it when they come.'

He bent his head and kissed her. He said, 'No messing about, OK?'

She shook her head. It was starting again, but two or three or twenty minutes on she murmured, 'Jago?'

'Mmmm?'

'I said we'd ring Viktor when we knew what the papers were.'

'Novak?' Jago kissed her again. 'Mmm. Let's do that. You got his number?'

She reached up for her bag. He reached up for the telephone. Somewhere amidst the kissing and caressing, she contrived to fish out the card and he to dial the number. A woman answered. Jago shouted, 'Hello. May I speak to Viktor Novak, please?'

The woman said, 'Moment,' so Jago kissed Holly some more.

'Hello?' That deep croak.

'Novak? Jago.'

'And Holly,' called Holly.

'Oh, fuck,' Novak sighed. 'How are you?'

'Fine, thanks. Listen, Holly's delivered the goods.'

'All intact?'

'All present and correct,' Holly called. 'They're at the British Library now, and everyone's getting very excited. You know what they are?'

'You know I bloody don't.'

Holly caught Jago's eye, and they chanted as one, 'A – cookery – book!'

'A *what?*'

'A cookery book,' Holly giggled. 'Catherine de Medici's cookery book, to be exact. She took a Prague chef with her to France. This is his book, annotated by her.'

'Great God in heaven,' Novak rasped. 'How much would that fetch?'

'Oh, hundreds of thousands for the manuscript,' Jago said casually, 'and a mass for the publishing rights, that's all.'

'I called the papers as instructed, Viktor!' Holly shouted. 'It'll be in *The Times* tomorrow!'

'Good, good. I hope now you understand, Mr van Zeller. It was not just for the jewels that you had to keep Ward guessing. If he'd had time to discover that the jewels weren't all they seemed, they'd have had a killing frenzy. They'd have wanted to take all of you to pieces to find what they wanted. Havlik wanted you to take the things for his reasons. I wanted you to take them because that gave you, Miss Byrne, time to get safely to London before they went mad and set off in pursuit of you. The decoy was necessary. Mr Pickering did not die for nothing.'

'No,' Jago nodded. 'No, I see that. So, do you reckon they might still come after us?'

'No, no. I talked to Ward today. I told him about the exhibition, about Havlik and Robinson. He wants to murder both of them a million times over, but those jobs have already been taken care of. So, when do we receive this national treasure from our generous benefactors Miss Holly Byrne and Mr Jago van Zeller?'

'God, the librarians are going to cry,' Holly said. 'Give them a week or two to play with them.'

'Two things, Novak,' Jago said.

'Yes?'

'First, Paul. If we're to be benefactors of the Czech Republic, Paul must be buried at Pardubice. OK?'

'I'm sure it can be organized,' Novak growled. 'What's the other?'

'I know a lot of publishers in this town. Someone's going to have to handle the deals. How about making me a literary agent for this book? As a special thank you.'

'What do literary agents get?' Novak snapped.

'Ten per cent.'

'So you get 7.5 per cent, I get 2.5 per cent. That way, I just think I might swing it.'

Jago and Holly unwrapped and enjoyed one another there on the floor before the fire. After the first couple of times, they poured more drinks and retired to bed. This time, he was glad to observe, it was she who first went to sleep, and with a contented little smile tugging at her lips.

Holly's face helped. She and Jago received a total of £82,000 from the various newspapers for their story. They sent half to Novak. The other half paid a lot of Zellers's debts.

Jago now has two very rich Czech sleeping partners and many rich Central and Eastern European clients. Business is booming. He is also a Knight Commander of the Ancient Order of St Jude, for what it's worth.

Queen Catherine's Cookbook will be published in October by HarperCollins both in Britain and in the States. Deals have also been arranged in France, Germany, Italy and Czechoslovakia.

Gargoyle Greetings Cards are also doing very nicely.

And, on the second Sunday of October last year, Jago and Holly visited Pardubice racecourse in the early morning, and laid a wreath on a grave at the centre of the racecourse. There were already many posies and tokens there.

Paul Pickering had come a long, long way to find honour, and friends.

Suit + shirt ✗

Belt

2 x W shirt. ✗

[illegible] cup

~~Belt~~ dk bloo ✗

2 x levis

shorts ✗

Blk ✗

Bloo ✓

cream ✓

[illegible] bloo

[illegible] ✓

T shirts

[illegible] Denim ✓

dk bloo Denim ✓

swimmers

Sox

Mix

Toiletries

Melatonin

Vits

Blk Boots

Brown

gym

[illegible]

shoes ✓

CD's

Books

X

Boot

Car

£

Comp

Tix

Pport

phone

Published or forthcoming

FEAR OF THE DOG

Neil Tidmarsh

In the art world, there's more than one way to make a killing . . .

Tony Acton, flamboyant and ruthless young art dealer, clocks up one blistering success after another. Artist Nicholas Todd should be delighted: Acton sells his work too. So why does he hate Acton? Hate him enough to consider the unthinkable? Enough to take pleasure in his early demise . . .

Fear of the Dog is a fiendishly clever thriller set in the darkest depths of London's art world. Neil Tidmarsh weaves a cunning web of love and hate, deception and forgery . . . and murder.

SIGNET

Published or forthcoming

HARD TARGET

James Adams

On a lonely back road in Moscow's hinterland, a collector of dog corpses picks up the last victim of the night. He cannot know that the next death will be his own, that it will be sudden, horrifying. Because Yagoda's bit part in a doomsday international drama is to suffer and die from a deadly escaped virus that simply isn't supposed to exist.

From Russia to America to Britain, one man from MI6 co-ordinates the race to stop the Russian mafia from marketing a stockpile of biological weapons. Loner David Nash knows his way around the post Cold War world. Yesterday's foes have gone, replaced by a ruthless new generation as skilled as Nash in the technology of tomorrow.

The combat is deadly . . .